European ESCAPES
ITALY

CAROL MARINELLI   LOUISE FULLER   SARAH MORGAN

MILLS & BOON

CONTENTS

The Italian's
Forbidden Virgin
Carol Marinelli

Carol Marinelli recently filled in a form asking for her job title. Thrilled to be able to put down her answer, she put "writer." Then it asked what Carol did for relaxation and she put down the truth—"writing." The third question asked for her hobbies. Well, not wanting to look obsessed, she crossed her fingers and answered "swimming"—but, given that the chlorine in the pool does terrible things to her highlights, I'm sure you can guess the real answer!

CHAPTER ONE

GIAN DE LUCA WAS the Duke of Luctano, yet he chose not to use his title. Others, though, could not quite bring themselves to let it go.

And as he finished up the working week in his sumptuous office suite, on the ground floor of his flagship hotel La Fiordelise, in Rome, his PA informed him that his date—for want of a better word—had arrived.

'I was supposed to meet her at the theatre,' Gian said, barely looking up as he signed off on some paperwork.

'Yes,' Luna agreed, for she was more than aware of his heavy schedule and that he kept his private life and work as separate as was possible, 'and a driver was ordered, but it would seem she wanted…'

Luna paused for slight effect, which told Gian she was about to quote directly.

'"To save the Duke the trouble."'

His pen paused and then Gian's final signature of the day appeared darkly on the page as the nib of his pen pressed in firmly. 'I see.'

'She also asked not to be treated as a hotel guest and made to wait in Reception. Given that pre-theatre dining is about to commence, she suggested meeting you in the restaurant.'

Gian held in a weary sigh. His restaurant was not a personal dining room for entertaining lovers. As soon as his dates started throwing around his title like confetti, or attempting to pull rank with his staff, or trying to get too familiar, it signalled the end for Gian. 'Tell her I'll be out shortly.'

'Except you have Ariana Romano in Reception waiting to see you.'

This time Gian could not hold in his sigh. His slate-grey eyes briefly shuttered as he braced himself for a mini-tornado, because it was always drama whenever she suddenly arrived.

If Ariana felt it, she said it.

'What does she want now?'

'A private matter, apparently.'

He kept his door open to her, given he was friends with her father Rafael and older brother Dante, in as much as Gian was friends with anyone. Growing up, he had been sent to Luctano each summer to stay with some distant aunt and her husband who, like his parents, hadn't much wanted him around. Those summers had often been spent hanging out with the Romanos.

Aside from the family ties, there were business connections too. Ariana was on the committee for the Romano Foundation Ball, which was held here at La Fiordelise each year. In small doses Gian chose to tolerate her, yet she was somewhat of an irritant. Rather like heavily scented jasmine in the flower arrangement in the foyer, or when lilies were left out just a little too long. Ariana had clung and irritated long after she had left and now, on a Friday evening, he had to deal with her in person.

'Bring her through then,' Gian said. 'Oh, and then take Svetlana through to the Pianoforte Bar to wait for me there...'

And there he would end their...*liaison.*

At thirty-five, Gian was considered one of Italy's most eligible bachelors.

His wealth and dark brooding looks were certainly a factor, but Gian was no fool and was aware that his title was coveted. He was the Duke of Luctano, even though his family had left the Tuscan hillsides generations ago and he had been born and raised in Rome. Or, rather, Gian had raised himself, for his hedonistic parents had had no time or inclination for their son.

Gian was, in fact, Italy's most *ineligible* bachelor for he had no interest in marriage or settling down and always stated up front with women that, apart from a handful of lavish dates, they would go no further than bed.

Gian had long ago decided that the De Luca lineage *would* end with him.

His sex life—Gian had never so much as contemplated the word 'love'—was rather like the stunning brass revolving doors at the entrance to La Fiordelise—wealth and beauty came in, was spoiled and pampered for the duration, but all too soon was ejected back out into the real world. Svetlana's behaviour was nothing unexpected: she had shown her true colours to his PA, and that was that.

They all did in the end.

Gian was jaded rather than bitter, and more than ready to get through this meeting with Ariana and then deal swiftly with Svetlana. So much so that he didn't bother to step into the luxury suite behind his office to freshen up for a night at Teatro dell'Opera; the gorgeous box with its pink-lined walls would remain empty tonight.

As would the luxurious suite behind his office.

His lovers never got so much as a toe in the door of his private apartment at La Fiordelise, for Gian was intensely private.

He sat drumming his fingers silently on his large black walnut desk, waiting for Ariana to arrive. But then, on a wintry and gloomy January evening, it was as if a vertical sunrise stepped into his office. Ariana's long black hair was slicked back into a low bun and she wore a suit and high heels. Except it was no ordinary suit. It was orange. The skirt sat just above the knee and the no doubt bespoke stockings were in exactly the same shade, as were the velvet stilettoes and large bag she carried over her shoulder. On most people the outfit would look ridiculous, but on pencil-thin Ariana it looked tasteful and bright... like a streak of burnt gold on the horizon heralding a new day.

Gian refused to be dazzled and reminded himself of the absolute diva she was. Ariana was the one who should be performing at Teatro dell'Opera tonight!

'Gian,' she purred, and gave him her signature red-lipped smile. It was the same smile that set the cameras flashing on the red carpets in Rome, but Gian remained steadfastly unimpressed—not that he showed it, for he was more than used to dealing with the most pampered guests.

'Ariana.' He pushed back his chair to stand and greet her. 'You look amazing as always.' He said all the right things, though could not help but add, 'Very orange.'

'Cinnamon, Gian,' she wryly corrected as her heart did the oddest thing.

It stopped.

Gian *should* be familiar. After all, she had known him all her life, yet she was suddenly reminded of his height and the deep tone of his voice. He wore a subtly checked suit in grey with a waistcoat, though his height meant that he wore the check rather than the check wearing him.

Of course her heart had started again—had it not she would have dropped to the floor—but it was jumping around in some ungainly trot as he walked towards her.

Pure nerves, Ariana decided. After all, she did have a huge favour to ask!

'I apologise for not coming out to greet you,' Gian said as he came around the desk and kissed her on both cheeks. 'I was just finishing up some work.'

'That's fine. Luna took good care of me.'

Except she felt far from fine. Ariana rather wished that the nerves in her chest would abate, yet they fluttered like butterflies—or perhaps fireflies would be a more apt description because there was a flash of heat creeping up her neck and searing her cheeks, but then Gian was, to say the least, rather commanding.

Cold, people called him.

Especially back home in Luctano, where gossip and rumour abounded. The history of the De Lucas was often whispered about and discussed in her home town—at times even by her family. Though a child at the time, Ariana could well remember the shock and horror in the village as news of the fire aboard their luxury yacht had hit in the early hours of a Sunday morning. And, of course, she still remembered the funeral held in Luctano for the Duke, the Duchess and the heir apparent...

People whispered about the fact that Luca hadn't attended the renewal of his parents' vows, and his lack of visible emotion at the funeral.

Yet, as Ariana sometimes pointed out, the fact that he hadn't attended had saved his life.

And, the villagers would add, happy to twist the truth, *his brother's death made him a duke*. As if Gian had swum out into the ocean and torched the boat himself!

'Basta!' Ariana would tell them.

Enough!

Ariana actually *liked* his steely reserve.

Her own self was so volatile that when life spun too fast, it was to Gian she turned for his distant, measured ways.

While rumour had it he melted women in the bedroom and endeared both staff and guests with his calm assertiveness, it was the general consensus that behind his polished façade there was no heart or emotion, just a wall of solid black ice. Ariana needed that wall of black ice on side so she kept her smile bright. 'Thank you for agreeing to see me.'

'Of course.' Gian gestured for her to take a seat as he did the same. 'Can I offer you some refreshments?'

'No, thank you.' Gosh, small talk was difficult when you had a huge favour to ask! 'How was your Christmas?'

'Busy,' Gian responded, then politely enquired, 'Yours?'

Ariana lifted her hand and made a wavering gesture, to show it had not been the best, though she did not bore Gian with the details, like how, in the manner of a tennis ball in an extended rally, she'd bounced between Florence and Rome. Gian already knew all about her parents' divorce and her father's subsequent marriage to the much younger Mia. After all the marriage had taken place here!

And he knew too that her father wasn't at home in Luctano but in a private hospital in Florence and so she gave him a brief update. 'Dante is hoping to have Papà moved here to Rome,' Ariana said, but left out the *hospice* word. 'That should make things a bit easier.'

'Easier for whom?' Gian enquired.

'For his family,' Ariana responded tartly, but then squirmed inwardly, for it was the very question she had been asking herself since her brothers had suggested the move. 'His children are all here, his Rome office...' Her voice trailed off. Though the impressive Romano Holdings offices were in the EUR business district of Rome, Dante had taken over the running of the company when their father had remarried.

Gian's question was a pertinent one—and confirmed for Ariana that she needed to speak with her father and find out exactly what it was *he* wanted for the final months of his life. 'It is not all decided,' she admitted to Gian. 'We are just testing ideas.'

'Good,' Gian said, and she blinked at the gentler edge to his tone. 'I visited him yesterday.'

'You visited him in Florence?'

'Of course. You know I have a sister hotel opening there in May?' Gian checked, and Ariana nodded. 'I always try and drop in on Rafael when I am there.'

For some reason that brought the threat of tears to her eyes, but she hastily blinked them back. Ariana was not one for tears—well, not real ones; crocodile tears she excelled at—but at times Florence, where her father was in hospital, felt so far away. It was an hour or so by plane and she visited as much as she could. So did her brothers, and of course Mia was there and the family home in Luctano was nearby...but at night, when she couldn't sleep, Ariana always thought of her father alone.

There was a break in the conversation that Gian did absolutely nothing to fill. A pregnant pause was something Ariana was incapable of. If there was a gap she felt duty-bound to speak. Any lull in proceedings and she felt it her place to perform. Gian, she felt, would let this silence stretch for ever and so of course it was she who ended it. 'Gian, there is a reason I am here...'

Of course there was!

Her slender hands twisted in her lap. She was nervous, Gian realised. This was most unlike Ariana, who was usually supremely confident—arrogant, in fact. It dawned on him then what this urgent appointment might be about. Did she want to bring her latest lover here, without it being billed to the Romano guest folio so as to avoid her father or brothers finding out?

It was often the case with family accounts, but if that was what Ariana was about to ask him...

No way!

There was no question he would facilitate her bringing her latest lover to stay here! 'What is it you want?' Gian asked, and she blinked at the edge to his tone.

'I have decided that I want a career.'

'A career?' His features relaxed and there was even a shadow of a smile that he did not put down to relief that she wasn't intending to bring her lover here. It was typical of Ariana to say she wanted a career, rather than a job. 'Really?'

'Yes.' She nodded. 'I've given it a great deal of thought.'

'And your career of choice?'

'I would like to be Guest Services Manager here at La

Fiordelise. Or rather I would like to be Guest Services Manager for your VIPs.'

'All of my guests are VIPs, Ariana.'

'You *know* what I mean.'

He had to consciously resist rolling his eyes. 'Why would I simply hand you such a position when you have no experience? Why would I let you near my VIPs?'

'Because I am one!' Ariana retorted, but then rather hurriedly checked herself. 'What I am trying to say is that I know their ways. Please, Gian. I really want this.'

Gian knew very well that whatever Ariana wanted, Ariana got—until she grew bored and dismissed it. Ariana should have been put over her father's knee many years ago and learned the meaning of the word 'no'. There was no way on God's earth that she was going to *play* careers at his hotel. So, rather than go through the motions, he shook his head. 'Ariana, let me stop you right there. While I appreciate—'

'Actually,' she cut in swiftly, 'I *would* like some refreshments after all. Perhaps, given the hour, some champagne is in order.' Her pussycat smile was triumphant as she prevented him ending their conversation.

Ever the consummate host, Gian nodded politely. *'Naturalmente.'* He pressed the intercom. 'Luna, would you please bring in champagne for myself and Ariana.'

Ariana's smile remained. No doubt, Gian assumed, she was thinking she had won, but what she did not quite understand was that Gian was always and absolutely one step ahead. Luna had worked at La Fiordelise even before his family had died and knew his nuances well. It was often what was *not* said that counted, and right at this moment Vincenzo, the bar manager, would be pouring two *glasses* of French champagne.

A bottle and ice bucket would *not* be arriving.

This was no tête-à-tête.

'I have brought my résumé,' Ariana said, digging in her suede designer *cinnamon* bag and producing a document, which she handed to him. He took it without a word and as he read through it, Gian found again that he fought an incredulous smile.

For someone who had practically never worked a day in her life, Ariana Romano had an impressive résumé indeed.

At least, it *read* well. She had studied hospitality and tourism management, although he knew that already. Naturally, she was on the Romano Board, and on the Romano Foundation Board too.

As well as that were listed all the luncheons, balls and functions which Ariana claimed to have planned and organised singlehandedly. Except—

'Ariana, you do not "create, design and implement the theme for the annual Romano Foundation Ball",' Gian said, and used his fingers to quote directly from her résumé. 'My staff do.'

'Well, I have major input.'

'No, Ariana, you don't. In fact, you barely show up for the meetings.'

'I always attend.'

'I can have Luna retrieve the minutes of them if you like. You rarely show up and you don't even bother to send an apology. The fact is you consistently let people down.'

'Excuse me!' Ariana reared, unused to him speaking so harshly, for, though cold, Gian was always polite.

Except here, today, they had entered unknown territory.

Usually when they discussed the Romano Ball, given the fact she was Rafael's daughter, Ariana's suggestions were tolerated, lauded even. Now, though, Gian refused to play the usual game of applauding her inaction, or nodding as she reeled off one of her less-than-well-thought-out ideas. He picked last year's ball as an example. 'You said you were thinking "along the lines of silver" and no doubt went off to plan your gown.'

He watched her lips press tightly together. Even clamped shut, Ariana had a very pretty mouth, but he quickly dragged his attention away from that thought and back to the point he was trying to make. 'Following your suggestion, my staff created a silver world, whereas you did nothing more than turn up on the night…' he held her angry gaze '…in a silver gown.'

'How nice that you remember what I was wearing,' Ariana retorted.

'Call it an educated guess.'

Ouch!

Suddenly, under his withering gaze, in this private meeting she had demanded, Ariana felt as gauche and naive as the virgin she was, rather than the temptress she portrayed. 'Well, I was the one who came up with a forest theme for this year,' Ariana reminded him.

'Tell me,' Gian pushed, 'what have you done to help implement the forest theme, apart from choose the fabric for your gown?'

Ariana opened her mouth to answer and then closed it. He watched her shoulders briefly slump in defeat, but then she rallied. 'I suggested ivy around the pillars in the ballroom.'

He looked as unimpressed with her suggestion as he had at the board meeting, Ariana thought. But, then, Gian considered decorations and themes and such somewhat vulgar.

'And berries,' Ariana hurriedly. 'I suggested a berry dessert. Fruits of the forest…'

Gian did not so much as blink; he just stared at her pretty, empty head.

Only…that wasn't right, and he knew it.

Ariana, when she so chose, was perceptive and clever, but he refused to relent. 'What about last month, December, the hotel's busiest time, and you reserved the Pianoforte Bar for yourself and your friends' exclusive use, yet forgot to let Reservations know that it was no longer required.'

'You were paid,' Ariana interrupted. 'My father—'

'Precisely.' It was Gian who now interrupted. '*Your father* took care of things. It is so very typical of you, Ariana. If something better comes along, then that is where your attention goes.'

'No!' Ariana shook her head, angrily at first but then in sudden bewilderment because he was usually so polite. 'Why are you speaking to me like this, Gian?'

'So that you understand completely why my answer to your request is no.'

It sounded as if he meant it, and Ariana wasn't particularly used to that so she tried another tack. 'I studied hospitality and—'

'I know you did.' Again, Gian cut her off. 'You might remember that it was necessary for you to do three months' work experience to pass your course and so I spoke to your father and offered for you to do your placement here.' His eyes never left her face. 'You failed to show up on your starting day.'

Ariana flushed. 'Because I decided to do my placement at the family hotel in Luctano.'

'And you didn't even think to let me know?'

'I thought my father's staff had contacted you.'

But Gian shook his head. 'The fact is, Ariana, you chose the easier option.'

'I wanted to work here, Gian,' Ariana insisted. 'But my parents wanted me at the family hotel.'

'No.' Gian shook his head, refusing to accept her twisted truth. 'You declined when I explained that your placement would consist of *working* in all areas of the hotel. You were to spend a week in the kitchen, a week as a chambermaid, a week—'

It was Ariana who interrupted now, her voice fighting not to rise as she cut in. 'I felt I would get more experience in Luctano.'

'Really?' Gian checked. 'You thought you would get more experience at a small boutique resort in the Tuscan hills than at an award-winning, five-star hotel in the heart of Rome?'

'Yes,' she attempted. 'Well, perhaps not as extensive as I would have had here but...' Her voice trailed off because her excuse was as pathetic as it sounded, but there was another reason entirely that his offer to work at La Fiordelise had been declined all those years ago. 'That wasn't the only reason I said no, Gian. The fact is, my mother didn't want me working here.'

'Why ever not?'

Even as she opened her mouth to speak, even as the words tumbled out, Ariana knew she should never be saying them. 'Because of your reputation with women.'

CHAPTER TWO

'PARDON?'

Gian was supremely polite as he asked her to repeat her accusation, but far from backtracking or apologising, Ariana clarified her words.

'My mother didn't want me working here because of your reputation with women.' She didn't even blush as she said it. If anything, she was defiant.

Still, such was the sudden tension that it was a relief when there was a knock on the door and soon Luna was placing down little white coasters decorated with La Fiordelise's swirling rose gold insignia and two long, pale flutes of champagne, as well as a little silver dish of nibbles.

The dish in itself was beautiful, heavy silver with three little heart-shaped trays, individually filled with nuts, slivers of fruit and chocolates.

It was easier to focus on incidentals because, despite her cool demeanour, Ariana could feel the crackle in the air that denoted thunder, and as the door closed on Luna, she stared at the pretty dish as she re-crossed her legs at the ankles.

'Ariana.' Gian's voice was seemingly smooth but there was a barbed edge to his tone that tempted her to retrieve her bag and simply run. Gian carried on, 'Before we continue this conversation, can I make one thing supremely clear?'

'Of course,' Ariana said. Unable to look at him any longer, she reached for a glass.

'Your mother had no right to imply or suggest that I would be anything other than professional with the work experience girl—or, in fact, any of my staff!'

'Well, you do have a formidable reputation...' Ariana started and raised the glass to her lips.

'With *women*,' Gian interrupted and then tartly added, 'Not teenage girls, which you were back *then*.'

Ariana nodded, the glass still hovering by her mouth. Even as he told her off, even as he scolded her for going too far, there was something else that had been said there—that she was different now compared to then.

She was a woman.

And Gian De Luca was a very good-looking man.

She had known that, of course. His undoubtedly handsome looks had always been there—something she had registered, but only at a surface level. Yet today it had felt as if she'd been handed a pair of magical eyeglasses and she wanted to weep as she saw colour for the first time.

He was beautiful.

Exquisitely so.

His jet-black hair framed a haughty face, and his mouth, though unsmiling, was plump in contrast to the razor-sharp cheekbones and straight nose.

She could not be in lust with Gian *and* work for him—that would never ever do!

She wanted to pull off those imaginary glasses, to be plunged back into a monotone world, where Gian De Luca was just, well...

Gian.

Not a name she wanted to roll on her tongue.

Not a mouth she now wanted to taste.

He was just Gian, she reminded herself.

The person she ran to when trouble loomed large.

She put her glass down on the small coaster as she attempted to push her inappropriate thoughts aside and rescue the interview. 'Mamma didn't mean it, Gian. You know what she can be like…'

'Yes.' Gian held in a pained sigh. 'I do.'

Too well he recalled joining the Romanos at their dinner table as a small boy. *'Straccione,'* Angela would say, ruffling his hair as he took a seat at the table. It had sounded like an affectionate tease; after all, how could the son of a duke and duchess be a ragamuffin and a beggar?

Except Angela had found the cruellest knife to dig into his heart, and she knew how to twist it, for Gian had always felt like a beggar for company.

Gian wasn't quite sure why Angela rattled him so much.

Ariana did too, albeit it in an increasingly different way.

He did not want Ariana working here. And not just because of her precious ways but because of this…this pull, this awareness, this attraction that did not sit well with him. 'Let's just leave things there, shall we?' he suggested. 'While we're still able to be civil. I could put you in touch with the director at Hotel Rav—' He went to name his closest rival but Ariana cut in even before he had finished.

'I was already offered a job there, and in several other hotels as well, but each time it was in return for some media coverage. I really don't want cameras following me on my first day.'

'Fair enough.' While he understood that, the rest he didn't get. 'What *are* you hoping to achieve by this, Ariana?'

'More than I am right now,' she said, and gave a hollow laugh.

He looked at her then.

Properly looked.

Ariana was, of course, exquisitely beautiful, with a delicate bone structure, but he suddenly noticed that rather than the trademark black eyes of her father and brothers, or the icy blue ones of her mother, Ariana's eyes were a deep navy-violet, almost as if they'd tried to get from blue to black, but had surrendered just shy of arrival.

Gian rather wished he hadn't noticed the beguiling colour of them and rapidly diverted his gaze back to her résumé.

'Why don't you formally interview me?' Ariana suggested. 'As if we don't know each other. Surely you can do that?'

'Of course, but if you want an honest interview, what happens if you are not successful?' She wouldn't be, he knew, but as he looked up she held his gaze as she answered.

'Then I shall walk away, knowing I tried.'

Walk away, Gian wanted to warn her, for there was a sudden energy between them that could never end well.

He scanned through her supposed work experience and attempted to wipe out a lifetime of history so they could face each other as two strangers. In the end, he reverted to his usual interview technique. 'Tell me about a recent time when you had to deal with a difficult client or contact...'

She wouldn't be able to, Gian was certain.

'Well...' Ariana thought for a moment. 'I wanted an interview with the owner of a very prestigious hotel, but I did not want to utilise my family contacts as I felt that would do me no favours.'

Gian felt his lips tighten when it became clear that she was speaking about trying to get in contact with him. 'Ariana,' he cut in, 'may I suggest that you don't make the person interviewing you the *difficult contact*.'

'But he was difficult. My goal was to get a full audience,' Ariana continued, 'and so I sent in my résumé, but when I heard nothing back...'

'You sent in an application?' Gian started scrolling through his computer, *almost* apologetic now, because an application from Ariana Romano *should* have been flagged—at the very least so he could personally reject her. 'Vanda has been on leave over the festive period...' He paused, for he could find nothing. 'When did you send it?'

'This morning,' Ariana replied, and then took a sip of her champagne.

'This morning.' Gian sighed, and leaned back in his chair. He looked upon the epitome of instant gratification. When Ariana wanted something she wanted it now!

'So, when I heard nothing back, I printed off my résumé and took it to him personally.'

'And what was the result?'

'I made him smile,' Ariana said.

'No,' Gian corrected, 'you didn't.'

'Almost.'

'Not even close.' He let out a breath as he tried to hold onto patience. 'Ariana, you asked for a proper interview, so treat it as if we've never met. Now, tell me about a time you were able to deal successfully with another person even when you may not have liked them.'

'Okay...' She chewed her bottom lip and thought for less than a moment. 'My father was recently given a terminal diagnosis. He still has months to live,' she added rather urgently, 'but...' She swallowed, for Ariana could not bear to think of a time months from now and dragged her mind back to the present. 'I am not a fan of his new wife.'

'Ariana, I am asking about professional—'

'However,' she cut in, 'I spoke calmly to her and said that I would like to be part of all interviews with the doctors and that for his sake, we should at least be polite.'

Curiosity got the better of him. 'How is that working out?'

She gave a snooty sniff and re-crossed her legs. 'We've both kept our sides of the agreement.'

Gian rather doubted it. Ariana and Mia were a toxic mix indeed! 'I was actually hoping you could give me examples that involve work, Ariana.'

'Oh, believe me,' she countered. 'Mia is work.'

Gian just wanted this charade over and done with. Both their glasses were nearly empty so he would ask one more question and then send her on her precocious way. 'Tell me about a time where you did something for someone else, not to earn favour, and without letting them know.'

'That would defeat the purpose,' Ariana deftly answered, 'if I later use it in an interview to show how benevolent I am.'

He liked her answer. In fact, were it a real interview, it might score her points, except he wasn't sure that Ariana wasn't simply being evasive. 'It's an important question, Ariana,' he told her. 'The role of Guest Services is to make a stay at La Fiordelise appear seamlessly unique. The aim is that our guests never know the work that goes on behind the scenes. So,' he added, 'I would like an honest answer.'

'Very well.' She was hesitant, though, for to tell him revealed more than she cared to. 'My brother...' She tried to remember that this was an interview and she should treat Gian as if he were a stranger. 'My twin brother, Stefano, is to marry soon—at the end of May.'

'And?'

'I have been somewhat excluded from the wedding plans.'

'Despite your extensive planning experience,' he added rather drily.

'Despite that!' Ariana answered crisply. 'They have decided that they don't need my help.'

He saw the jut of her chin and that her hands were rigid in her lap, and suddenly Gian did not like the question he had asked, for he could see it was hurting her to answer.

'Eloa,' Ariana continued, 'Stefano's fiancée, had her heart set on the wedding being held at Palazzo Pamphili...'

'Where the Brazilian Embassy is housed.' Gian nodded. He knew it well, for the superb building was across the square from the hotel, and even with his connections he knew how hard it would be to arrange a wedding there.

'I sorted it,' Ariana said.

'How?' Gian frowned, quietly impressed.

'That is for me to know,' Ariana responded. 'However, to this day, Eloa and Stefano think that they arranged the reception venue by themselves.'

'You haven't told them that you were behind it?'

'No. They have made it clear they don't want my help and it might sour things for them to know I had a hand in it.'

She watched as he put down her résumé and she continued to watch his long fingers join and arch into a steeple. He slowly drew a breath and Ariana felt certain that he had not been persuaded, and that she was about to be told that his answer was still no. 'I really do want to work, Gian.' There was a slightly frantic note to her voice, which she fought to quash, but there was also desperation in her eyes that she could not hide. 'I love the hotel industry and, you're right, I should have done my placement here...' It wasn't just that, though. 'I want some real independence. I'm tired of—' She stopped herself, sure that Gian did not need to hear it.

Yet he found that he wanted to. 'Go on,' Gian invited, casting his more regular interview technique aside.

'I'm tired of living in an apartment my family owns, tired of being on call when my mother decides I can drop everything for her. After all,' she mimicked a derisive tone, 'I couldn't *possibly* be busy.' She screwed her eyes closed in frustration, unable to properly explain the claustrophobic feeling of her privileged world.

Oh, many might say that life had been handed to Ariana Romano on a plate.

The trouble was, it wasn't necessarily a feast of her choosing.

While she had a family who seemingly adored her, even as a child Ariana had always been told to take her toys and play somewhere else.

To this day it persisted.

While she had access to wealth most people could only dream

of, there was a perpetual feeling of emptiness. For Ariana, the golden cup she drank from was so shot through with holes that no gifts—no trust-funded central Rome apartment, no wild party, no designer outfit or A-list appearance—filled her soul.

'I want a career,' Ariana insisted.

'Why now?' Gian pushed.

'It's a new year, a time when everyone takes stock...' She suddenly looked beyond Gian to the window behind him and saw white flakes dance in the darkness. 'It is starting to snow.'

'Don't change the subject,' Gian said, without so much as turning his head to take in the weather. It was Ariana he was more interested in. 'Why now, Ariana?'

Because I'm lonely, she wanted to say.

Because before Mia came along, I thought I had something of a career at Romano Holdings.

Because my days are increasingly empty and there surely has to be more to life than this?

Of course, she could not answer with that, and so she took a breath and attempted a more dignified response. 'I want to make something of myself, by myself. I want, for a few hours a day, to take off the Romano name. Look, I know what I'm asking is a favour, but—'

'Let me stop you right there,' he cut in. 'I don't do favours.'

There was from Ariana a slight, almost inaudible laugh, yet Gian understood its wry gist and conceded. 'Perhaps I make concessions for your father, but he was very good to me when...'

Gian didn't finish but Ariana knew he was referring to when his brother and parents had died and, to her nosy shame, Ariana hoped to hear more. 'When what?' she asked, as if she didn't know.

Nobody did silence better than Gian.

Surely, not a soul on this earth was as comfortable with silence as he, for he just stared right back at her and refused to elaborate.

It was Ariana who filled the long gap. 'I didn't get my father to lean on you, Gian,' she pointed out. 'I'm trying my best to do this by myself.'

'I know that,' Gian admitted, for if she had asked her father to call in a favour, then Rafael would have had a quiet word with him when he'd visited yesterday.

'I won't let you down, Gian.'

But even with Ariana's assurances, Gian was hesitant. He did not want Ariana to be his problem. He did not need the complication of hiring and, no doubt, having to fire her. And yet, *and yet*, he grudgingly admired her attempt to make something of herself, aside from the family name she'd been born into.

She broke into his thoughts then. 'Perhaps you could show me around?'

'I do not give guided tours to potential staff, that is Vanda's domain...'

'Ah, so I'm "potential staff" now?'

'I did not say that.'

'Then, as a family friend, you can show me around.'

Gian took a breath, and looked into navy violet eyes and better understood the predicament her parents must find themselves in at times. How the hell did you say no to that?

CHAPTER THREE

To the surprise of both of them, Gian agreed to the tour of La Fiordelise.

Ariana's clear interest in the hotel pleased him, and if it had been a real interview, her request would have impressed him indeed.

'Just a short tour...' he nodded '...given you are my final appointment for the day.'

Perhaps it was the single glass of champagne on a nervously empty stomach, but Ariana was giddy with excitement as she stood up. There was even a heady thought that perhaps they might conclude the tour in the restaurant, and then dinner, of course.

And there Gian would offer her the role of VIP Guest Services Manager!

Oh, she could just picture herself in the bespoke blush tartan suits and pearls that the guest services managers wore!

It felt very different walking through the foyer with Gian at her side. Ariana was more than used to turning heads, but there was a certain deference that Gian commanded. Staff straightened at his approach, and guests nudged each other when he passed. There was a certain *something* about Gian that was impossible to define. Something more than elegance, more than command.

Ariana would like to name it.

To bottle it.

To dab her wrists with the essence he emanated.

Soon they had passed Reception and the Pianoforte Bar where, unbeknownst to Ariana, Svetlana sat drumming her fingers on the table, her silver platter of nuts empty, as was her glass. Vincenzo was taking care of that, though, and shaking another cocktail for her, yet Gian barely gave her a glance. He was working after all.

'You know the Pianoforte Bar...' Gian said rather drily, thinking of the array of colour Ariana and her friends made as they breezed in on a Friday night for cocktails to get the weekend underway. 'No doubt your friend Nicki shall be here soon.'

'She shan't be,' Ariana said. 'Nicki is away, skiing with friends.'

'Don't you usually go?'

'Yes, but I didn't want to be stuck on a mountain with Papà so unwell so I told them to go ahead without me.'

'They're staying at the Romano chalet?'

'Of course.' Ariana gave a tight shrug. 'Just because I can't go it doesn't mean I should let everyone down. It's our annual trip.'

That took place on her dime, Gian thought.

He loathed her hangers-on, and all too often had to hold his tongue when her entitled, self-important friends arrived at La Fiordelise courtesy of her name.

He could not hold his tongue now. 'Your partner was asked to leave here the other week.'

'My partner?' Ariana frowned, wondering who he meant. 'Oh, you mean Paulo...'

'I don't know his name,' Gian lied.

Absolutely he knew his name, and those of her so-called friends who added their drinks to the Romano tab, even when Ariana was not here. Gian had even spoken to Rafael about it and had been disappointed with his response: 'Any friend of Ariana's...'

Could Rafael not see his daughter was being used? No, because in his declining years it was easier for Rafael not to see!

'Paulo was never my partner,' Ariana cut in. 'He and I, well...' She shrugged, uncertain how to describe them. 'It's just business, I guess.'

'Business?' Gian checked.

'The business of being seen.'

Oh, Ariana...

Still, she was not here for life advice, so Gian brushed his fleeting sympathy aside and got on with the tour.

'This is the Terazza Suite. It caters for up to thirty and is used for smaller, very exclusive functions...'

'Is this where my father married *her*?' Ariana asked, refusing to use Mia's name. She had been invited to the wedding, but of course neither she nor her brothers had chosen to attend.

'Yes,' Gian said, without elaborating about the wedding. 'It opens out to a terrace adjacent to the square, though it is too cold to go out there now.'

'I would like to see it.'

The Terazza Suite was empty, but it took little imagination to see that the gold stencilled walls and high ceilings would make a romantic venue indeed.

One wall was lined with French windows and when she pushed down on a handle Ariana found that of course it was locked. *'Per favore?'* she asked. She sensed his reluctance, but Gian first pressed a discreet alarm on the wall then took out his master key and unlocked a door.

As she stepped out it was not the frigid air that caught her breath, more the beauty of the surroundings. There was the chatter and laughter from the square, which was visible through an ornate fence.

'In spring and summer there is a curtain of wisteria that blocks the noise,' Gian explained, looking up at the naked vines, 'but it can be dressed for privacy in winter.' He told her about a recent Christmas wedding with boxed firs for privacy, only Ariana wasn't really listening.

Instead, her silence was borne of regret for not being here to support her father...

'Certainly,' Gian continued, 'it is perfect for more intimate gatherings...'

'You mean weddings that no one wants to attend,' Ariana said, shame and regret making her suddenly defensive.

'You are showing your age, Ariana,' Gian said.

'My age?' Ariana frowned as they stepped back into the warmth and he locked up behind them. 'I'm twenty-five.'

'I meant in brat years,' Gian said, and left her standing there, mouth gaping in indignation as he marched on, just wanting this tour to be over. 'You already know the ballroom...' He waved in its general direction as she caught up, but Ariana had more than a ballroom on her mind.

'Did you just call me a brat?' She couldn't quite believe what he had said.

'Yes,' he said. 'I did.'

'You can't talk to me like that.'

'You're almost right. Once I employ you I can't tell you what an insufferable, spoilt little madam you are...'

But though most people would have burst into tears at his tone, Gian knew Ariana better than that. Instead he watched her red lips part into a smile as realisation hit. 'You're going to take me on, then?'

'I haven't quite decided yet,' Gian said. 'Come on.'

'But I want to see the ballroom.'

'They are in the final preparations for a function tonight.'

'I would so love to see how others do it,' she said, ignoring

Gian and opening one of the heavy, ornate doors and gasping when she peeked in. 'Oh, it looks so beautiful.'

'It is a fortieth wedding anniversary celebration,' Gian told her.

'Ruby,' Ariana sighed, for the tables were dressed with deep red roses and they were in the middle of a final test of the lighting so that even the heavy chandeliers cast rubies of light around the room with stunning effect. 'I know I get angry about my parents' divorce,' she admitted—although as she gazed into the ballroom it was almost as if she was speaking to herself— 'and it is not all Mia's fault, I accept that, but I was always so proud of their marriage. Of course, it was not *my* achievement, but I was so proud of them for still being together when so many marriages fail...'

She gave him pause. Gian looked at her as she spoke, and could almost see the stars in her eyes as she gazed at the gorgeous ballroom.

'I should have gone to Papà's wedding,' Ariana said, for the first time voicing her private remorse. 'I deeply regret that I stayed away.'

Gian was rarely torn to break a confidence. The truth was, Rafael had been relieved that his children had not attended the nuptials. It was a marriage in name only, a brief service, followed by drinks on the terrace, then a cake and kiss for the cameras...

As the owner of several prestigious hotels, Gian was the keeper of many secrets.

So outrageous were the many scandals that Gian was privy to that the Romanos and their rather reprobate ways barely registered a blip. But it would be a seismic event if Ariana found out the truth about her parents.

Their marriage had been over long before their divorce.

Angela Romano had been with her lover for decades. Prior to the divorce, Angela and Thomas had often enjoyed extended midweek breaks at La Fiordelise.

Rafael would not blink an eye if he knew; in fact, Gian, assumed that he did. For those long business lunches Rafael had enjoyed with Roberto—his lawyer—had, in fact, been rare public outings for a devoted couple who had been together for more than fifteen years.

As for Mia...

Well, Gian to this day did not understand Angela's hatred towards her, when close friends all knew that Mia was Rafael's beard—a prop used to prevent the world from finding out in his declining years that Rafael Romano was gay. Perhaps, if Ariana could have this necessary conversation with her father, it might lead him to reveal his truth before it was too late or, worse, before she inadvertently found out.

'Why don't you tell your father that you regret not being at his wedding?' Gian suggested. 'Talk to him about it...'

'I try to stay upbeat when I visit him.'

'Tell him how you feel,' Gian gently pushed, and saw that she was thinking about it.

'I might.' She nodded and then turned to him with a question no one had ever dared ask. 'Were your parents happy?'

It was just a question, and it flowed from the context perhaps, but he had to think for a long moment, to cast his mind back, to the parties, to the laughter, to the inappropriate mess that had been them, and for once he did not choose silence. 'Yes,' Gian finally answered. 'They were happy because they followed only their hearts and not their heads.' When she frowned, clearly nonplussed, Gian explained further. 'Their happiness was to the exclusion of all else.'

'Including you?'

He did not answer and Ariana knew she had crossed the line, but now they were in this odd standoff.

They looked at each other. His thick black hair was so superbly cut that as she looked up at him she felt the oddest temptation to raise her hand and simply touch it, and to see if it fell back into perfect shape, but of course impulse had no place here, and anyway it was just a thought. But that made it a red button that said *do not touch*, and consequently made her itch to do so. 'Including you?' she persisted.

'This is an interview, Ariana, the purpose of which is to find out more about you, not the other way around.'

Under her breath she muttered, 'Your life is an interview then.'

'Pardon?'

'It just dawned on me, Gian, that you know an awful lot about me, but I know practically nothing about you.'

'Good,' he clipped.

It wasn't good, though. Suddenly there was a whole lot that Ariana wanted to know about him, and her heart suddenly stopped with its ungainly trot and kicked into a gallop.

He angered her.

Only that wasn't quite right, because anger didn't make her thighs suddenly clamp, or her lips ache. And anger didn't make her knickers damp or give her an urge to kiss that haughty, arrogant face. This was something else entirely, though her voice when she spoke was indeed cross. 'Are you going to hire me or not, Gian?'

'I am hesitant to.'

While he wanted to afford her a new start, Ariana working here spelt Trouble.

In more ways than one.

Yes, she was airy and spoilt and brattish, but he could almost feel the prickle of her under his skin and that was an attraction that was safer to deny. 'If it doesn't work out—' he started.

'It *will* work out,' she broke in. 'I shall make it so!'

And I will push all thoughts of fancying you aside, Ariana hurriedly thought.

'You would still have to do the twelve-week induction.' He wasn't asking, he was telling. 'It is mandatory that all my guest services staff have personally worked in every area of the hotel.'

'Yes.' Ariana nodded. 'I'll do the induction.'

'If you are successful in your introductory period then there might be a position as a guest services *assistant...*'

'But—'

'My managers earn their titles, Ariana.' He watched two spots of colour start to burn on her cheeks. 'And there will be no favours and no concessions. From this point on, the trajectory of your career is in your hands. You will report on Monday at seven to Vanda, who deals with staff training, and any issues you have, you take to her, not me.'

'Of course.'

He wasn't sure she got it, though. 'Ariana, this is my hotel, and I separate things, so if you work here you must understand that I don't deal with the grumbles of minor staff. I don't want to hear about your day; I simply do not want to know. I don't want to hear you can't handle vomit or difficult guests. You take it up with Vanda. Not my problem...'

'Of course.'

'And there shall be no stopping by my office for champagne. That stops today! In fact, as of now there will be no need to drop by my office at all.'

She pouted. 'You said I could always come to you.'

He had.

And over the years *she* had.

Not all her confessionals took place in his office, though. They went way further back than that.

Once in Luctano, an eight-year-old Ariana, too scared to confide in her older brother Dante, had admitted to an eighteen-year-old Gian that she had stolen chocolate from the local store. She wouldn't tell him why, just pleaded with him not to tell her father or Dante.

'First, explain to me why you stole,' Gian had persisted. 'You have the money to pay.'

'Stefano dared me to,' Ariana had admitted. 'I haven't eaten it, though. The chocolate is still under my bed, but I feel ill when I try to say my prayers...'

Gian had taken her in to the store and Ariana had duly apologised and paid for the chocolate, and, no, he had not told Dante or Rafael. Instead he'd had a quiet word with Stefano. 'You want to steal,' he had said to the young boy, 'then at least have the guts to do it yourself.'

Another time, some years later, Stefano had been caught smoking and Ariana had arrived here in Gian's office and begged him to impersonate her father when the school inevitably rang.

'Why would they ring here?' Gian had frowned.

'Because I told Stefano to say that Papà is here at La Fiordelise on business.'

Ariana was a minx and far too skilled at lying. Gian had of course declined to cover for Stefano, and had spoken to Rafael himself.

There was *always* drama surrounding Ariana, though it was not always of her own making—just two years ago, in the midst of her parents' scandalous divorce, she had found out that her father was ill and Ariana had sat in Gian's office, being fed tissues but not false promises.

Yes, he had kept his door open to her, but—

'If I hire you,' Gian said, very carefully, 'all that stops.'

And suddenly, if the safety net of Gian was going to be removed, Ariana didn't know if she wanted her career any more—not that he seemed to notice her dilemma.

'Who the hell orders champagne at a job interview?' Gian mused.

'It was my first ever interview,' Ariana admitted. 'I sensed your irritation and was trying to drag things out.'

'Well done, you, then,' Gian said, and then sighed because he did not need Ariana under his precious roof, and the drama that would undoubtedly entail. 'Why here, Ariana? Why La Fiordelise, Rome?'

'Because I love it,' she admitted. She looked up at the high ceilings and the gilded mirrors and the beauty that never failed to capture her heart. There was a sense of peace and calm that Gian had created, a haven that somehow made her feel safe. 'I am sure your other hotels are stunning—in fact, I have stayed in the London one several times—it is just...' She tried her best to explain it. 'There is so much history here, so much...' She faltered and then pushed on. 'It was your great-great-grandfather's?' she checked.

'You will learn the history in your induction.'

'Can you at least give me the condensed version?' Ariana asked, running a hand along a marble column and frowning at an indentation, a mar in perfection.

'That is a bullet hole,' Gian told her, 'from when the hotel became a fortress in the Second World War.'

She breathed in, shivering at the history and aching, actually aching, to know more. But Gian was glancing beyond her shoulder now, and Ariana sensed she was running out of her allotted time. 'Can I see the penthouse suite? The original one?'

'No.'

'Please.'

God, Gian thought, she was incessant. 'There might be guests.'

'I'm sure you would know.'

He sighed. 'You are most persistent.' He took out his phone and though he knew there were no guests due in the most expensive suite until tomorrow, he double-checked just to be sure, and almost sighed when he saw that indeed it was vacant. 'Very well, but only briefly.'

As they took the elevator up, Ariana had a question. 'Is your apartment on the penthouse floor?'

'No, though it is where I grew up,' Gian told her, 'but when I took over La Fiordelise, I decided I could not afford the luxury of misappropriating the hotel's most valuable asset.'

As well as that, the penthouse floor had been the loneliest place in the world for Gian. He would sometimes glimpse his parents drifting off to some event, or hear first the laughter and merriment of parties, and then lie drenched in dread as the gathering flared and got out of hand.

But as dark as his memories were, the penthouse floor was an asset indeed. This was confirmed by her gasp as she stepped into the main suite.

Rome was spread out before them and from this vantage she looked down at the square and across to Palazzo Pamphili, where her brother's wedding would be held, but that was not all that held her gaze. She wandered the vast space, taking in the ornaments and oil paintings that surely belonged behind a rope in a gallery and yet they were there for the luckiest guests to take in at their leisure.

'This corridor can be closed off,' Gian explained as she peered into the spare bedrooms, each as exquisite as the next; there was even a gorgeous library that had a huge fire, just waiting to be lit.

And then he showed her the master suite and it felt as if she wasn't just in Rome but was at the very centre of it. The bed was draped in gold, the intricately painted ceilings a masterpiece of their own, and it was as if the walls had their own pulse. Ariana was rich, but there was, of course, a pecking order, and the Penthouse Suite was not Ariana's domain. 'Is this where my parents would stay for the Romano Ball?'

Her question went unanswered, for Gian never commented on the sleeping arrangements of his guests and anyway, her eyes would fall out if he told her the truth.

'And now Dante?' she persisted.

Still he said nothing, and it was Ariana who filled the gap. 'I could live here for ever,' she sighed, sinking onto a plump lounge and kicking off her stilettoes.

'Believe me...' Gian started, but did not finish.

Certainly, he would not be sharing with Ariana that he loathed coming up here. There were just too many memories that resided here. Instead, he pointed out another of its disadvantages. 'It takes for ever to clean, which you might soon find out,' Gian said with a wry edge, and he watched as she tucked her slender legs under her. 'A full two days to service properly.'

'Let me dream for a moment,' she sighed. 'So this was built for the Duke's mistress?'

'Incorrect.'

'Correct me then,' Ariana said, her voice dropping to huskiness as, for the first time in her life, she officially flirted. Not that Gian even noticed, for he proceeded to give her a history lesson.

'It was officially built for the Duke and the Duchess,' Gian told her. 'It was actually first called La Duchessa,' Gian said, 'well, officially, but the locals all called it La Fiordelise…'

She watched as he pulled back some ornate panelling to reveal a heavy door and in it a silver key. 'Fiordelise lived through here.'

He turned the key and pushed open the door to reveal another completely separate penthouse suite, in feminine reds and with a view of the square and a personality of its own. Yet he was somewhat surprised when the rather nosy Ariana did not untangle her long legs and pad over to look at the sumptuous boudoir. Instead she screwed up her nose. 'The poor Duchess.' Her sloe eyes narrowed. 'How awful to live with just a wall between you and your husband's mistress.'

'You don't find the story of La Fiordelise romantic?'

'History makes it *appear* romantic.' Ariana shrugged. 'I find it offensive.'

Of course, given her father's *supposed* affair with Mia, he guessed that infidelity would be one of her hot buttons, but he sensed that her thoughts had been formed long ago. There was a side to Ariana he had never seen: a free thinker was in there, though somewhat suppressed.

'Why do you find it so offensive?' Gian asked. 'Things were very different back then.'

'I doubt *feelings* were different,' Ariana said. 'And I hate it that the Duchess had to vie for his attention. You would hope, once married, all that would stop.'

'All what?'

'Being shut out. It should have been the Duchess on his mind, not Fiordelise.'

Gian looked at her thoughtfully. 'You have a very idealistic view of marriage.'

'Absolutely I do,' Ariana agreed. She stood and padded over to where Fiordelise had once resided and, standing in the doorway with him, peered into the opulent, sensual, feminine suite. Yet she did not set as much as a foot inside, just faced him in the doorway. 'And that is why I am still single.'

His eyes never left her face as she continued to speak. 'My mother has spent the last quarter of a century planning my wedding—any old billionaire will do—but I shall only marry for love.' She smiled at him then and teased him a little. 'Do you even know what that word means, Gian?'

'No,' he replied, 'and I don't care to find out.'

'As is your prerogative, but it is mine to feel sad for the Duchess. What was her name?'

'Violetta,' Gian answered, 'like…' He hesitated, for he had been about to compare the name to Ariana's eyes. For several reasons, that would not be a sensible thing to do. Neither was the way he was looking into them right now.

Yes, he had noticed the huskiness of her voice and the earlier batting of her eyelashes. There was a friction in the Ariana-scented air, and his hand wanted to know for itself the softness of her cheek—so much so that Gian had to focus on not lifting his hand and cupping her face.

Gian, despite his formidable reputation, had scruples, and to kiss her, as he now desired to, while still involved with Svetlana was not something he would do.

And, aside from that, this was Ariana Romano.

The daughter of a man he respected and the little sister

of his lifelong friend. And soon to be an employee. A casual affair she could never be, and that was all Gian wanted or knew.

Ariana Romano was completely off limits.

CHAPTER FOUR

'VIOLETTA.' ARIANA REPEATED the name of the forgotten Duchess while gazing into his eyes. 'That's beautiful.'

She practically handed him a response—*and so are you*—except Gian refused to rise to the bait.

Or rather he fought not to rise.

They stood facing each other in the doorway, their bodies almost as close as when they danced their one duty dance each year at the Romano Foundation Ball.

And he was as turned on as he had been while holding her in that dress of silver.

Of course it had been more than an educated guess, for she had looked utterly stunning that night.

Gian was well aware of his past with women.

And he was decided on his future too.

Casual, temporary, fleeting, there were many ways to describe the nature of his relationships, except entering into any of the above with Ariana was an impossible concept. If they were seen out more than a couple of times the press would soon get hold of it and her mother would too. As much as Angela resented Gian for holding Rafael's second wedding here, she would forgive him in an instant to have a title in the family.

No, there could be no kisses, though certainly the moment was ripe for one...

'What?' Ariana said. She could feel a sudden charge in the air, a slight frisson that had her on her guard. She assumed he was displeased and wondered if perhaps she shouldn't have brought up the Duchess's name, or been so derisive of Fiordelise.

Ariana could not read men.

Well, not real men, which Gian undoubtedly was.

She could read fake men, who wanted to be seen with her just for appearances' sake. And though she tried to convince herself they cared, she could never bring herself to take it beyond anything other than a tasteless kiss.

Despite popular gossip, Ariana was completely untouched.

Her flirting was all for the cameras.

No, she could not read *this* man, who stared into her eyes and gritted his jaw and, in the absence of experience, she assumed he was displeased. 'I've offended you,' Ariana said. Completely misreading the tension, she shrugged, not caring in the least if she had upset him by refusing to rave about the mistress, Fiordelise.

'You haven't offended me,' Gian said, snapping back into business mode. 'I'm just telling you the history of the place—as you asked.'

'Well, I've enjoyed hearing it.'

It was nice to be here with Gian.

Nice to have a conversation that was about more than the latest fashion or who was sleeping with whom.

It was, quite simply, nice.

'Tell me more,' Ariana said, walking back through to the master bedroom and resuming her place on the lounge. Bending over, she pulled on one of her suede stilettoes.

'There's not much more to tell.'

'Liar.' She smiled and caught his eye. 'Go on,' she persisted, 'tell me something that no one else knows.'

'Why would I do that?'

'Why wouldn't you?' she asked, peering up at him through her eyelashes as she wedged the other shoe on.

Usually, Gian could not wait to get out of the Penthouse Suite, yet Ariana was so curious and the company so pleasing that he decided the world could surely wait and he told her a titbit that very few knew. 'The Duke had a ring made for Fiordelise.'

'A ring?' That got her interest and Gian watched as her pupils dilated at the speed of a cat's. 'What was it like?'

'It is the insignia of the hotel,' Gian told her. 'The Duke would only ever let her look at it, though; she never once put it on. He held onto it on the promise that one day he would marry her.'

'I'm liking the Duke less and less,' Ariana said, smiling.

'Then you'll be pleased to know that when the Duchess died and he offered Fiordelise the ring, she declined it.'

'Really?'

'Yes. By then she had fallen in love with a servant. The old Duke was too tired to be angry, and too embarrassed by her rejection to ever admit the truth. Fiordelise saw out her days in her boudoir with her manservant tending to her needs…'

'Good for her.' Ariana smirked.

'Don't tell the guests, though.'

She laughed, and it sounded like a chandelier had caught the wind.

Right there, in the presidential suite of his signature hotel, something shifted for Gian.

Ariana was more than beautiful.

And she was more complex than he had known.

More, he admired her for the mutinous act of trying to shed her pampered existence—with conditions of course. 'Come on,' he said, trying to keep the reluctance from his tone as they left the vast and luxurious cocoon of the suite.

'What's down there?' Ariana asked as they came out into the corridor and she saw that there was a door on the other side. 'Is there *another* penthouse suite?'

'No, there's a butler's room and kitchen and some storage space...' His expression was grim as she wandered off to explore. What was now the butler's room had been home for his many nannies. 'What's this one for?' she asked, and peered into a dour windowless room, unaware it was where Gian had slept as a child. There were shelves holding spare laptops, computer screens, chargers, adaptors, magnifying mirrors, straightening irons, and anything else a guest might have forgotten or need. 'Miscellaneous items.' Ariana concluded.

'Precisely.'

Oh, that frisson was back, only it felt different this time, and Ariana was quite sure that this time he really was displeased so she closed the door on the windowless room.

They were soon in the elevator. That clinging scent she wore was reaching him again, and he turned rather harshly towards her. 'If you do commence work at La Fiordelise you should know that perfume is banned for staff. It is not pleasant for the guests as some have allergies.'

'*You* wear cologne,' Ariana rather belligerently pointed out, for those citrus and bergamot notes had long been the signature of his greeting and the scent she breathed once a year when they danced.

'Yes, but I am not servicing the rooms. Please remember not to wear perfume for work.'

'I don't wear perfume.'

'Oh, please.'

'But I don't.' Ariana frowned. 'My skin is too sensitive.'

He wanted to debate it, to point out that the small elevator smelt of sunshine and rain and an undernote that he could not define, but the doors opened and he stepped out to the relative neutrality of Reception. He would have a word with Vanda, Gian decided. She could talk to her about perfume and such, because policing Ariana would no doubt be a full-time job! 'Are you sure you aren't just coveting the suit and pearls that my guest services managers wear?' Gian checked, as Bianca, one of his senior staff, smiled a greeting as she passed.

'Of course, not.' Ariana shook her head and flushed at her own lie, because the gorgeous blush tartan outfits were divine. 'I'm not that shallow. I really want this, Gian.'

'Well, I mean it, Ariana. If you blow this, I shall not be giving you another chance. You are to be here at seven on Monday morning,' Gian said. 'If you're late, if you're ill, if your arm is hanging off, I still don't want to hear it. Any problems, any issues, any *excuses* are no longer my concern. Vanda shall deal with you.'

And no doubt Vanda would soon fire her. 'I will say goodbye to you here,' he said.

'I need to collect my bag from your office.'

Of course she did!

He tried not to notice the feeling of the sun stepping into his office again as they walked in. 'Thank you for the tour.' Ariana smiled, 'I absolutely loved hearing about the Duke and Duchess, and Fiordelise, even if I do not approve. I'm glad she never got to wear the ring.'

He should conclude the meeting. They were already running over her unallotted time and Svetlana was waiting impatiently in the Pianoforte Bar, yet such was her enthusiasm, so unexpected the brightness of her company that instead of dismissing her Gian headed to the safe hidden in his wall.

He rarely opened the safe. In it were documents and rolls of plans, and there were also the coroner's and police reports from the deaths of his parents and brother, but there was also one thing of beauty nestled atop them.

'Come here,' Gian told her.

Those words sent an unfamiliar shiver through her, so unfamiliar that Ariana did not ask why, or what for. Instead, she followed his command and walked over.

He removed a faded velvet box from the safe. It might once have been gold, but it had faded now to a silver beige, yet it was beautiful still. The box was studded with gold tacks and the clasp was so intricate that she wondered how he flicked it open so easily.

'Look,' Gian said.

Fiordelise's ring was the rarest of treasures. It was a swirl of stunning Italian rose gold, and in the centre was a ruby so deep and so vibrant it made her breath hitch.

'I've never seen a ruby of that colour,' Ariana breathed. 'It's the colour of a pomegranate kernel, although it's bigger...'

'It's called pigeon-blood red,' Gian corrected. 'The colour of the first drops after a kill.'

'Don't.' Ariana shuddered. 'I like pomegranate better.'

'Then pomegranate red it is.' Gian smiled and then closed up the box. 'I found this five years after I inherited the place.'

'Where did you find it?'

'Under the very spot you were seated a short while ago,' Gian told her. 'When the suite was being renovated they pulled up the floor. There was a hidden basement and in it was a box. There was a shawl and some sketches of Fiordelise, and also this...'

'What happened to the sketches?' Ariana asked.

'I had them restored and framed.'

'And the shawl?'

'I gave that to an aunt. But this...' He replaced the box in the safe. 'God alone knows it would have been easier to have found this some five years earlier.'

'You'd have sold it?' Ariana frowned. She knew that he had inherited his estate from his family in the direst of conditions, and that La Fiordelise had been on the brink of collapse, yet she could not believe he would have sold something as precious and sentimental as this ring.

But Gian was adamant. 'Absolutely I would have.'

'I don't believe you.'

'Then you don't know me,' Gian said, closing up the safe. He turned to her. 'I shall have Luna bring your coat.'

'Thank you,' Ariana said, trying to quash the thud of disappointment that he hadn't suggested, given the hour, that they have dinner together. Well, she would soon see about that. 'Gosh, it's almost seven!' Ariana exclaimed. 'No wonder I'm so hungry.'

'Indeed,' Gian said. 'I should let you get on.'

She tried to stall him again. 'What about my uniform? Don't I need to be measured?'

'You'll be working as a chambermaid for the first few weeks of your rotation. That uniform comes in small, medium or large, I believe.'

There was the tiniest wrinkle of her pretty nose and then she shrugged. 'I lied,' Ariana admitted. 'I do want the tartan and pearls.'

'I know you do.'

'And I *shall* get them one day. I shall be the best guest services manager you've ever had.' She pictured her pretty pink business cards with her name embossed in rose gold: *Ariana Romano, VIP Guest Services Manager.*

Perhaps she shouldn't be so vocal with her dreams, but when she looked up she was startled by the glimmer of a smile softening his mouth.

It was a smile she had never seen on him before.

Ariana had known him for a long time. If there was trouble in her life—and all too often there was—it was Gian she ran to. And when, inevitably, she thanked him for sorting whatever problem she had placed in his lap, he would nod and give her his grim, somewhat weary smile. There was another smile she knew: each year they sat side by side at the Romano Ball, and each year he performed a duty dance, and so of course she was privy to his duty smile.

Yes, his duty smile, she called it, for that was exactly what it was.

She saw it used on guests, on dignitaries and on herself as recently as this evening when she had first walked in. *This* smile, though, was different. This *off-duty* smile felt as if it was just for her, though it was fading now and his grey eyes returned to guarded.

'I really do need to get on,' Gian said as Luna appeared with her coat.

As she and Gian walked out, Ariana saw the stunning woman from the Pianoforte Bar smile over at him. 'I'll be with you in just a moment.' Gian nodded to her and from the lack of affection in his tone she assumed he had another client.

'I thought I was your last appointment,' Ariana said.

'You were.'

He stalked off then to the waiting woman, who lifted her face to him, clearly expecting a most thorough kiss, but instead Ariana heard his slight rebuke. 'I said I would meet you at the theatre, Svetlana.'

'I thought we might have dinner in the restaurant,' Svetlana purred and needlessly fiddled with the lapel of his jacket. 'You still haven't taken me there.'

Oh!

Ariana's face was on fire, yet she could not look away. It was unsettling to see him with a woman when of course it should not be, given his reputation. It just felt different seeing it first-hand and flicked a little knife toward her heart.

'Maybe after…?' Svetlana persisted.

Gian was not enamoured of women who purred, or those who felt the need to pick an imaginary piece of lint from his lapel, and Svetlana had been doing a lot of both of those of late.

He had already decided they were over, and was about to tell Svetlana, but with Ariana so close, for reasons he did not care—or dare—to examine, he chose not to. 'Come,' he said, 'we'll be late.'

He didn't even glance in Ariana's direction as he headed off.

After all, if he stopped to say goodbye to each member of staff, he would never get out of the door.

Ariana Romano as staff?

Ariana in his hotel each and every day…

Instantly, he regretted his decision to take her on.

But then, on Monday morning, an hour after Ariana *should have* commenced her first shift, he received a text.

Gian, I am sorry! There has been an Extraordinary Board Meeting called!!!! Can I start in the afternoon instead?

Very deliberately, Gian didn't respond.

He didn't even scold her for her excessive use of exclamation marks; after all, Ariana personified them. This could never, ever work, and when she came in, hours late, on her very first day, Gian would tell her exactly why.

At lunchtime, rather than text she called him, no doubt with yet more excuses.

'Gian—'

'I don't want to hear it,' Gian cut in abruptly. 'Ariana, I simply do not want to know. Even after I gave explicit instructions not to do so, you still think you can call and text me with excuses for why you're late or not coming in. I don't deal with junior—'

'Gian, please, just listen to me…'

She was starting to cry, but Gian was way too used to her crocodile tears. 'I knew on Friday you were unsuitable for the role and your behaviour today merely confirms it. This could never have worked.'

'Gian…' she sobbed, but though he refused to be moved his mask slipped and he forgot to be polite. 'You sat in this office and pleaded for a start, and I gave you one. The contracts were drawn up and waiting to be signed, but clearly something more enticing has come along. I don't want to hear about extraordinary board meetings. The only extraordinary thing was that I actually thought you had changed your precocious, self-serving ways, but clearly you have not.'

Problem solved, Gian thought as he terminated the call. He was a little breathless, and barely holding onto his temper but he also felt a strange disappointment that, yet again, Ariana had let herself down. She was incapable of seeing things through. She was absolutely devoid of any sense of responsibility. She was always onto the next best thing the second it showed up.

Yet there was a mounting sense of disquiet to have heard her tears, for there had been an unfamiliar rasp to them that had, on reflection, sounded real.

She'd probably been putting it on, Gian told himself. If Ariana really wanted a career then perhaps she should have considered acting.

The ridiculous thing was, as he sat there, he was envisioning her in the blush pink tartan suit and the string of pearls that she had admitted she secretly desired.

Ariana, whether he wanted her to or not, made him smile, and for Gian that was rare indeed.

His private phone was buzzing and he saw that it was Dante who was calling, no doubt hoping to sway Gian from his decision.

'*Pronto,*' Gian said.

There was silence for a moment.

'Dante?' Gian checked. 'Look, if you're calling to excuse Ariana and ask—'

'Gian,' Dante interrupted. 'I don't know what you're referring to. I just wanted to call you before word got out. I'm sorry to have to tell you, but a short while ago my father...' Dante cleared his throat. 'Rafael has passed away.'

CHAPTER FIVE

GIAN DE LUCA MIGHT BE the last Duke of Luctano, but to him Rafael Romano had always been King.

In modern times, Rafael Romano had put Luctano on the map far more than the De Lucas, who had long ago sold off their land and moved to Rome.

This cold grey morning he flew in to bid farewell to a man Gian considered not just a brilliant business mind but a man he had been proud to call a friend.

The landscape beneath his navy helicopter was familiar. A lattice of bare vines weaved across the hills and down into the valley but, deep in winter, the poppy fields were bare and silver with ice. The lake, beside which Rafael was to be buried, was at first a black, uninviting mirror, but now rippled as his helicopter neared its location.

It was to be a private burial, for Rafael's wife and children only, and Gian was there just for the church service.

The family would now all be at the house, and though Dante had invited him to have his pilot land there, without Rafael, Gian felt he would be invading on this solemn day.

A driver had been arranged to meet him and as he took the steps down from the helicopter Gian felt a blast of bitterly cold air: the weather in Luctano was always more extreme than in Rome. He wore a long black wool coat over his tailored black suit. His thick black hair had not quite been due for a trim, but his barber had come to his apartment that morning to ensure a perfect cut and he was particularly close shaven.

With good reason.

As a car took him to the church, he recalled Rafael's words from long ago. 'Look immaculate,' Rafael had once told him. 'You are not a university student any more but the owner-manager of a five-star hotel. Get your hair cut, and for God's sake, shave.' His advice had not ended there. 'See a tailor, buy fine shoes...'

At the age of twenty, Gian had been studying architecture and living in the residences, having turned his back on his family two years previously. His scholarship had covered accommodation and his bar work funded books and food, but barely stretched to a haircut, let alone designer clothes. 'I can't afford to,' a proud Gian had dared to admit.

'You can't afford not to. Now, listen to me, it is imperative that you look the part...'

But Gian had held firm. After the tragic death of his family, he'd discovered the financial chaos his parents had left behind and the many jobs that depended on him. 'No, the accounts are a disaster. Before the fancy suits, first the staff are to be paid.'

'It doesn't work like that.'

Rafael had taken a reluctant Gian to Via dei Condotti—a fashionable street in Rome—where he had met with artisan tailors and been fitted for bespoke Italian shoes in the only true handout that Gian had ever received. But better than the trip had been the glimpse of having if not a father then a mentor to advise him.

The day had ended at a Middle Eastern barbershop, with hot

towels and a close shave. Rafael continued with the sage advice: 'You need to attract only the best clients.'

'How, though?' Gian had asked, staring at his groomed reflection and barely recognising himself. 'La Fiordelise's reputation is in tatters and the building is in disrepair.' Gian loathed the destruction of history—how there were only a few decent areas remaining in the once elegant building. The rest was cordoned off and for the most part the hotel was faded and unkempt.

But Rafael remained upbeat. 'La Fiordelise has survived worse. It has a new owner now and its reputation will recover: all we need is a plan.'

A couple of weeks later they had contrived one.

A plan that, to this day, few knew about.

Yes, Rafael Romano had been far more of a father to Gian than his own, and Gian would miss him very much indeed.

Arriving at the church, he could feel eyes on him as the absent Duke made a rare return. Gian declined the offer of being guided to a pew and instead stood at the back of the small church and did his level best to keep from recalling the last time he'd been here—at his own family's funeral. He pondered his handling of Ariana when she had tried to tell him her father had died. Of course he had tried to call her back and apologise, but had been sent straight to voicemail...

Gian's words, though, had been an unwitting lifeline.

It was Gian's deep, calm voice on this terrible morning that brought Ariana a little solace.

'Ariana,' Dante snapped as they all stood in the entrance hall of their father's home, preparing to head out for the funeral procession. It was exquisitely awkward as of course it was Mia's home too. Her older brother was in a particularly picky mood. 'Surely you can get off your phone for five minutes?'

But Ariana ignored him as she listened again to Gian's message.

I should have let you speak. Ariana, I apologise and I am

so deeply sorry for your loss. Call me if you want to, if not...'
His deep voice halted for a few seconds. *'You will get through this, Ariana. You are strong. Remember that.'*

Ariana didn't feel very strong, though.

She was weak from having to comfort her mother through the day, and at night, though exhausted, she could barely sleep. She felt as if she were holding a million balls in the air and that at any moment one might drop, for her family, scattered by Mia's presence, had not been under one roof since the divorce, let alone the roof of a church.

Surely her mother would not create a scene?

Or her aunts or uncles...

As well as the worry of that, as she headed out to the waiting cars, the loneliest morning of her life felt even more desolate when Dante decided to take a seat in the front vehicle with Mia, rather than make her travel to the church by herself. That left Ariana with Stefano and Eloa, which lately felt like the equivalent of being alone.

As the cortège moved through the hills to the village, Ariana tried to come to grips with a world without her father while acknowledging a disquieting truth.

Since her father had found Mia, he too had pushed her aside.

For two years, she had felt like a visitor in the family home and later at his hospital bedside. Perhaps she could have accepted Mia more readily if they had accepted her more into their world. Yes, she regretted now not going to the wedding, but the truth was her father hadn't exactly pushed for her to attend.

In fact, he'd seemed a touch relieved when Ariana had declined.

Once she had been the apple of her father's eye and they would talk and laugh. They would fly to the London office together, and she had felt there was a real place for her on the Romano board, but since Dante had taken over all she had felt was supernumerary.

Ariana didn't just miss her father today; she had missed him for the last two years of his life. And now she would miss him for ever, with no time left to put things to rights.

'We're here,' Eloa announced, breaking into her thoughts, and Ariana looked up and saw they were at the church.

The doors were opened and the trio stepped out. Her legs felt as if they had been spun in brittle steel wool, and might snap as she walked over the cobbles and into the church. Her heart felt like a fish flopping in her chest that might jump out of her throat if she let out the wail she held in. The sight of her father's coffin at the front of the church, though expected, was so confronting that she wanted to turn around and flee, unsure whether she was capable of getting through the ceremony.

But then, just as she felt like panic would surely take over, came an unexpected moment of solace.

Gian was here.

Of course he was, but it was the actual *sight* of him, the glimpse of him, that allowed Ariana to draw a deeper breath.

He looked more polished and immaculate than she had ever seen; his black hair was brushed back from his face and she could see both the compassion and authority in his grey eyes.

Yes, authority, for him standing at the back with a full view of proceedings instantly calmed Ariana.

Gian would not let things get out of hand.

He would keep things under control.

And then she knew that it wasn't the hotel, or the haven in Rome that Gian had created, that calmed her.

It was Gian himself who made the world safe.

The look they shared lasted less than a moment—Gian gave her a small, grim smile of sympathy, a nod of his noble head, more by way of understanding than greeting—but time had taken on a different meaning, for the velvet of his eyes and the quiet comfort they gave would sustain her through the service.

You are strong.

He had told her so.

And so she did her best to get through the eulogy and the hymns and the hell.

Gian had been through this before, Ariana reminded herself as she did her level best not to stare at the coffin.

There had been three coffins in this church when his family had died. Pink peonies on his mother's, white lilies on his father's and a huge spray of red poppies on his brother's.

'I don't like this, Papà,' she had whispered, for she'd been ten years old and the chants and scent of incense had made her feel a little ill.

'I know, bella, but we are here today for Gian,' her *papà* had said.

'Shouldn't we sit with him, then?' Ariana had asked, for even beside his aunts and such he had looked so completely alone.

'We are not family,' her *papà* had said. *'Hold my hand.'*

His warm hand had closed around hers and imbued her with strength, but she had looked over at Gian and seen that there was no one holding his.

And there was no one holding Ariana's today.

It was an emotional service, but Gian refused to let it move him and stood dry-eyed even as the coffin was carried out to the haunting strains of his favourite aria—Puccini's 'O Mio Babbino Caro'. *Oh, my dear Papà...*

Ariana looked close to fainting, but her damned mother was too busy beating at her chest to see.

'Hey,' Gian said. To the frowns of the congregation, he broke protocol and joined the family on the way out. 'You are doing so well,' he murmured quietly.

'I am not.'

'You are, you are.' He could feel her tremble. As the family lined up outside the church, instead of guiding her to join them, he took Ariana aside and held her.

She leaned on him for a moment, a blissful moment that smelt of Gian, and she learned something more about him. There were no tears in his eyes, he looked a little pale but unmoved, yet his heart beat rapidly in his chest and she could *feel* his grief as he held her in his arms.

As they held each other.

'You'll miss him too,' she whispered.

'Ever so.'

It was the closest she had ever been to him, this blissful place on a terrible day, and she wanted to cling on, to rest in his arms a while longer, but he was pulling her back and returning to his usual distant form.

'Gian.' It was so cold to stand without him, especially when she wanted the shield of his arms. 'I don't think I can face the burial.'

'Yes, Ariana, you can.'

But hysteria was mounting. 'No. I really don't think so...'

'Would it help if I came with you?'

It would, but... 'You can't.' She gave a black laugh. 'Stefano practically had to put in a written request to Dante to have Eloa attend, and she's his fiancée. Mamma has been denied. God, Gian, I don't...'

'Take this.'

From deep in his coat pocket he handed her a *cornicello*... a small gold amulet. 'Your father gave me this to hold when I buried my family. You *can* do this, Ariana; you will regret it if you don't.'

It was the most private of burials.

Mia, who could barely stand, held a single lily.

And Dante, who loathed Mia possibly the most of all Rafael's children, was the one who had to take her to the graveside so she could throw the flower in.

Stefano wept and was comforted by Eloa, and that left Ariana standing alone, holding onto the little sliver of gold.

Ariana had never felt so cold as when she returned to the house and stood by a huge fire, grateful for the large cognac

someone placed in her hands. Looking up, she saw it was Gian.
'Thank you.'

'How was it?' Gian gently enquired.

'It is done,' Ariana responded, without really answering and
then held out the amulet. 'Here, I should give this back to you.
Thank you.'

'Keep it.'

'He gave it to you,' Ariana said, suddenly angry at his lack
of sentiment. This man who would sell a priceless ring, this
man who would let go of a gift from her father. 'Why would
you give it away?'

'Did it help?' he asked, and she nodded. 'Then you yourself
might pass it on someday when someone else needs your father's strength.'

Never, she thought.

Never, ever.

For it was her first gift from Gian and it almost scared her
how much that meant.

'It seems strange to be here without him,' Gian admitted, trying to gauge how she felt, but for once the effusive Ariana was a
closed book. She gave a tired shrug and her black lashes closed
on violet eyes highlighting the dark shadows beneath them.

'It has felt strange to be here for quite some time.' Her eyes
opened then and came to rest on Rafael's widow, and Gian followed her gaze as she spoke. 'My father and I used to be so
close.'

'You were always close,' Gian refuted.

'No.' She shook her head. 'It fell away at the end.'

He would like to take her arm and walk her away from the
funeral crowd, to walk in the grounds and gently tell her the
difficult truth—the real reason her father had pulled away from
his family and from the daughter he had loved so very much.

It was not his place to do so, though.

Oh, today he loathed being the keeper of secrets, for the truth
would surely help her to heal.

'How long are you here for?' Ariana asked, determinedly changing the subject, then wishing she hadn't for the answer was not one she liked.

'I'll be leaving shortly. I just wanted to see the house one last time and…' He hesitated but then admitted the deeper truth. 'To see how you were after the burial.'

Stay longer, she wanted to say, yet she dared not.

'And,' he added, 'I wanted to properly apologise for how I spoke to you on the day you called. I was completely out of line.'

'Not completely,' Ariana said, and he watched her strained lips part into a brief glimpse of her impish smile. 'Not to come in because of a board meeting *was* inexcusable on my first day…'

'Oh!' Her burst of honesty and the explanation surprised him. 'I thought you must have had word that your father was ill.'

'No, no,' she said. 'That wasn't till later.'

'Well, even so, I'm very sorry for the way I spoke to you.'

'It's fine,' Ariana said. 'I would have been annoyed with me too.'

He watched the dart of anxiety in her eyes as he looked around the room, filled with low murmurs of conversation and her veiled *mamma*, sitting weeping on a chair against the wall surrounded by aunts. 'Mamma and Mia have never been under the same roof…'

'Everyone is behaving,' Gian pointed out.

'For now they are,' Ariana said, and let out a nervous breath, unsure how long the civility might last. 'There is the reading of the will soon.'

'It will be fine,' Gian assured her, though he quietly thought Ariana's concerns might be merited and she didn't even know the half of it! Roberto, the family lawyer, had also been Rafael's long-term lover and he was reading the will. With the current wife and widow in the room, one could be forgiven for expecting fireworks.

'Do you want me to stay until afterwards?' he offered.

'I would like that,' Ariana admitted. She looked up at the

man she always ran to, always turned to, yet the moment was broken by the sound of her mother's voice.

'Gian, I was hoping that you'd come back to the house...' She placed an overly familiar hand on his arm, and Gian would have liked to shrug it off. He loathed the sudden fake friendliness from Angela, although of course it was for a reason. 'Could I ask you to take me back to Rome with you? I simply cannot stand to be here.'

'It would be my pleasure,' Gian politely agreed, for even if he did not particularly want Angela's company, he would do the right thing.

'I have to stay for the reading of the will,' Angela explained, 'but if we could leave after that? Ariana will be coming with us also...'

'But, Mamma, Stefano and Eloa are heading back to Zio Luigi's...' Ariana started, but clearly her desires had no importance here and Gian watched her shoulders slump as she acquiesced. 'If that is what you want.'

Naturally, Gian did not enter the study for the reading of the will. Instead, he poured himself a brandy from Rafael's decanter, as his friend had often done for him, and silently toasted his portrait.

What a mess.

He looked at the portrait and wondered if Rafael's truth would be revealed in the will.

Of course Angela had long since known the truth about her husband, and had fought like a cat to prevent it getting out, more than happy to let the blame for the end of their marriage land on Mia.

He looked at the pictures above the fireplace—family shots. There was a surge that felt almost like a sob building when he saw his own image there, for he had never considered he might appear on anyone's mantelpiece. Certainly there had been no images of him at his childhood home.

Yet here he was, fourteen or fifteen years old, on horseback, with Dante.

Good times.

Not great times, of course, because the end of the holidays had always meant it would be time to head back to Rome and his chaotic existence there.

The door of the study opened and the subdued gathering trooped out; Gian quickly realised that Rafael's truth had not been revealed.

'How was it?' he asked Dante, who was the first to approach him.

'Fine. No real surprises.'

And then came Ariana. She looked pale and drained, as if all the exuberance and arrogance that he was coming to adore had simply been leached from her.

'How did it go?' Gian asked.

'I don't even know how to answer,' she admitted. 'I am taken care of. I have an apartment in Paris and I will never have to work.' She gave a tired shrug. 'Does that mean it went well?'

'Ariana,' he cut in, and his hand reached for her arm but she pulled it back.

Not because she didn't want physical contact, more because of how much she did. 'I should go and say my farewells.'

'Are you sure you want to come back to Rome tonight?'

'Not really.'

'Your family are all here,' Gian pointed out. 'Wouldn't it be better to spend time with them?'

'Yes, but I think Mamma needs me. She feels so out of place here.'

It was a subdued little group that flew back to Rome. Gian's car was waiting at the airport and he gave Angela's address to the driver.

'Ariana, darling,' her mother said, 'I have the most terrible headache. I think I might just head home to bed. After I've been dropped off, Gian's driver will take you home.'

'But, Mamma, I thought I was to stay with you tonight.'

Gian heard the strain in Ariana's voice. She was clearly asking to be with her mother, rather than offering to take care of her, although Angela, just as clearly, chose not to hear it as that. 'Ariana, I know you're worried about me but right now all I really need is some peace.'

Gian gritted his jaw because he could see the manipulative behaviour, pulling Ariana away from the rest of the family just because she could when she'd always intended to spend the evening with Thomas, her lover.

He knew now that he loathed Angela because she was as selfish as his own mother had been.

'I'll call you tomorrow,' Angela said to her daughter as she got out of the car. 'Thank you, Gian, for seeing us home.'

Eternally polite, usually he would have wished her well and forced himself to kiss her cheeks, but the best he could manage was a curt nod.

As the driver closed the door, he looked over at Ariana. She was staring straight ahead and there was the sparkle of unshed tears in her eyes that he knew were waiting to fall the very second she was alone. 'Let's get you home,' Gian said as the car pulled away.

'I don't want to go home.' Ariana shook her head and blinked back the tears. 'I might call Nicki.'

Ariana's friend Nicki ran rather wild and she would undoubtedly prescribe a night of drinking and clubbing as a cure for Ariana's troubled heart. 'How come Nicki wasn't at the funeral?' he asked.

'She only got back from skiing this afternoon.' Ariana scrabbled in her purse for her phone. 'She'd have come if she could.'

Gian doubted it.

Nicki liked the galas and balls, and the spoils of being Ariana's friend, but where was she now when her friend needed her most?

Gian did not quite know what to do.

If it were Stefano, or Dante, or even Angela—who he didn't even like—Gian would suggest a drink at the hotel, or a walk perhaps. Conversation or silence, whatever they chose.

But this was Ariana.

He wished he hadn't noticed her beauty, or the colour of her eyes.

Gian wished he could snap his fingers and return them to a time when she had been just the annoying little sister of a friend, the daughter of his beloved mentor... That thought had him stepping up to do the right thing, for he did not want Ariana in questionable company tonight. 'Would you like to come back to La Fiordelise for a drink, or something to eat perhaps?'

'I...' His offer was so unexpected. Gian usually made her feel like an annoying presence, always trying to cut short their time together, and now it was he who was offering to extend it. 'I don't want to impose.'

'It doesn't normally stop you...' Gian teased, but then, seeing her frown, realised that even the lightest joke wasn't registering. 'It would be my pleasure,' he said. 'I just need to make a quick call.'

Ariana pretended not to listen as he cancelled his date for the night. And his date for the night did not take it well.

'Svetlana,' he said, and Ariana blinked at the slight warning edge to his tone as she looked out at the dark streets. 'Not now.'

And that slight warning edge had her stomach clenching and a small flush rising to her cheeks. She looked at Gian, who appeared incredibly bored at the unfolding drama.

Yes, drama, for she could hear the rise in Svetlana's voice, and foolish, foolish Svetlana, Ariana thought, for she literally watched his impassiveness transform to disdain.

'Svetlana, I am unable to see you tonight,' Gian said, and then, when it was clear she had asked why, rather drily he answered, 'Because I am unable to see you tonight.'

His lack of explanation must have infuriated Svetlana for

even with the phone to his ear, Ariana heard her angry retort. 'When then?'

'Do I have to spell it out, Svetlana?'

It would appear that he did, and Ariana listened as very coldly and firmly he ended their relationship.

'Gian,' she said as they pulled up at La Fiordelise, 'please, call her back. I can go home. I really didn't want to make trouble for you…'

'Forget it.' He gave a dismissive shrug. 'We were always going to end.'

In fact, he hadn't seen Svetlana all week.

Somehow they had bumped through the concert at Teatro dell'Opera but instead of returning to the sumptuous suite behind his office, Gian had taken her home.

'Why did you break up with her?' Ariana asked as they stood outside the car beneath the bright entrance lights.

'Because she wanted more.'

'More?'

'She had started to drop into the hotel unannounced,' he said. Ariana just frowned. 'And she wanted to come up to my residence…'

Her frown deepened.

'As well as that, she wanted to come with me to your father's funeral.'

'Oh?' Ariana said, but it was more a question, because she didn't really understand.

'As if we were a couple.' Gian attempted to explain his closed-off life, but clearly still bewildered, Ariana gave the tiniest shake of her head and so he elaborated. 'She wanted things to progress and that was not what we had agreed.'

'What did you agree to?'

'Only the best parts.' Gian did not soften his words. 'Dinner in a nice restaurant, a trip to the theatre…'

'I assume sex?'

'Correct.'

'So if not in your residence...'

'Ariana, I am not discussing this with you. Suffice it to say I never want a relationship.' He ended the matter. 'You're cold, let's go in.'

'To the restaurant?' Ariana asked.

'I thought the Pianoforte Bar...'

Her eyes narrowed, recalling Svetlana being denied a seat at his restaurant. Despite his kind invitation to keep her company, she knew she was also being kept at arm's length.

'No, thank you.' She shook her head. 'I don't need the noise of a bar tonight, even one as elegant as yours...' Ariana fished and she fished, but Gian did not take the bait, nor upgrade her to restaurant status, even as she stood there and sulked. 'I think I might go for a walk.'

'In heels?' Gian frowned.

'I have my flats in my bag. I'll be fine on my own,' she said, waving him away as she took off her heels and went to put her flats on, but where was a marble pillar when you needed one?

Gian would not be waved off, though, and neither was he Prince Charming, for he did not go down on his knees to help, instead offering his arm. 'Lean on me.' He took one black stiletto that she handed to him and passed her a flat, and then it was all repeated with the other foot.

'Let's walk,' Gian said.

For Ariana, it felt like the right choice. Piazza Navona, the grand, elegant square overlooked by La Fiordelise, was beautifully lit. Its fountains were hypnotic and a little of the tension of the day left as they strolled.

It felt different at night.

Or rather it felt different being here with Gian.

His presence was a comforting warmth in the chilly night air and his voice felt like a welcome caress, as he enquired how things were with her brothers.

'Dante is...' Ariana let out a long sigh. 'I don't know. He's just been so focused on the funeral. I think it will all hit him afterwards. He and my father were close.'

'Yes,' Gian agreed.

'Well, they were until Mia came along.'

'They grew close again, once your father became ill,' Gian pointed out. 'And Stefano?'

'I wouldn't know,' Ariana said tightly. 'You would have to ask Eloa.' She heard the bitterness in her own voice and screwed her eyes closed, because she had told no one, not even Nicki, how left out she felt. 'Sorry, I didn't mean that.'

'Yes, you did,' Gian said gently. 'I know the two of you are close.'

'*Were* close,' she corrected. 'I know it sounds childish, but we used to speak every day. Now he calls Eloa, and that's correct, of course, and how it should be; they're getting married in May. However...' She didn't know how best to describe the loneliness that had descended almost the moment Eloa had been introduced to her and Ariana had felt shut out.

'You miss him?'

'Yes.' She nodded. 'And especially now.'

'Since your father died?'

'Before that,' Ariana admitted. She looked at the moon lighting up the square. If ever there was a time for honesty it was tonight. 'When our parents broke up it was Stefano I turned to. Papà had eyes only for Mia; he didn't want me around so much...'

Gian stayed silent, for he knew that wasn't quite the case. Rafael had found out he was dying and wanted his final years to be spent in peace with Roberto; Mia had been a front of respectability. Of course he could not reveal that and just listened as she continued. 'But Stefano met Eloa around then,' Ariana said. 'I just felt as if everyone I was close to disappeared. I know I have Dante, but he is so much older...'

'Ancient,' Gian agreed drily, for he and Dante were the same age.

'I have Mamma, of course, but...' She wished he would interrupt, or finish her sentence for her, because it was perhaps not something she should say out loud, yet his continued silence compelled her to speak. 'I have Mamma, though only on her terms, and it can be a little stifling at times.'

Still he remained silent as they walked.

'And a little solitary at others,' Ariana admitted. 'I thought things were different with Stefano. He's my twin; I'm used to him being there and I thought, no matter what, we'd still be in each other's lives. I'm happy for him, I honestly am. I'm just not so happy for me. I'm being selfish, I know. Childish...'

'Ariana.' Gian thought for a moment and then decided he could be honest about this much at least. 'For what it's worth, I think Stefano is wrong to shut you out.'

Her head turned towards him, her eyes wide with surprise. She'd expected to be scolded or told she was being petty or jealous. Instead he seemed like he was on her side. 'Really?'

'From everything I can observe, since Eloa came along he's dropped everyone and everything. I didn't realise until today that that also extended to you. Don't you and Eloa get on?'

'That's the ridiculous part,' Ariana said, relieved to speak about something other than death, and also relieved to share what had been eating at her for months. 'I like Eloa, I really do. They just don't seem to want to spend any real time with me.'

'I'm sorry.'

'It doesn't matter.' She gave a tight shrug, at first closing the conversation but then opening it up in a way he had not anticipated. 'Were you close to your brother...' She had to think for a second to recall his name. 'Eduardo?'

'No,' Gian said. At first his answer was final, but she had shared so much with him that he felt it right to share a little more. 'We were for a while.'

'Oh.'

'For a long while I looked up to him. Admired him...'

'And then?'

'And then I didn't.'

He gave her no more.

'Wait there,' Gian said. She assumed he had to make a call, perhaps to Svetlana… Maybe he was bored already with the company he had chosen tonight.

Alone for the first time that day, Ariana quietly admitted her deep feelings for him.

Ariana wanted more of Gian.

She wanted to know his kiss. She wanted…more.

More than his kiss…

To know his touch…

To sit holding hands at his table…

The more she admitted to herself, the more honest her admissions became…

She wanted Gian to hold her and she wanted to know how it felt to be made love to by him.

For Gian De Luca to be her first…

It was a reckless thought, though, for by his own admission Gian came with a warning.

But since when had Ariana heeded warnings?

She stared up at Fontana dei Quattro Fiumi—the Fountain of Four Rivers, said to be the most complex of the many fountains in Rome. She looked at the four river gods and then up, ever up, to the tall obelisk that topped it. Her feelings were spinning in her mind as the crush she had on Gian transformed into need.

She loathed being twenty-five with barely a kiss to her name.

Yet while kisses did not excite her, the mere thought of Gian's kiss did.

'Here.' His voice startled her and she looked at the paper cone filled with hot chestnuts that he held out. 'You looked cold.'

'You got these for me?' Gian watched as her pale face broke into a smile, and her eyes shone as if he were handing her a purse of gold. 'Thank you.'

Hot chestnuts on a cold night had never tasted so good as they sat at the base of the fountain, biting into the salty treats.

'These are the best I have tasted,' Ariana said, every single time she ate one.

'They're just chestnuts.' Gian did not really get her enthusiasm for such a familiar winter treat. 'I used to come down here at night as a child and buy these.'

'You would sneak out?' she nudged.

'No sneaking required.'

'What do you mean?'

'Just that...' Gian said, and he looked at Ariana, quietly watching the world go by. He knew why he had not left her alone tonight. He knew better than anyone how it felt to be alone in Rome after dark, that frantic search for company, any company, that compelled you to speak to a stranger or hang out with a wayward friend, anything other than return to your room and lie there alone. 'So...' he changed the subject and looked over at the stunning Palazzo Pamphili, where the wedding was to be held '...you arranged the wedding reception.'

'I managed to secure the venue,' Ariana corrected.

'Good for you.' He smiled.

His smile was like being handed the earth.

'Come on,' he suggested, when they had finished eating, 'let's walk.'

They passed the impressive building where a few months from now the wedding would take place. It seemed so wrong that such a celebration would take place and their father would not be there.

'Are you going?' she asked, because the idea of him being there really helped. She was so out of the wedding loop she had no real idea if he'd been invited, let alone responded.

'No,' he admitted. 'It's the weekend of the opening of my Florence hotel so I shall be sending my apologies. I am sure I shan't be missed.'

You shall be missed, she wanted to say, but did not know how. 'I'm kind of dreading it,' she said, hinting a little that his presence might help.

'You'll be just fine,' Gian said assuredly, and gave her hand a squeeze, yet her fingers were cold beneath his so he held onto them as they walked.

Gian did not do hand-holding.

Ever.

Yet tonight he did.

For a second, Ariana felt as if she were walking in the Tuscan fields in the middle of summer, not sad and frozen in Rome. But then she remembered the reason for his kindness this night, and wondered how it had been for him. 'You must miss your parents...' she ventured, though immediately knew she had said the wrong thing for he dropped her hand like a hot coal.

'I didn't know them enough to miss them,' he said, but Ariana refused to be fobbed off.

'What about your brother?' she probed, but he was equally unforthcoming.

'Leave it, Ariana.'

She refused. 'How did you find out about the...?' She hesitated, unsure what to call a raging fire on a yacht in the middle of the ocean. 'The accident?' she settled for.

'Hardly an accident,' Gian retorted, and she heard a trace of bitterness to his tone. 'With the amount of alcohol and class-A drugs my family consumed, I think it could be called inevitable.'

Ariana was stunned.

She had heard whispers, of course, like little jigsaw pieces of scandal that had been gathered together over dinners and parties, but all too soon scooped up and put away. But now it was Gian himself putting the pieces together and giving her a glimpse.

'They were renewing their wedding vows?' Ariana checked.

God, she was persistent. Perhaps it was the emotion of the day, but he found that tonight he didn't mind. 'Yes. It sounds romantic, doesn't it, like the Duke and Fiordelise, but the truth is it was an excuse for a party. They renewed their vows every couple of years,' Gian said drily. 'They would fight, they would make up, they would say never again... I got off the hamster wheel and left before then. I was at university, studying architecture. I was asleep in the residences...'

'You didn't live at La Fiordelise then?'

'God, no.' He gave a hollow laugh. 'I was more than happy to leave it all behind. Luna came with the police and woke me...'

'Luna worked for your parents?'

'She was actually working her notice,' Gian said. 'They had been late again paying her and she had resigned, but after they died Luna said she would stay until things were more stable.' Gian gave her a tight smile. 'Fifteen years later, she still reminds me on occasion that she is working her notice.' He shook his head and closed the subject.

Except Ariana wanted to prise it back open. 'Tell me...'

'Tell you what?'

'How you felt when they died?'

'As I told you, I barely knew them.'

'They were your parents, your brother...'

'Just leave it,' he warned. 'Ariana, I respect your boundaries. Why can't you respect mine?'

'Because I want to know you some more...'

He kept right on walking, though a little faster than before. 'Wait...' Ariana said, and grabbed his coat to slow him down, except her hand found its way back into his. 'I'm sorry for pushing. I just wonder...' she didn't know how best to say it '...when the grief goes?'

'I can't answer that,' Gian admitted. 'I grieved for them long before they died.' He should close it there, but her hand was warm and he sensed she would walk for ever just to hear some more. 'Eduardo and I were both repulsed by their ways. He was older, the one who would look out for me when I was small, make sure my nanny was paid, that sort of thing...'

She stayed silent in the hope he would continue and her reward was great, for he revealed more.

'Then he took up their ways and I ended up looking out for him.'

Still she stayed silent but she felt the grip of his hand tighten and it seemed like the darkness of his truth guided her through her own pain.

'I found Eduardo one morning; I thought he was dead. I couldn't rouse my parents. The hotel doctor came and for all the hell of that morning, by that evening the incident was forgotten.'

Now she spoke. 'Not by you.'

'Never by me,' Gian said. 'It happened several times again. I said to Eduardo one day, "I won't always be there to save you." And it was then that I stopped...'

'Stopped what?' Ariana asked.

'I can't answer that,' Gian admitted. 'And I'm not being evasive, I just...' He shrugged. 'Stopped.'

Ariana stopped asking, which he was grateful for, because revelations like these were hard.

He had stopped...not loving, not caring, just stopped all feelings.

Stopped hoping for change.

Stopped trying to control their chaos.

'I like order,' he admitted, and looked over at her. 'Why do you smile?'

'Because it's hardly a revelation. I know you like order, Gian.'

'You know too much,' he said, and dropped a kiss on the top of her head as they walked.

It was a tiny kiss, but when it came from Gian, it felt as if he had just picked her up and carried her.

It felt so perfect that she actually let out a little laugh and touched her head to feel where his lips had just pressed, for her scalp tingled. 'You're crazy, Ariana,' he told her.

'A bit.'

It was unexpected bliss on the saddest of nights, to be walking on a cold Rome night, hand in hand, along Piazza d'Arecoli, their breaths blowing white in the night air. Ariana had run out of words, and she was terrified that he might drop her hand.

His hand was warm and it was so unexpected and so nice and just everything she needed tonight.

Gian too was pondering the light weight of her fingers that wrapped around his and how, on the near-empty street, when they could easily walk apart, they were strolling like this.

It was Ariana Romano.

She's a friend, he told himself.

He was simply doing what any friend would.

Except he did not have friendships of this type.

And he never confided in anyone, yet he just had.

Still holding hands, they took the stairs and there before them, ever beautiful, was the Altar of the Fatherland. Soldiers stood guarding the tomb of the unknown soldier and Ariana knew she should guard her own heart with the same attention and care.

'Oh,' she gasped as they took in the altar of the goddess of Rome.

His stomach growled and he turned her to face him. There were tired streaks of mascara, like delicate lace, smudged on her cheeks. Her mouth, rarely devoid of lipstick, was swollen from days of tears. She smiled briefly and it lit up her face for a moment. He wanted to capture it, to frame it and hold onto it—and he did so with his hands.

She felt the brush of his fingers on her cheeks and then the soft pressure as he held her face. Surely the eternal flame flared, because something lit the sky and seared her as his lips made first contact.

Just the gentlest brush at first then soft and slow and exploring.

His kiss made her slightly giddy in a way no other had. His touch was both tender and firm and she felt she could fall right now and be caught, even though his hands barely held her.

Only once did she peek. Ariana opened her eyes, while praying that she wouldn't be caught, for she did not want to break this spell. Gian's eyes were closed, though, as if savouring the most exquisite wine. He continued to hold her cheeks, so firmly now that her head could not move. He kissed her thoroughly and his lips were like velvet, his tongue so shockingly intimate it felt charged as each stroke shot volts of ecstasy to her own. His hand moved into her hair, holding the back of her head and knotting into her scalp as his tongue danced with hers.

A craving for more built in her but he pulled back. Gian looked at her wet lips and dilated pupils and the frantic, somewhat startled look and he tried to rein in his usual common sense. 'I should get you home...'

'Please,' Ariana said, but her voice was low and husky and told them both what she wanted.

Ariana's decision was made.

Gian De Luca would be her first.

Perhaps that was the reason she had held on for so long, because there was no one else who held a candle to him. No one who made her shiver, even without touching her, no one who made her mouth want to know his kiss...

'Ariana.' His voice was gruff. 'When I said home, I meant to your door.' Gian was serious. A kiss was one thing, but bedding her was out of the question. 'If we were so much as seen out together...'

'That would get them talking.' Ariana smiled as Gian clearly hated the thought. 'Mamma would have us married in a moment if she knew her virgin daughter was out with the Duke...' Her voice trailed off, unsure how Gian would receive the news of her inexperience, but he gave a low laugh.

Ariana was not, he knew, dropping in his title; instead she was capturing her mother's thought process and agreeing with exactly how it would be if they were seen. 'Exactly. Though,' he added, 'I'm sure all mothers think their daughters are virgins.'

'But I am one.'

He almost laughed again, and then realised she wasn't laughing. He almost hauled her off him, but decided that reaction might be a bit extreme and so instead he offered her his smile.

His duty smile, which she determinedly ignored.

'Let's get you home...' Gian said.

'Yes,' Ariana agreed. 'Take me to bed.'

'Absolutely not.'

And he meant it, for he was headed down the steps. Ariana did not quite know what she'd done wrong, just that everything had changed.

'Gian.' Now she really did have to practically run to keep up with him. 'Why are you being like this? Didn't you like our kiss?'

'It was a kiss,' Gian snapped, 'not an open invitation.'

But Ariana would not relent. She had made up her mind and was all too used to getting her own way. 'I want my first to be you.'

'Well, it won't be. If we are even as much as seen, people will talk and it will be...' He had to be cruel to be kind. 'They will turn it into something bigger than it is.'

'I know that.'

'Do you?' Gian checked. 'Do you understand that I don't do relationships? That the very last thing I want is to be involved in someone else's life?'

'You're always dating.'

'Yes.'

'So what's the difference?' Ariana frowned. 'I might be innocent in the bedroom, but I am not stupid, Gian...'

'I never said you were.'

'I'm not asking for love. I don't want lies to appease and promises that you won't keep,' Ariana said. 'I'm all too familiar with them, but I do want you to make love to me.'

'Ariana—'

'No,' she broke in, and they argued in loud Italian all the way home. 'Don't make me ashamed for admitting it. I'm twenty-five and a virgin. I don't want to be married, Gian. Do you not think my mother has endless suitors in mind for me? I can't have a casual relationship or it will be a kiss and tell. You know that...'

He looked at the spoilt, immature Ariana speaking like the woman she was.

'Surely there have been kisses…?'

'Yes,' she admitted, 'plastic kisses from plastic men, but your kiss nearly made me come.'

He laughed because she fascinated him.

Like a stunning portrait, like a song you had to pause just to go back and listen to the lyrics again.

He loved how she stated her case.

They argued all the way to the swish apartment block where she lived. 'I get that I'm not as experienced or as worldly as Svetlana…'

'Stop,' Gian said. 'Just stop right there. Why would you sign up for inevitable hurt, Ariana?' Gian asked. 'You know it'll go public, and you know your family will find out, and I know that I'll end things…'

'How?' Ariana asked. She wasn't begging or persuading, more genuinely perplexed. 'How do you know?'

'Because I never want to get too close. I date women who understand from the get-go that we'll never progress further than we did on the very first night.'

'So I would get no more than a kiss and a cone of hot chestnuts,' she teased. 'Well, rest assured, you wouldn't have to worry about dumping me, Gian. I would grow bored with you very quickly.'

He didn't smile at her joke and he would not relent, but rather than face being alone she turned off the voices in her head and tried to argue with a kiss. She put her arms around his neck and pressed her mouth to his, but there was no longer solace there for his was pressed closed and unyielding, and she sobbed as he pulled his head back.

'Go in!' he warned her.

'Please, Gian, I don't want to be lonely tonight.'

But when he remained silent, Ariana got the message. He did

not want her, so she scrabbled around for her dignity. 'Thank you for seeing me to my door.'

'Get some sleep.' Gian said.

'Oh, please,' Ariana scoffed as she huffed off. 'As if that's going to happen.'

He watched her leave, and by honouring Rafael he felt like he'd failed her. 'Ariana…' Gian called out, and it troubled him how quickly she turned and was back at his side.

He would not sleep with her, no matter how much they both wanted it.

He would do the right thing by Rafael *and* Ariana.

'I'll come in, but I'm taking the sofa.' She nodded, both regret and relief flooding through her as he spoke on. 'You don't have to be alone tonight.'

CHAPTER SIX

THEY PASSED THE dozing doorman and took the elevator, although Gian stood like a security guard to the side of her, rather than like a man who had almost kissed her to orgasm.

She was all dishevelled in her head as they stepped into her apartment. 'Thankfully,' Ariana said as she closed the drapes, 'it was serviced while I was away, or we would be knee-deep in...' Her voice trailed off.

Knee-deep in what? Gian wanted to ask, for there was no real evidence of her here. He could be walking into any well-heeled woman's apartment in Rome—and Gian had walked into many—and the décor would be much the same. It was all very tasteful with plump sofas and modern prints, yet it was rather like a show home and there was barely a hint of Ariana. Even her bookshelves offered no real clues, for there were a few classics on the shelves as well as elegant coffee table books. There were at least some photos up, but even they seemed carefully chosen to show, so to speak, only her best side.

'Do you want a drink?' Ariana offered.

'No, thank you.'

Now that she had him here, Ariana didn't quite know what to do with him. It was, she thought, a bit like stealing a bear from the zoo, making it your mission to get him home and then…

'I'll show you around,' she offered, 'where you're sleeping. Given that you'd rather it wasn't with me.'

'I don't need a tour,' Gian responded. 'I will stay here.' He pointed to the sofa.

'I do have a guest room.'

'I'm not here to relax.'

'You are *such* a cold comfort.'

'Better than no comfort at all. I do have some scruples, Ariana. I am not going to make love to you on the night of your father's funeral when you are upset and not thinking straight.'

'Oh, believe me, I am thinking straight. Life is short, Gian, life is for living, for loving.'

'Then you've come to the wrong man because, as I've repeatedly said, I don't do love.'

She wanted to stamp her feet. She knew she was being a bit of a diva but she was beyond caring.

When Ariana wanted something, she wanted it now, and when she'd made up her mind…well, it was made up.

'Can you unzip my dress, please?' Ariana lifted her hair and stood with her back to him, waiting for the teeniest indicator—a run of his finger, a lingering palm, him holding his breath—as he found the little clasp at the top of the velvet dress and undid it. Yet Gian was a master of self-control and without lingering he tugged the zip down so that her back and the lacy straps of her black bra were exposed.

'There,' he said, with all the excitement of an accountant relocating a decimal point.

She turned around and her dress slipped down, exposing her shoulders and décolletage, but he looked straight into her glittering eyes and smothered a yawn. 'It's been a long day,' Gian said. 'Perhaps you should go to bed.'

'So much for the playboy of Rome,' she sneered as she headed for her room, embarrassed that he clearly did not want her.

No wonder, Ariana thought as she stood in the bathroom and looked at her blotchy tear-streaked face.

She cleansed her skin and then ran a brush listlessly through her hair. She pulled on some shorts and a T-shirt and then climbed into bed. Sulking, she pulled the covers up to her chin.

'Do you want milk or something?' Gian called.

'I'm not ten!' she shouted through the darkness. It was worse having him here like this than being alone. Except, as she lay in the dark, Ariana knew that wasn't strictly true. She loathed the dark and the night, especially since her father died, and now it did not seem quite as dark and the place not quite so lonely.

In fact, there was comfort just knowing that Gian was near.

Finally, whatever it was that had possessed her, that had had her angrily demanding sex, left her.

Oh, Papà!

Gian listened to her cry, and knew that for once it was not for attention. Though it killed him not to go to her, Gian knew they were necessary tears.

He opened the drapes and looked for something to read. Some might call it snooping, but really he was looking for somewhere to charge his phone when a cupboard *fell* open and he could see that this was where *Ariana* had been hiding. It was rather chaotic and piled high with photos, wads and wads of them, and dated boxes too. Ah, so she must have been knee-deep in photos, Gian realised, trying to choose some favourites for the funeral montage. As well as that, there were fashion magazines and blockbusters and recipe books…

An awful lot of them!

Gian selected one and tried to block out her tears by reading. He just stared at the method for tempering white chocolate until finally she fell into silence.

He was reading how to make cannelloni when he heard her again.

It was almost hourly, like some tragic cuckoo clock, but Gian kept the door between them closed for he would *not* sleep with her on the night of her father's funeral. Surely only foolish decisions were made then…

Gian was completely matter-of-fact about sex. To him it was as necessary as breathing. Perhaps it was an exaggeration, but he felt he would not have lived to the age of twenty-five without the escape of it, and he knew he could give her that, but only when her head was clear.

To know she trusted him was significant, for the thought of her misplacing her trust in someone else left him cold.

He watched the black sky turn to a steel grey and, even though Gian knew his logic was flawed, when the silver mist of a new day dawned and he heard her little cry, Gian went through and sat on the bed.

Ariana was far from a temptress at dawn. She covered her face with one hand as he came in, and little bits of last night played like taunting movies.

'Did I make a complete fool of myself?' she asked in a pained voice.

'Of course not,' he said magnanimously, then teased her with a slow smile. 'You just pleaded with me to make love to you.'

'Perhaps it was the cognac,' she said hopefully, but they both knew it had been a small sip and that had been back in Luctano. There had been a lot of walking and talking since then and she could hardly blame the chestnuts! 'I'm sorry for my behaviour. I don't actually fancy you, Gian.'

'Really?'

'Well, sometimes a bit, but then I remind myself that you are just a hunk of good-looking…' She liked his slow smile. 'I remind myself how mean you can be…'

'Mean?'

'*One* glass of champagne at my interview!'

He smiled for he thought she hadn't noticed the absence of a bottle.

'Ah, that.'

'A meal at your bar instead of your restaurant...'

'You make it sound like the local dive.'

'Perhaps, but even so I *deserved* five stars last night. Anyway,' she continued, 'when I do find myself fancying you, I remind myself how remote you can be and how humourless you are.'

'Well, it's good you've come to your senses,' Gian said, 'especially as I don't have condoms with me. I tend not to keep them in my funeral suit.'

She stared back and resisted smiling, determined to prove her humourless point.

'Except we wouldn't need them.' He held up a purple foil packet of contraceptive pills. 'What are these for?'

'You've been snooping.'

'Not really, I wanted toothpaste. I just wondered what you were doing on the Pill if you're not sleeping with anyone...'

'Yet!'

His jaw was set in a grim line. He had this vision of Ariana chasing some bastard who sensed her fragility, yet she was not fragile now. Ariana was looking right at him and there was none of last night's desperate need for comfort, just the desire that had always been beneath it.

'So?' he asked. She looked at the purple Pill packet and was about to lie, as she so often did, and say she was on the Pill for her skin, or so that it made her cycle more predictable, or whatever she would say if her mother found them.

But Gian was certainly not her mother.

And with Gian there was no reason she could see to lie.

'I went on it because I feel like the only person in the world without a sex life, and when I go away with friends I don't want them to know I'm the only one...' She shrugged. 'Pathetic, huh...'

'No more pathetic than when I was younger and would have condoms on me, just to have them on me...'

'Really?'

'Yes.'

They shared a smile in the thin dawn light but then hers wavered. 'Look, I'm sorry I've made things even more awkward between us. I should never have foisted myself on you. I was all a jumble.' She looked at his suave good looks and then at his chest. His tie was gone and his shirt unbuttoned, though just at the top—enough to see a glimpse of chest hair—but she reminded herself of how empty a vessel his chest was and again tried to salvage some pride. 'And it's not as if I enjoyed kissing you last night. In fact, it was like kissing a screen. I felt nothing...'

'Really?'

The thin morning light disappeared as his face came closer, but she refused to be moved by the brush of his lips and the softness of his mouth, just as he had refused to be moved by hers.

Except his kiss was more refined, more skilled, more measured and she found she could not quite catch her breath as her mouth fought not to relent.

'Like kissing a screen?' he checked.

'Yes,' she said, and felt the scratch of his chin drag on hers. As his fingers came to her jaw, his tongue slipped in, and she absolutely refused to moan at the bliss. In fact, she held her mouth slack as his tongue moved in and out. He tasted divine, all minty and fresh, but there was nothing clean about his kiss—it was filthy, in fact. Thorough, probing and potent with skill, his tongue felt like it ran a wire straight down between her legs and she bunched her hands into fists rather than reach for his head.

'Still nothing?' he checked, and now his hand was stroking her breast through her top and Ariana was sure that if she hadn't been lying down she might have fainted.

'Nothing,' she lied.

'Do you want me to stop?'

'No.'

'Do you understand it is just this once?'

'Oh, stop with the lectures,' she said, as his fingers slid inside her top. 'I accept the terms and conditions...'

He laughed.

Gian actually laughed. Not that she saw it, for he was pulling her T-shirt over her head, and Ariana was loose limbed and compliant and letting him.

'Please get naked,' she said. 'I want to see you.'

'For a virgin, you certainly know how to provoke me,' Gian commented as he rose from the bed and started to undress.

'Because you provoke me,' Ariana responded. She felt a blush spread across her chest as he removed his shirt and discarded his clothes.

Oh, God. She had always known he was stunning, but he looked so toned, and so male—his chest hair, the thick line on his stomach—and she was holding her breath in nervous, excited anticipation as he unzipped.

He was the most beautiful thing she had seen and she was far from shy, just staring with hungry eyes. It made her blood feel too heavy to move through her heart as he took her hand and closed it around his thick length.

He was warm and hard and he felt like velvet and he let her explore him. Gian kissed her neck, and he kissed down her chest and when his mouth met her breast she wept inside.

'Help me,' she said, because he made her so frantic with desire and his warm hand was on her stomach, which made her want to lift her knees.

'Does that help?' he said, and she moaned as his hand moved down and he stroked her.

'Not enough,' she gasped. 'God, Gian...' And then she whimpered, for the soft vacuum of his mouth on her breast and the relentless pressure below created a feeling akin to both panic and bliss building inside her.

And though his intention had been to bring Ariana to the edge and then take her, instead he indulged in the pleasure of watching her orgasm build.

Her eyes opened to his for a moment, and she had never felt more bathed in attention, or so in tune with another person.

Then she gave up watching him and shut her eyes, arching her neck as she surrendered to the sumptuous pleasure he so easily gave. He kissed her then so slowly that it felt like a revival but then his thighs were between hers and his mouth was by her temple as her hands held his hips, holding him back, digging him in, both wanting and conflicted. She was desperate for fusion and for the initiation she would allow only Gian to give her.

It hurt, and yet it did not.

He squeezed into her tight space and it was both pleasure and a pain that must surely end. Yet her lungs were expanding and cracks of light returning to the blackout he had brought upon her, and everything multiplied as he moved slowly inside.

'Gian.' She said his name as she had wanted to since her interview. She rolled it on her tongue and tasted it as he moved deep inside her.

She felt crushed, she felt covered, she felt found. 'Gian,' Ariana said again, as he moved faster, but his name was more like a warning now, for he was tipping her towards the edge and she almost did not want to go.

For then they would end.

'Let go,' he told her. He could feel her slight panic and the mounting tension, and then when she shattered he shot into her in relief.

Both breathless, both dizzy, they lay there, catching their breath.

He adored her inexperience, not just because of the honour of being her first but because she could never know that, even while making love, he held back.

CHAPTER SEVEN

THEY LAY THERE together in silence. Ariana examined her conscience and heart for regret and found none.

Not a jot.

For Gian, there was rare peace as he lay there, their limbs knotted together. Only one thing missing. 'We need food.'

'I have none,' Ariana happily admitted. Her world had been turned upside down since the death of her father, and anyway she tended to eat out. 'Well, I have some ice cream.'

'Ice cream?'

'A lot of ice cream!' Making it was her hobby, her absolute guilty pleasure. Wearing a small wrap, she padded to the kitchen. There she defrosted two croissants and filled them with ice-cream in flavours of cardamom and pistachio and a dark chocolate one too while she waited for the mocha pot to boil and wondered how best to take back her heart.

How to accept his terms and conditions and somehow let him go with grace.

Gian lay there breathing in the scent of brewing coffee, trying to pinpoint the moment he had started wanting her.

On the day of her farcical interview, when he'd first noticed the true colour of her eyes? No, a more honest examination told him it had been before that, and even Ariana herself had voiced it: the night of the silver ball.

Or had it been when she'd swept into the planning meeting and said she wanted silver as a theme?

Instead of gritting his teeth, he had found himself smiling, at least on the inside, for Gian rarely showed how he truly felt.

But, no, while *it* might have started then, for Gian things had really changed the night she had worn silver. Rafael had not been there, and Gian had stood by Ariana's side as she played host. He'd been in awe of how long she'd smiled with the guests and carried on with grace.

He'd wanted to take her aside and tell her that he knew how hard this was, and how proud of her he felt. Instead, they had danced their duty dance and he had held her back from him with rigid arms so she would not feel how turned on he was and how he had ached to drop a kiss on her mouth, on her bare shoulder.

And he was hard for her again.

'Colazione!' Ariana announced breakfast as she came into the room and blinked at his obvious arousal. 'Good grief,' she said. 'I'm far too sore for that.'

'Sore?'

She nodded. 'Nicely sore, the best sore ever.' Oh, God, she wanted him again, but then the ice cream would melt and her phone had already pinged in several messages. She had Nicki coming round *and* she had to do this without starting to cry. 'Eat,' she told him. 'You can have the chocolate one.'

It sounded like she was making a concession, but Gian could tell when she was lying. 'I want the other one.'

'No, no,' she said, 'I'll *let* you have the chocolate one.'

'But I want the pistachio.'

'And cardamom.' Ariana sighed and handed the one she really wanted to him. 'I put in extra when I made it.'

Gian, though used to breakfast in bed, was not used to this—just sitting in bed, eating and tasting food with a woman, and taking bites of each other's.

Bites so big she nearly lost her fingers to his mouth, and they laughed as they fought over food. 'You really made this?' he checked.

'Not the croissant, just the ice cream. I'm going to make salted roast chestnut next, and I shall get them from the same vendor. They were the best I've tasted…'

'They're just chestnuts.'

'No,' she said, and then she gave him the speech she had prepared in her kitchen. 'They kept me warm. *You* kept me warm last night, Gian, even if you did not share my bed. You cared for me last night and then again this morning and I thank you.'

She had surprised him, and then she surprised him further when, with breakfast done, it was Ariana herself who suggested he leave. 'You'd better go. Mamma might drop in.'

'Doesn't she call first?' Gian asked.

'No,' Ariana said. 'I always ask her to but then she reminds me that she's my mother and shouldn't need an appointment…'

'I'll get dressed then.'

'Have a shower,' she offered.

He declined, or he would be trailing a floral boutique all day if he used her scents. 'I'll have one back at the hotel.'

It was odd, Ariana thought as she lay watching him dress, that he did not call La Fiordelise home.

'I like you unshaven,' she admitted. 'You're always so…' she fought to find the right word '…well-presented and groomed.'

'It's my job to be.'

'Perhaps, but…' She shrugged and his eyes narrowed, trying to interpret yet another of her actions, for those slender shoulders could say many things.

'But what?'

'Nothing.' She smiled wickedly. 'There are other sides to you, I'm sure. I guess I won't find out now.'

'You could. Why not tell the doorman to lie and say you're out?'

'He's so lazy he'd forget,' Ariana rolled her eyes and tried to sound casual, when in truth she wanted to cry and cling onto his leg and beg him to never leave.

Not a good look, that much she knew!

'You really ought to go,' she said as he buckled his belt, though she wanted to reach up and unbuckle it so she was only half listening as he spoke.

'So how do you have a private life, with her dropping in and out? How do you have a…?' And then his voice faded. After all, this morning had been her sex life to date. 'You'll be okay?' he checked as he did up the buttons of his shirt and half tucked it in.

'Yes.'

'If you're not…'

'Gian,' Ariana broke in. 'I have my family and I have my friends.' He hovered on the edge of both of her inner circles but was not fully in either. She felt the indent of the mattress as he sat down and bent over to do up his laces, and though she ached to reach out to him, Ariana told him of the practicalities of her day. 'Also, Nicki is dropping by to tell me about her holiday…'

He sat up and looked right at her. 'As opposed to coming by to see how you're faring after the loss of your father?'

'Of course she's coming for that.' Her eyes narrowed as she took in his sulking mouth; she knew he didn't like Nicki. 'It's a bit early in the relationship for you to be dictating who I see. Oh, that's right, it's not a relationship, and even if it were…' she gave him a tight smile '…that still wouldn't give you a right to say who my friends are, Gian.'

'Fine.' He put up two hands to indicate he was dropping it.

And he was!

Ariana was right. It was not his place to call out her friends but, still, that Nicki got his goat.

All of Ariana's hangers-on did.

'Look,' he said, and Ariana could feel him weighing things up before he spoke. 'I think you were right about working. I do think you'd be an asset for the hotel and if we can both…' He reached over and toyed with a thick coil of her black hair that sat on her collarbone as he spoke, but she pushed his hand away and her response was sudden.

'No!'

She could not work for him; far too much had changed.

'I can't work for you, Gian,' she said, and used another inevitable truth to disguise the real reason. 'Mamma's going to need me now more than ever.'

CHAPTER EIGHT

HER MOTHER DID indeed need her more than ever.

In the tumultuous weeks following her father's death, Ariana's mother's demands were relentless.

It was still by appointment only—Angela Romano liked her make-up, jewellery and the day's carefully chosen wig perfectly arranged before even her daughter dropped around.

Yet the lunches were endless.

As she sat there, twirling a shred of prosciutto on a fork, Ariana fought to quell a surge of anger as her mother called over the sommelier to tell him that the champagne was a little flat. She wondered how someone so supposedly bereft with grief would even notice, let alone have the energy to complain!

'I'm fine, thank you,' Ariana said, placing a hand over her glass. 'I really do need to get going, Mamma,' she said, reaching for her bag. 'I'm meeting Dante.'

'Oh, he can wait.'

'Mamma, please, I said I'd be there at three.' She tried to temper her irritation. 'I really do have to go...' Her voice trailed off because she didn't want to worry her mother, but Dante's mood of late was pretty grim and nothing seemed to be getting done for the Romano Ball—the invitations hadn't even gone out and it was just a few weeks away. 'Would you like me to come over this evening?'

'No, no.' Angela shook her head. 'I have the priest coming over tonight.'

'Well, take care.' Ariana kissed her on both cheeks. 'I shall see you soon.'

'Tomorrow,' Angela checked. 'Here? Or perhaps we could go shopping...' She ran a disapproving eye over Ariana's navy shift dress and espadrilles. 'We could get you something a little less last year.'

Ariana had never felt more stifled and wished not for the first time that there was more purpose and structure to her day. She took a taxi to Romano Holdings in the EUR district, craning her neck as they passed La Fiordelise. She wished she was working there.

And then she flushed with sheer pleasure when she recalled the very reason she now could not.

It was her favourite memory, a harbour in troubled times she could return to, yet there was confusion there too—how, from the very moment they had kissed, Gian had started the countdown to the end.

She had stopped having drinks there on a Friday. Well, Paulo had been banned and Nicki said they should no longer go in solidarity with their friend.

Except Ariana had loved going there...

'Signorina?'

The voice of the driver startled her and Ariana realised they had arrived. Time tended to run away whenever she thought of Gian, and so she determinedly put him out of her mind as she walked into the plush office building.

Sarah, Dante's PA, gave her a smile. 'Go through,' she said and then added, 'Good luck.'

'Do I need it?' Ariana joked, but then all joking faded when she saw him. 'Dante!' She could not keep the surprise from her voice when she saw her older brother, looking less than his put-together self, for his complexion was grey and his shirt was crumpled and there was just such a heavy air to him. 'How are you doing?' she asked as she went over and kissed his cheeks and gave him a hug. 'I've barely seen you. Mamma is saying the same.'

'Well, work has been busy.'

'I'm sure it has.' She nodded. 'What's happening about the ball?'

'It's all under control. I'm meeting with Gian at five to finalise the details...' His voice trailed off. There was a strange atmosphere in the office, and for an appalling moment she wondered if Dante had found out about their one illicit night, or rather illicit morning.

'And?' she asked with a nervous laugh. 'What are the final details?'

Dante said nothing.

'How are we addressing Papà's passing?' Ariana pushed.

'I'm sure Gian will take care of that.'

'But in the will Papà asked that his children take care of the ball,' Ariana said, but then stopped and sat chewing the edge of her thumbnail. She was worried about Dante. Though not as close to him as she had always been to Stefano, she knew there was something wrong. He was grieving for their father, but she couldn't help but think there was more to it than that. 'Is everything okay, Dante?' she ventured.

'Of course.'

'You can talk to me. I might just understand.' He closed his eyes, as if she couldn't possibly. 'Look, why don't I meet with Gian?' There was genuinely no ulterior motive, just a need to get the ball right for their father. 'I can take over the ball...'

'Would you?' Dante's relief was evident.

'Of course.' Ariana nodded.

It was only then that her nerves caught up!

* * *

Ariana walked by the *laghetto* for a full hour. The cherry blossoms were in full bloom and the park looked stunning, and if there was a little trepidation about coming face to face with Gian it was soon displaced as something else took hold. Excitement. It felt like for ever since her brain had been put to work.

Sitting on a bench, looking at the blossom swirl and float like pink snow, it was the perfect place for her imagination to wander. Scrabbling in her bag, she took out a journal and started to make notes.

It was exhilarating, cathartic, and there were tears in her eyes as memories danced while words formed on the page. It was right that she take over the ball, Ariana knew, for she knew how best to celebrate her father.

Ariana wasn't even nervous about facing Gian.

She had so much to tell him.

'I have Ariana Romano in Reception to see you,' Luna informed him.

'Ariana?' Gian frowned. 'But I thought I was meeting with Dante...'

'Well, Ariana is here instead.'

'Fine.' Gian did his level best to act as if it were of no consequence that it was Ariana who had just arrived. It was an informal meeting, but also a very *necessary* meeting. One that Gian had pushed for, given Dante seemed to have—both figuratively and literally—dropped the ball. 'Send her through.'

Damn.

Gian usually had no qualms about facing an ex-lover, but with Ariana it felt different indeed.

It was because they were family friends, he told himself, steadfastly refusing to examine his feelings further than that.

It had been weeks since the funeral and to his quiet surprise he had heard nothing from Ariana. He had expected the demanding, rather clingy Ariana to drape herself like bindweed around one of the columns in Reception, or at the very least find an *accidental* reason for her to drop by.

And now she was here.

He was curious as to her mood, and very determined to get things back on a more regular footing, as if they had never made love.

As if they had not sat eating ice cream naked in her bed.

She stepped into his office, and brought with her an Italian spring. He had to consciously remind himself to greet her the same way he would have before...

'Ariana...' He stood and went round his desk and of course kissed her cheeks. There were dots of pink blossom in her hair and he had to resist lifting his hand and carefully picking them out. 'This is unexpected...'

'I know.' She gave him an apologetic smile and an eye-roll as she took her seat but she was too excited to be awkward around him. 'Dante and I agreed that I will take over the final preparations for the ball. Believe me, I did not engineer it...'

He knew she spoke the truth.

For Ariana with a secret agenda would be immaculate, rather than bare-legged and a little tousled. Plus, she was more animated than he had ever seen her and dived straight in.

'Firstly, I don't want to go with the forest theme...'

'Thank God,' Gian said. 'What theme do you have in mind?'

'None,' Ariana said. 'I want the ballroom to speak for itself, and I want gardenias on each table. He loved them.'

'Yes.'

'And orchids...' she said, but Gian reacted with a wavering gesture with his hand.

'Not together,' he said.

'Perhaps by his photo?'

Gian nodded.

'And I want to change the menu.' She handed him a sheet of paper she had torn from a pad.

He said nothing as he read through it, for Ariana did all the talking. 'These were my father's favourites,' she said. 'I thought we could use some produce from his estate...'

'One moment,' Gian said. She sat tapping her feet as, suddenly in the midst of this most important meeting, he simply got up and walked out. 'Sorry about that,' he said a moment later when he returned. 'Now, where were we?'

'I don't think it should be a solemn night, but if we can acknowledge him in the food and wine...'

She spoke for almost two hours. There was no champagne brought in, just sparkling water, which she took grateful sips of between pouring out ideas. There was no flirting, no reference to what had happened, no alluding to it, just a determination to get this important night right.

'What about the wording for the invitations?' Gian said. 'Mia is technically the host...'

'No!' Only then did she flare. 'We don't even know if she's coming.'

'I'll work on the wording,' Gian agreed. 'Leave Mia to me. I think your ideas are excellent. There's a lot to do but I agree it has to be perfect. Why don't we try the dinner menu now?'

'Now?' she frowned.

'I asked Luna to give your menu to my head chef. He is preparing a sample menu...'

She had her dinner invitation.

He never took dates to the hotel's restaurant, but Ariana wasn't his date. It was business, Gian told himself as they were shown to his table. It looked out onto the restaurant but was private enough for conversation to take place.

'I wish I was better dressed,' Ariana admitted as a huge napkin was placed in her lap. Her clothes were better suited for lunch, or even a gentle lakeside walk, certainly not fine dining in La Fiordelise.

'You look...' He hesitated, for he did not tell his business dates they looked stunning or beautiful. 'Completely fine.' Gian settled for that, yet it felt as flat as the iced water that was being poured, and as shallow as the bowl in which a waterlily floated. 'You look stunning,' Gian admitted. 'Especially with pink blossom in your hair.'

Ariana laughed and raked a hand through her mane. 'I was walking by the office; the blossom is out and it's so beautiful.'

'And so fleeting.'

Like us, she wanted to say as she dropped a few petals from her hair into the water lily bowl between them. 'Yes, so fleeting,' Ariana agreed, 'but worth it.'

It was the briefest, and the only reference to what they had shared.

The starter was ravioli stuffed with pecorino with a creamy white truffle sauce and it brought a smile to her lips as it was placed on the table and she signalled the waiter to rain pepper upon it.

'Taste it first,' he told her.

'Why?' she said. 'If it is cooked to my father's taste then to my mind it needs more pepper and a little less salt.' She signalled to the waiter for even more.

'You love your pepper.'

'I do! And he loved this pasta so much.'

'I know,' Gian told her. 'It was served on the night La Fiordelise came back to life.' He put down his fork and though he had never told another living soul the details, if ever there was a time to, it was now. 'Your father saved La Fiordelise.'

'Saved it?'

'Yes. It was practically empty of guests and running on a skeleton staff when my family died.'

She looked up.

'Papà gave you a loan?'

'Not as such.'

Ariana frowned.

'I inherited a disaster,' Gian said, 'and, believe me, the banks agreed...' He hesitated at how much to tell her and decided, for this part of Rafael's life at least, there was no need for brevity and so as the main course was served he told her what had happened. 'Your father suggested buying into the business.'

'Really?' Ariana hadn't known that. 'But he didn't?'

'No.' Gian shook his head. 'I refused his offer.'

'Can I ask why?'

'I prefer to rise or fall alone,' Gian said. 'I did not see that the hotel could be saved. Still, not everyone was aware that it was on the brink of going under, and I told your father about a request to host some royalty on their trip to Rome. Top secret, of course...

'I couldn't consider it, but your father said it was a chance to turn things around. The Penthouse Suite was still incredible—my parents always kept the best for themselves—and the dining room was, of course, in good shape. And so word got around...'

'How?' Ariana frowned. 'If it was top secret?'

Gian smiled. 'He told your mother.' There was a tiny feeling of triumph to see Ariana laugh. 'Before we knew it, the hotel was at full quota for a certain weekend in February.'

'Really?'

'The helicopter brought in the best produce from your father's estate and the best wines. And my staff worked like they never had before. That's why now I only hire staff who can work in all areas. I had the chief bartender making up suites. Luna herself got the Penthouse Suite ready...'

'My goodness.'

'It was the biggest charade and it went off superbly and La Fiordelise shuddered back to life.'

'Just like that?'

'Not just like that,' Gian corrected. 'Years of hard work.'

The main course was just as delicious but when it came to dessert, Ariana could not choose from her father's favourites, which were all being served.

'I think we choose the two best, and of course ice cream,' Gian said, 'though not this.' He frowned as his silver spoon sliced through a quenelle of ice cream from her menu and pulled a face as he tasted it. 'Tutti-frutti?'

'It was his favourite,' Ariana said. 'Every summer, in the evening, he would send me to the shop to get a cone for him.'

'Really?' Gian checked, and he watched a little flush of pink spread up her neck. 'Because I seem to remember that you would go to the store for ice cream and when you came back with this flavour your *papà* always declined his cone.'

'No.' She shook her head. 'You have it wrong.'

'And Stefano would complain that he didn't like tutti-frutti either, and so you would end up having to eat all three.'

'You're getting mixed up,' Ariana said haughtily, and she dipped her spoon into the quenelle. He watched as she took a taste and closed her eyes in bliss, then opened them to him and looked right at him. 'He *loved* that ice cream.'

Rafael probably had, Gian conceded. Not so much the sickly-sweet candied ice cream, more the little games Ariana constantly played.

'Well, it's not going on the menu,' Gian said. 'It's...' He dismissed it with a wave of his hand. 'A simple *affogato* is a better way to round off the meal.' He watched her pout. 'Ariana, you are one of the few people in the world who like tutti-frutti ice cream. Trust me on that.'

'I suppose you know best,' she said in her best pained voice.

'There is no suppose about it.'

'It would mean so much to me, though...'

Wearily he took another taste and, as he did so, Ariana did her sneaky best and pulled on all her inner resources so that crocodile tears pooled in her violet eyes.

It did nothing to move that black heart, though.

'No,' Gian said, and put down his spoon and, as if to prove how awful her dessert of choice was, took a drink of water before speaking again. 'Would you like some *amaro* or a cognac?' Gian suggested, but Ariana shook her head.

'No, thank you.'

'Are you sulking?' he asked.

'A little bit,' she admitted, and then smiled despite herself. 'Of course not. I just ought to get home...' She looked away then, because the reason she could not stay was surely there in her eyes.

She wanted her cognac.

But not here.

Ariana wanted to curl up with him elsewhere, to talk, to kiss, but most dangerous of all she actually ached to know him better.

And if she stayed she would cross a line. The business meeting had surely concluded and to keep it at that, she needed to leave. 'Thank you for a lovely dinner.'

'I'll arrange a car—'

'Gian,' she cut in, 'the concierge can do that.'

'Then I'll walk you out.'

They stood at the entrance and tried to pretend that they had never tumbled naked into bed, had never been more than old friends.

'Your ideas are excellent,' Gian said as the doorman blew his whistle to summon a vehicle.

'Except for dessert.'

'Except for dessert,' he agreed.

'And you think it's okay not to have a theme?'

'I think it's better.' Gian nodded. 'It's going to be a tricky night...'

'Yes,' Ariana agreed.

They had been over this already. The car pulled up and it was time to stay or leave.

'Gian—' she started, for she wanted so badly to ask why there was no possible hope for them.

'I'll say goodnight,' Gian cut in, because if he didn't he would break his own rules about separate lives and kiss her beneath the lights and take her to his private apartment where no lover had ever gone. And they would take things further than he'd ever dared, for no one was permitted a place in his closed-off heart.

And so he kissed her on both cheeks, and as he did so a little pink petal that had been hanging temptingly from a strand of her jet-black hair, just waiting for him to pick it off, glided down to his lapel. Her eyes drifted down. 'You're wearing my blossom.'

He glanced down. 'Yes.'

She would not be Svetlana, Ariana decided, and pick it off. Or one of the doubtless many others that had come before her and dared to demand more. She bunched her fist so hard that her nails dug into her palm, and smiled. 'You'd better tidy yourself up then.'

To her everlasting credit, Ariana got into the car and went home alone.

CHAPTER NINE

BY AND BY, the Romano Ball drew closer.

Gian had quickly forged a strictly business code.

There were emails and phone calls and even a couple of face-to-face meetings, but there was no low-level flirting or alluding to *them*.

For there was no them.

If anything, it was all so professional that Ariana actually wondered if she'd completely misread the mood that night after dinner, if it really had all been just business to him.

Sometimes she wondered what might have happened if she hadn't asked him to leave her apartment that morning, because she'd been unable to grasp at the time that it really was to be the end of them.

Sometimes she just stared into space for a whole afternoon, blinking as she realised it was getting dark, just wondering about him.

A man who did not want love.

Everyone breathed a private sigh of relief when Angela Romano, unable to bear Rome at the time of the Romano Ball, headed off on a cruise.

Phew!

Ariana lay in bed, so relieved not to have to do lunch and placate her mother as well as focus her attention on both Stefano and Eloa's wedding, which she was now helping with a little, and organise the ball.

Even when the final menu cards came, Ariana merely fired back a confirmation, saying that they looked wonderful and she was certain her father would approve.

There was not as much as a breath of tutti-frutti between them.

Or references to pink blossom.

Or hints about a moonlit night and a deep kiss by the eternal flame.

It was just:

Gian, regarding the orchids, Roberto will bring them on the day...

Blah, blah, blah...
And in turn Gian, kept to his side of the deal. Or he tried to.

Ariana, regarding the seating plan...

But two days from the big day, he was finally so irritated that he picked up the phone and called her. 'I don't understand the problem with Nicki,' Gian said. 'We managed to find her a seat...' He chose not to add that Nicki was being accommodated at the exclusion of a potential paying guest and this ball was a very high-end ticket indeed. 'What is her issue?'

'The table is near the back,' Ariana explained, 'and with Paulo not coming because you banned him—'

'I will ban anyone who is abusive to my staff, which he was.'

'Well, she doesn't know anyone she's seated with. She was hoping to bring a friend.'

'*You're* her friend,' Gian rather tersely pointed out. 'Would you like me to move you to sit with her, because there simply isn't room at the top table.'

'Don't be ridiculous,' Ariana said. 'Has Mia RSVP'd yet?'

He knew, even before she asked, that Nicki must have asked her the same question 'Because, if she doesn't come then there'll be a space.'

'Ariana.' It was the first time they had crossed to anything remotely personal. 'I told both you and Dante that you are to leave Mia to me.'

'Yes, but if she isn't even coming…'

'You cannot give Mia's place to…' *to one of your freeloaders*, he was tempted to add, but refrained and reminded himself that this was a business discussion. In truth, if the Romanos wanted a flock of geese seated at the head table then it was his job to accommodate it. He took a breath. Where Ariana was concerned, it was almost impossible to draw the line and differentiate between personal and professional. 'However,' Gian said, 'if you want Nicki at the top table so desperately then she can have my seat.'

'But where would you sit?' Ariana asked, loathing the thought of him not being next to her. Gian was always seated by her side at the Romano Ball, but now it seemed like he was willing to break that tradition.

'In the seat to which she is currently assigned. I'll be working the room anyway. Nicki can have my seat, if that is what you want.'

'No, no,' Ariana rapidly broke in, blushing as she declined his cold and practical solution to salvage her seat beside Gian. 'Just leave it as it is.'

'Very well,' Gian clipped. 'Anything else?'

'I don't think so. Should there be?'

'No.' Gian was assured. 'Everything is under control.'

Except himself, but he was working on that, determined to erase that forbidden morning from his thoughts.

He did not need the complication of Ariana Romano in his life, he insisted to himself. He just had to get past the ball.

It wasn't just Ariana that was worrying him, though.

Trouble loomed in another Romano direction…

'Dante!' Gian shook his friend's hand and invited him to take a seat when he arrived unannounced the day before the ball. 'I just spoke with Ariana this morning…'

'I hear it's all under control.'

'She's done very well,' Gian agreed. 'I expect the ball to be a huge success. Your sister has an eye for detail—'

'Has Mia responded?' Dante cut in.

'Not as yet,' Gian said. 'As I said to Ariana, even if she arrives unannounced, she will be greeted as if she had always been expected and made to feel most welcome.'

'Well, if that's the case, could you ensure she gets this gift just before she heads down to the ball?' He handed Gian a black velvet box and envelope. 'I thought it better to take care of the hostess gift myself, rather than leave it to Ariana.' He gave a black laugh. 'Or it would be a doll full of pins…'

Dante was his close friend, yet Gian found himself smiling his on-duty smile. 'Of course. I'll see to it personally.'

'And perhaps it would be best not to upset Ariana with such details…'

'*Naturalmente,*' Gian said.

Damn, he thought.

By and by, the Romano Ball loomed ever closer.

Gian wanted the ball over and done with; he wanted Ariana gone, instead of her voice, her emails, her thoughts all dancing in his mind.

He wanted his life back to neat order, with sex when he required it and no silent demands for a future.

Gian could feel how much she wanted him, which was usually a turn-off.

He found, though, that he liked it that she craved him and yet kept herself under control. He did his best to ignore it as another damned message pinged into his box, with an attachment.

And there, smiling at him, was his friend Rafael.

It was a slight shock.

Unexpected.

He stared back at Rafael and silently swore that he would stay the hell away from hurting his daughter.

Ariana. Yes, the photo you found of Rafael on Ponte Vecchio was most suitable. Kind regards, Gian

Ariana scoured in between the lines for even the slightest sign, the tiniest clue, that he might linger there in the memory of them, but there was not a single needle she could glean in the haystack.

There were no veiled clues or promises.

His briefly open heart had, it would seem, ever so politely, closed.

By and by, a silver car pulled up outside La Fiordelise in the late afternoon on the day of the Romano Foundation Ball.

And trouble loomed large.

'Ariana Romano is here,' Luna informed him. 'You wanted to see her when she arrived.'

'Yes.'

'Shall I send her through?'

'Of course.'

'Gian!'

She smiled her red-lipped smile and for someone running later than the Mad Hatter, she still looked pretty incredible in a loose top that showed one shoulder and a skirt that showed a lot of leg.

Gian, though, did not look his usual self.

'You look...' she started, but then stopped. It was none of her business that the immaculate Gian was unshaven and that his tie was pulled loose. No doubt he was saving his shave for the evening, but the unrufflable Gian looked, well, ruffled.

She wanted to hold him, to climb onto his knee and kiss that tense face, but instead she stood stock still.

'Ariana...' He got up and they did the kiss-kiss thing.

'Careful,' she warned, so he didn't crush the orchids. 'Damn things,' she added as he re-took his seat but Ariana did not sit down. 'Who knew flowers could cause so much trouble. Roberto is sick and can't come,' Ariana explained, nerves making her mouth run away. 'And these were the orchids he was supposed to bring...' She held up her free hand in an exasperated gesture. 'I've been standing on a platform at Roma Termini, waiting for a courier to deliver them.'

'It's fine.' He tried not to want her; he tried to treat her as he once would have. 'Do you want a drink?'

'I don't have time for a drink,' Ariana pointed out. 'I have to be greeting guests in a couple of hours. What did you want to see me about?'

He was silent for a moment as he poured his own drink while wondering how best to broach things. 'Mia is here.'

'So?' Ariana shrugged and turned to go. 'What do I care? There was no need to drag me to your office. You could have told me that in a text.'

'Yes.' He watched the tension in her jaw and the press of her lips and knew she was struggling to process the news. Aside from that, there was also a whole lot more she didn't know.

Dante and Mia had the adjoining presidential suites.

And Dante had the key.

Yes, Gian De Luca was the keeper of many secrets and at times it was hell. 'I want to speak to you,' he said. 'About tonight.'

'You're going to tell me to behave and be nice. Don't worry.

I've already had the lecture from Dante. Poor Mia is struggling to face us all tonight. Poor Mia—'

'Ariana!' He spoke more harshly then, but that was like holding up a red rag to a bull, Gian knew, for nothing tamed her. 'Do you remember how you felt at your father's funeral, as if everything might get out of hand? Well, Mia is surely feeling that way...'

'*Poor* Mia, you mean.' She looked at him then, really looked, and she could see the fan of lines beside his eyes and feel his tension. She assumed he was concerned about Mia; it never entered her head that his concern might be for her. 'Why do you always take her side?' Ariana asked, jealousy rearing its ugly head. 'Don't tell me you have a thing for her too...' She simply could not bear it if that was the case, and spite got the better of her. 'Well, I guess at least she's closer to your age than Papà's.'

'Enough!' Gian cut in. 'Why do you have to be so petty and cruel whenever you speak about her?'

'Because I hate her.' Ariana shrugged. 'And I hate it that my parents divorced. I'll never forgive her.'

'You forgave your father when it was he who had the affair. Mia, at the time, was single.'

'Stop it,' Ariana said, loathing his logic. 'And please stop telling me what to think and how to feel. We slept with each other once—that doesn't give you licence to police my friends and now how I interact with my family.'

'You're insufferable, Ariana.' He strode over and took her bare arms. He wanted to shake some sense into her, but even as he scolded her Gian actually understood her anger more than she knew.

Ariana was only ever given half-truths.

Or a quarter.

Or an eighth.

The Romanos were masters at smoke and mirrors and Ariana had grown up stumbling blind through their labyrinth of lies, and he loathed it that he was only giving her a tiny sliver of the truth now.

'I'm trying…' He held on to his words, because if he said one thing more it might well be too much. 'I'm trying to ensure that this night goes well.'

'Have you delivered Mia this pre-function lecture?' Ariana goaded. 'Have Stefano and Dante been summoned too? No!' She answered for him. 'Because you don't trust me.'

'No, because I—' Gian abruptly halted himself, because he didn't want to admit, even to himself, that he cared about Ariana more than he wanted to. 'Because I know how you feel about Mia, and I also know that you want the night to be a success.'

'Then we want the same thing,' Ariana replied tartly.

They did indeed want the same thing and now they were face to face in no way that could be construed as professional.

She looked up at him through narrowed eyes. She wanted to exit in a huff, but his hands were on her bare arms and she liked the odd comfort of him, of someone, the first person ever, pulling her back before she went too far.

They were both breathing hard, as if they had just kissed.

Ariana looked at his mouth and unshaven jaw and felt his fingers holding the top of her arms. He turned her on so easily that she could feel the heat at the top of her legs, and the ache of her breasts in her flimsy bra. She knew he was hard, she just knew, the same way she did not need to look at the sky to know it was darkening.

'Ariana,' Gian said in a voice that sounded a touch gravelly, 'if there are any issues tonight, then you are to come to me.'

She always did, Ariana realised.

Whether it was stolen chocolate, or her father's widow showing up, she always leaned on Gian, yet she could not when it came to the urgent matter of her heart, for he was the one who was quietly stealing it.

'I need to get on,' Ariana croaked.

'Of course,' Gian politely agreed.

'And you need to shave.'

When she had gone, Gian opened up the safe and took out the black box and envelope.

He would not break his own rules and deliberately did not look inside.

He would go and get ready and then drop off the gift to Mia, and then get through this night and once that was done, hopefully he wouldn't have to see Ariana for some considerable time.

Except that was easier said than done. First he had to dance with her and hold her and for the first time ever he found he wanted someone in his life.

And so he reminded himself of all the reasons why he did not want someone in his life.

When he should have been meeting with the barber in his apartment and then seeing to the final preparations for this important night, instead he took out the official papers he did his level best to avoid.

It was all there.

The drugs, the debauchery, the *findings*… The absolute hell of love.

For he had loved them.

Even if his parents had not wanted him.

And he had loved his brother Eduardo, even if it had been safer to stop caring, to detach and close off his heart.

To refuse all drama.

And Ariana really was pure drama.

'Gian?' Luna knocked on his door a long time later and found him sitting almost in the dark. 'Should you still be here?'

'No,' he admitted, and stood. 'Luna,' he said, 'can you…?' He was about to hand over the papers to shred. 'It doesn't matter,' Gian said, and returned them to the safe in case he ever needed another reminder of why he refused to let someone into his life.

And, by and by, the Romano Foundation Ball was here.

CHAPTER TEN

ARIANA WORE BLACK.

A simple black velvet halter neck and the diamond studs her parents had given her for her eighteenth.

She put on her red lips, though, and lashings of mascara. There was a ridiculous pit of anticipation building at the thought of dancing with Gian, for she was still floating from the encounter in his office and getting her hopes up as she made her way down for the ball.

His warning, however poorly she'd taken it, meant that Ariana was at least slightly prepared when her father's *widow* made her entrance. And what an entrance. Mia was standing at the top of the stairs in crimson! Her blonde hair was piled up, and heavy diamond earrings glittered at her ears as she made her way down. Ariana saw red—as red as the dress that Mia wore.

'So much for the grieving widow,' she hissed to Dante.

She was, in fact, grateful to Gian for the heads-up and even managed a somewhat stilted greeting to the widow in red, but then all rancour drained from her when she saw Gian approach.

He was still unshaven, but sexily so.

His attire was immaculate and his black hair gleaming but it was such a change from his more regular suave appearance at such an event that she felt a pull, down low. He simply hollowed her out with desire.

'Eloa,' he said in that low, throaty drawl. Even the happily engaged, blissfully-in-love Eloa had the hormones to blush when bathed in his attention. 'You look exquisite.' He kissed her cheeks and then shook Stefano's hand. 'Dante.' He nodded to his friend. 'I trust everything is satisfactory.'

'Absolutely.' Dante agreed.

He turned to Ariana, finally acknowledging her. Sort of. His eyes did not as much as dust over her body, and she felt the chill of a snub, even as he spoke politely. 'Ariana, you look beautiful.'

They were the same words he said every year when he greeted her at the ball, and he kissed her on the cheeks as he always did when they met, except he barely whispered past her skin.

As if she were an old aunt, Ariana thought.

'Thank you,' she said. 'Everything looks beautiful.' And then she leaned in and murmured, 'Even the grieving widow.'

He didn't smile, and neither did he return her little in joke.

There was an edge to him that she couldn't quite define, an off-limits sign she could almost read. He was essentially ignoring her.

Damn you, Gian, she thought as she headed into the ballroom. But really she was cross with herself. Somewhere, somehow, she had lost sight of the clear message he had given right at the start and had been foolish enough to get her hopes up.

The ballroom could never be described as understated, but without hanging moons and ivy vines tonight it looked its elegant best, and Ariana caught the sweet scent of gardenias as she took her seat. Mia entered and took her seat at the table too, Gian sitting between them. He was, of course, his usual dignified self and made polite small talk alternately with both Mia and Ariana.

Like a parent wedged between two warring siblings and trying to give both equal attention, Ariana thought.

'I shouldn't have worn red,' Mia said as the pasta was served. 'It was the gown I had for last year...'

'You look stunning,' Gian told her—*again*. And Ariana gritted her teeth.

Gian tried his level best to be his usual self, as Ariana smouldered beside him. The drama of waiting for her to explode was painful, but he told himself she was not his problem. He told himself that the Romanos, the whole lot of them, were each a theatre production in themselves.

The bed-hopping, the scandals—Dante and Mia doing their best not to make eye contact. He was rather certain that the heavy earrings she wore had been in the box that he had earlier delivered to her door. Rafael's lover was too ill to attend but his orchids took pride of place. Eloa and Stefano were desperate for the night to be over so they could be alone.

And don't get me started on Ariana, he thought.

He could feel her, smell her, hear her when she spoke, and of course she was asking for more pepper.

She jangled his nerves and she beguiled him, because for once she behaved.

Almost.

She turned her back when Mia tried to speak, which he did his level best to ignore and gloss over.

And then the appalling Nicki came over between courses and moaned about her seat. 'Ariana, you really have stuck me beside the most boring people and I'll never hear the speeches back there.'

Gian stared ahead, but said in a low voice for Ariana's ears, 'My offer still stands.'

He would move, Ariana knew. Right now, Gian would get up and stalk off and it was the last thing she wanted. She looked at her friend and, for the first time ever, stood up for herself.

'Nicki, the sound engineer is the best in Rome. I'm sure you'll be able to hear.'

Well done, he wanted to tell her. *Well done, Ariana.*

But he stayed silent. It was not his place.

Yet he wanted it to be.

There was just one unkind comment, as dessert was being served, when Eloa spoke of her wedding that was now just a few short weeks away. She told Mia, 'Ariana is helping us organise a few things,' clearly trying to feed her into the conversation.

'Yes.' Ariana flashed a red-lipped smile at Mia. 'It's going to be amazing. Anyone who's anyone has been invited...'

Meaning—*not you!*

Gian caved.

Ariana felt his hand on her thigh, and the grip of his fingers actually halted her words.

'That's not a good idea,' she said to Gian, while looking ahead. 'If you reward me each time I go too far...'

'Would you prefer the discipline method?'

She threw her head back and laughed.

Even with Mia at her table, Ariana found that with Gian beside her she could still have such a wonderful night.

And it was then that she got another reward, for as the desserts were served and shots of coffee were tossed over ice creams, there was a special dish, made just for her. Tutti-frutti.

Ariana gasped.

'Yes.'

It was better than being handed chestnuts on a freezing night; it was better than a sliver of gold when she could not face her father's funeral alone.

'Thank you.'

She wanted to cry as she tasted the sweet candied ice cream and remembered how her father had, over and over, let her get away with buying three cones, just so she could devour them all.

Happy memories reigned as little shots of sugar burst on her tongue and when she finished she had to dab at her eyes with her napkin. 'Ice cream has never made me cry before,' she admitted to Gian as the waiter cleared her very clean plate. 'Happy tears, though. It was beautiful, thank you.'

'Shall we get it over with?' Gian asked as the band struck up.

'Get what over with?' Ariana said, as if she didn't know.

'The duty dance.'

It had been months since she had known the bliss of his arms, and for Gian it had been months with no feminine pleasure.

He'd known he would only be thinking of her and, besides, no one else had her scent.

'Your perfume,' he said, as he held her at a distance and resumed their old wars.

'I've told you,' she said, 'I don't wear any.' She looked right at him. 'You're the only one who complains.'

'I'm not complaining.'

'Why do you always hold me at such a distance?'

'You know why,' he said, and pulled her deep in so she could feel him hard against the softness of her stomach. She flared to the scent of citrus and bergamot and testosterone and the roughness of his skin seemed to burn her rouged cheek. 'You didn't shave…'

'Because you like me unshaven.'

'Gian.' She was trying to breathe and dance and deal with the change all at the same time. She simply didn't understand him. 'You've ignored me most of the night…'

'I tried to,' he admitted.

'You've ignored me for weeks…' He shook his head, but then nodded when she quoted his impersonal sign-offs. '"*Kind regards, Gian*"?'

'How else could we get the ball done?'

'And after tonight will you ignore me again?'

He didn't answer because he didn't know. He could not afford to think of tomorrow now.

The judgements of the coroner's report should be flicking

through his mind, except tonight those violet eyes turned his warning systems off.

He gave her no promises, just told her the card for his private elevator would be in her bag and left her to stumble her way through the rest of the evening.

The speeches were brilliant, the whole night was perfect, but it felt as though she might faint with desire as she said farewell to the guests.

'We should go for a drink in the bar,' Nicki said.

'It will be closed.'

'I meant the bar in your room.' Nicki smiled, but Ariana shook her head. 'I'm exhausted, Nicki.'

It was a lie.

Ariana felt as alive as an exposed wire as she slipped away and took the private elevator to his floor and let herself in.

It was not the view that she craved, or the stunning surroundings; it was the glimpses of him.

There were paintings, the sketches of Fiordelise he had told her about, his history and lineage all there on the walls.

The older Dukes and Duchesses too, and it went right down to his parents, his brother...

But where was Gian?

Her eyes scanned the walls.

Where was the man she adored?

Then she found him, in a suit, at the desk in Reception, and she frowned at the one single image of him, but her thoughts faded as she heard the whir of the elevator. And her heart moved to her throat as he stepped through the door.

It had been agony not to touch him, but both were relieved of that agony now.

As they reached for each other, almost ran to each other, it was like falling into another dimension.

He was undoing her gown so it fell like a black puddle on the floor. His tongue was cool and his kisses hot as she impatiently pushed down the sleeves of his jacket, and they were so *desperate* for each other, for more than this.

He picked her up, dressed only in her underwear, and deposited her onto a vast gold bed.

His eyes never left her face as Ariana removed her bra and lay on her back, propped up by her elbows and watching him undress.

He threw off the tie as though it was choking him and she gave a satisfied smile when the cufflinks dropped silently to the carpet for he was as desperate as she.

He slowed down to take off her strappy high heels. First the right, and he was so annoyingly slow with the strap that she took her other high heel and pressed it into his toned stomach.

Gian caught her calf.

She could see his erection, the one that had been pressed against her on the dance floor, and she almost writhed in frustration as he took off her left high heel. Now the soles of her feet were on his stomach as he slowly pulled her silk knickers down, revealing her to him. Finally, he buried his face in her.

'Gian!' She was shocked at the delicious roughness of him, at the sounds of him, at her own reaction to him, for she was coming as quickly as that.

Suddenly she was pulsing as he devoured her and then she was falling where she lay, but with him atop her.

'We need condoms…' she said frantically, for she had cursed herself after the last time.

'There's been no one since.'

Those words made her too weak for reason.

He was holding her naked as she tumbled through space, and for all the terrible decisions she had made in her lifetime, this, Ariana knew, was not one of them.

He kissed her mouth and her face, the shells of her ears, and the tender skin of her neck as he took her.

He devoured her and rained kisses and words on her that

should not be said to someone you were not prepared to love the next day.

'You make me crazy,' he told her.

And that made her heart sing.

He told her how he had wanted her all night, how he had wanted her for weeks, in fact, all this as he moved within her and stared right into her eyes. The prolonged intensity astounded her, the focus, the climb, the ache of want and the desire to give. Her hips moved involuntarily with his and they were wild for each other, rolling and tumbling across the bed. He took in her flushed features and brushed the damp hair back from her face as he drove into her and gazed at her.

Help, Ariana thought, for she had never seen Gian so tender before.

There was passion and there was desire, but there was something else too.

He was also aware of it, this slip into a deeper caring, this moment, when he rolled her onto her back again, and one lesson in tenderness moved to the next.

He was up on his forearms, his body sliding over hers, each intimate stroke of him winding her tighter and tighter. His pace built and built and she wrapped her legs around his hips and simply clung on as he took her to wherever he chose.

He took her to bliss, pounding her senses, making her more his with each thrust.

For Gian it was a dangerous space. He knew that as he looked down at her, her black hair splayed on his pillow, her body tight around his. He would regret this later, Gian knew, but at that moment he didn't care.

Especially as he swelled that delicious final time and filled her. Completely.

And this time it was Gian shouting out her name.

He dragged her into an orgasm so deep and intense that for a moment she existed there with him.

It was dizzying…too much…never enough, and she was crying as it was fading.

And he kissed her back to consciousness.

'I loved my ice cream,' she told him, and then stopped, because there was another thing that Ariana knew she loved too.

Don't say it, she told herself as he turned off the lights with a single bedside switch and Ariana curled into him, loving the feel of being utterly spent yet curiously awake in her lover's arms.

Ariana usually hated the dark and the night, but not this night. The thud-thud-thud of his heart and the sound of Gian collecting his breath brought Ariana a sense of contentment in the soft thrum of her body as she came down from the high he had taken her to.

'Why are there no paintings or sketches of Violetta?'

'There are a couple but they need to be restored.'

'And why are there no photos of you?' Ariana asked a question that could only be asked in the dark, in that black hole where gravity did not apply, where words floated and drifted in nonsensical patterns, before logic applied.

'There are,' he said. 'There's one in the gallery, taken during the royal visit to La Fiordelise—in the entrance hall.'

'You mean the Employee of the Month photo?' Ariana said, mocking his formal business photo. For some reason her words made them both laugh.

But then the laughter faded.

'Why are there no photos with your parents?'

'I was not a part of their plans.'

'What were their plans?'

'To party,' Gian said. 'And a late baby nearly put paid to that.'

'But it didn't?'

'No,' he admitted. 'They carried right on.'

'With a baby?'

'Without,' Gian said. 'A lot of nannies, a lot of time in Luctano… It's better this way, though. It taught me independence, so by the time they were gone, there was nothing to miss. They were never a necessary part of my life, or I of theirs.'

She could not imagine it.

Sure, her father had pulled back, but that had been in her twenties, and her mother still called her every day.

And even though she and Stefano were not as close now as they once had been, she would die if he pulled away so completely.

Even Dante, always remote and distant, was still a vital part of her world.

To have no one.

To miss no one.

'I don't believe you,' she admitted. 'I can't believe you don't miss them.'

'Truth?' Gian said, still floating in that void where there were no sides and no barriers hemming you in. 'I have missed them from the day I was born.'

'Gian?' She lifted her head when he fell silent.

'Go to sleep,' he said, but she wanted to ask him how they were supposed to be with each other in the cold light of day.

'What?' he asked her, when her head stayed up and her eyes remained focused on him.

Self-preservation struck—or was it sanity?—and Ariana, even with little experience in the bedroom, knew that pushing the issue with Gian would be something she would live to regret.

'I'm cold,' she said, though she had never felt safer or warmer.

Ariana knew when, and how, to lie.

CHAPTER ELEVEN

GIAN WOKE TO DISORDER.

Not just the knot of limbs and the scent of sex, for that he was used to, but the exposure of thoughts and the deep intimacies of last night had brought disorder into his mind.

He did not want to love her.

Ariana awoke to a cold empty bed and the sound of the shower.

She could almost feel the weight of his regret in the air.

There was no sense of regret from her. In fact, she wanted to stretch like a cat and purr at the memory of their lovemaking.

She had thought nothing could beat the first time, but again Gian had surprised her.

In his arms, as he'd driven her to the very edge and then toppled them, it had felt as if they were one.

Not now, though.

She looked over to the bedside table and the cufflinks he had dropped last night; his tux was hanging over the suit holder.

Order had been brought to the bedroom.

Except for the hot mess that lay in his bed, Ariana thought.

Yes, an utter hot mess, because despite assurances and promises, both to Gian and herself, she had completely fallen for him.

Well, that was a given…

No, this was bigger.

This feeling was almost more than her head could contain.

It was a cocktail of affection and craving and desire and hunger but she refused, even to herself, to call it love.

It was lust, Ariana told herself.

He had turned on her senses, introduced her to her body, and she must not allow herself to believe that the kisses and intimacies shared last night were exclusively known to her.

Except it had felt as if they were.

It had felt, last night, when she had been trapped in his gaze, being kissed, being held, as if this feeling had been new to them both.

She heard the shower being turned off, and she imagined him in there naked, the mirrors all steamed up. She willed him to come out and face the woman who should not be in his bed and she hoped he wasn't wondering how to get rid of her.

Oh, God, this was going to be a million times harder than the first time. Then, it had felt like she had been party to the rules, but this time, naked in his bed, she had to find the armour to brazen out a smile and leave without revealing her heart.

He came out of the bathroom with a distinct lack of conversation and a thick white towel wrapped around his lean hips.

'Buongiorno,' Ariana said, and looked at Gian with his black hair dripping and unshaven face.

Unshaven, for Gian had barely been able to bring himself to look in the mirror.

He had got too close, and what had felt like a balm last night now felt like an astringent. He couldn't bear to let anyone in.

More, he couldn't bear that he was about to hurt her.

'I'll call for breakfast,' he said in a voice that attempted normality but failed. She noted that he did not get back into bed.

Ariana gave a half-laugh at his wooden response in comparison to the easy flow of words last night. 'You sound like the butler.'

He said nothing to that and Ariana pulled herself up from the bed. 'I'll have a shower.' It served two purposes: one, she refused to force a conversation on an unwilling participant and appear needy and pleading; and, two, she felt the sudden sting of tears and desperately wanted to hide it.

'Sure.' Gian said, fighting with himself not to dissuade her. He stepped back as she brushed past and he only breathed again when she closed the bathroom door.

Why the hell was he like this?

Gian generally fought introspection, but he sat on the bed and wrestled with his demons.

The panicked part of Gian wanted the maids to come in and service the apartment so he could get back his cold black heart, instead of fighting the urge to go into the bathroom and join her in the shower before spending a lazy Sunday in bed.

The buzz of his phone had him glancing at the bedside table. Luna calling at such an early hour on a Sunday morning would generally cause him to curse, yet now he leapt on the distraction and took the call.

It was not good news, to say the least.

Ariana, he knew, would freak.

When he'd ended the call, he made a couple of his own and by then Ariana had come out.

'Don't worry about breakfast,' Ariana said, her voice a little shaken, though she was clearly doing her best to control it and keep things light. She had given way to a moment of tears in the shower but she'd pulled herself together and let the hot jets of water flow over her. She would serve herself better to wait until she got home so she could weep alone.

'I'm not really hungry. I might head down to my own suite...' She wouldn't even bother putting on her gown. Wearing the robe and with wet hair, anyone who spotted her would assume she had been for a swim in the luxurious pool in the hotel spa. 'If you could just send my things down to my suite, please...'

'Ariana, wait.'

As she headed for the door, she stiffened, fighting the surge of hope that he was calling her back to apologise for the shift in mood and the silent row that had taken place. Slowly she turned around.

'It's better that you hear this from me,' Gian said, and his voice was deadly serious.

'Hear what?'

'There was a photo taken last night at the ball...'

'There were many photos taken.'

'I mean, there has been an image sold to the press. It hasn't got out yet and my team are doing all they can to suppress it, but I fear it is just a matter of time.'

'What sort of photo?'

'One of Dante...'

'Dante?' Ariana frowned. 'What has Dante got to do with anything?' Dante's behaviour had been impeccable last night. He had delivered a speech that had encapsulated the essence of their father and he had worked the room like the professional he was. Though Dante was rather well known for his rakish ways, that had all been put on hold last night.

Or so she'd thought.

'There is an image of Dante and Mia in the atrium.'

'And?' Ariana was instantly defensive. Dante was her brother after all. 'He's allowed to speak to her, for heaven's sake. He told us himself to be polite. She's my father's widow...' Her voice faded as Dante handed her his tablet and there, on an eleven-inch screen, was an image that washed away any further excuses.

Her father's very young widow was locked, groin to groin, with her elder brother, and raw, untamed desire blazed in both their eyes. Oh, she recognised that desire for what it was, because it was exactly what she had shared with Gian last night.

But Dante and Mia?

Her brother and her stepmother?

'No!' Her lungs and head shouted the denial, but the single word caught in her vocal cords and it came out a strained, husky bark. 'He would never,' she implored. 'It's been doctored, cropped...'

'Ariana, the image is real. I called Dante just now and apologised that such an invasion of his privacy took place in my hotel. My legal team are onto it, as are my security team. We are doing all we can to stop the photo getting out and,' he added darkly, 'I shall discover the culprit.'

But Ariana didn't care who had taken the photo, only that this moment in time had ever existed.

Oh, Papà!

She wanted to weep at the insult to his memory. She wanted to hurl a thousand questions at her brother, who went through women like socks. Except surely this woman, the widow of his father, should have been out of bounds?

'How long have they been together...?' Her accusing eyes looked at Gian.

'Ariana, you are asking the wrong person.'

'I'm asking exactly the right person. You're a who's who of all the scandal in Rome!' She wanted to claw the hair from her scalp. 'Did. You. Know?'

'Yes.'

He might as well have stabbed her for she put her hands to her chest and moaned exactly as if he had. 'Traitor!'

'Stop it.' Dante pointed a warning finger and moved swiftly into damage control. But this time he was moving swiftly to protect not his hotel's reputation but Ariana from the fallout that was surely to come. 'Look at me,' he said, and waited till finally she met his eyes. 'It is not so terrible.'

'But it is.'

'Because you make it so! Remember how you accused me last night, how you said Mia and I were closer in age...?'

She blinked as she replayed her own accusation.

'Your brother is my age.'

'She's his stepmother...'

'So will say the headlines, but that's just click bait... Listen to me, Ariana.' He could feel her calming just a touch. 'Think of how Dante will be feeling right now.'

She nodded, and looked down the barrel of recent weeks. 'I knew something was wrong. I thought he was just missing Papà, not just...'

'I know what you mean. Ariana, it must have been hell for him.'

'I need to speak to him.' Though still frantic, he could feel her calm beneath his touch. 'Both of them...'

'Yes,' he agreed, 'but without accusation. He and Mia have taken off to Luctano...'

'You've spoken to him.'

'Just now,' Gian said.

'Can you take me there?'

'Of course. I'll have Luna arrange the pilot. Go down to your suite and get dressed and I'll meet you there.'

She took the elevator down to the spa floor and then stepped out and took the guest elevator back up to her own. There she pulled on some underwear and a pretty dress. Gian's calm manner was somehow infectious, for she even dried and styled her hair.

But then her phone rang and she saw it was her mother, just back from her cruise.

'How much more can I be shamed?' her *mamma* shouted.

'Mamma, please,' Ariana attempted. 'Maybe there is some explanation.'

'Mia and Dante. My son!'

'Mamma, you should surely hear what Dante has to say. They are closer in age...' Ariana pleaded, repeating Gian's words, but nothing would placate her.

'That woman!' she sobbed. 'She has killed my family, my joy, my life. She takes and she takes and she leaves me with nothing.'

'You have me,' Ariana pleaded. 'Mamma...' But she had run out of excuses for Mia and Dante. 'I'm going now to speak with him.'

'Well, you know what to say from me.'

If Ariana didn't know, she was specifically told.

'Okay?' Gian checked as they headed up to the rooftop, except she barely heard him. All she could hear was her *mamma*'s acidic, angry words.

'I wanted the ball to be perfect for Papà.'

It was all Ariana said.

Sitting in his helicopter, Gian looked from her pale face down to the rolling hills and the familiar lace of vines. Now they were deep into spring and the poppy fields were a blaze of red, and there was foliage on the once bare vines.

He turned back to Ariana, who sat staring ahead with her headphones on, her leg bobbing up and down. He didn't doubt that she was nervous to be facing her brother.

Gian was sure that it would soon be sorted out. He knew how close the Romano siblings were. At least, they had been growing up. And surely even Ariana could understand that grief and comfort were a heady cocktail. Hell, she'd sought comfort herself on the night of the funeral after all.

He spotted the lake and soon they were coming in to land. Only then did Gian wonder how it might look that he was arriving with Ariana.

Would it be obvious they had spent the night together?

Did it announce them as a couple?

Gian was nowhere near ready for that. If anything, a couple of hours ago he'd been ready to end things, as was his usual way.

But, as it turned out, Ariana wasn't expecting anything from Gian, other than the equivalent of a rather luxurious taxi ride.

'Wait there,' she said, as she took her headphones off. 'I shan't be long.'

'What?' Gian checked, unsure what she meant.

She was more than used to entering and exiting a helicopter, and the second it was safe to do so, the door opened and the steps lowered and Ariana ran down.

'Wait…' he called, and then looked in the direction she ran.

Dante, even from this distance, looked seedy and was striding towards her, no doubt surprised by her unannounced arrival.

If Gian had thought for a moment that Ariana Romano had finally grown up, he was about to be proven wrong, for she was back to the spoiled, selfish brat of old. Only, instead of being placed over her father's knee, it was Ariana delivering the slaps.

He watched her land a vicious hit on her brother's cheek and then raise her other hand to do the same, but Dante caught it.

The scene carried echoes of another world, one Gian had loathed—champagne bottles on the floor, fights, chaos, all he had sought to erase, and the scars on his psyche felt inflamed.

Ariana heightened his senses. Gian was more than aware he had let down his steely guard in bed last night and it had shaken him. For a moment he had glimpsed how it felt to need another person, to rely on someone else, and that could never be.

Right now, though, her actions plunged him straight back into a world that had spun out of control—the chaos and fights between his parents, finding his older brother unconscious on the floor and shouting frantically for help, and their smiles and the making up that came after, the promises made that were never, ever kept.

Always they had taken things too far, and it was everything that he now lived to avoid.

'Hey.' He was speaking to the pilot, about to tell him to take off, for he wanted no part in this. Yet some odd sense of duty told him not to leave Ariana stranded, and so he sat, grim-faced, as a tearful Ariana ran her leggy way back to the helicopter and climbed in.

'We can go now,' Ariana said once her headphones and microphone were on. 'I'm done.'

And so too was he.

And he told her so the minute they stood alone back on the roof of La Fiordelise.

'You never cease to disappoint me, Ariana.'

He watched her tear-streaked, defiant face lift and her angry eyes met his as he gave her a well-deserved telling-off. 'I thought you were going there to speak with your brother, to find out how he was…'

'He shamed my mother!' Ariana shouted. 'She went on a cruise to get away from the ball and had to return to this!'

'Ah, so it was your mother talking.' He shook his head as he looked down at her, realising now what had happened between her leaving his suite and boarding the helicopter. 'And there was me thinking you had a mind of your own. How dare you put me in the middle of this? I would never have offered to take you if I'd known your plan was to behave this way.'

She had the gall to shrug. 'You have no idea what she did to us.'

'I have every idea!' Gian retorted.

'Meaning?'

But Gian was not about to explain himself. 'You know what, Ariana? I don't need your drama.'

It felt like a kind of relief that he could finally walk away without the painful struggle with his demons he had faced earlier when considering how to draw a line under all that had happened between them.

Except Ariana Romano ran after him.

He didn't want to hear her sobbing or begging for forgiveness, except Gian received neither. Instead he was tapped smartly on the shoulder and was somewhat surprised by the calm stare that met him when he turned around.

'You should be thanking me, Gian.'

'Thanking you?'

'Absolutely,' she responded. 'You were about to give me my marching orders this morning, and you were fumbling for an excuse. I handed you this on a plate.'

'You don't know that.'

'But I do.' Ariana was certain, for she could clearly recall the heavy atmosphere and the absolute certainty that Gian had been about to end things. Well, she'd given him the perfect reason to now. 'It isn't a relationship you're avoiding, Gian; it's emotion.'

Ariana struck like a cobra, right to the heart of his soul. He looked at her and all he could see was the chaos she left in her wake. He thought of the knife edge he had grown up on, the eternal threat of disaster that had hung over his family, and the eternal calm he now sought.

'Don't worry, Gian,' she said to his silence. 'I'm out of here. You keep your cold black heart and I'll carry right on.'

CHAPTER TWELVE

IT WOULD BE NICE, Ariana thought early the next morning, to pull the covers over her head as she nursed her first ever broken heart.

Officially broken.

She knew that since they had first made love she had been holding onto a dream. The fantasy that Gian would bend his rules for her and decide it was time to give love a chance…

Because it felt like love to Ariana.

Now she had to let go of that dream. Her mother called and then called again, but Ariana ignored it.

But then Stefano called and Ariana could never ignore a call from her twin…

'There's an extraordinary board meeting at nine,' he told her.

'Pass on my apologies,' Ariana mumbled, but Stefano was having none of it. 'We are to meet at the offices at eight,' Stefano told her. 'A driver has been ordered for you; he should be with you soon.'

'Eight?' Ariana checked.

'Mamma wants to speak to the three of us before the board meeting.'

'She's coming to the offices?' Ariana frowned. 'But she hasn't been there since...'

Since the news of her father and Mia's affair had broken.

This was big, Ariana knew as she quickly showered, squeezing in eye drops to erase all evidence of tears. She selected a navy linen suit and ran the straightening iron through her hair, trying to look somewhat put-together while she pondered what was about to take place. Ariana arrived at Romano Holdings and took the elevator up to where her family were waiting for her.

Her *mamma* was as pale as she had ever seen her, and Stefano looked grey. She could barely bring herself to look at Dante, but when she did she saw the bruise beneath his eye and felt sick that it had come from her own hand.

'I'm sorry,' she said to Dante. 'I just...'

'I get it,' Dante said, and gave her a hug. 'Ariana, I know how confusing this has all been, but there's something you need to hear, both you and Stefano...' He turned to their mother. 'It's time, Mamma,' he said.

This *was* big.

Gian knew that, because even as he tried to focus on his weekly planning meeting with Luna, little pings from his computer had him looking over. The press were gathered outside Romano Holdings, where an extraordinary meeting was being held, and in an unprecedented move Angela Romano was seen entering the building.

Gian watched as Ariana duly arrived in a silver car and he scanned the short piece of footage for a clue, a glimpse, as to what lay behind the mask she most certainly wore.

Her parting shot to him yesterday had seriously rattled him and he had spent most of the night simultaneously disregarding and dwelling on her words.

You keep your cold black heart and I'll carry right on.

Yet he was struggling to carry on, knowing that Ariana must be suffering now. For the first time, Gian wanted *more* information on the details of a woman's private life. He was fighting with himself not to call Ariana to see what was going on, how she was coping, what she knew...

Her brief appearance told him nothing. She was immaculate. Ariana really should be on the stage, for there was no hint of tension in her body language.

She wore a navy linen suit and her hair was smooth and tied back in a slick ponytail. She even paused and smiled her gorgeous red-lipped smile for the cameras.

'This can wait,' he told Luna, and wrapped up their morning meeting so he could focus on the news. 'If you could just bring coffee.'

'Of course.'

Throughout the morning, the little pings became more and more frequent for there was drama aplenty. Dante Romano and Mia were engaged to be married! Gian could not imagine that going down well with a certain hot-headed lady, but there Ariana was, still smiling for the cameras as she left the building and climbed into a car.

Ariana would come to him.

Of that Gian was certain.

Despite their exchange yesterday, Gian was quietly confident that Ariana would arrive in his office, because whenever there was drama in Ariana Romano's life, inevitably Luna announced she was at his door and a mini-tornado would burst in.

'Any messages from Ariana Romano?' he checked with Luna.

'None.'

'If she arrives here,' Gian said, 'please send her straight through.'

Ariana did not arrive, though, for she *refused* to run to him.

The car was mercifully cool and, rather than stare ahead, Ariana looked out of the window and smiled at the cameras as if the drama surrounding Dante and Mia hadn't affected her in the slightest. In fact, their engagement was the merest tip of an iceberg that had just been exposed to her in all its blinding glory. Ariana was having trouble taking it all in.

'Home?' the driver checked.

'No...' She hesitated, not quite ready for the emptiness of her apartment and the noise of her own thoughts. 'Just drive, please.'

She took a gulp of water from a chilled bottle the driver handed to her and tried to come to terms with the fact that her life, her childhood—in fact, all she had ever known—had been built on a lie. Her parents' marriage, of which she'd been so proud, had been a sham. They'd both had other partners and the marriage had been in name only, so much so that she and Stefano had been IVF babies.

It felt as if she was the very last to know.

They drove for ages. It was rush hour in Rome, all the workers spilling out, some rushing for transport, others taking their time for a coffee, or to sit in a bar.

She felt like an alien.

A stranger in her own body.

As they passed La Fiordelise she had never been more tempted to ask the driver to pull in, to push through the brass doors and escape to the cool calmness of Gian's office and unburden herself, as she would usually do. Except, thanks to their argument yesterday, that refuge was denied her now.

Instead, Ariana asked to be dropped off where they had walked that lonely night. She wandered there, too shocked and stunned for tears. It was a sticky late spring day and she drifted a while, ignoring the buzz of her phone.

Finally she glanced at the endless missed calls.

He came first and last.

Gian.

Mamma.

Gian.

Gian.

Mamma.

Gian.

Stefano.

Gian.

She had nothing to say to any of them, at least not until she had gathered her thoughts. Eventually, drained from walking and with a headache creating a pulse of its own, she wandered listlessly home.

'Hey,' she said to the doorman, who was dozing behind his cap. She took the elevator up, jolting when she saw a very familiar face. Gian was leaning against the wall, but came to his full height as she approached.

Her heart did not lurch in hope or relief. In fact, it sank, for right now Gian felt like another problem to deal with, another person to hide her true self from.

For her true self was hurting and dreadfully so—and her emotions were clearly too much for him.

'What are you doing here, Gian?'

'You didn't respond to my calls…'

'No.' She didn't even look at him. 'Because I was not in the mood to speak to anyone. How did you get up here?' She let out a mirthless laugh as she answered her own question. 'I really am going to fire that doorman.'

'I told him we were friends.'

'Friends.' She let out a mirthless laugh at his description of them. 'Well, however you described yourself, the doorman shouldn't have let you up.' She opened her door and her words dripped sarcasm as she invited him in. 'Come through, *friend.*'

She did not rush around making him welcome or offering a drink. Instead, she dropped her bag and headed straight to the kitchen, where she went to a drawer and took out two headache tablets and poured a glass of water.

For herself.

Gian watched as she downed the tablets and wondered how she still managed to look so put-together, even though he was sure her world had just been turned upside down. 'I saw you leaving Romano Holdings…' He tried to open the conversation, but Ariana didn't respond.

She was in no mood for conversation, and for once she didn't fill the silent gaps, offer drinks, or make him welcome. In fact, it was Gian who finally broke the tense silence.

'What happened?'

'We've been having a family catch-up and filling each other in on a few things.' She had been holding it in all day, sitting through revelation after revelation, and then a formal board meeting, always having to find a way to smile. 'Dante and Mia are expecting. That's for family's ears only,' Ariana needlessly warned, for she knew, because of his damned discretion, she might as well be telling it to the wall. 'There is to be a marriage in May, so that makes two Romano weddings.' Her voice rose and she almost let out an incredulous laugh, that both her brothers, who had always been indifferent to marriage, would soon both have all she had ever craved for herself.

But there was far more on her mind than her brothers. 'Gian, there's a reason I didn't take your calls. I have nothing to say to you. Nothing polite anyway.' Her confusion at the unfolding events was starting to morph into anger and she turned accusing eyes on him. 'Did you know?' she asked, her eyes narrowing into two dangerous slits.

'I told you—'

'I'm not talking about Dante and Mia.' She put down the glass with such a bang that he thought it might shatter, but Gian didn't even blink. 'Did you know that my father was gay?'

'Yes.'

'For how long?'

'Since I took over the hotel, I guess.'

'You guess?' she sneered.

'I wasn't taking notes, Ariana.'

'And what about my mother's affair?'

'I knew about that too. Look, your parents didn't sit me down and tell me, but given the nature of my work, they rightfully expected discretion. I would never gossip or break a confidence. I didn't even tell Dante and he is my best friend...'

'We were lovers!' Finally she shouted. Finally a sliver of her anger slipped out. 'I had every right to know.'

'Oh, so in your perfect world the fact we were sleeping together meant we should have started holding hands and gazing into each other's eyes and *sharing*?' He spat the last word with disdain. 'Tell me, Ariana, when was I supposed to tell you? The first time we made love? The second...?'

'If we were ever to have a relationship—' She stopped herself then, her nose tightening as she fought to suppress the tears building in her eyes, because a relationship, a real one, a close one, was the very thing he didn't want. 'You could have at least told me as a friend.'

'I wanted to,' he admitted. 'But it was not my place. They were not my secrets to tell. I tried to get you to speak to your father, that day of the interview—'

'You didn't try hard enough then.' Her anger, however misplaced, she aimed directly at him. 'For two years I felt pushed away by Papà. Now I find out that he just wanted to live out his days in peace with Roberto. My God! I was led to blame Mia. I was goaded and encouraged to hate her by my mother, just because she didn't want the truth getting out.'

'Ariana...' He tried to calm her down. 'Your mother came from a time—'

'I don't care!' She swore viciously in Italian and told him what rubbish he spoke. 'I'm his daughter. I deserved to know...' He crossed over as she swallowed down a scream that felt as if it had been building since her father died. 'If I'd known the truth, I could have spent quality time with him. Had *you* told me...'

She was almost hysterical and for once he was not trying to keep a lid on the drama or stop a commotion. It was not for that reason that he pulled her into his arms, but to comfort her. But she thumped at his chest and then scrunched his perfect shirt in her fist, knowing it wasn't his fault, knowing that the truth could only have come from her father.

'It was all just a farce...' She was starting to cry now in a way she never had before. Angry, bitter tears, and Gian held her as she drowned in his arms. 'I was so proud of their marriage, but it was just a sham. Even Stefano and I were conceived by IVF to keep up the charade...' All she had just learned poured out in an unchecked torrent he allowed to flow. 'They didn't really want us...' It was then Gian intervened.

'No.'

'Yes!' she insisted. 'It was all just a sham.'

'You were wanted,' he insisted, but Ariana would not be mollified.

'You don't know that...'

'But I do.' He was holding her arms and almost shaking her in an effort to loosen her dark thoughts before they took hold. 'I know for a fact you were wanted and loved.'

'Oh, what would you know?' Ariana responded. 'What would a man like you know about love?'

'Nothing!'

She stilled in his arms at the harsh anguish in his voice.

'I know nothing about love!' He hated to tell her, for Gian was loath to share, but he would expose his soul if it saved her from the dark hole she was sinking into. 'I wasn't wanted, Ariana. I was a regretful mistake and they never let me forget that fact. When Eduardo caved to their lifestyle, I brought myself up. I could see my mother's loathing on the rare occasions she actually looked me in the eye. You know how your mother called me a beggar? Well, I was one. I walked the streets at night, just for conversation, for contact...'

Her stomach clenched in fear at the thought of a child out there alone.

'They didn't even notice or care that I was gone. You want the truth, Ariana? I wanted to disappear...'

She couldn't breathe. So passionate was his revelation that there was not even the space to take in the air her lungs craved.

'No!' she refuted. It wasn't that she thought he lied, more that she could not bear his truth.

'Yes,' he said, 'so while I have never known love, I know what it looks like, and I know how much you were wanted and loved...'

They were the words she was desperate to hear, but she wanted to hear them from him. She was so desperate that she managed to twist her mind to pretend that Gian was saying *he* wanted her, that *he* loved her.

'Gian...' His name was a sob, a plea that she could hold onto the dream that those words were for her. Ariana honestly did not know who initiated their kiss but it was as if he read her cry in his name. For a man who knew nothing of love, he knew a lot about numbing pain. The room went dark then as their mouths melded, hot angry kisses to douse the pain. As his mouth bruised hers, as their teeth clashed, Ariana reacted with an urgency she had never known.

She kissed him as if it were vital.

And Gian kissed her to a place where only they remained. His hands were deft, shedding her jacket and lifting her top, pushing his hands up and caressing her breasts through her flimsy bra, his palms making her skin burn, then leaving her smouldering as he tackled her skirt.

He scalded her with desire, his hands hitching up her skirt so impatiently that she heard the lining rip. And Ariana, who had thought desire moved more slowly, could not begin to comprehend that she might simply seize what she craved.

He offered oblivion in the salty taste of his skin as she undid his shirt and buried her face in him. He offered escape as she unbuckled his belt and trousers.

'Ariana,' he warned, for he had not come for this. He had come to offer more, yet it was a poor attempt at a protest for he was lifting her onto the bench and tearing at her knickers as their mouths found each other again.

She had not known that the world could feel empty and soulless one moment and then find herself wrapped in his arms and drowning in the succour he gave.

He spread her thighs and she let out a shout as he pushed inside her. It was not a cry of pain but of relief, for here she could simply escape and be.

'Please,' she sobbed, because she never wanted it to end, yet they were both building rapidly to a frantic peak.

The glass she had slammed down spilled and her bottom was cold and wet, but it barely registered. There was only him, crashing against her senses again and again, a mass exodus of hurt as he touched her deep inside and somehow soothed the pain.

'Gian!' It was Ariana who offered a warning now, for she was trembling on the inside, her thighs so tight it felt like cramp. A sudden rush of electricity shot down her spine and she clenched around him, dizzied by her own pulses, and she was rewarded with his breathless shout.

They were both silent and stunned as their breathing gradually calmed. Ariana was grateful for the empty space between her thoughts. It was the first time she had felt even a semblance of quiet since her phone had shot her awake that morning. Gian too was silent, somewhat reeling at his own lack of control, for he had come here to speak, to talk, to offer Ariana comfort...

Now, though, he lowered her down from the bench and tidied himself. Ariana twisted the waistband on her skirt so the damp patch was at the side, and she even smoothed her hand over her hair, as if order could somehow be resorted.

Except it was chaos, Ariana knew, for she had made love to him again.

She had convinced herself, once again, that Gian might one day change and want her the way she wanted him.

'Ariana.' He cleared his throat. 'I didn't come here—'

'What did you come here for then?' she interrupted. 'A chat?'

'Yes,' Gian said, as the blood crept back to his head. 'A proposal.'

She looked at him with wide, nervous eyes, for this was new territory to Ariana. How one moment they could be locked in an intimate embrace, and the next attempting to speak as if his seed wasn't trickling down between her thighs. 'A proposal?'

He nodded. 'I thought a lot about what you said yesterday, and you're right, Ariana, I do avoid emotion...' He smiled a pale smile. 'Which is impossible around you.'

She swallowed, unsure where this was leading, but hoping... Hoping!

'What you said about moving...' Gian ventured.

'I meant,' Ariana said, 'I'm not going to live in an apartment my mother feels entitled to use as a second lounge.' Her decision was crystal clear now. 'I want to take the Romano name off for a while. I want to work on myself.' She gave a hollow laugh. 'I want to actually *work*...'

'I get that,' Gian agreed. 'And, as I said, I have a proposal for you. Fiordelise Florence hotel opens at the end of May. What if you do your training here, and then work as Guest Services Manager there?'

'Sorry?' Ariana frowned, though clearly not for the reason he was thinking.

'I know I said you would start as an assistant, but I agree, you have an exceptional skill set and would be an asset.'

'Your *proposal* is a job.'

'More than a job,' Gian said.

'A career then?'

'No!' She was missing the point, Gian thought. Though he could understand why, given his usually direct style of communication. He was not good at this relationship game. 'We could see each other...*more* of each other,' he said. 'Away from your family.'

'Without them knowing?' Ariana frowned.

'Of course,' he agreed. 'We both know that would cause

more problems than it would solve so we would have to be discreet. I'll have an executive manager there, so I would not be so hands-on in running the place. There would be no impropriety at the hotel and far less chance of being seen out. I would, of course, get to Florence as often as I was able.'

Oh, she understood then. 'I'd be your mistress, you mean?'

'I never said that.'

'Perhaps not in so many words, but...' Her lips were white but still turned up into the kind of practised smile she flashed for the cameras all the time, all the brighter to disguise how she was breaking down on the inside. 'Tucked away, my family in the dark, no one finding out...that sounds an awful lot like a mistress to me. Well, I won't be your Fiordelise.'

'You're complicating matters.'

'Then I'll make it simple. Where would this lead, Gian?'

'Lead?' Gian frowned. 'Why does it have to lead anywhere?'

'Because that's what my heart does.' Ariana could say it no more honestly than that. 'My heart wants to know where this might go one day.'

'I'm offering you the best parts of me, Ariana.'

'No, you're offering to keep me tucked away, to flit in and out of my life whenever it's convenient. Gian, I want my lover by my side. I want to share my life with him, not live a secret. God knows, my parents did enough of that and look how it turned out.'

'That is so you,' Gian said. 'You have to get your own way. Everything has to be now—'

'I'm not asking for now, Gian,' Ariana interrupted. 'I'm asking if there's a possibility that this might lead to more. You want directness,' she said. 'You tell your lovers up front that it will go no further. Well, I'm being direct too and I'm telling you that I want at the very least the possibility of more.'

'I have no more to give.'

She had known that getting involved with Gian would ultimately hurt her, so why did she feel so unprepared to deal with the pain he so impassively inflicted?

'No, thank you.' Her voice was strangely high.

'Think about it…'

'I already have.' She was staring down at the barrel of a future spent mainly alone. Christmases, weddings, the birth of Dante and Mia's baby, christenings and even funerals…all the things she would have to deal with alone.

Her love unacknowledged and unnamed.

'I won't be your mistress, Gian.' Her response was clearer now, her decision absolutely made. She started to show him the door, but then changed her mind. 'Actually, before you leave, I have something I need to put to you.'

Gian frowned. He was not used to being told no in this way, particularly when he had offered Ariana more than he'd ever offered anyone. 'What?'

'I can't pretend,' Ariana said. 'And I don't want to keep making the same mistake again.'

'You think that was a mistake?' He pointed to the bench where they had both found a slice of heaven just moments ago.

'Not at that time I didn't,' Ariana said. 'Even now, no, I don't think it was, but if we make love again then, yes, that would be a mistake.'

'You make no sense.'

'I want you to stay away,' Ariana said. 'Not for ever, but at least until…' She swallowed down the words, loath to admit how he turned her on merely by his presence, how with one look, one crook of his manicured finger, she would run to him. 'Until I can act as if nothing ever happened between us.'

As if I don't love your soulless heart.

'I can't face you in front of my family until I can look at you as if nothing ever happened between us. I have to get to that place where we can do the kiss-kiss thing and…'

She took a breath to steady herself. Right now it seemed like an impossible dream, that one day she might merely shrug when she heard that Gian had arrived.

'I'd like you to stay away from my brothers' weddings...'

'I'm already not going to Stefano's, but Dante...' He shook his head. 'Dante is my closest friend...'

'Oh, please.' Ariana found a new strength in her voice then, a derisive one, a scorn-filled one. 'What would do you care about that? You've told me relationships are the very thing you don't want.'

He couldn't deny that.

'So, please, Gian.' She said it without derision now. 'If you care about me at all, then do the decent thing and stay away.'

Gian did as she asked.

He stayed away from Dante's wedding, citing an urgent issue at La Fiordelise Azerbaijan, which he had to deal with personally.

That meant Ariana could smile her red smile at the wedding and have fun with her regular posse of friends.

Yet, despite him acquiescing to her request, she missed him so much: the little flurry in her stomach that existed whenever there was the prospect of seeing him; the small shared smiles; the occasional dance; and, most of all, the prospect of a late night alone with him...

Instead, she stood in the grounds of what had once been the family home and tried to push Gian out of her heart and focus on the nuptials. Mia looked utterly gorgeous and Dante looked so proud and happy as his bride walked towards him.

'That didn't take long, did it?' Nicki nudged.

'What?'

'She's showing!' Paulo said.

Ariana pressed her lips together. Only family had been let in on the secret that Mia was pregnant. Dante had assured them all that nothing had taken place before Papà died, although for four months Mia did appear rather, well, large.

'It must have been going on for quite some time,' Nicki whispered. 'Your pa only died in January...'

'Thanks for pointing that out,' Ariana sniped, but Nicki didn't notice for she had moved on. 'Where's Gian? I thought he'd be here.'

'I've no idea,' Ariana said, practising her shrug, as if Gian De Luca was the very last person on her mind.

As the vows were made, and Nicki jostled to take photos on her phone, Ariana asked herself why she hadn't told Nicki about what had happened with Gian. Neither had she told her the truth about her parents…

Paulo she wasn't so close to, but she and Nicki were supposed to be best friends.

It was a question of trust, Ariana realised.

Deep in her soul, Ariana realised that she did not trust the woman who sat by her side and it had nothing to do with Gian's opinion of Nicki…

The answer had arrived in its own time and the conclusion Ariana came to was all hers.

Ariana said nothing, of course. She just smiled through the proceedings and raised a glass when Dante announced in his speech that he and Mia were expecting twins—likely the reason for her showing so much. Not that Nicki corrected her earlier assumption. 'You're going to be an aunty…twice!' Nicki screeched, and called to the waiter for another bottle of champagne.

'Make that two bottles,' Paulo said, and Ariana's eyes actually scanned the room for Gian, as if hope and need might make him somehow appear.

He did not.

Apart from his absence, it was a wonderful wedding, their love so palpable it made Ariana both happy and pensive.

'It will be your turn soon.' Nicki smiled as they took a break from the dancing. 'And I shall be your bridesmaid…'

'You'll be the oldest bridesmaid in Rome if you wait for me,' Ariana said. 'I want a career.'

'Why?' Nicki frowned. 'It's not as if you need to work. You have Daddy's trust fund. Didn't he leave you an apartment in Paris? We should go there and check it out...'

'It's not enough—'

'Please,' Nicki scoffed. 'Poor little rich girl.' Her narrowed eyes snapped back to wide and friendly and she pushed out a smile. 'Let's join Paulo.'

'You go,' Ariana encouraged. 'I'll just sit here awhile.'

Her rare absence on the dance floor did not go unnoticed. 'Get off your phone, Ariana,' Dante called. 'Come and dance...'

Except it wasn't her own phone that Ariana was going through, it was her friend's. Some might call it dishonest, or an invasion of privacy, a breach of trust...

Except, from where Ariana now sat, those titles belonged to Nicki.

There was a sneaky little shot of Mia in profile as she made her vows, a definite confirmation of the pregnancy that had been announced only to family and friends. That could be excused, though, as lots of people had been taking photos.

What could not be excused was an earlier image of Mia and Dante, locked in a passionate embrace. It was the photo that had been taken at the ball, the one that had caused so much pain.

To a heart that Ariana had thought could not be broken further, the knowledge that her friend had betrayed her added another river of pain.

The ridiculous part was that the one person in whom she would have confided, Ariana had asked not to attend.

She missed him.

Even with his selfish guidelines as to what a relationship with him might entail, she *needed* him tonight.

'Ariana!'

Her name was being shouted by lots of people now.

Maybe she had grown up some, because instead of confronting Nicki and causing a scene at her brother's wedding, she did the right thing.

Ariana put down the phone, topped up her lipstick...

...and danced.

CHAPTER THIRTEEN

ARIANA WASN'T AVOIDING sorting out her life.

If that had been the case, then she would have said yes to Gian's offer to be his mistress. She would have left her chaotic family and Janus friend and headed for Florence to be wined and dined and made love to over and over.

Instead, she faced the mountain that at first had looked far too high to climb. Yet, bit by bit, she found the tools to tackle it, some of which had been given to her by Gian.

The doorman received a stern warning that from now on Ariana's whereabouts were to remain private and heaven help him if an unannounced guest arrived at her door. She declined nights out with Paulo, *to be seen*, for she had felt Gian's exasperation and knew he was right.

It wasn't just Gian's suggestions she followed, though. She also took Dante's perpetual advice and finally turned off her phone.

Apart from Eloa's hen night, where red lips were certainly required, most were spent sitting on her apartment floor, eating ice cream and finally sorting out her photos into albums.

Ariana chose to withdraw from the endless vacuous socialising and learned to rely on her own company, arranging her past into a more honest shape as she prepared for a new future. Finally, she was ready for a couple of nights in Luctano, where she spoke at length with Roberto and got to know her father, a little too late, but a whole lot more.

'He loved you,' Roberto said.

'I know.'

She did.

On the Thursday before she headed for home, ready now to visit his grave, Ariana spread an armful of gorgeous hand-picked daffodils, which meant truth, rebirth and new beginnings, and a little sprig of violets, for peace in the afterlife, and told him about Stefano and Eloa's wedding, which was just two days away.

'I am his wedding *padrihnos*, or wedding bridesmaid,' Ariana told her father. 'It basically means I am Stefano's best man.' She knew that would make him smile, wherever he was now. 'And Nicki is coming over tomorrow and I shall be telling her she is not welcome at the wedding and I don't want to see her any more.' Ariana swallowed. 'I still haven't told Dante about the photo.'

It wasn't her brother's wrath that worried her, more that he would, of course, tell Gian. She couldn't bear the thought of him rolling his eyes, for he had warned her about Nicki more than once.

There was something else too, something she hadn't told anyone yet, not even herself, but she admitted it out loud now. 'I am in love with Gian, Papà.'

She wouldn't be the first in her family to act in her own interests and keep it secret, were she to become his mistress, but despite how she felt about Gian, she could not reconcile herself to it. Not now she was finally becoming someone she could be proud of.

* * *

'You're not ready!' Nicki frowned, when she saw Ariana dressed in a pale grey dress and flat sandals and with her hair wild and her eyes all puffy and swollen.

'Actually, I am ready,' Ariana corrected. She had been up all night, completing the finishing touches to gifts for her loved ones, and she had worked through the day, only stopping to refuel with coffee, thinking about what must be done. 'Come in, Nicki.'

It was up there with the hardest things she had ever done, because Ariana had truly thought of Nicki as a forever friend. Confronted with the evidence of what she had done, Nicki attacked her friend, and Ariana didn't have the energy to muster a defence against the tirade of abuse she was subjected to. Instead she listened and then said, 'I think you should leave now.'

'But we have the wedding tomorrow,' Nicki flailed. 'It'll look odd if I'm not there and we have our trip to Paris—'

'*I* have a wedding tomorrow,' Ariana interrupted. 'You're no longer welcome at Romano family events.'

It hurt and it hurt and it hurt, and once Nicki had gone, she cried for a while. But Ariana wanted this chapter of her life firmly closed, which meant that she had to tell Dante and Mia that it had been her friend who had invaded their privacy and outed them to the press.

And in turn they would tell Gian.

Only that wasn't right, Ariana knew. It wasn't up to Dante to tidy up after her. It was *her* friend who had caused this, and it was Ariana's mess to clean up. With that thought in mind, she grabbed a wrapped parcel from her bed. She had intended to mail it, but that was a cop-out and so she walked, or rather marched, her way down cobbled lanes and packed streets then pushed through the gorgeous brass door of La Fiordelise and towards his office, where she was met by his gatekeeper, Luna.

'Gian is in a meeting at the moment,' Luna said.

'It's my fault for arriving unannounced...' Ariana shook her dizzy head '…but if he can spare me a moment when he's done it would be very much appreciated.'

'Of course.' Luna nodded. 'Would you like some refreshments while you wait?'

Ariana guessed she was being sent to the Pianoforte Bar, or, as his lovers should name it, the Relegation Bar, and her braveness evaporated. 'It's fine.' Ariana had changed her mind. 'I'll catch up with him another time.'

'No, no…' Luna said, and it dawned on her that she was not being sent to the Pianoforte Bar. Instead, Luna gently suggested that she freshen up and pointed her towards a powder room. 'Still or sparkling?' she asked.

'Sorry?' Ariana frowned.

'Acqua,' Luna said patiently. 'Would you like still or sparkling?'

She must thank Luna one day, Ariana thought as she splashed her face with water and ran a comb through her hair, because she still had a morsel of pride left, enough to know she had been saved from facing him looking so terrible.

Terrible.

Ariana hadn't so much as glanced in a mirror since her confrontation with Nicki. It looked as if she'd rolled out of bed this morning and just pulled a dress on.

She had.

As if she hadn't brushed her hair.

She hadn't.

Her skin was all pale and blotchy, and her lips were swollen from crying so there was no point painting her usual red lipstick on. Still, she was grateful for the reprieve and the chance to freshen up somewhat, as Luna would no doubt have told him that yet another of his exes had shown up in a state of distress…

No, not she!

'I have Ariana Romano in Reception, asking to see you.'

Gian was just packing up his laptop, about to head to Florence. He had no time for theatrics. And yet, with each day that passed, he found that he missed the colour she had brought to his world, the drama and emotion she always brought to his table, to his bed...

He wanted them.

It had been hell missing his friend's wedding because, despite his supposed lack in the heart department, under any other circumstances he would have moved heaven and earth to have been there.

'I can tell her that you are due to fly out—'

'It's fine,' Gian cut in.

'I should warn you then, Gian, she seems distressed...'

'Was she short with you?' Gian asked, almost hopefully, because if Ariana was throwing her weight around with his staff, he could at least be aggrieved, but Luna shook her head.

'Of course not. Ariana is always polite with me.' Luna suddenly laughed.

'What's so funny?'

'Ariana always makes me smile,' Luna said. 'Anyway, I'm just letting you know that it looks as if she's been crying.'

He nodded and nudged a leather-covered box of tissues to her side of the desk in preparation for her arrival. 'Send her through.'

Gian was certain he knew what this would be about. It had been a few months since the funeral, and there had been the ball, and of course what had taken place in her kitchen. Whatever way he looked at it, Gian was sure he was about to be told he was to be a father.

Yes, there were always consequences, and not once, but on three separate occasions he had not taken the level of care he usually would, relying on her to take the Pill. It was his own fault entirely and he would handle this with grace, even if a pregnancy was everything he had always dreaded.

Gian did not know how he felt.

When she arrived in his office, she was most un-Ariana-like.

Her dress was crumpled, her espadrilles tied haphazardly, her hair, dared he say it, a day past needing a wash, and her make-up but a distant memory. And yet, to his eyes, this was the real Ariana, the one who shot straight to his heart. To see her so fragile and clearly distraught had him fighting not to go straight over and take her in his arms.

Instead, for now, he kept his arms to himself.

'Ariana.' He rose to greet her and they did the kiss-kiss routine she had referred to so painfully in their last conversation. He gestured for her to take a seat as they both tried to go back to a world where they hadn't done more. 'Can I offer you some refreshments?'

'No, no...' She shook her head. 'Thank you, though.'

'Some champagne?' Gian suggested. 'A bottle this time.'

But she did not smile at his little reference and instead shook her head. 'No, thank you.' She took a breath. It wasn't just La Fiordelise and the oasis he made that calmed her; it was Gian himself.

Despite there being so much on her mind, there was a chance to pause, to just sit in the calming low light of his office and take a moment.

That was what he gave her.

Always.

This tiny chance to pause, and it was in that moment Ariana knew that she really did want things resolved between them. No matter her blushes, it was time to face things head on.

'Before I say what I came to say—' before he got angry about Nicki '—I just want to clear the air. I'm sorry for asking you to miss Dante's wedding. It wasn't fair of me to do that.'

'There were extenuating circumstances and it was right that you did,' Gian said. 'I'm sure we'll get to managing steely politeness at family gatherings soon.'

'Yes!' She shot out a laugh and tried to glimpse a time when she wouldn't want him, but it was such an impossible thought that her smile slid away.

'Dante understood,' Gian said. 'The wedding was at such short notice. He dropped by the other day, we had lunch, and he told me about the twins. So we're all good...' He was so certain that Ariana was here to tell him she was pregnant that he kindly gave her an opening. His eyes never left her face as he watched carefully for her reaction. 'Twins must run in the family...'

'Oh, please.' Ariana gave a mirthless laugh. 'Twins don't run in my family, Gian. I assume my mother had more than one egg put back. Anything to keep up the charade!'

'It wasn't all a charade, Ariana.'

'I know that now.' She gave him a thin smile.

'Are you talking?'

'Of course we are,' Ariana said. 'I am hurt, yes, but I love her.'

Lucky Angela, Gian thought, to have her Ariana's unconditional love.

A love he himself had discarded.

'I have something for you,' Ariana told him. 'I've been sorting out some of my father's things...' She handed him a leather-bound book as she explained what she had done in recent days. 'I've made one each for my brothers and one for my mother. The contents are different in each, of course...' She was talking a little too fast, as she did when she was embarrassed, unsure if he would even want her gift.

'An album?'

'Yes, there were a lot of photos, and I thought you might like the ones you were in. But please don't look at it now: that's not what I'm here for...' She took a breath. 'Gian, there's something I have to tell you. I wasn't going to; I've tried to deal with it myself, but you do deserve to know...'

Gian braced himself to hear the inevitable.

'I've had my suspicions for a couple of weeks.' Ariana's voice was barely above a whisper, and she cleared her throat. 'I should perhaps have come to you sooner but I wanted to be sure myself...'

'You could have come to me,' Gian said. 'You can always come to me. You know that.'

'Yes.' She nodded. 'I just wanted to be very sure before I said anything, and so this afternoon I confronted her.'

Gian frowned, not sure what Ariana meant by that. 'Confronted...who?' he asked, surprised. 'What do you mean?'

'I've just come from speaking with Nicki.' Ariana ran a shaking hand through her thick dark hair and then forced herself to look at Gian and simply say it. 'It was Nicki who took the photo of Mia and Dante at the Romano Ball...'

That was it?

Ariana wasn't here to tell him she was pregnant! Instead, she had found out who had sold the photos to the press! Gian waited to catch the smile of relief that should surely be spreading over his face.

Except the smile didn't come, and the anticipated relief didn't course through his veins, as he looked at Ariana sitting tense and hurt, let down by a friend she had trusted.

'You're sure it was her?' Gian checked.

Ariana nodded. 'At Dante's wedding she was acting strangely, and when I got a chance I looked through her phone. I'm so sorry, Gian.'

'*You're* sorry?'

'Nicki was my guest on the night of the ball. I know the photo caused problems for you—'

'It's fine,' Gian cut in. 'Well, it's not, of course, but don't worry about me.' He wanted to go over and take her hands, which still twisted in her lap. 'I'm sorry she let you down.'

Ariana nodded.

'Does Dante know?'

'Not yet. It's taken me a couple of weeks to get my head around it all, and I decided I would tell you first.' She looked at the man she had always run to with troubles that seemed too big for this world. 'I might leave it until after Stefano's wedding. Really, I don't think Dante will be too upset. After all, the photo forced things out into the open. I know it angered you, though, and that it was damaging for the reputation of the hotel.'

'The only reputation that has been damaged is Nicki's,' Gian said kindly. 'What did she say when you confronted her?'

Ariana let out a pained, mirthless laugh. 'Plenty.'

He saw a fresh batch of tears flash in her eyes and knew that the confrontation hadn't been pleasant and so he asked again. 'What did Nicki say?'

'That it was my fault. That I treated her poorly and always made her feel second best...'

'No.'

But his words couldn't comfort her now. She was still shaking from the recent encounter with someone she had considered to be her friend, someone she had defended so often to this man.

'I'm sorry,' Gian said.

'I know you never liked her.'

'I mean, I'm sorry you had to go through that.'

'I should have listened to you in the first place. In fact, I'm starting to think you might be right...about the value of not letting people get too close.'

'Never take relationship advice from me,' Gian said. 'As you have undoubtedly seen, I am not particularly good at them.'

'I don't know about that.' Ariana smiled. 'You made me feel pretty wonderful, at least for a while.' But she hadn't come here to discuss her time with Gian. She'd said what she'd come to say. 'Anyway, thank you for being so gracious. I just thought it was something you should know. I don't know if Nicki will have the audacity to come here again...'

'It'll be fine. I'll let my security team know.' He looked at her swollen eyes and knew Nicki had said plenty more. 'What else did she say?' Gian asked.

Ariana was rarely silent.

'Tell me,' he pushed.

'That I'm spoiled...'

'You deserve to be spoiled.'

'You do too, Gian.'

'What do you mean? I have everything I could possibly want or need.'

'You really don't get it, do you?' He was so self-assured and yet so remote, just so impossible to reach. She ached, literally ached, to shower him with kisses, to bring him ice cream in bed, to be there at the beginning and the end of his day… 'It's not about the best bits, Gian.' He just stared back at her, nonplussed.

It was time to let go of her fantasy that he would change his mind, that he would see her as anything more. It was time to go.

She stood to leave, but it was Gian who delayed her. 'Are you ready for the wedding tomorrow?'

'Yes.'

He wanted her to elaborate, as she usually did. Gian wanted to know if she was dreading tomorrow, if she was speaking with Mia, and lots more besides, but it would seem he had lost his front row seat to her thoughts.

'Good luck with the opening,' Ariana said.

'Thank you. Enjoy the wedding.'

'I intend to.'

This really was it, Gian realised.

The tears she had shed and her sudden appearance hadn't been about him. It had been about Nicki and a friendship lost.

There was no baby, no emotional issues to deal with, it really was just time to move on.

Gian was usually very good at that. So why did he feel this way?

The opening of La Fiordelise Florence was a tremendous success and on the Saturday night esteemed guests mingled and celebrated. While he should be quietly congratulating himself, he had never felt more alone in a crowded room.

The best food, the best champagne, and if it was sex he wanted, well, there would be no shortage there, for there were beautiful women vying for his attention.

The problem was him, because instead of enjoying the spoils of his own success Gian found himself slipping away not long after dinner, sitting in his impressive suite leafing through a leather-bound book... There were several pictures of him fishing or riding with Dante and later with the twins. There was one of a teenage Gian rolling his eyes while Dante kicked a stone to Stefano as a very spoiled Ariana sat on a fat little pony, the absolute apple of her parents' eyes.

But then Ariana faded from the images as life took its twists and turns and he had headed to university. There were a couple of years without any images while the disasters that had unfolded back then had played out.

He had never really liked Angela Romano, but there was a picture of him smiling at her the night La Fiordelise had been saved. Angela was dripping jewels and being her usual affected self, as she stood with her husband and Gian.

This really was a gift without an agenda, Gian knew, for there was even a picture of Gian standing with the Romano family on the night Ariana had attended her first ball. He knew Ariana had made this album purely for his benefit because she would prefer that this picture of herself be relegated to burn in a fire for she looked scowling and awkward.

It was a slice of time he had forgotten.

Even now, as he looked at the photo, there was no flash of memory.

He would have been in his mid-twenties then, and Ariana at that awkward age of fifteen, her hair done in a way that now looked very much of its time, and she had been wearing too much make-up.

They had all been there for him throughout his life, and he couldn't help but wonder what each of the Romanos was doing now.

How Ariana was coping with the nuptials.

He turned back the pages and looked again at a podgy little Ariana sitting on a podgy little pony, only he saw it differently this time… Not the pony, or the pampered heiress, just the absolute adoration on her face as she smiled at her parents and pleaded with them, with her eyes, to be loved, loved, loved…

It could have been a cone full of chestnuts they had given her; it wasn't the pony she had craved, it had been attention and love.

Gian went out onto the balcony and gazed on the Ponte Vecchio, the gorgeous old bridge that was the soul of Florence, and sung about in 'O Mio Babbino Caro'.

Yet it was not the music that filled his soul tonight, for he would never look at this bridge and not think of her.

Ariana.

Yes, he was proud of his new hotel, but tonight his heart was in Rome.

CHAPTER FOURTEEN

'COLOUR,' ELOA HAD SAID.

A Brazilian wedding was a colourful affair, and that was evident even before the nuptials had started. Even though Gian was not in Rome this weekend, he had ensured La Fiordelise was at their disposal. The reception area was a blaze of colour and forbidden perfume, Ariana noticed as she walked through Reception and headed up to her suite to get changed.

Ariana would have preferred to wear black, as she had to the Romano Ball, to denote that she was in mourning. For her father, of course, but the end of a relationship also felt a whole lot like grief. She awoke with a weight of sadness in her chest that never quite left, and she felt Gian's presence beside each and every thought. Yet she must push it all aside today, so she chose a dress as red as her signature lipstick. She wore her jet-black hair up, teased, with a few stray curls snaking down, meaning that she looked far more vibrant than she felt.

As Stefano fiddled with his tie, Ariana stepped out for a moment onto the balcony and looked down at the square beneath and remembered the night of her father's funeral, that desperately lonely night made so much better by Gian.

Why had she insisted that he stay away, when the truth was that she missed him already?

Half the congregation were clipping their way across the square to the venue and Ariana watched the colourful display from the balcony of Stefano's suite. The sun seemed at odds with the greyness of her world, and the flowers looked like placards from angry protesters to her tired eyes, yet they waved their petals and demanded she sparkle.

And so Ariana put on her best smile and stepped back inside. 'We should head over soon,' she told him.

'Before we do, there's something I want to say,' Stefano said. 'Ariana, I'm sorry for shutting you out.'

'Stefano, we don't need to do this now. It's your wedding day...'

'And I want it to be perfect,' he said. 'I want the air to be cleared between us. Gian suggested—'

'Gian?' Ariana frowned.

'He called me this morning to wish me well and apologise for not being here. We got to talking...' He took a breath.

Even though he wasn't physically here, Gian was still looking out for her, Ariana realised. He was still fixing the pieces of her life that he could, and she was so grateful to him as Stefano spoke on and finally gave her his reasons for keeping his distance. 'You see, I knew Mamma was having an affair, and I was having suspicions about Pa and Roberto. I was worried I might let things slip when I spoke to you and so I stayed away as much as I could. I was wrong...'

'No,' Ariana corrected. 'You did what you thought best at the time, and the air is clear now.' Clear, if a little thick with unshed tears when she thought of Gian and this moment he had created to bring her and her twin back together.

'We have some catching up to do,' Stefano prompted.

'We do...' Ariana smiled '...though it can wait till after your honeymoon.' But certain things would wait for ever. They were close again, but it would never be like it was before. Gian had changed her, she realised. She was far more independent now and did not need to run and tell Stefano everything, certainly not about herself and Gian.

It was her secret to keep.

'Do you have the rings?' Stefano asked for maybe the twentieth time.

'I have the rings.' Ariana smiled as she checked again for maybe the thirtieth time! 'Are you nervous?'

'Very,' Stefano admitted, and looked at his sister. 'I miss him.'

'I know you do.'

'It's the bride who should be crying...' Stefano said as he took a deep breath. 'I'm so happy yet I miss him so much today.'

'Hey,' Ariana soothed, and then she did something she never thought she would do. She reached into her purse and took out a tiny sliver of gold she had sworn she would never give away, but that Gian had told her she might. 'Papà gave Gian this for strength when his family died...'

'Really?'

'And he gave it to me when I felt weak at Papà's funeral, but I don't need it any more.' She put it in his top pocket. 'Papà is with you today.'

Ariana got on with her designated job: getting her brother to the embassy on time and remembering the rings.

Eloa was a stunning bride and the day brimmed with happiness. Well, that was what Ariana determinedly showed, even if there was a squad of elves holding down the cork on a vat of tears she would later shed.

'No Nicki?' Dante checked after the service as he handed her a glass of cachaça—a rather smoky Brazilian rum that made her eyes water. Ariana shook her head, deciding that she would tell him another time about the photo.

Tonight was a celebration after all.

And then Mia had a question for her new husband. 'No Gian again?'

'His new hotel,' Dante said. 'The opening was booked before the wedding date was decided and couldn't be changed...'

It was a throwaway sentence as he took his gorgeous wife off to dance and Ariana stood there, wondering how she would get through not just tonight but every future Romano family event at which Gian should be present.

Because Mia was right, Gian should be here.

The Romanos loved him like their own and he belonged here amongst them.

And when the next one happened, and the next, Ariana had to somehow work out how *not* to tumble into bed with him afterwards.

For. The. Rest. Of. Her. Life.

Oh, those elves were working overtime, yet she refused to cry and so she danced with Pedro, who was a cousin of the bride, and she danced with Francisco, who was a friend of an aunt, and Ariana laughed and danced and determinedly refused to give in to a heart that was breaking.

'Come on, Ariana...' They were all dragging her to the centre, where it would seem it was a Brazilian tradition to dance around Eloa's gold shoes. Really, Ariana had no idea what she was doing, but she swayed her hips and laughed and did a sort of Spanish flamenco around the shoe, tapping her feet and swishing the ruffles on her dress.

He had almost missed this, Gian thought when he saw her.

He had almost missed another Romano wedding and another night with people he could only now admit to himself were family.

The usually unruffled Luna had nearly thrown a fit when Gian had declared that he was flying back to Rome and asked if she could arrange it urgently, as well as a couple of other small assignments he wanted her to swiftly organise. 'I need to be there tonight.'

Fortunately, Ariana had arranged the reception just across from La Fiordelise so, with his helicopter landing late into the night, it was a simple matter of checking everything was in place and feeding some official documents through the shredder.

Gian didn't need reminders of the past.

It was a future he wanted now.

And with the past shredded, he walked across the square to Palazzo Pamphili and found, to his pleasant surprise, he was still on the guest list.

Walking through the grand building with its intricate ceilings and formal galleries, there was a moment to gather himself in such esteemed surroundings. It felt deserted, yet finally he could hear the laughter and merriment as if calling for him to join in. And even without his feelings for Ariana, it was right that he was there tonight for, perfect or not, these people had been more of a family to him than his own.

'Gian!' Dante caught up with him as he congratulated the bride and groom and apologised for arriving so late. 'It is good that you made it.'

It was said completely without implication or malice that he had missed theirs, Gian knew; Dante and Mia were simply pleased to see him.

Gian was back in the fold, as easily as that, and he stood watching the celebrations for a moment, taking it all in. He did not have to strain to locate Ariana; she was completely unmissable, of course.

Dressed in red, she was the belle of the ball, dancing and laughing and having the time of her life, so much so that even Gian could not see the hurt he was certain resided within.

He wasn't vain enough to believe it was all to do with him. There was the loss of her father, her relationship with her mother, Nicki, Stefano...

He was proud of his diva and her acting skills, proud of her resilience, and also aware of an unfamiliar sensation tightening his chest as she danced happily in another man's arms.

And another!

Damn it, Ariana, Gian thought, *I get it. Your life will go on without me, but please tone it down!*

He had never cared about anyone enough to know jealousy before, yet he learned there and then to breathe through it, even smiling as she kicked up her heels.

No longer able to resist, he caught Ariana's arm as she stamped past him, and saw how startled she was in her violet eyes when they locked with his.

Gian was here.

Damn!

Just as she did her best to move on and prove to herself she could party without him, the best-looking spanner in the world was suddenly thrown into the works.

'I'm busy dancing,' she told him, and reclaimed her arm.

'It's a Brazilian wedding, Ariana,' he told her. 'Not a Spanish one.'

'I know that.'

'Yet you're doing the flamenco.'

'So I am...' Her heart was hammering because she could not quite believe that he was here. 'These cachaças are very strong.' She was trying to act normally, or rather how she would have acted a year ago at a family event when Gian De Luca suddenly showed up. 'I thought you had to be at the La Fiordelise Florence, opening—'

'I left early and gave myself the rest of the night off...'

'Why are they all called La Fiordelise?' she snapped. It had always annoyed her and she let him know tonight. 'It's hardly original.'

'Your father said the same.'

'Well, you should have listened to him. La Fiordelise, London. La Fiordelise, Azerbaijan...' *Gosh those cachaças must be strong*, she thought, because she allowed a little of her resentment to seep out. 'Perhaps you could send me there...'

He just smiled.

But it was a smile she had never seen before. Not his on-duty smile, or his off-duty one; it was just a smile that let her be, that simply accepted her as she was and, she felt, suddenly adored.

'Hey, Ariana...' Pedro was waving her to join in another odd-looking dance.

'Your boyfriend is calling you to dance with him again,' Gian said, and with those words let her know he'd been watching her for a while. 'You're very popular tonight.'

'Yes, I am,' Ariana said, and she'd never been happier to be caught dancing and smiling and laughing, even if she was bleeding inside. 'I am in demand!'

'Have you time to dance with me?'

No.

She had to practise saying no to him, had to have that tiny word fall readily from her tongue.

For. The. Rest. Of. Her. Life.

Except that tiny word felt far too big when she looked into those beautiful slate-grey eyes. She would start tomorrow, Ariana decided, and allow herself just one tiny dance tonight. 'One dance,' Ariana said, and found herself back in his arms. 'For the sake of duty.'

Yet this was no duty dance, for his arms were no longer wooden and his hands ran down her ribs and came to rest on her hips and there was slight pressure there to pull her against him. He moved like silk and this time it was Ariana who was the one holding back.

'Dance with me,' he moaned.

'I am.'

'Like we did.'

'No,' she said. 'My mother is looking.'

'Let her look.'

'You know what she can be like.'

'Tell her that your sex life is none of her business.'

'I have.' Ariana laughed. 'But we no longer have a sex life, so there's nothing to tell.'

She felt the heat of his palm low on her hips and heat somewhere else as he pulled her hard up against him. His voice was low in her ear and made her shiver. 'You're sure about that?'

This wasn't fair, Ariana thought as they danced cheek to cheek with their bodies meshed together. He wasn't being fair after all that had passed between them.

'They will guess…' Ariana started.

'Stop worrying about them,' Gian said, and for a little while she did. Her family all danced with their various partners and she danced with a man who was always there for her. There was something so freeing about Gian's acceptance of her, and the way he lived life on his terms. It was something she was starting to embrace herself and so she wrapped her arms around his neck and told him a little of her new world. 'I've told my lazy doorman that he's not allowed to let guests up without my permission, not even my mother, and I shall petition the other residents to have him removed if he doesn't improve.'

'Good for you.'

'And I have an interview next week with your rival company. I used my mother's maiden name, so I know I got the interview on my own merit.'

'Very good,' Gian said.

'And I will never give up on love.'

'I'm pleased to hear it.' He was serious suddenly. 'Can we go outside?'

'It will cause too much gossip and rumour…'

'I don't care.'

'Well, I do,' Ariana said. 'I'm not leaving Stefano's wedding to make out with you.'

'That is a revolting term,' Gian told her, 'but fair enough.' For though he was desperate to speak with her, she was right not to leave during her brother's wedding reception. 'Will you come over to La Fiordelise afterwards?' Gian asked.

'No…' she said slowly. Her reply was tentative, but with practice she would perfect it, Ariana decided. 'No.' She said it more clearly this time.

No. No. No.

Easy as pie.

'Come to me tonight.'

They were still cheek to cheek, though the music had ended, yet they carried on dancing. She could feel herself weakening at his touch. 'No,' she told him as he reached into his inner pocket and slipped a cold thin card where the ruffle of her dress parted. It was all discreetly done, yet Ariana knew she should have slapped him there and then, but lust moved faster than anger where Gian De Luca was concerned. It took a moment for her to form the proper reply. 'Leave me alone, Gian.'

'I can't.'

'Ariana!' Her *mamma* was laughing and calling her over. 'Gian!' In fact, she was calling them both, for the music had restarted and upped its tempo and the bride and groom were about to be waved off into the night.

It was loud, it was fun, and it was over.

Stefano and Eloa were officially married and it was kisses and final drinks and then they all spilled out of the venue into the square. She was so happy for Stefano and Eloa, especially now the air had been cleared between her and her twin.

And happy for Mia and Dante too, Ariana thought as she watched them walk hand in hand into the night.

If it was possible to be lonely and happy at the same time, then she was lonely and happy for herself too, for Gian had already gone.

She wanted not just to be part of a couple, but she wanted to be part of that couple with Gian.

Walking hand in hand in public, kissing without secrets, in love for all to see.

The square had never looked more beautiful. There was a carousel all lit up and the stunning fountains were gushing and spouting. It was a special place indeed, where they had eaten hot chestnuts on the night she'd said farewell to her father, and where she now stood so confused and so wanting to go into La Fiordelise if it meant another night with the man she loved.

She would always want him.

That was a given.

If, somehow, forty years from now, they were here at Stefano and Eloa's ruby wedding celebration, there would still be a longing and an ache for what could have been. If learning the truth about her family had taught her anything, it was that regrets were such a waste of a life. She didn't want to have any regrets when it came to Gian.

She would start saying no on Monday.

Not caring if she was found out, Ariana slipped away and found herself in the reception area of La Fiordelise, heading straight for his bed and the bliss he would temporarily give.

Life was better with Gian in it than not.

Yes, she was turning into Fiordelise, Ariana decided as she took the elevator up.

He opened the door and, before she fell into his arms, she stated her case. 'There will be rules,' Ariana said.

If she was to be his mistress then there would be rules and *she* would be the one making them.

'We shall discuss them,' Gian agreed.

'If you cheat on me, you die.'

He laughed. 'I'm saving you from prison then. I never cheat.'

'Liar.'

'Never. Even at your interview when I wanted to kiss you but Svetlana—'

'Stop!' She halted him. 'Don't ever try to redeem yourself with another woman's name.' She was way too needy to ignore it though. 'You wanted to kiss me then?'

'All over,' he told her. 'Come, there's something I want to show you...'

Down his hallway they went and she smiled when she saw there were pictures of Gian. 'When did you do this?' she asked.

'Tonight. The maintenance man has been busy.'

'Oh, Gian.' Her eyes were shining and happy to see his childhood finally featured on the wall, but then her smile died. 'What the hell is this doing here?' It was the most appalling, awkward photo of her at her first Romano Ball. She had been tempted to tear it up, but had decided it wasn't just her memory to delete.

'No!' She was appalled. 'That photo was for your eyes only, I look terrible!'

'You do and, believe me, your mother had nothing to worry about then... It was here that things started to change for me...'

Her breath stopped, as there she was, in a silver dress, standing next to Gian, in an informal shot of a night that had been more difficult than the picture revealed.

It was the first Romano Ball without her *papà*. He had been a last-minute withdrawal due to a deterioration in his health. On the one hand, she had been relieved that she wouldn't have to see him with Mia.

On the other hand, it had meant her *papà* was getting worse.

Gian had steered her through it, though. He always did.

He had held her in those wooden arms and told her that she was doing well, and it had meant the world.

'I think,' Gian said, 'well, I know, that for me things changed that night...' She swallowed as he went on. 'You were right. I easily remembered what you were wearing, for my eyes barely left you that night, and I think things changed for you too, Ariana. You didn't come by my office so much after that...'

'No...' She flushed as she admitted to herself something that for so long she had denied. 'I have liked you for a lot longer than you realise, than even I dared admit.'

'Come,' he said, 'I have something for you.'

Of course that something was in the direction of the bedroom, and as they walked there, she said, 'I'll make a terrible mistress, Gian. I talk too much, I'm not very discreet...' But then her voice trailed off for there on the bed lay everything she had once thought she wanted: a blush tartan suit, a silk cowl-necked cami, a string of pearls and even a little wallet for her business cards.

'Gian...' She wanted to weep, for he made her so weak.

This time when he unzipped the back of her dress, his fingers lingered and she closed her eyes as he peeled it off and slowly kissed her shoulder.

'Turn around,' he said in that voice that made her shiver. She was a little bewildered and a lot in lust as she complied.

He undressed and then dressed her.

She lifted her arms as he slid on the silk cami, and she lifted her feet as he negotiated the little kilt. The only resistance was in her jaw as he put on the jacket, for it was everything she had wanted, and yet Ariana knew she deserved more.

He dressed her neck in a string of pearls and she closed her eyes as he secured the clasp, then turned her around and knelt as he dressed her feet in the gorgeous neutral stilettoes that his guest managers wore. 'We can't work together, Gian.'

'We can.'

'No, because I'm not going to spend my career worrying about when my time will be up...'

'It will never be up.'

But Ariana had too much to say to stop and listen. 'I don't want to be hidden away, and I don't want hide my love.'

'You won't be hidden away,' Gian said. 'And you don't have to hide a single thing.'

'It would be unprofessional,' Ariana insisted, 'to be sleeping with a member of your staff.'

'I think it would be perfectly reasonable for the owner to love his wife, who just happens to be a guest services manager.'

She swallowed and then corrected him. 'VIP Guest Services Manager.'

'Absolutely.' He smiled. 'Ariana, Duchess of Luctano, VIP Guest Services Manager...'

'Stop.'

'Well, we might leave off the title on your business card...' He looked at her frowning face. 'I'm asking you to marry me.'

'Please, stop,' Ariana said, for she did not want him playing games with her heart.

'No,' Gian said, and from the bedside drawer he took out a box she recognised. 'I don't want to stop, and I don't want my lineage to end. I want ours to be a different legacy...'

She looked at the most beautiful ring, in shades of pomegranate, and it was so unexpected, but not as unexpected as what he said next. 'When you walked into my office yesterday, I thought it was to tell me you were pregnant...'

'Gosh, no.'

'I think I wanted you to be.'

Her world went still as that black heart cracked open and revealed all the shining hope for their future inside.

'I don't want to be like that old fool who left it too late,' Gian said. 'I want the woman I love by my side. I love you,' Gian clarified, and she felt the blood pump in every chamber of her heart as it filled with his words. 'You are the most important person in my day.'

It was the one thing Ariana had wanted her whole life—to be the centre of someone's world, to be wanted, to be cherished, for exactly who she was.

'Ariana,' Gian said, 'you are the love of my life. Will you be my wife?'

Her answer was a sequence of squeaks, a 'Yes,' followed by 'Please,' as an ancient ring slid onto a slender finger, and because it was Ariana, she took a generous moment to properly admire it. 'I love it,' she said, and he watched massive pupils crowd the violet in her eyes. He adored her absolute passion for his ring. 'You would never have sold it...' She scolded the very thought.

'No,' he said, 'it belongs with me, as do you.' He was silenced by her kiss, a kiss that held nothing back but showered him in frantic love. Another 'I do, I do,' she said, and then followed that with another needy, necessary question. 'When?' she asked. 'When can we marry?'

'Soon,' Gian said, and got back to kissing her, but Ariana had something else on her mind.

'And can we have...?'

'You can have the Basilica, if you want it,' Gian said.

'No,' Ariana said, 'can we have tutti-frutti and salted chestnut ice cream for dessert...?'

He laughed. 'Trust you to have chosen the dessert by the end of the proposal.' And then he kissed her to oblivion, and behind closed doors he took his newly appointed guest services manager and made love to her as the Very Important Person she was.

To him.

For life.

EPILOGUE

'YOU HAVE ANOTHER phone call.' Gian gently shook a sleeping Ariana's shoulder. 'Stefano,' Gian added, watching her eyes force themselves open, knowing she could never not take a call from her twin.

And certainly not on an important day such as this.

'Stai bene?' Stefano urgently asked if she was okay.

'Of course.' Ariana smiled sleepily as she sat herself up in bed. 'We are doing wonderfully.'

'Have you decided on a name for her?' Stefano asked.

'We are waiting until you arrive to announce the name,' Ariana said. 'I want us all to be together when we do.'

Eloa and Stefano and little George were in Brazil and soon to board a flight to Florence. Dante, Mia and the twins would fly in with their mother and Thomas tomorrow, and all would meet the newest member of the family. But, tired from an exhausting day, Ariana was grateful that for now it was just the three of them.

'How is Stefano?' Gian asked when she ended the call.

'Excited to meet her,' Ariana said, gazing over to the little crib that held their sleeping daughter.

She was so beautiful, with dark hair and a little red face, and tiny hands with long delicate fingers.

They were both aching for her to wake up just to look into those gorgeous blue eyes again and hear her tiny cry.

'I wish Papà had got to see her,' Ariana said. Her father was the only part of her heart that was missing. 'I wish he had known about us.' She would get used to it, of course, but she couldn't help but think how happy he would be today. 'I am glad we had her in Florence,' Ariana said. 'I feel closer to him here.'

'I know you do.'

La Fiordelise Rome was no longer where Gian resided. For the first time he had a home—a real one—a luxurious villa just a little way out of Florence, with a gorgeous view of the river.

This morning, as labour had started, Ariana had stood on the terrace, taking in the morning, the pink sky, and the lights starting to go off in the city they both loved and thinking what a beautiful day this was for their baby to be born.

And now she was here and it was right to have a little cry and to miss her *papà*.

'I have something for you,' Gian said, and he went into his pocket and pulled out a long, slim box. But instead of handing it to her, he opened it and took the slender chain out and held up the pendant for her to see.

She smiled as he brought it closer, but she didn't immediately recognise what it was.

'Gian?' she questioned as she examined the swirl of rose gold and saw that instead of an F for Fiordelise, there was an A, sparkling in diamonds. 'It's beautiful, but...'

'Take a look,' Gian said, and he pulled back the heavy drapes that blocked out the world and the city skyline. Her eyes were instantly drawn to the sight of La Fiordelise Florence, for it was lit up in the softest pink.

And there was something else different.

The elegant signage had been changed. Oh, there was still the familiar rose gold swirl, but like her pendant the letter in the centre was now an A.

'The hotel has had a name change,' Gian said. 'It is now Duchessa Ariana.'

'But...' She was overwhelmed, stunned actually, that this private man would share their love with the world.

'I've been planning it for months,' Gian said. 'Even the letterhead has all changed. The last time I saw your father, like you, he told me I could do better with the hotel names and, like me, he thought your name should be in lights. I think he knew the way the wind was blowing, perhaps even before we did.'

She liked that thought so very much, and then, better than any insignia, came the sweetest sight of all: their daughter stretching her little arms out of the swaddle of linen. They both smiled at the little squeaking noise she made.

Gian clearly wasn't going to wait for her to cry.

'Hey, Violetta,' he said, and gently lifted her from the crib.

They had named her after her great-great-grandmother, the forgotten Duchess, somehow lost in all the tales of Fiordelise.

Well, she was forgotten no more.

Violetta's restored picture was mounted on the gallery wall of their home in Rome, and soon it would be joined by her namesake's first photo.

Ariana buried her face in her daughter's and breathed in that sweet baby scent, and then lifted her head and gazed down at her.

'I cannot believe how much I know her already,' Ariana said, playing with her tiny fingers, 'and at the very same time I cannot wait to get to know her more...'

That was, Gian thought as he looked at his wife, a rather perfect description of his love.

* * * * *

Italian's Scandalous Marriage Plan

Louise Fuller

Louise Fuller was a tomboy who hated pink and always wanted to be the prince—not the princess! Now she enjoys creating heroines who aren't pretty pushovers but are strong, believable women. Before writing for Harlequin, she studied literature and philosophy at university, then worked as a reporter on her local newspaper. She lives in Royal Tunbridge Wells with her impossibly handsome husband, Patrick, and their six children.

Books by Louise Fuller

Harlequin Modern

Craving His Forbidden Innocent
The Rules of His Baby Bargain
The Man She Should Have Married

Secret Heirs of Billionaires

Kidnapped for the Tycoon's Baby
Demanding His Secret Son
Proof of Their One-Night Passion

Passion in Paradise

Consequences of a Hot Havana Night

The Sicilian Marriage Pact

The Terms of the Sicilian's Marriage

Visit the Author Profile page
at millsandboon.com.au for more titles.

To my mum X

CHAPTER ONE

STANDING ON TIPTOE, Juliet reached up and shoved her small suitcase into the overhead locker.

It was difficult, though, what with all the other passengers pushing past on their way up the plane. Frowning, she shoved again. But it was catching on something—

'Here. Let me.'

The voice had a definite Italian accent, and it was male—very definitely male. As strong hands made space for her bag she was suddenly aware of the pounding in her heart and the onset of panic.

'There.'

Turning, Juliet felt her panic die and her cheeks grow warm as she gazed up into a pair of eyes the colour of freshly brewed arabica coffee.

'Thank you,' she said quietly.

The man inclined his head and then smiled. 'It was my pleasure. Enjoy the flight. Oh, and let me know if you need a hand getting it down. I'm just back here.' He gestured to several rows behind her seat.

'That's very kind of you.'

Heart still pounding, she slid into her seat. Her skin was tingling. Stupid, *stupid*, *stupid*, she thought, glancing out of the window at the dull grey runway. Not for thinking it was Ralph but for wishing it was—for letting her romantic dreams of love momentarily overrule cold, hard facts.

Her husband was cheating on her and, aside from the legal paperwork, her marriage was over.

Only, unlike her famous namesake and her Romeo, they hadn't been torn apart by warring families. They had been the ones to destroy their own marriage.

But then they should never have been together in the first place...

Her hands were suddenly shaking and, needing to still them, she leaned forward and pulled out the safety instructions card from the pocket in front of her. She stared down at the cartoonish pictures of a young woman jumping enthusiastically down an inflatable slide.

That was exactly what she had done.

Leapt into an unknown, trusted in fate, stupidly hoping that, despite all the odds stacked against her, everything would be all right. That this time the promises would be kept.

Some hope.

Blood flushed her cheeks for the second time in as many minutes as she thought back over her six-month marriage to Ralph Castellucci.

They had met in Rome, the city of romance, but she hadn't been looking for love. She'd been looking for a cat.

Walking back from the Colosseum, she'd heard it yowling. Just as she'd realised it was stuck down a storm drain it had started to rain—one of those sudden, drenching January downpours that soaked everything in seconds.

Everyone had run for cover.

Except Ralph.

He alone had stopped to help her.

And got scratched for his efforts.

In the time it had taken to walk with him to the hospital and get him a tetanus jab she had found out that his mother was English and his father Italian—Veronese, in fact.

She had also become *innamorata cotta*—love-struck. And it had been like a physical blow.

Wandering the streets of Rome, she'd felt dazed, dizzy, drunk with love and a desire that had made her forget who and what she was.

All it had taken was those few hours for Ralph to become everything to her. Her breath and her heartbeat. She had craved him like a drug. His smile, his laughter, his touch...

They had spent the next three weeks joined at the hip—and at plenty of other places too.

And then Ralph had proposed.

It had been at the hospital that she had first noticed the ring on his little finger, with its embossed crest of a curling *C* and a castle, but it had only been later that she'd discovered what it meant, who his family were—who he was.

The Castelluccis were descended from the Princes of Verona, and from birth Ralph had lived in a world of instant gratification where his every wish was immediately granted, every desire fulfilled.

Her skin tingled.

And he had desired her.

Whatever else had proved false since, that was undeniable.

Right from that very first moment in Rome the heat between them had been more scorching than Italian summer sunshine.

What she hadn't known then was that wanting her wouldn't stop him from wanting others—that for Ralph Castellucci sexual nirvana wasn't exclusive to the marital bed.

It was just what rich, powerful men had been doing throughout history, all over the world. Taking one woman as their wife, and then another—maybe even a couple more—as their mistress.

Only, idiot that she was, she had been naive and smug and

complacent enough to believe that the heat and intensity of their passion would somehow protect her. That they were special.

Remembering the agonising moment when she'd spotted her husband climbing into a car with a beautiful dark-haired woman, she tightened her fingers around the armrest.

It wasn't as if she hadn't been warned.

It was what they did—his set.

She'd heard the gossip at glossy parties, and then there were the portraits dotted around his *palazzo*…pictures of his ancestors' many mistresses.

As an outsider, with no money or connections, she had got the barely concealed message that she was lucky even to be invited through the front door. She certainly didn't get to change the rules.

Rules that had been made perfectly clear to her.

For the Castelluccis, as long as it was kept away from the media and out of the divorce courts, adultery was acceptable and even necessary for a marriage.

Not for her, it wasn't.

Her stomach twisted.

Maybe if Ralph had been willing to have a conversation she might have given him a second chance. But he'd simply refused to discuss it. Worse, after she'd confronted him, he'd still expected her to get dressed up and join him at some charity auction that same evening.

And when she'd refused, he'd gone anyway.

Her body tensed as she remembered the expression on her husband's face as he'd told her not to wait up.

Now there was only one conversation left to have. The one in which she said goodbye.

But first there was the christening to get through.

A shiver ran down her spine.

When Lucia and Luca had asked her to be Raffaelle's godmother she had been so pleased and proud. Unfortunately for her, Ralph was Luca's best friend, so of course they had asked him to be godfather. He would be there in the church and then at the party afterwards, so she was going to have to see him.

There was no way around that, and she had accepted it. But as for the ball...

She breathed out shakily.

The Castellucci Ball might be the highlight of the Veronese social calendar, but a herd of wild horses couldn't drag her there.

She would act the good Castellucci wife for the sake of her friends at the christening, but her cheating husband could go whistle.

Her mouth twisted.

Ralph would never forgive her for not going.

Good. That would make them equal.

The thought should have soothed her, but even now—five devastating weeks after she had fled from the glittering palace in Verona—it hurt to admit that her marriage was over. And with it her dreams of having her own baby.

An air steward had begun running through the pre-flight safety demonstration, and as she fastened her seat belt she curled her fingers into her palms.

More than anything she had wanted a baby. Ralph had too. She'd been planning to come off the pill. Only fate had intervened...

Her father-in-law, Carlo, had been rushed to hospital, and somehow she had simply kept on taking it out of habit.

She hadn't told Ralph—not keeping it from him intentionally...it just hadn't come up. How could it when they never had a conversation?

And later she had been scared to stop taking it.

With Ralph absent so often, and without a job of her own or any real purpose to her days, it had been the one area of her life where she'd still had some control.

And then she had seen him with his mistress, and suddenly it had been too late.

She had been tempted to do what her mother had done. Get

pregnant and live with the consequences. But she was one of those consequences and she'd had to live with the aftermath of her mother's unilateral decision. And unhappily married couples, however wealthy, didn't make happy parents...

The flight arrived in Verona on time. It was a beautiful day and, despite her anxiety, Juliet felt her spirits lift. A baby's christening was such a special occasion, and she was determined to enjoy every moment.

She held out her passport to the bored-looking man behind the glass at Immigration.

It would be awkward seeing Ralph, but she was willing to play the wife one last time, for Lucia and Luca's sake.

'Grazie.'

As she headed towards the exit she slipped her passport back into her bag and pulled out a baseball cap and a pair of sunglasses. Cramming her hair under the hat, she slid on the glasses.

She would behave.

And Ralph would do the same.

Her husband might be a philandering liar, but first and foremost he was a Castellucci. And more than anything else his family hated scandal.

There was no way he would make a scene.

'Scusi, Signora Castellucci?'

Her brown eyes widened in confusion as two uniformed officials, both female, neither smiling, stepped in front of her, blocking her path.

Plucking off her sunglasses, she glanced at their badges. Not police...airport security, maybe?

'Yes. I'm Signora Castellucci,' she said quickly.

The younger woman stepped forward. 'Would you mind coming with us, please?'

Her heart started to race. It had been phrased as a question, but she didn't get the feeling that refusing was an option. 'Is there a problem?'

There wasn't.

There couldn't be, because she had done nothing wrong.

But, like most people confronted by someone in uniform, she felt instantly guilty—as though she had knowingly broken hundreds of laws.

'Do you need to see my ticket? I have it on my phone—'

Her cheeks felt as though they were burning. After weeks of speaking nothing but English she knew her Italian was hesitant, and it made her sound nervous...guilty.

The second woman stepped forward. 'If you could just come this way, please, Signora Castellucci.'

Juliet hesitated. Should she demand an explanation first? Only that might slow things down, and really what she wanted to do was get to her hotel and have a shower.

Her shoulders tensed as the first woman turned away and began speaking into a walkie-talkie.

Even though she looked nothing like a Castellucci wife, there was just a chance that somebody would recognise her, and the last thing she wanted right now was to draw attention to herself.

Perhaps she should call Lucia first and ask her to...

What? Hold her hand?

Lucia was a good friend, and during the first few months of her marriage, when everything had been so strange and scary, she had been a lifeline—at times literally holding her hand.

But she was a big girl now, and Lucia had an actual baby to look after these days.

Besides, she knew her friend. If she called her now, Lucia would insist on coming to the airport. And what would be the point of that? Clearly this couldn't be anything but a mix-up.

'Follow me, please,' the second woman said.

Stomach flip-flopping nervously, Juliet nodded.

They left the arrivals hall and began walking down a series of windowless corridors. People passing glanced at them curiously, and some of her panic returned, but surely it was too gloomy for anyone to recognise her.

'This way, please.'

She walked through a pair of sliding doors, blinking at the sudden rush of daylight.

And then she saw the car.

It was sleek and dark, both anonymous and yet unnervingly familiar—as was Marco, the uniformed chauffeur in the driver's seat.

But it wasn't the car or the driver that made her heart lurch.

It was the tall, dark-haired man standing in the sunlight. Even at a distance, the cut and cloth of his dark suit marked him out. He had his back to her, and she stared at the breadth of his shoulders, her nerves jangling.

No. Not him. Not here. She wasn't ready.

There was no need for her to see his face. She would know him in the darkness, would find him in a crowd with her eyes blindfolded. It was as if she had some invisible sixth sense that reacted to his presence like a swallow following the earth's magnetic fields.

Ralph.

But it made no sense for him to be here.

She had told no one which flight she was catching. Even with Lucia she had kept her travel plans deliberately vague.

Yet here he was. Her husband. Or rather her soon-to-be ex-husband.

She stared at him in silence. Not so long ago she would have run into his arms. Now, though, a voice in her head was urging her to turn and run as fast and as far away from him as she could. But every muscle in her body had turned to stone and instead she watched mutely as the younger official stepped forward.

'*Vostro moglie, Signor Castellucci.*'

Your wife, Mr Castellucci.

Her breath hitched in her throat and then her hands started to tremble with shock and disbelief.

She was being delivered.

Like a parcel. Or some mislaid luggage.

Her fingers twitched against the handle of her bag as Ralph slowly turned around.

'Grazie.'

His eyes flickered across the Tarmac and he inclined his head, just as if he was dismissing a maid from the tennis-court-sized drawing room of his fifteenth-century *palazzo*.

As she stared at him in silence, she was dimly aware of the two officials retreating. It was five weeks since she had last seen her husband, and in that time she had transformed him into some kind of pantomime villain. Now, though, she was blindsided by the shock of his beauty.

Eyes the colour of raw honeycomb, high cheekbones and the wide curve of his mouth competed in the sunlight for her attention. But it wasn't just about the symmetry and precision of his features. Plenty of actors and models had that. There was something else—something beneath the flawless golden skin that made everyone around him sit up and take notice.

He had a specific kind of self-assurance—an innate, indisputable authority that had been handed down invisibly over hundreds of years through generations of Castelluccis. It came from an assumption that the world had been set up to meet *his* needs. That *his* happiness took precedence over other people's.

Her shoulders tensed. *Even his wife's.*

He was moving towards her and her eyes followed his progress as though pulled by an invisible force of nature. She felt her heartbeat jolt.

She hadn't forgotten the smooth lupine grace with which he moved, but she had underestimated the effect it had on her.

Only why?

Why was she still so vulnerable to him?

Why, after everything he'd done, did this fierce sexual attraction persist?

He stopped in front of her and she felt her breath catch as he tipped her chin up and plucked the cap from her head.

'Surprised to see me?' he said softly.

Mutely, she watched as he lifted his hand in the imperious manner of a Roman emperor, and then the chauffeur was opening the door for her. More out of habit than any conscious intention to obey, she got in.

The door closed and she waited as Ralph crossed behind the car. Then the other door opened, and he slid in beside her.

Moments later, the car began to glide forward.

She felt her stomach muscles clench as he shifted into a more comfortable position.

'Good trip?' he said softly.

His words flicked the tripwire of her nervous anger. He made it sound as though she'd been on holiday, when they both knew she'd run away.

The note she'd left for him when she'd fled Verona five weeks earlier might have been brief and vague.

I need some space...

But the voicemail she'd left him a week ago had been less ambiguous. She'd told him she would be returning to England after the christening and that she wanted a divorce.

Afterwards she had cried herself to sleep, and during the days that followed she'd been awash with misery, panicking about his possible reaction.

But she needn't have bothered.

Ralph clearly didn't believe she was serious.

To him, all this—her leaving, asking for a divorce—was just a storm in an espresso cup that required only a little of the famous Castellucci diplomacy. And so he'd turned up at the airport to meet her, assuming she would back down as every other Castellucci wife in history had done.

Fine, she thought savagely. If that was the way he wanted to play it, so be it. Let him realise she was serious when he got the letter from her solicitor.

Tamping down her anger, she forced herself to meet his gaze. 'Yes, thank you.' She kept her voice cool. 'But you really didn't need to do this. I'm perfectly capable of taking care of myself.'

'Clearly not.'

Her eyes narrowed. 'What's that supposed to mean?'

'It means that, despite knowing the risks, *bella*, you didn't follow the rules.' His gaze was direct and unwavering. 'If I hadn't intervened you would have walked out of the airport unprotected and—'

'And caught a taxi.' She glared at him. 'Like a normal person.'

Something flared in his golden-brown eyes. 'But you're not a normal person. You're a Castellucci and that makes you a target. And being a target means you need protection.'

Her heartbeat accelerated as a flicker of heat coursed over her skin like an electric current. She did need protection, but the man sitting beside her was a far bigger threat to her health and happiness than some random faceless stranger.

He stretched out his legs and the effort it took her not to inch away from him fuelled her resentment. 'If you've finished lecturing me—'

'I haven't,' he said calmly. 'By not following the rules you're not just a target, you're also a liability. You make it harder for the people responsible for your safety to do their job.'

Heat scalded her cheeks and she felt a wave of anger ripple over her skin.

But he was right.

It had been one of the first conversations they'd had when he'd finally told her about his family—how being a Castellucci was a privilege that came with enormous benefits, but that there were some downsides to being an ultra-high net worth individual.

She could still remember him listing them on his fingers. Stalkers, robbery, kidnapping, extortion...

Cheeks cooling, she edged back in her seat. Except the risk today was minimal, given that he'd clearly had her followed the entire time she was in England.

How else would he have known that she was catching this flight?

Her heart bumped behind her ribs.

Besides, if he wanted to talk about rule-breaking, she could name a few he'd broken. Like the vows he'd made at their wedding when he'd promised to be true to her.

'People in glass houses don't get to throw stones, Ralph,' she said crisply.

He held her gaze. 'But I don't live in a glass house or any other kind of house, *bella*. I live in a palace. As do you.'

For a few half-seconds she thought about the beautiful home they had shared for six months. The timeless elegance of the vaulted rooms with their frescoes and sumptuous furnishings, the creeper-clad balconies overlooking the formal gardens and the rest of the *palazzo*'s estate.

And then she blanked her mind.

Did he really think that was all he had to do to get their marriage back on track? Remind her of what she would lose? Didn't he understand that she'd already lost the only thing that mattered to her? His heart.

Battening down her misery, she reached up and slowly twisted her hair into a loose ponytail at the nape of her neck. 'Why are you here, Ralph?' she said quietly.

Honey-coloured eyes locked with hers as his mouth curved at one corner. 'I take care of what belongs to me.'

She looked at him incredulously. How could he say that after what he'd done? He had broken her heart.

But in the grand scheme of things the compensations of being a Castellucci more than made up for a little heartbreak and a bruised ego.

Or that was what everyone kept telling her.

Only none of those things—his wealth, his connections and social status—were what mattered to her. They never would. That was why she had left and why she would be leaving again.

And this time she wouldn't be coming back.

'You have people here. They could have done it for you,' she persisted.

He shrugged. 'I wanted to meet my wife at the airport.' He held her gaze. 'You are still my wife, Giulietta,' he said softly.

Her chin jerked upwards, his words jolting her.

Everyone else called her Letty. He alone called her by her full name, but in the Italian form, and the achingly familiar soft intonation felt like a caress.

The narrowed gaze that accompanied it, on the other hand, felt like sandpaper scraping across her skin.

Her eyes found his. The anger and the bruised ego were there—she could see it simmering beneath the surface.

But that was the problem. He would never show it. He was always so in control.

Glancing across the seat, she felt her pulse skip and her breasts tighten as her body, her blood, responded to the memories stirring beneath her skin.

He was not always in control. Not when they made love.

Then he was like a different man. Every breath, every touch, unrestrained, urgent, unfeigned.

Her breathing slowed as images of his naked body moving against hers crowded into her head. She felt her skin grow warm.

Back in England she had felt so certain, so sure that it was all wrong between them, but being alone with him now was making her second-guess herself.

Only there was nothing to second-guess.

She had seen it with her own eyes.

He was having an affair.

Heart thumping against her ribs, she stared at him mutely, the knot of anger hardening in her stomach. He had deceived and betrayed her, lied to her face. And, judging by the fact that he'd not even attempted to get in touch with her over the last five weeks, he'd clearly been having far too much fun with his dark-haired lover to care about her absence.

The thought of the two of them together made her feel sick, and suddenly she was done with playing games. What was the point of delaying the inevitable? Why not confront him now?

Lifting her chin, she met his gaze head-on. 'Not for much longer.'

There was a long silence.

Glancing up, she saw the glitter in his eyes and it made a shiver run down her spine.

He raised an eyebrow. 'You think?'

A tiny part of her wished she already had the paperwork from her solicitor, so she could throw it into his handsome, arrogant face. The rest of her was too busy trying to ignore the effect his casual question was having on her nerve-ends.

'Did you not get my message?' she asked.

'Ah, yes, your message…'

Slouching backwards, he nodded slowly, as though he was a record producer and she had sent him a particularly uninspiring demo.

'It was all so sudden. I assumed you were being…' He paused, frowning and clicking his fingers for inspiration. 'What's the word? Oh, yes, dramatic. London's theatreland rubbing off on you.'

She held his gaze. 'I want a divorce.'

If she was looking for a reaction she didn't get one.

He merely inclined his head. 'That's not going to happen, *bella*.'

His voice was soft, but there was an unequivocal finality to his words.

'It's not up to you, Ralph.' She was battling with her anger.

He stared at her steadily. 'Now you really *are* being dramatic.'

She wanted to hit him. 'I want a divorce, Ralph. I don't want anything else.'

It wasn't just words. She really didn't want anything from him. It was going to be hard enough getting over her marriage as it was. It would be so much harder if there were reminders of him everywhere.

'I'm not looking for any drama or some cash prize. I just want a divorce.'

His expression hardened, his eyes trapping hers. 'And what are you expecting me to say to that, Giulietta?'

'I'm expecting you to say yes.' Her fingers curled into her palms. 'Look, we both know this isn't working. *We* don't work as a couple.'

Probably because they weren't a couple any more, she thought dully. Now there were three of them in the marriage.

'And that's what you do, is it? When something doesn't work.' His eyes locked with hers. 'You just discard it.'

She stared at him incredulously, feeling an ache spread through her chest like spilt ink. How could he say that after what he'd done? After what he'd thrown away.

Her eyes blazed. 'Our marriage hasn't meant anything to you for months.'

'And yet you're the one who's walking out,' he said slowly.

She took a breath, trying to control her escalating temper. 'Because you are having an affair!'

Even just saying the words out loud hurt, but his gaze didn't so much as waver.

'So you said. And I denied it.'

Her head was pounding in time with her heart. 'Look, I've made up my mind, so you can stop lying to me now—'

His eyes narrowed almost imperceptibly. 'I didn't lie. I told you I wasn't having an affair. That was true then, and it's still true now. Only you chose, and are still choosing, not to believe me.'

She stared at him, the memory of that terrible argument replaying inside her head. Although usually an argument required the participation of more than one person...

Remembering her angry accusations and his one-word denials, she felt a beat of anger bounce across her skin. 'There was no choice to make, Ralph. I believe what I believe because I saw it with my own eyes.' She drew a deep breath. 'Now, are we done?'

'Not even close.' His jaw tightened. 'You didn't see what you thought you did.'

'Of course I didn't.' She hated the bitterness in her voice, but it was beyond her control. 'So explain it to me, then. What exactly did I see?'

He was silent for so long she thought he wasn't going to answer.

Finally, though, he shrugged. 'She doesn't threaten you—us.'

His reply made her breathing jerk. 'Oh, I get it. You mean it's not serious?' She shook her head, her chest aching with anger and misery. 'And that's supposed to make it all right, is it? I should just put up and shut up.'

'You're twisting my words.'

Her head was hurting now. She was so stupid. For just a moment she'd thought that finally she'd got through to him. But it was all just the same old, same old.

'You know what, Ralph? I'm not doing this with you. Not here, not now.' Leaning forward, she tapped on the glass behind Marco. 'Can you drop me at this address, please?' Glancing down at her phone, she read out a street name. 'It's near the hospital.'

'What do you think you're doing?' His voice had become dangerously soft.

Forcing herself to hold his gaze, she took a deep breath. 'I'm going to my hotel.'

He raised an eyebrow. 'Hotel?'

'Yes, Ralph. It's a place where people stay overnight when

they go away.' Watching his eyes narrow, she gave him a small smile. 'I think it's for the best if we keep our distance from one another.'

He stared at her for a long moment. 'You mean you're worried you won't be able to resist me.'

Her skin prickled. 'No, I just don't want you turning up at the christening with a black eye,' she said stiffly. 'But you don't need to worry. I'll play my part at the ceremony, and the party, and I made the hotel reservation in my maiden name.'

Something primitive darkened his expression. 'Show me,' he demanded.

Feeling all fingers and thumbs, she tilted the screen towards him.

'I don't know this hotel.'

Of course he didn't. For Ralph, like all his family and friends, there was only one hotel in Verona. The five-star Due Torri.

She shrugged. 'It's only for one night. I just want somewhere clean and quiet.'

'I'm sure it's both, but…'

He paused and she felt a shiver of apprehension. There was something wrong—a disconnect between his reasonable tone and the glitter in his eyes.

'But what?'

'But if it isn't it won't matter.'

As his gaze drifted lazily over her face a chill began to spread through her bones.

'Because you won't be staying there.'

Her eyes clashed with his. 'Oh, but I will. And there's nothing you can do about it,' she added hotly as he started to shake his head.

He met her gaze with equanimity. 'It's already done. I've had someone cancel your reservation. It's time to come home, *bella*.'

CHAPTER TWO

WATCHING HIS WIFE'S brown eyes widen with shock, Ralph felt a savage stab of satisfaction. *Good*, he thought coolly. Now she knew what it felt like.

Although there was obviously no comparison between her shock and his...

Gritting his teeth, he replayed the moment when he'd walked into their bedroom and seen the envelope on his bedside table. Even now he could still feel his anger, his disbelief, at returning home and finding his bed empty and his wife gone.

Although, in the scheme of things, that was one of her lesser crimes.

He glanced over at his beautiful, deceitful wife. An oversized linen blazer disguised the curves beneath her dark jeans and white T-shirt, and she was make-up-free aside from the matt nude lipstick she loved.

She looked more like a gap year student than the wife of a billionaire. But, whatever she might say to the contrary, she was still his wife. And that wasn't about to change any time soon. Make that *ever*.

It was five weeks since she had bolted from his life, leaving no clue about her motives or plans except a two-line note. But he hadn't needed any note to know why she had fled. She'd still been steaming over that row they'd had. A row he knew he could have done more to mitigate.

Except why should he have to mitigate anything?

He had told her the truth. Vittoria was not his mistress. Their relationship was complicated, but completely innocent. As his wife, Giulietta should have believed him. In fact, she shouldn't even have asked the question.

Most women in her position—his cousins' wives and his aunts for example—would have understood that.

But his wife was not most women.

He glanced over at her, watching the flush of anger colour her sculpted cheekbones.

When he'd first noticed Juliet Jones on that chilly afternoon in Rome, it hadn't been for those glorious cheekbones, her bee-stung lips or glossy tortoiseshell hair. In fact, her hair had been hanging down in rat's tails and she hadn't looked that different from the half-drowned cat she'd been trying and failing to rescue.

No woman he knew would have been out in that downpour, much less halfway down a storm drain.

But then Giulietta was not like any other woman he knew.

He had fallen for her beauty and the fire in her eyes—fallen deeper for her smile and her laugh. And then she had made *him* laugh. There had been no doubt, no hesitation in his heart. She was his soulmate. He knew what she was thinking, what she was feeling...

Or he had thought he did.

Remembering the empty packet of contraceptive pills in the bin, he felt his jaw tighten. It didn't make any sense. They'd been trying for a baby—

Except apparently they hadn't.

Hadn't she known how much it meant to him to have a child?

Had he not made it clear how important it was to him to have a son or daughter of his own?

It made no sense, her behaviour. She'd wanted a baby as much as he did—had been eager to start trying. Or so she'd said.

But women—some women anyway—were very good at keeping secrets.

'You had no right!' She practically spat the words at him, her eyes flaring with fury.

'To protect my wife?' He frowned. 'Most husbands would disagree with you.'

She scowled at him. 'Well, it doesn't matter anyway. I'm just going to rebook it.'

With her hair tumbling free of its ponytail and her flushed cheeks she looked the way she had in Rome that first day, when they had kissed their way upstairs to her room.

His stomach muscles tightened. He'd missed her—missed her fire and her spirit—and for a moment he considered running his finger over her soft, flushed curves.

But he still had scars from the last feral cat he'd cornered...

'I thought you might,' he said mildly. 'So I took the precaution of booking all the available rooms.'

Her eyes widened with shock, and then she rallied. 'Then I'll book another hotel.'

'You can try.'

She stared at him, her mouth an O of disbelief. 'You can't have booked out the whole of Verona, Ralph.'

For a moment he thought about toying with her, stringing her along as she had strung him along for months now.

'I didn't need to,' he said finally. 'In all the excitement you appear to have forgotten that the opera festival starts this weekend. You'll be lucky to get a manger in a stable.'

His people had reserved the few remaining rooms that had still been available, but he would have booked every room in the city if it had been necessary. He had the wealth and the power to surmount any obstacle in his path. And when it came to his wife he was prepared to use any and all means at his disposal to get her back where she belonged.

Sighing, he pulled out his phone.

'I suppose you'd better stay with Lucia. I know she has her family and Luca's there. And, of course, she's got Raffaelle's christening to organise, but...'

He watched the emotions chase across her beautiful face, ticking them off inside his head.

Confusion.

Outrage.

Then, last but most satisfying of all, resignation.

'Okay, then.' It was almost a shout.

Snatching the phone from his hand, she threw it onto the seat between them and slid as far from him as physically possible.

'Does that mean you've decided to come home with me after all?'

Momentarily the flicker of fury in her dark eyes reminded him of the flickering candles in the simple trattoria where she had treated him to dinner the night they'd first met.

'I hate you.'

'I'll take that as a yes,' he said softly.

Shifting back against the cool leather, he let his gaze skim over her rigid profile, then down to her tightly closed fists.

She wasn't exaggerating. She really did hate him.

And maybe if they'd been anywhere else in the world he might have been worried. But this was Verona, a city where hate and love were inextricably linked. All he needed to do now was remind his Juliet of that fact.

'Buongiorno, Signor Castellucci. Benvenuto a casa, Signora Castellucci.'

They had arrived at the Palazzo Gioacchino.

Striding into the imposing hallway, Ralph nodded at the small, balding man who was waiting for them.

'*Buongiorno*, Roberto. Signora Castellucci and I will take coffee on the terrace.'

Giulietta had followed him inside, but now he felt her hesitate. A ripple of irritation snaked over his skin. She had no idea what she had put him through these last few weeks, or how hard it had been to give her the space she'd requested. But he had done it. He'd made himself wait.

Knowing the mistakes his father had made with his mother, how could he not have done?

His hands curled into his palms. He had given her a week, thinking he was doing the right thing, and then two. Two had become four, then five, and then suddenly she was asking him for a divorce.

A divorce.

Listening to her message, all he'd been able to think was, *This cannot be happening. This can't be what she wants.*

Even now it blew his mind—and he knew they would have a short, edifying conversation about it soon. But it would have to wait until after the christening. Luca and Lucia didn't need their special day overshadowed by some bump in his marriage.

And, whatever Giulietta might think to the contrary, that was all this was. A bump.

There would be no divorce. Not now. Not at any point in the future.

'Is there a problem, *bella*?' he said roughly.

She was staring at him as if he'd suddenly grown an extra head. 'You mean other than you forcing me to stay here?'

Anger and frustration clouded her features, and if she'd had a tail it would have been flicking from side to side.

Frowning, he glanced pointedly round the opulent hallway. 'This is your home. I shouldn't need to force you to stay.' He let his gaze rest on her face. 'But if that's how you feel, *mia moglie*, then maybe you need to rethink your priorities.'

Her priorities.

That was the problem.

Surely her priorities should run in tandem with his? She'd certainly led him to think that was the case.

But the empty blister pack he'd found said otherwise...

He heard her take a breath, could see the pulse jumping at the base of her throat as she glared at him.

'You have to be kidding. You know all those beautiful Venetian mirrors in the drawing room? Well, you need to take a good look at yourself in one of them. Because it's not me who needs to rethink their priorities.'

If she'd been angry before, she looked as if she wanted to hit him now. Only why? He'd given her the space she'd demanded. Why couldn't she do the same? Why couldn't she back off and just accept what he'd told her? That what she'd seen didn't threaten their marriage.

But, no, she had to go flouncing back to England.

He shook his head slowly. 'And yet you are the one behaving like a petulant child.'

Her mouth dropped open, but without giving her a chance to reply he spun on his heel and walked away from her.

As he strode through the rooms, past the rare French and Italian tapestries on the walls, he tugged off his jacket and tossed it onto a chair.

'In what way is that true?' She had followed him. 'Tell me.'

They were outside now. She blinked in the sunlight.

'What? I'm being childish because I had the effrontery to get upset that you cancelled my hotel room?'

'Which I did for obvious and understandable reasons.'

Her eyes flared. 'In other words, you were protecting the Castellucci brand.'

His jaw tightened, but he resisted the urge to tell her that as her surname wasn't ever going to change *she* was part of that brand.

'My decision to cancel your booking had nothing to do with

my family.' Why was she so determined to think ill of him? 'I was thinking about our friends and how they would feel if their son's christening got turned into a circus by his godparents.'

He took a step towards her.

He had been thinking, too, about his wife.

His chest tightened. It had been hard enough when she had been in London, but knowing she was here in his city, sleeping in some strange bed instead of by his side...he couldn't let that happen.

'I was careful,' she said.

But the colour had drained from her cheeks and he could hear the catch in her voice.

'Not careful enough,' he said quietly.

Even after six months as a Castellucci she still didn't get it. She still hadn't accepted that her life was not like other people's. And, like his mother, apparently she wanted something different—something more.

The thought made his stomach muscles tighten painfully. 'What if the taxi driver had recognised you? Or someone at the hotel? That's all it would take.'

There was a long silence. She was biting her lip.

'I thought it would be awkward...me staying here.'

He studied her face: the full, soft mouth, the dark arch of her eyebrows, the eyes the colour of molten chocolate. Eyes that had lost their anger.

A pulse of heat danced across his skin as the silence lengthened. Did she know how beautiful she was? How much he wanted her? He didn't even need to touch her to get turned on.

But that didn't mean he wasn't interested in touching her.

He was.

He was very interested.

As though reading his thoughts, she lifted her chin and their eyes collided. Around them the air was pulsing in time with his blood surging south.

Reaching out, he touched her cheek, let his hand slide through her hair, feeling the glossy weight. 'Does this feel awkward to you, *bella*?'

Heart pounding, Juliet stared at him, shivers of anticipation tingling across her skin. One second she had been standing in front of him, blinded not just by sunlight but by anger, the next his hand had been caressing her cheek.

Stop this now, she ordered herself, her hands pushing against his chest.

Except they weren't pushing.

Instead, her trembling fingers were splaying out, biting into the cool cotton of his shirt.

And now time had stopped, and everything was fading into the background, and she was conscious of nothing but the man and the pulsing wayward urges of her body.

Her heartbeat accelerated as she silently answered his question. *No*, this part of their life had never been awkward. Not even that first time—her first time.

Her skin tightened as she remembered those magical hours in Rome.

The tangle of sheets and their bodies blurring over and over again in that stuffy little bedroom.

Before Ralph she'd done things with guys, but always something had stopped her from going all the way. Her nerves, their clumsiness, a lack of the chemistry she assumed would and should be there. But mostly it had been an unspoken need for her first time to matter. Or, more accurately, for *her* to matter.

That was the difference between her and her friends. Obviously they had wanted their first time to be a good experience too, but they'd grown up believing they mattered, so for them it had been more about getting their virginity 'out of the way'.

It had never been in the way of anything she wanted.

Her pulse dipped.

Until she'd met Ralph.

And he had been worth the wait.

From that first caress everything had flowed like water. At some point they had become one, and by then there had been no barriers between them.

Remembering his smooth, sleek skin, and the tormenting pleasure of his touch, she felt her body grow warm. She had known that sex could be quick or slow, tender or passionate, but she hadn't known that it had the power to heal. That it could make you feel whole.

Her eyes fluttered over his body. He had taken off his jacket and he was close enough for her to see the definition of hard muscle and the hint of hair beneath his immaculate handmade shirt.

So close that she could feel the heat of his skin.

Feel the heat racing along her limbs.

But she was over him.

Wasn't that why she had walked out of this glittering palace and away from their life? Why she had told him she wanted a divorce? So she could walk away for ever and move on with her life.

And yet she could feel herself leaning closer, feel her body starting to soften, her pulse to slow. It would be so easy to move nearer, to thread her fingers through his tousled hair, sink into his body and feel that perfect curving mouth against her lips.

There was the clink of china behind her back. For a moment she felt her body sway like a pendulum, and then she took a step backwards, glancing over to where Roberto was putting down a tray on the glass-topped table.

The skin on her palms felt as though it had been burned. Her cheek, on the other hand, felt cool without Ralph's hand there. She took a shaky breath, her pulse ragged with shock and exasperation.

One touch! Was that all it took to make her forget all sense of self-preservation? *Clearly she had been out in the sun too long.*

'Would you like me to pour the coffee, *signor*?'

'No, it's fine, Roberto.' Ralph was shaking his head, but his eyes stayed locked with hers. 'We can manage—can't we, *cara*?' *We.*

She felt her stomach flip over. His choice of word was deliberate, and she waited impatiently, nerves jangling, for Roberto to leave the terrace.

'Won't you join me?' he asked.

She turned, her eyes narrowing, as her husband dropped down into a chair and sprawled out against the linen cushions.

'What are you doing?' she said hoarsely.

'I'm sitting down.'

'I meant before. What was that all about?'

He stared at her steadily, his face impassive. 'You said we didn't work as a couple. I was just reminding you that we do.'

She glared at him, the truth of his words only making her angrier with both him and herself. 'We don't.'

'So what was that, then? And please don't tell me it was a mistake,' he said softly.

'It was nothing.'

She wanted to move further away, to get more distance between them, but that would simply suggest that the opposite of what she was saying was true.

'Nothing happened and nothing is going to happen,' she said stiffly.

His golden gaze was direct and unwavering. 'You can't fight it, *bella*. It's stronger than both of us.'

His cool statement made her breathing jerk.

It scared her that he might be right. That years from now, maybe decades, she would still crave Ralph as she did now. It didn't matter that she would never admit that to him—she couldn't lie to herself.

And what made it worse—*no*, what made it wrong—was that her hunger for him was unchanged even though she knew he'd been unfaithful.

Surely that should have diminished her desire? Eased the ache inside her?

The fact that it hadn't scared her more than anything else. She didn't want to be that woman—to be vulnerable.

Only she was vulnerable where Ralph was concerned.

She knew how easy it would be to give in to the heat of her hunger, to go where he wanted to take her, just as she'd done at the airport.

Her hands tightened into fists.

But it was bad enough that Ralph had betrayed her. She didn't need to betray herself too.

'That doesn't make it right,' she said. 'Just because you want something—*someone*—it doesn't mean it's okay to act on that desire.'

She felt a spasm of pain, remembering the moment when she'd seen Ralph guiding his mistress in the street, the intensity of his gaze, the urgency of his hand on the car door.

Lifting her chin, she locked her eyes with his. 'But obviously I can see why you might find that a difficult concept.'

Watching her face, Ralph felt his shoulders tense. On the contrary, he thought. He'd spent five weeks *not* acting—five long weeks tamping down his anger. Now he could feel it rising to the surface.

He wanted to shake her.

Gazing up at her flushed face and the glossy hair spilling free of its ponytail, he felt his groin harden.

Actually, no. He wanted to kiss her.

Here, now, he wanted to pull her into his arms and cover her soft mouth with his, to strip her naked and make her what she had been before and would be soon enough again.

His.

But he resisted the temptation to act on his desire. There was plenty of time. What mattered was that she was here and not in some shabby hotel on the outskirts of the city.

Everything was going according to plan.

Tomorrow they would arrive at the christening together.

Afterwards they would leave together.

Later in the week she would be by his side like a good wife, welcoming guests to the Castellucci Ball.

And then he would get answers to the questions that had been swirling like storm clouds inside his head.

But for now he would be patient.

Not that his beautiful, baffling wife would believe that was possible...

He stared at her steadily, his mind searching its own corners for words that could douse her fire and fury—temporarily at least.

But why did he need eloquence? Simple and honest might actually work best.

Sighing, he gestured towards the sofa. 'Look, I get that you're angry with me, and we clearly need to talk, but could we just put this particular conversation on hold? For our friends? For Lucia and Luca?'

Her face was stiff with tension, but he could see she was listening.

'It's their son's christening. Our godson's christening. And we might not be in agreement about much right now, but I know neither of us wants to do anything that might impact on Raffaelle's special day.'

There was a beat of silence as her dark eyes searched his face, and then she sat down stiffly on the sofa opposite him. He felt a rush of triumph, and relief.

'Coffee?' he said.

She nodded slowly. 'But, so we're clear. Just because I've agreed to stay here, it doesn't mean I'll be sharing a bed with you.'

Sitting down, he picked up his cup and took a sip of coffee, deliberately letting the silence swell between them.

The Castelluccis had been, and still were, one of the most

powerful families in Italy. For that reason alone most women would have burned a path across the earth to share his bed.

Not his wife, though.

His pulse skipped a beat.

It was tempting to haul her across the sofa's feather-filled cushions and demonstrate that a bed wasn't necessary for what he had in mind. But, much as he wanted to do so, what mattered more was that she came to him willingly, wantonly, as she had before.

Remembering the softness of her skin, the urgency of her touch, the smooth dovetailing of her body with his as she melted into him, he felt his groin tighten. And then, blanking his mind, he shrugged.

'That won't be a problem. There are twenty-five bedrooms here, *bella*. I'm sure one of them will meet with your satisfaction.'

Roberto would have had her case taken to their room, but that was easily resolved. The butler had worked for the Castellucci family for thirty years. He was both quietly efficient and discreet when it came to family matters—as were all members of the household staff.

'But you will dine with me tonight?' he said.

He held her gaze…could almost see her brain working through a flow chart of possible outcomes.

Finally, though, she nodded. 'I suppose we both have to eat.' Smoothing down her jeans, she stood up, her eyes dark and defiant. 'I'm going to freshen up. I'll see you at dinner.'

Forty minutes later she was staring at her reflection and wondering why she hadn't just said no.

It was crazy.

She could easily have had a tray sent up to her room.

But, then again, she was going to have to see him at the christening anyway, and it was clear she needed to practise pretending that everything was fine between them.

Blotting her lips, she checked her reflection again.

And she wanted to prove to herself and to Ralph that what had happened out on the terrace had been a one-off. A moment when the past and present had overlapped.

Picturing the up-curve of his mouth and the familiar blunt expression on his face as he'd stared down at her, she felt her breath hitch in her throat.

She knew time couldn't stop or stand still, but just for those few seconds it had felt as though the laws of physics had been disrupted and they were back at the beginning, before everything unravelled.

Her mouth thinned.

And maybe that was a good thing.

Those few seconds had amply proved just how naive she had been, assuming an explosive sexual chemistry like theirs could simply be switched off.

Looking back at the mirror, she adjusted the neckline of her dark blue sleeveless shirt dress.

But, as she'd told Ralph, it wouldn't happen again—whatever she wore tonight needed to reinforce not undermine that message, and this dress was perfect.

For a moment she considered putting a thin cardigan over the top, but that might imply that she needed additional barriers between them.

Plus, it would remind her of Rome…

Her lip curled. *No.* Rome was the past.

If she thought about Rome then it would be all too easy to let good memories persuade her that his betrayal had been a momentary lapse. Particularly now that she was here in Verona… in the home they shared.

Only it wouldn't be her home for much longer.

She swallowed against the lump in her throat. It hurt to let go of the past and the passion. But there was no point in holding it close. In thinking that things would change. That people changed.

Her body tensed.

Been there, done that.

And not just once, she thought, closing her eyes.

For a few half-seconds she let herself go back…let memories float up through the darkness.

Other children had been raised by their parents. She had been forged. So often she had been out of her depth, and always it had felt as if she was waiting and hoping. Waiting for the inevitable. For things to go wrong, for the latest set of promises to be broken. Hoping that this time would be different. Only that had just made the disappointment worse.

She opened her eyes and stared at her pale, set face in the mirror.

Ralph had been right.

Some things were too relentless, too immutable to fight. And, no matter how much she wanted to stay and keep fighting, she knew from experience that the only way to survive mentally, emotionally, was to walk away.

So, however much it hurt, however desperately she wanted to hold on to the dream of her marriage, that was what she was going to do.

Walking downstairs, though, took more courage than she'd thought. Her beautiful home seemed both different and yet familiar, so that she felt as if she was sleepwalking in a dream.

'*Buonasera, Signora Castellucci.*' Roberto greeted her as she walked into the drawing room. 'Signor Castellucci is waiting for you on the terrace.'

'*Grazie*, Roberto.'

She walked outside, her breath tangling in her throat. They hadn't often eaten alone in the evening. He'd worked long hours—longer after Carlo had been taken ill. And on the rare occasions when they hadn't been attending a party or a charity event there had been numerous family commitments.

Her heart twisted.

It was ironic that only a few months ago she'd actually longed for an evening when it would be just the two of them.

She felt her pulse stutter as she spotted Ralph. He was standing with his back to her, as he had at the airport, his gaze directed towards the yellowing lights of Verona. Gone was the dark suit of earlier. Instead he was wearing pale chinos and a dark brown polo shirt that hugged his broad shoulders.

As he turned towards her, she stared at him mutely. The Castelluccis might live in palaces, but they had a horror of the baroque or flamboyant. Ralph's clothes were a masterclass in the kind of high-end stealth-wealth camouflage loved by his family. Inconspicuous, logo-less, but eye-wateringly expensive.

She hadn't realised that in Rome. She'd been too smitten, too dazzled by his beauty and confidence to think about his clothes. He'd told her he was taking a few days off and his jeans and sports jacket had reflected that.

Now, though, she knew that, however casually her husband was dressed, he was rarely off duty or off guard.

She walked towards him, her skin tightening as his gaze drifted slowly over her dress down to her sandaled feet.

'You look beautiful,' he said quietly.

She accepted his compliment. Her plan was to stay cool, but polite, to eat, and then to excuse herself as soon as possible. 'Thank you.'

'What would you like to drink?'

'Sparkling water would be lovely.'

She was careful to avoid his fingers as she took the glass from his outstretched hand.

Glancing across to the table, she felt a flutter of relief. There were candles, but there was still enough daylight to offset any seductive overtones from the fluttering flames.

'Shall we?' Ralph gestured towards the table. 'Unless you—?'

'No, let's eat,' she said quickly.

The sooner this was over the better.

He stood behind her, waiting while she sat down. And, nerves tightening, she held her breath until he was safely seated opposite her.

'So, how was England?' he asked.

She had half thought he might pick up their conversation from where he'd left off earlier, but if he wanted to talk about England that suited her fine.

Ralph's chef, Giancarlo, had run an award-winning *cantina* in Venice, and his food was innovative, quintessentially Italian and delicious. But her stomach was tight with nerves and each mouthful of her ravioli with lobster and saffron was harder to swallow than the last.

'Relax, *bella*. It's just some pasta in a sauce.'

His lazy smile made her chest ache with an unsettling mix of regret and longing.

'But don't tell Giancarlo I said that. He still hasn't forgotten when I asked him to make a Hawaiian pizza for my seventh birthday.'

Her laugh was involuntary. 'Did he make it?'

'Of course. I always get what I want,' he said softly.

Her blood turned to air as he reached over and lightly traced the curve of her mouth.

'You have such a beautiful smile. I'd forgotten just how beautiful, and that's my fault.' His mouth twisted. 'All of this is my fault. I know that. But I want you to know that I can change, and if you give me a chance I will prove that to you.'

The pull of his words was making her breathless. She so wanted to believe him, but—

She batted his hand away. 'I'm sorry, but that's not what I want.'

'And *I'm* sorry, but I don't believe you.' His eyes didn't leave her face. 'Giulietta, we have something special.'

'*Had* something special,' she corrected him.

Or maybe they hadn't. She didn't know any more. That blissful certainty of finding her one true love had been no more than pyrite—fool's gold—and she would be a fool to go back to the pain of loving him again.

'Please, Ralph, there's no purpose to any of this.'

'No purpose to fighting for our marriage?' He frowned. 'We promised to be there for one another, for better and for worse.'

She opened her mouth, then closed it again. She didn't want to think, much less talk about their wedding day, or the vows he had unilaterally broken. What was the point?

'Giulietta—?' he prompted her.

'*What*, Ralph?' Her voice was vibrating with reproach and accusation. 'What do you want me to say?'

His eyes hardened. 'Look, I know this has been a tough time, but all marriages go through rocky patches.'

She knew they did. A lifetime in and out of foster care was proof of that.

But, looking at his face, she felt her heart twist. This wasn't about reconciliation. It was about pride and power. Ralph Castellucci simply didn't understand the word *no*.

She stood up from the table and took a step back 'They do, but not everyone wilfully steers the boat onto the rocks.'

Ralph stared at her in exasperation.

Moments earlier she had smiled a smile he remembered and missed…a smile of such sweetness that he could almost taste it in his mouth.

And, watching her, he had felt a sudden rush of hope that maybe he didn't have to be alone with the truth any more. That maybe he could finally confess to her and then everything would go back to how it used to be.

But how could he tell her the truth? She wouldn't even meet him halfway, even though she was the guilty party. She had lied and deceived him, only apparently all this was his fault.

'It's not me who steered the boat onto the rocks. I can sail with my eyes shut.'

Her eyes narrowed. 'I'm not talking about the *Alighieri*.'

'Neither am I,' he said softly.

She glared at him, her teeth bared. 'What's that supposed to mean?'

It was on the tip of his tongue to tell her. To upend her world as she'd upended his. But he wanted time and privacy for this conversation. Fortunately, he had just the place in mind.

For a moment a strained silence hung between them, and then she took another step backwards. 'I think we're done here, don't you?'

Watching her stalk back into the house, Ralph picked up his glass and downed the contents.

They weren't done. Far from it. But he could afford to let her go. Afford to wait until the time was right. And then he would prove to her just how seriously he took his marriage vows.

CHAPTER THREE

'*EHI*, CASTELLUCCI! OVER HERE!'

Glancing over the heads of the guests gathered outside the beautiful Romanesque church, Juliet felt her lips curve upwards as she spotted a smiling Lucia holding Raffaelle. Beside her, Luca was waving and grinning.

She looked up at Ralph. 'They're over—'

'I can see them.'

Her body tensed as his hand caught hers, but he was already tugging her forward. 'This way.'

How did he do this? she wondered. There was an incredible number of people milling around in the square, and yet the crowd was parting like a Biblical sea as he guided her towards Lucia and Luca.

Following in his footsteps, she had the usual feeling of being both protected and horribly conspicuous—as if every eye was tracking her through the crowd, judging her hair, her clothes, her weight, her suitability as a Castellucci bride.

She had never really got used to it—no more than she had got used to the bodyguards who were an integral part of life for the super-rich. And now, after five peaceful, anonymous weeks back in England, she felt extra naked.

Not a particularly relaxing sensation to have around Ralph, she thought, feeling his gaze and his fingertips on her back.

'Amico!'

As Luca grabbed Ralph in one of those complicated one-armed man hugs, Lucia kissed her on both cheeks. 'Letty, you look beautiful. I love that dress.' Her eyes widened. 'And those shoes!'

Glancing down at her dark red heels, Juliet laughed. 'I'm happy to swap. Truly. I nearly broke my neck just walking here from the car.'

Lucia breathed out shakily. 'I'm so glad you're back. Promise me you won't disappear like that again.'

It was a simple exchange between friends, and yet Juliet could feel a tingling warmth creeping down her spine. From somewhere over her shoulder, she was aware of Ralph's gaze boring into the back of her head.

She hesitated, not wanting to lie, but also wanting to reassure her friend. Only the stubborn need to remind her husband that he wasn't calling the shots forbade her from doing so.

'I didn't disappear,' she said quickly, sidestepping the question. 'But I did miss you and…' she glanced down at Raffaelle '… I missed this little one too.'

Reaching out, she gently stroked his cheek, feeling something unravelling inside her as the baby grabbed her fingers with one chubby hand. With his dark, silky hair and huge brown eyes, he was utterly gorgeous.

'Hey, *ometto…'*

Even without hearing his voice, she knew that Ralph was standing beside her. She could feel his eyes picking over her face, looking at her hand in Raffaelle's, and the sharp ache in her heart made her feel faint.

Watching the baby's lips flutter into a smile, Juliet felt her heart contract. She'd wanted a baby so badly. Ralph even more so. Although perhaps it might be more accurate to say that he'd wanted an heir.

A sharp pulse of pain made her press her fingers against her forehead. Was all this her fault? Would it have been different if she'd got pregnant?

Yes. No...

Truthfully, she didn't know. But she did know that if she'd kept on playing by his rules their child would have grown up in Ralph's gilded world. Heir to a fortune, and surrounded by unimaginable luxury and opulence.

Except that wasn't enough.

Not if that world required her son or daughter to grow up as she had—surrounded by lies and compromise and broken promises.

Gazing down at the baby, she felt her throat tighten. She knew how painful that was—knew too that you could never outrun the damage it caused.

Why else had she married a man like Ralph?

A man whose carelessness with people's feelings matched— no, *surpassed* that of her parents.

As a child she'd had no control over her life. She hadn't understood then that her parents' choices had required her to give up something of herself. But she did understand now that if her marriage continued she would be pitched back into the pain and uncertainty of her childhood.

Only she wasn't a child now. She was an adult. And she couldn't—she wouldn't—go there again.

She wouldn't be trapped in a loveless marriage.

Not even for Ralph.

Shifting the baby in her arms, so that Ralph could kiss her, Lucia grimaced. 'He's not so little now. He's actually the biggest baby in our mother and baby group,' she added proudly.

'That's because he takes after his *papà*.' Leaning forward, Luca blew on his son's neck, grinning as the baby squirmed and giggled in delight. 'We Bocchetti men inspire superlatives.'

'Yes, you do.' Ralph grabbed his friend round the shoulders. 'Like dumbest and most uncool.'

Lucia burst out laughing, but Juliet barely registered the joke. It was the lazy smile pulling at Ralph's mouth that had captured her attention and was holding it with gravitational force.

Around her, she felt the women in the crowd crane forward, like flowers turning towards the sun, and despite her resentment she completely understood why.

It was a smile that promised and delivered unimaginable pleasure.

Other promises, though, he found harder to keep.

And yet seeing him with his friends made it hard to remember that.

Her heart began beating a little faster.

She hardly ever saw this side of him—perhaps only ever with Luca, his childhood friend…the one person he seemed able to relax around.

With his family—particularly the older members—he was serious and formal. And his cousins Nico and Felix were too in awe of his status as heir, too anxious both for his attention and his approval to fully relax with him.

Perhaps he had been different with his mother?

But Francesca Castellucci had died just over a year ago, and although Ralph had told her about his mother's illness he hadn't offered any insights into their relationship.

Her heartbeat accelerated. It was something they had in common, that reluctance to talk about their mothers. Although not, she was sure, for the same reasons.

She had no desire to talk about any of her parents. Not her numerous foster parents and particularly not her biological ones.

Nancy and Johnny had collided when Nancy was just seventeen. Their marriage had been an unhappy mix of easy sex and complicated emotion, and almost exactly nine months from the day they'd met they'd become parents.

Juliet felt a familiar nausea squeeze her stomach.

By then there had already been fault lines in the relationship, and they'd got deeper and wider after her arrival.

For weeks at a time, sometimes months, it would work. But sooner or later it had always fallen apart, and she had always been waiting for that moment to happen, body tense, all five senses on high alert, trying to anticipate every potential flash point.

An empty milk carton.

Money missing from a purse.

A dropped call.

She swallowed. Telling Ralph about her childhood hadn't been an option. She had shared the bare bones with him, but she knew he would never understand the chaos, the lack of control, the insecurity.

How could he? He'd grown up in a palace, the pampered heir to a fortune, and he was part of a large and close family.

Correction: they were close to *him*. To her they were polite, but clearly baffled as to why someone like Ralph had chosen someone like her.

Her stomach churned.

And, judging by his behaviour, Ralph was starting to agree with them.

'Are you ready?'

She turned at his voice. Ralph was looking down at her steadily, the corners of his eyes creasing, and she felt suddenly as if the crowds had parted again and it was just the two of them, standing outside in the mid-morning sunlight.

As usual, he looked ridiculously handsome. Like every other man there he was wearing a suit—handmade, dark, Italian design, of course—but Ralph looked nothing like any of them.

For starters—perhaps thanks to his mother's genes—he was taller. His hair was lighter too, and of course he had those incredible golden eyes.

And yet it was more than just his physical appearance that set him apart.

Around him everyone was talking expansively, hands moving, gesticulating, heads tipping back to roar with laughter, but Ralph was quiet and calm: the eye of the storm.

He had been her one place of safety—only that wasn't what she needed to be thinking right now.

'It's time to go,' he said softly.

'Yes, of course.' She nodded, then felt a rush of panic bubble up inside her as he held out his hand. But this wasn't the time or place to be proving a point and, ignoring the pulse of heat that jumped from his skin to hers as their fingers entwined, she joined the guests walking into the church.

The service followed its usual pattern, and then the priest smiled at Lucia and Luca and it was time for the christening.

Taking a breath, Juliet walked towards the font.

Although she knew it was a simple ceremony, she was slightly worried about saying her lines, but everything went perfectly. Raffaelle was utterly angelic, gazing solemnly at the priest and not even crying when the water was poured over his head.

It was beautiful, she thought, tears pricking her eyes.

And then suddenly it was over, and they were back in the midday sunshine, and everyone was smiling and clapping.

'Thank you.' Lucia was hugging her. 'Both of you.' She hugged Ralph. 'He's such a lucky boy, having two such wonderful godparents.'

Juliet smiled. 'It's an honour to be asked.'

'And you're coming in the car with us,' Lucia said firmly. 'I love my family, but after two solid days of living with my mother, my sisters and...' leaning forward, she lowered her voice, '...my *mother-in-law*, I just need a few minutes to recover.'

Tucking her arm through her friend's, Juliet laughed.

The christening reception was being held at the Casa Gregorio Hotel, twenty minutes outside of Verona. Although the word 'hotel' didn't really capture the magic of the Gregorio,

Juliet thought as she slid into the cool, air-conditioned interior of the limousine.

Set in idyllic countryside, the exclusive, exquisitely renovated monastery offered a tranquil retreat from the bustle of city life, and these days the legendary kitchen garden was being put to mouth-wateringly good use by two Michelin-starred chef, Dario Bargione.

'Just sit back and enjoy the party,' she advised her friend. 'Everything is under control. You don't need to do a thing.'

Eyes suddenly bright, Lucia reached over and squeezed her hand. 'I know, and we're so grateful to you and Ralph for making this reception possible. It was so generous of you both.'

'It was our pleasure.'

Juliet felt Ralph's words skimming across her skin. You could hear it in his voice, she thought. Hundreds of years of Castellucci patronage.

How had she ever thought they would work?

Paying for Raffaelle's christening party was no big deal to him, whereas she felt uncomfortable when strangers thanked her at fundraisers and charity balls.

But then, when it came to money, the Castelluccis were in a league all their own. And, thanks to his talent for unearthing tiny start-ups that turned into commercial behemoths, Ralph had personally redefined the concept of wealth.

As well as the *palazzo* in Verona, he owned a villa in the French Riviera and penthouses in Rome, New York and London. For him money was almost irrelevant. Put simply, there was nothing he couldn't buy.

Except her.

'No, we mean it, *amico*. We can't thank you enough.' For once Luca's face was serious.

Juliet opened her mouth, but before she could speak Ralph said, 'But you have. You chose us to be godparents to Raffaelle. You're trusting us to help raise your beautiful son.' He paused.

'Aside from love, there's no gift more precious than trust. Don't you agree, *mia moglie*?'

Her heart thumped against her ribs as his eyes locked with hers. She knew he wasn't talking about Lucia and Luca.

He was talking about her.

More specifically, he was talking about her refusal to trust him, to take his word over the evidence of her eyes.

Her breath caught in her throat. *Trust.* It was such a small word and yet it encompassed so much. Confidence. Security. Hope. *And betrayal.*

Ignoring the misery filling her chest, she held his gaze.

'Ralph's right. Trust is the most precious gift.' She forced a smile onto her face. 'So thank you, both, for trusting us.'

Snatching a glass of prosecco from a passing waiter, Ralph stared across the heads of the other guests, his eyes seeking out his wife like a wolf tracking a deer.

His gaze narrowed as he caught a flash of dark red.

There she was.

His stomach tightened.

All through the ceremony she had avoided his gaze, focusing instead on the priest and then on Raffaelle. But as she'd made her vows her eyes had met his, and suddenly he had been fighting the temptation to reach out and touch her—to press his lips against hers.

Gritting his teeth, he stared across the terrace to where his wife was talking to Luca's mother. It was a cute dress—pleated, one-shouldered, with a flippy little skirt. From a distance the print looked floral, but it was actually tiny cherries.

And then there were her shoes...

Shiny patent red heels, the colour of the Marostica cherries that grew on the hillsides in the town down the road in Vicenza.

For a moment he let his gaze drop, and felt his body hardening exponentially as his eyes drifted slowly down the length of her legs, then back up, drawn to the hollow at the back of her neck that was just visible beneath her smooth chignon.

Even now it caught him off balance. Not her looks—in his world beauty was the norm, although with that hair and face, *those legs*, it was hard not to feel as though the floor was unsteady beneath his feet—what had got under his skin that first day they'd met in Rome, and what still blew his mind even now, was how she drank in life, lived so completely in the moment.

A pulse of heat beat across his skin. Even when she was soaking wet, with her head stuck in a storm drain.

And look at her now.

Glancing across the terrace, he watched as she leaned forward to choose a canapé. He had seen her look at beautiful jewellery with the same attention and excitement. It was a quality he'd never encountered in anyone but Giulietta. The unique ability to free herself from time and place and other pressures to edit her emotions, her actions, her thoughts.

In contrast, he was both burdened with the past and preoccupied with the future. He had grown up in a world where nothing had been what it seemed. There had been mirrors that were doors, and windows that were walls, and the people had been the same.

Giulietta was different. Transparent. He had *known* her—

His mouth twisted. Except clearly he hadn't.

He watched as she caught Lucia's arm, gestured. Even at a distance it was clear that she was offering to take the baby, and his heart thumped as Raffaelle took the decision into his own hands by lunging towards his wife.

Watching her tuck the baby against her body, he felt his anger and frustration rise up inside him like mercury in a heatwave.

How could she have lied to him about wanting a baby? And why had she deceived him?

The same questions had been burning inside his head for weeks now, and he still had no answers.

Soon, he promised himself. Just a couple more hours. But first...

His shoulders tensed.

His wife was walking away from Lucia back towards the hotel.

Without so much as a beat of hesitation he began moving smoothly after her, tracking her progress through the guests mingling in the sunshine.

'Signor Castellucci?'

Ralph swore silently as Giorgio, the hotel manager, popped up beside him, smiling nervously.

'I hope you're enjoying the celebrations, *signor*. I just wanted to check that everything is to your satisfaction.'

Ralph nodded. 'It is. Thank you.' Despite his irritation, his voice was even, his smile polite.

'No, thank *you*, Signor Castellucci, for choosing Casa Gregorio for this most special of celebrations.'

Still smiling, Ralph darted his eyes over Giorgio's shoulder. If this carried on they would still be standing there thanking one another at Raffaelle's eighteenth birthday party.

'I look forward to returning very soon. Now, if you'll excuse me, I need to speak to my wife,' he said firmly.

'Ah, yes, Signora Castellucci has taken the baby to have a nap. As you requested, we have reserved a suite for that exact purpose.'

The suite was on the first floor, away from the noise of the party. He didn't need the room number. The two dark-suited bodyguards on either side of the door told him that was where he would find his wife.

He nodded to them briefly and opened the door.

After the heat of the terrace, it was blissfully cool. But it wasn't the drop in temperature that made him stop mid-step—it was the sound of his wife's voice.

She was singing softly, some kind of lullaby, and the sound was so intimate, so tender, that he felt as if he was intruding.

For a moment he almost retreated, but the softness in her voice pulled his legs forward with magnetic force.

The room was decorated in a style that might be described as 'minimalist luxe': clean lines, a neutral colour palette, and artisan furnishings with impressive ethical credentials.

A simple iron bed with a canopy of ethereal white muslin dominated the room. Through a doorway, he could see the cot that had been set up for Raffaelle.

But the baby was not in the cot.

Giulietta was holding him.

He stared at his wife in silence. Her face was soft with love and she was gazing down, entirely absorbed. Holding his breath, he stood transfixed, fury and confusion merging with desire in a maelstrom of emotion.

He was sure that he'd made no sound, and yet something made her turn towards him—and as she did so her face didn't so much change as turn to stone.

The creamy skin of her bare shoulder tugged at his gaze like a headstrong horse, and the rise of her small, rounded breasts transformed her from tender to sexy.

'What do you want?' she said hoarsely.

Behind her, a light breeze riffled the muslin, giving him a glimpse of a crisply folded sheet, and he felt his body harden with an almost unbearable hunger.

I want to take you bending over that bed, and then against the wall, and then again on that desk, didn't seem like a reply he could make.

'Luca said I need to start pulling my weight.' It wasn't quite a lie. Luca had teased him about never having changed a nappy. 'So I thought I'd see if you needed any help.' He glanced over at the sleeping baby. 'I also thought this might be an opportunity to hold him without it turning into a circus, but I can see he's settled.'

There was a moment's silence. Then, 'You can put him down if you want.'

'I'd like that,' he said quietly.

She didn't meet his eye as she handed the sleeping baby over to him, but he could feel the tension in her body as he briefly brushed against her.

Despite what Lucia had said about his size, Raffaelle seemed incredibly small and light to him. He felt his heart contract as he looked down into the baby's peach-soft untroubled face, and a primitive, unbidden instinct to protect surging through his veins.

Leaning over the cot, he gently laid the baby on his side. 'He's so perfect,' he murmured, gently touching one of the tiny thumbs.

Giulietta had followed him into the room.

'He is, isn't he?' Her eyes found his.

He smiled. 'It's hard to believe he's going to be like Luca one day.'

Personally, he thought Raffaelle looked more like Lucia. But it was the first time she had willingly agreed with him about anything since returning to Italy, and he didn't want to lose this fragile connection between them.

'Perhaps he won't be.' She gave him a small, stiff smile. 'Not everyone grows up to be like their parents.'

She turned and walked out of the room and he stared after her, his spine tensing, picturing the handsome, patrician face of his father, Carlo Castellucci, and his mother, Francesca.

Guilt rose up inside him—guilt and shame and an anger that he couldn't seem to shift.

No, not everyone did grow up like their parents.

Blocking his mind against where that thought would lead, he followed her out of the room, leaving the door slightly ajar.

Someone had loosened the thick linen curtains, so the room was half in shade, and Giulietta had chosen to stand in the darkened half.

His chest tightened. Was that why she wanted a divorce? Did she think she could hide from him? From the truth?

'Well, in Raffaelle's case it wouldn't be a bad thing, would it?' he said.

She didn't answer, and he felt a rush of irritation.

'Is that it? You're done with the small talk?' He shook his head. 'And I thought one of your jobs as godparent was to lead by example. It's not a promising start, is it?'

Her eyes narrowed. 'It's not just small talk, Ralph. I'm done with talking to you, full-stop. And as for setting an example— I'm not sure cheating on your wife is the kind of life lesson Lucia and Luca are hoping you'll share with Raffaelle.'

Swearing softly, he crossed the room in two strides, so fast that she took a clumsy step backwards. 'For the last time, I did not cheat on you.'

'I know.'

He stared at her in confusion. 'I don't understand—'

Her eyes were fixed on his face. 'I didn't understand either at first. I thought you were lying to me. But you weren't. You're not even lying to yourself.'

She lifted her chin, and now he could see that her eyes were dark and clear with hurt and anger and determination.

'You actually believe that adultery is a part of marriage. That having a mistress doesn't cross any boundaries. But I don't think like that and I can't live like that. So can we just agree to end it here—now?'

Slowly he shook his head. 'No. Not here. Not now. Not this side of eternity, *bella*.'

Her hands curled into fists. 'But I don't want to be your wife any more.'

'*Too bad*. You see, I'm not the only one who made promises. And I'm not talking about *till death us do part*.'

He took a step closer. '*"Indivisa, etiam in morte."* The Castellucci family motto. It means "Undivided, even in death".'

Holding his breath, he pushed back the memory of his father weeping at his mother's grave.

'And that's why you want to stay married?' Giulietta asked. 'Because of some stupid medieval family motto?'

Her voice was shaking, and he could see the pulse at the base of her neck hammering against the flawless, pale skin.

'It's one of the reasons, yes.'

She was staring at him incredulously. 'Well, it's not enough. It doesn't count—it's not a real reason.'

'And that's what you want, is it?' Goaded, he closed the gap between them. 'You want something real? I'll give you real.'

And, lowering his mouth to hers, he kissed her.

He felt her body tense, her hands press against his chest, her lips part in protest—but then, even as he moved to break the kiss, her fingers were curling into his shirt and she was pulling him closer.

His hand wrapped around her waist and for a few half-seconds he was conscious of nothing but the hammering of his heart and how soft her lips were. And then he was closing the gap between them, his hand anchoring her tightly against his torso.

Oh, but she tasted so good. Soft and sweet, like *dulce de leche*. And her body was soft too…soft and pliant…so that it felt as if she was melting into him.

And where she was soft, he was hard.

Harder than he'd ever been in his life.

He groaned, sliding his fingers through her hair, his hands at her waist, pushing her up against the wall. He felt her fingers tighten in his shirt, her nails catching on the fabric as she pulled it free of his waistband, and he breathed in sharply as her hands splayed against his bare skin—

There was a sharp knock on the door.

Beneath his hands, he felt Giulietta tense.

'Excuse me, *signor*, but the nanny is here.'

He closed his eyes, wishing he could block out the bodyguard's voice as effortlessly. *Not now.*

But it was too late. His wife was pushing away from him,

smoothing her hair back from her face in a gesture that was an unmistakable shorthand for *We're done here*.

'Giulietta—'

He reached for her, but she sidestepped him with such speed and agility that he was still tucking in his shirt when he heard the door open and her voice telling the nanny to 'go on in'.

Breathing shakily, Juliet pulled out her phone and checked the time. The taxi firm had said twenty past and it was a quarter past now.

Her heart felt as though it was going to burst through her ribcage.

What had she said to Ralph? *'Not everyone grows up to be like their parents.'*

Obviously *she* had.

She moaned softly. Wasn't it bad enough that she had let Ralph kiss her? Had she had to kiss him back?

Remembering how she had pulled at his shirt, how her hands had pressed against his skin, she felt her face grow hot.

And not just kiss him…

Quelling a bout of panic, she checked her phone again. Just one minute to go. And then this would all be over.

Her flight wasn't for another three hours, but once she was at the airport she could check in and then— She felt her pulse accelerate.

Oh, thank goodness. It was here. The taxi was here.

Holding up her hand in greeting, she watched, relief flooding through her, as the car came to a halt.

'*Ciao*. The airport, please.'

She opened the door—but as she leaned into the taxi a hand closed over her wrist.

'Not so fast.'

In one smooth movement Ralph had slammed the door and pulled her away from the car.

The next moment one of the bodyguards stepped forward,

bending down to the driver's window. Before she'd even had a chance to open her mouth in protest the taxi had sped off.

She shook herself free. 'What do you think you're playing at?'

His face was impassive, but there was a dangerous glitter in his eyes. 'I could ask you the same question. Only there's no need. You're making quite a habit of this, *bella*. Sneaking off without saying goodbye.'

He was right. She was sneaking off. But how could she have stayed after what had just happened? After what she'd let happen?

'It's got nothing to do with you.'

'Wrong. You're my wife. I think you sneaking away from a christening party for *our* godson has got everything to do with me.' He shook his head in mute frustration. 'How do you think Lucia and Luca would feel when they realised?'

Her stomach twisted with guilt. She couldn't meet his eye. Of course she had wanted to say goodbye—but then she would have had to tell them that she was leaving Italy for good.

'They'd understand,' she said, cringing inside at how callous she sounded.

He clearly thought so too; the contempt on his face made hot tears burn the back of her eyes.

She took a step backwards. But how dare he try to shame her? 'You know what, Ralph? You're so keen to keep reminding me that I'm your wife, but maybe if you hadn't forgotten that you're my husband this wouldn't be happening.'

His face hardened. 'Really? You want to do this now? Here?'

'I don't want to do it anywhere,' she snapped. 'I want to go the airport.'

He was staring at her as if she had said she wanted to go to the outer ring of Saturn.

'You want to leave? You want to go back to England? After what just happened?'

Her pulse accelerated. 'Why wouldn't I? What happened didn't change anything.'

He swore softly. 'I kissed you. And you kissed me back. You wanted a reason to stay and I gave you one.'

She felt pinpricks of heat sweep over her body. 'Well, you probably confused me with someone else. Like your mistress. I certainly confused you with someone else. Someone with scruples. Someone who wasn't going to lie to my face.'

'I'm not lying,' he said quietly.

She watched, frozen with misery, as he lifted his hand and, seemingly out of nowhere, a familiar sleek dark limousine drew up beside them. A second car followed a beat behind.

'Please get in the car, Giulietta.'

Planting her feet firmly on the Tarmac, she lifted her chin. 'I told you—I'm going to the airport.'

A muscle flickered along his jawline. 'Fine. My car is here, ready and waiting.'

She straightened her back. 'And it'll carry on waiting unless you tell me who she is.'

'I've told you she's no threat.' His voice was expressionless.

'Just tell me. Do you love her?'

His silence wrapped around her throat, choking her. She couldn't breathe. The ache in her chest was swallowing her whole. No pain had ever felt like it.

Suddenly she felt exhausted. It was over. All this was just her fighting the inevitable. Fighting the knowledge that she was the problem. She had failed as a daughter, and now she had failed as a wife.

But she couldn't fight any more. She was done.

'Goodbye, then, Ralph.'

She spun on her heel, but as she started to walk away he blocked her path.

'She's not a threat,' he said again. And then he closed his eyes, as if he too had stopped fighting.

Suddenly she didn't want to hear the truth. She didn't want

to hear about this woman who had captured his heart and broken hers.

'Don't, Ralph, please...' she whispered, turning away.

Swearing softly, he spun her round, his hand tipping up her chin. 'She's not my mistress. She's my sister.'

She looked at him for one long, excruciating moment and then she pushed his hand away. 'You don't have a sister.' She shook her head, rage mingling with misery. 'You don't have any siblings.'

His skin was stretched taut over his cheekbones, like a canvas on a frame. 'She's my half-sister.'

Half-sister.

She stared at him mutely. That couldn't be true—but why lie?

'What's her name?'

He hesitated, then sighed. 'Vittoria. Her name's Vittoria Farnese.'

She felt a rush of confusion, almost like vertigo. The name sounded familiar.

'So why hasn't anyone mentioned her?' Her tone was accusatory. 'Or am I supposed to believe your entire family is suffering from some kind of collective amnesia?'

'They don't know about her.'

There was tension in his frame now, as though speaking each sentence required an effort of will.

She looked at his face, trying to fill in the gaps, to make sense out of what made no sense at all, unless... 'Are you saying—do you mean Carlo had an affair?'

He shook his head. 'It was my mother. She had the affair.'

Her heart hammered against her ribs. 'So Vittoria is her daughter?'

There was a stretch of silence and then he shook his head again. 'No, Vittoria is my half-sister on my father's side.'

He stared past her, letting his words sink in.

'But you said your father didn't have an affair...' she said slowly.

'He didn't.'
And now she could hear the pain in his voice.
'But Carlo Castellucci is not my biological father.'

CHAPTER FOUR

FOR THE SECOND time in less than twenty-four hours Juliet found herself climbing into the limousine on automatic pilot. But this time it was not so much habit that propelled her as shock.

She watched numbly as Ralph leaned into the driver's side window to talk to Marco. Her head was spinning. Questions were bubbling inside her so fast and so violently that she felt as though a dam had burst and she was being carried along in the surging water.

Breathing out shakily, she tried to put her thoughts in some kind of order—but it was hard to do that when she felt as though she'd been kicked in the stomach.

Her fingers tightened around the smooth leather armrest as Ralph sat down beside her. She was stunned…confounded by what Ralph had told her. But most of all she felt swamped with guilt for not having been there for him.

For weeks now, she had been so sure that he was having an affair. And, given that she'd spent most of her married life waiting for their relationship to fall apart, it had been easy to stay sure even when he'd denied her accusations repeatedly.

Her pulse shivered.

Easy to convince herself that his denial was simply the reflex of a wealthy man not used to having to justify his actions. After all, the Castellucci male's right to variety in his marriage was not just hearsay. It was well-documented in art and history.

But if what he said was true then she was wrong.

Her husband hadn't been unfaithful.

She breathed in against a sharp rush of adrenaline.

And, perhaps more shockingly, Carlo was not his father.

Glancing at Ralph's set face, she felt her heart begin hammering inside her chest.

And as the silence stretched out in the air-conditioned chill of the limo she knew there were no 'ifs' or 'buts' about it.

It was true.

She could see it in the tension around his jawline and the rigidity in his shoulders.

And in that moment her own anger and hurt were instantly superseded by the emotions she knew her husband must be feeling.

How had he discovered the truth?

And who was his real father?

Gritting her teeth against the weight of questions forming in her throat, she said quietly, 'When did you find out?'

His hesitation was so brief she might not have registered it had it not been for the slight tensing around his eyes. Then he turned to face her.

'My mother told me. Not long before she died.' His eyes locked with hers. 'She'd wanted to tell me sooner, only she never found the right time.' Pain, mostly masked, shimmered for a moment. 'I think she realised she'd run out of time.'

Juliet stared at him mutely, the strain in his voice pinching her heart. She'd had difficult conversations with her own mother—the last one in particular had been in a class of its own. The only positive was that she had initiated it, so that the time and place had been of her choosing.

Pushing aside the memory of that appalling day, she said hesitantly, 'Does anyone else know? Does your father—?' She stumbled over the word. 'Sorry. I mean, does Carlo know?'

Carlo Castellucci.

She could still remember the first time she had met her father-in-law. Her stomach lurched at the memory. Would it have been any less intimidating if she'd known then what she knew now?

Probably not, she concluded. At the time she'd been dazed—dazzled, really—by the glamour of the Castelluccis and the lives they led. And as the resident patriarch of the family, Carlo's unlined face and languid, cocktail party smile had perfectly embodied that glamour.

He had kissed her on both cheeks, welcomed her to the family, but despite his words she had sensed his well-bred disbelief.

Her hands curled in her lap, her fingers grazing the huge yellow diamond that Ralph had given her to make up for the lack of an engagement ring.

Part of her hadn't blamed Carlo. After all, Ralph was his adored son. Only now it appeared that he wasn't.

She felt again that same shock of something fundamental being turned on its head, like a storm of hailstones beating down on a sunny beach in July.

Her heartbeat stuttered as Ralph shook his head.

'No one knows except me and Vittoria. And now you. My mother didn't—' his jaw tightened '—couldn't tell my father.' His voice sounded as if it was scraping over gravel. 'She knew how much it would hurt him. '

'And she didn't think it would hurt you?'

The words were out of her mouth before she could stop them, propelled by a spasm of anger that had nothing to do with Francesca Castellucci's infidelity. It was an anger that came from having had to deal with adult truths at an age when she had been ill-equipped to deal with them.

Chest tightening, she smoothed a crease from the skirt of her dress. But when would any child be ready for something like this? It was the most basic, essential truth—one you unthinkingly took for granted. Your mother and father were your parents. To learn that was a lie...

His expression didn't change, but something flickered in his eyes. 'She thought it was important that I knew the truth.'

Now Juliet felt a sharp pang of empathy for Francesca. Telling the truth sounded so easy. All you had to do was say what was in your head or your heart. But countless family therapy sessions had taught her that it was a whole lot more complicated than just opening your mouth and talking.

In practice, it was more like balancing an equation—facts had to be weighed up against the feelings they inspired, and often the process had to be done in the blink of an eye.

She watched as Ralph glanced away to where the sun was starting to dip down into the hills. His head didn't move. 'She wanted to give me the chance to get to know my biological father, Niccolò Farnese. If that was what I wanted.'

And was it?

A sudden silence filled the space between them. Inside her head, her heartbeat was deafeningly loud as a mix of panic and misery mingled uneasily in her stomach.

Once she'd thought she knew instinctively what Ralph wanted, but for months now she'd had no idea what he was thinking, and she didn't understand what mattered to him or why. It was as if there was some invisible barrier between them, blocking that immutable private bond they had once shared.

Correction: that she'd *thought* they had once shared.

She took a breath, needing to process her thoughts, his words. *Niccolò Farnese.* That name was definitely familiar, and now she was putting a face to the name...the face of a handsome, smiling man, waving to the crowds...

She stared at Ralph, the image frozen in her head. 'Are we talking about Niccolò Farnese the politician?' Politician, philanthropist and media tycoon.

He nodded. 'We are.'

His slightly accented voice was quiet, but firm. He had a beautiful voice...

Glancing at his profile, she felt her breath tangle in her throat. Before bumping into Ralph in Rome, she'd spent a few days on her own, exploring the city. Rome was bursting with things to see and do, and she had devoured all the sights as greedily as she had the *supplì*—the deep-fried rice croquettes sold in pizzerias across the capital.

It was truly the eternal city. Everywhere she'd looked she had seen ancient ruins rubbing up against modern concrete curves. She had been smitten...speechless. But it had been the ceiling of the Sistine Chapel that had left her reeling. It was mesmerisingly beautiful. Each time she'd looked up, something else had held her captive.

Her eyes fluttered across the car. Only in comparison to Ralph even the artistic power and brilliance of Michelangelo felt muted. He was so close, so solid beside her...

She breathed in and felt her stomach muscles tighten, responding to the pull of his beauty and the hint of leashed power. Her body was remembering the feel of his mouth on hers, the way he kissed, touched, caressed—

Her heart began beating unsteadily.

And he hadn't been unfaithful.

She reached across the seat and took his hand, felt a pulse of hope ticking over her skin as his fingers tightened on hers.

Maybe she'd had to push him, kicking and screaming, into doing so, but he was talking to her now—talking in a way that he had never done before.

Her pulse dipped. Her marriage wasn't over. They could work this out.

She squeezed his hand. 'And is it what you want? To get to know him? Niccolò?'

He made an impatient sound. 'You don't need to worry about that.'

'But what if I did?'

His features tightened. 'I wouldn't tell you. This is my problem and I will find a solution.'

He looked across the car but his expression was distant—as if he wasn't really seeing her. Watching him lean back in his seat, she felt her a trickle of ice run down her spine. He might not be Carlo Castellucci's biological son, she thought dully, but the casual dismissal in his voice was a pitch-perfect match of the man who had raised him.

Replaying his words in her head, she felt her mouth tighten. Surely he wasn't being serious? They needed to talk about this. Didn't he want to talk to her about this? She was his wife...

For a few half-seconds she thought back to their wedding ceremony and how his eyes had meshed with hers as he slid the single gold band onto her finger.

Her throat tightened and she thought of the blind, limitless happiness of their wedding day bleaching out to nothing.

She might be his wife, but he couldn't make his message any clearer short of parading in front of her with a placard.

As far as he was concerned, she knew *enough*. Everything else was beyond her pay grade.

He'd given her the basic facts, just as he might to a child. But she wasn't a child. She was an idiot.

A chill was creeping over her skin, and with it the unwelcome but inescapable awareness that, far from being a turning point in their relationship, this was simply another example of how far apart they were.

His confession had never been about confiding in her. It had been an exercise in damage limitation.

Glancing helplessly down at her hands, she took a deep breath, hating him, and hating herself for being so naive as to think that he could change...that he even *wanted* to change.

'You're right,' she said. Smiling thinly, she slipped her hand free of his. 'It's none of my business.'

She stared down at her dress, remembering how she had smoothed out the pretty cherry-printed fabric just before the sky fell in. Just before it had become clear that he was willing to commit them both to this marriage for no better reason than—what? Pride? The need to maintain a public façade?

She was done with this. With him. There were no more questions she needed or wanted to have answered. Not any more. And not because she didn't care, but because she did. And it was too dangerous to let herself keep caring about this beautiful, baffling man.

Caring was a hoax. Her parents had taught her that. It was a game played by the heart to distract the head from looking too closely at the facts. Or, in this case, one diamond-hard fact that she had chosen to ignore.

Her fears about Ralph's infidelity had simply been a distraction from the bigger picture. From their fundamentally different beliefs about what made a happy, healthy marriage.

She felt the car slow.

Outside, the sounds of the real world bumped against the solid body of the car. Men shouting…some kind of machinery humming…

As she looked up, her eyes clashed with his.

He raised an eyebrow. 'None of your business, *bella*? How so? You're my wife.'

So now she was his wife?

She could feel anger rising in waves inside her. Marriage was supposed to be a partnership of equals. But with Ralph everything had to be played out on his terms. He got to make the rules and change them as and when it suited him to do so.

Catching sight of her wedding band, she felt her heart being squeezed as though by a fist. She'd kept it on, telling herself that she had to for appearances' sake. But the truth was that, despite telling him she wanted a divorce, a part of her had still been hoping that she could make her marriage work.

Now, though, she knew nothing she did or said could make that happen.

She forced herself to speak past the frustration twisting in her throat. 'Fat lot of difference that makes.'

His golden gaze bored into her. 'Meaning?'

'Meaning that wives are not just for sex and providing heirs. Not this wife, anyway. So when I get back to England I will be filing for divorce.'

She reached for her wedding ring, struggling to loosen it from her finger.

His hand covered hers. 'Leave it on.

Pulling her hand free, she glared at him. 'Why? I'm not staying married to you, Ralph.'

Tilting his head back, he stared at her in silence. The silence stretched and stretched, and when finally he spoke she could hear a note of exasperation in his voice.

'Enough of this, Giulietta.' His voice rose. *'Enough.'*

He made a gesture that was familiar to her. It was the same gesture he made in a restaurant, when he dismissed a waiter. Like waving away a particularly persistent fly.

'There will be no divorce—as you very well know. You made accusations and you were wrong. But fortunately for you I'm willing to forget your behaviour.'

She gaped at him mutely, a ripple of anger, smooth and hot like lava, snaking sideways across her skin. 'Well, I'm not willing to forget yours,' she said slowly.

His gaze was direct and unwavering. 'Did you not understand anything of what I just told you? I haven't been having an affair—'

'I know.' She cut him off. 'And I'm sorry that I thought you were. But it doesn't make any difference—'

Now he cut her off. 'You're kidding me?' His mouth curved upwards at the corners, but there was nothing humorous about his smile.

As she started to shake her head he pressed his hand against his eyes, as if doing so might change what he was seeing.

'Let me get this right. You spend days accusing me of being

unfaithful with another woman. Not only that, you storm off to England for *five weeks* because you need "space".'

His voice was quiet—soft, even—but it crackled with an authority that made it impossible for her to look away.

'According to you, nothing I say or do matters except the truth. So I tell you the truth. Only now you're saying it makes no difference.'

He practically chewed the words and spat them out at her.

'It doesn't…'

Her heart was racing with panic and pain. He was right. When she'd gone to London she'd thought all she cared about was finding out for certain if he was having an affair. Threatening to divorce him had been the only thing she could think of that would push him into telling the truth.

But in these last few minutes she'd finally accepted that what they'd shared had never been strong enough to survive outside of that small hotel room in Rome.

Marriages needed solid foundations.

They needed transparency and trust.

Ralph didn't trust her, and she sure as hell didn't trust him.

Not with her heart or her future.

Nor could she risk giving him a second chance—not when she knew first-hand how easy it was for that second chance to slip into a third, and then another and another.

But one look at his face told her that trying to explain that to this man would be a fruitless exercise.

'There's no point in trying to do this here…now. Let's leave it to the lawyers.'

Ralph would have access to some of the finest legal brains in the world, but she had everything she needed with her. Her passport was in her handbag. She wanted nothing from the house. Her broken heart was all the reminder she needed of her failed marriage.

As she opened the car door she heard him call her name, sensed him reaching out for her.

But it was too late.

It had always been too late.

Stepping out onto the kerb, she froze, her mouth hanging open. She had been so preoccupied by their conversation that she had barely glanced out of the window during the journey, but naturally she'd assumed they were heading to the airport.

But they were not at the airport.

Nor were they in Verona.

They were at the marina in Venice.

She gazed up at the huge, gleaming white yacht, her skin prickling with shock and disbelief.

Not just any yacht.

Ralph's yacht. The *Alighieri*.

Ralph had got out of the car.

She spun round to face him, a wave of fury cascading through her body. 'You said you were taking me to the airport.'

He shook his head. 'I think you'll find that I didn't. Besides, why would you want to leave now? We're in the middle of a conversation.'

'We are not in the middle of anything. We are at the end,' she snapped.

Her voice was rising, and on the other side of the road a couple of men loading equipment onto another boat turned towards her, their eyes sharp with curiosity.

'So, unless you want me to cause a truly memorable scene that will make your illustrious ancestors roll over in their graves, I suggest you take me back to Verona right now.'

Although she knew there was every chance she would miss her flight…

'That's not going to happen.'

His face was impassive, and his cool, untroubled expression made her want to scream.

Stomach curling with apprehension, she glared at him. 'I'm warning you, Ralph. I won't hold back.'

He stared at her for a long moment, his golden eyes locking with hers. 'Oh, I know, *bella*,' he said softly. 'You're always very vocal…'

She felt her breath catch, her pulse fluttering. Ralph knew exactly how to make her lose control.

Only she didn't need reminding of that now.

'We're not doing this, Ralph,' she said stiffly.

'Really?' He raised one smooth dark eyebrow. 'I thought you weren't going to hold back?'

His eyes gleamed with the satisfaction of having proved a point, and suddenly she hated him more than she had ever hated anyone.

How did he always manage to make it so that she ended up on the wrong foot? If only for once she could get under his skin, make him see red, lose his head, lose control…

But she didn't have to stand here and wait for him to stop playing his silly games. She was perfectly capable of getting herself back to Verona. Alone.

She spun round, but as she started to walk away, he blocked her path.

'We need to talk,' he said softly.

He sounded calm, but there was something flickering in the dark gold gaze. Like a warning beam from a lighthouse. *Danger. Rocks ahead.*

But she was too awash with misery and humiliation to care. 'I gave you a chance to talk and you threw it in my face.' Her eyes narrowed, her body vibrating from the close proximity to his. 'And, frankly, I don't have anything left to say to you,' she hissed.

'That suits me fine.' His voice was infuriatingly calm. 'It means I can talk without interruption.'

And, without missing a beat, he plucked her handbag from her fingers, tossed it to his bodyguard and scooped her up into his arms.

* * *

Gritting his teeth, Ralph ignored his wife's flailing fists and, shifting her body, tipped her over his shoulder.

'Put me down!'

'Oh, I will—just as soon as you're safely on deck.'

She had threatened to make a scene. If that was what she wanted, then that was what she was going to get, he thought savagely, tightening his grip.

'Let me go! You can't do this!'

'Apparently I can,' he said softly.

After he'd stepped on deck he moved swiftly through the boat, nodding briskly at Franco, the skipper, and the crew members.

They reached the master cabin and he walked across the room and dropped her onto the bed.

She swore graphically.

He frowned. 'I'm not sure if that's anatomically possible.'

From somewhere down below a low hum rose up through the boat as the engines started.

Her eyes narrowed as she looked past his shoulder at the open door.

'Don't!' he said warningly.

'Or what?' she raged. 'You're already kidnapping me.'

He shrugged. 'I'm not asking for a ransom, so technically it's more of an abduction—'

As she swore again, he watched her, like a cat with a mouse.

Actually, he thought, this was retribution. It was payback for the hypocrisy of her behaviour. She had no idea what she had put him through these last few weeks, but she was going to find out now.

Her chin lifted pugnaciously, and despite his own simmering anger he couldn't but admire her defiance. And the indignant swell of her high-riding breasts...

'You had this coming, *bella.*'

'Why? For having the temerity to want more than you're offering?'

Fighting an urge to pick her up again and toss her overboard, he narrowed his eyes. Was she serious? Was that what this was about?

'You live in a palace,' he said coolly. 'You have access to a private jet, this yacht, a limousine. You have an unlimited expense account. Do you know what most women would give to have your life?'

'Well, they can have it—and you.' She glared up at him. 'There's more to life and marriage than palaces and private jets, Ralph.'

Yes, there was. A whole lot more.

Her soft brown eyes were muddied with anger and resentment, and the set of her jaw held more or less the same message as her eyes. But, glancing down at her, he felt his heartbeat quicken and his groin tighten.

Probably it was her hair, he thought distractedly. Gone was the smooth chignon. Now her long tawny hair fell about her shoulders in disarray. Like it did in bed. When she rode him. Head thrown back, small upturned breasts bared to his gaze, face taut with the fierce, animal passion that would melt away into surrender at the moment of climax.

He felt his breath catch.

In the time it had taken for his brain to conjure up that picture, his body had hardened as if in a forge, and the speed at which his anger had turned to hunger did little to improve his temper.

Ignoring the ache in his groin, he stared at her steadily. 'Like what?'

She scrambled to her feet, her glossy hair fanning out behind her. 'Like honesty.'

Honesty?

The word vibrated in his head.

Ma che cazzo!

His fingers twitched. He wanted to shake her. Or kiss her. Maybe both.

How could she look him in the eye and talk about honesty? She had been lying to him for months. Not in words, maybe. But in her actions. Pretending that they were trying for a baby when she'd known the whole time that it would never happen.

He took a step towards her. 'I have been honest with you. I have told you about Vittoria.'

And she had no understanding of how hard that had been. How impossible it had been to say the words out loud.

His family were not like other families. The Castellucci name was not just a name, it was a brand. They lived in the public eye. Every birth, marriage and death was given round-the-clock news coverage and everything in between was meticulously managed.

And this scandal would not just be about him, but his entire family.

He had kept the secret to himself to protect the people he loved most in the world and he'd been so careful.

But then Giulietta had seen him with Vittoria. And it hadn't mattered what he'd said—she wouldn't let it go.

She should have trusted him. Like he'd trusted her.

His pulse twitched and he thought about the empty blister packet in his pocket. He'd been carrying it around with him for months now—carrying around the pain and shock of her deceit, waiting to confront her as she had confronted him.

She was staring at him, her lush eyelashes flaring around her widened eyes.

'Only because I made you tell me,' she said.

Her hands were clenched—not into fists, but as if she were trying to hold on to something.

'I don't understand…' The words sounded as if they were caught in her throat. 'You're acting like there's some kind of need-to-know basis and I don't have clearance.'

The catch in her voice snagged at something in his chest. He had hurt her, and he didn't like how that made him feel. But she was wrong. He had been planning to tell her the truth.

Not at the beginning—not when they'd first met in Rome.

Later, though, in those first few months of their marriage, the honeymoon period, he'd fully intended to tell her. Only each time something had happened. First Carlo had been rushed to hospital with a kidney infection, and then Raffaelle had been born by emergency C-section.

For a split second he replayed the moment when he'd noticed the gleam of silver in the bin, remembering his confusion, and then the headrush of shock, the pain of betrayal.

Another betrayal.

And this one worse, somehow, for not being refracted through his father.

After that there had been no way he could trust her with the truth about his parentage.

His throat tightened. He still didn't understand why she'd done it. Why mislead him like that? Why let him think they were trying for a baby?

He thought back to that moment in the hotel when he had seen her holding Raffaelle. It had been like a painting brought to life, everything in the room retreating so that it was just the woman and the child illuminated in the early evening sunlight.

Her gaze had been fixed on Raffaelle's face, her eyes soft with love and longing, and in that moment he had known with absolute conviction that she wanted a baby of her own.

But that meant there was only one possible explanation for why she had been taking the contraceptive pill.

His fingers curled into fists. She didn't want a baby with *him*.

Had that been how his mother had felt about Carlo?

Having realised too late that she'd married the wrong man, had she deliberately chosen to get pregnant? To keep a piece of her lover for herself?

The thought of Giulietta having a baby with another man made him want to smash the cabin to pieces with his bare hands.

'What else is there to know?' he asked. His voice echoed harshly round the room, but anger had stifled all other emotions.

'What else?' she repeated. 'Oh, I don't know, Ralph… How about what you're thinking. What you're feeling.'

His feelings. He felt his chest tighten. *No way.*

To share how it had felt to have his whole life upended, to watch history being redacted and rewritten? His history?

Ever since that day it had felt as if he was walking through a minefield. Every step carried an unseen risk. Nothing was what it seemed. Looking at his reflection, he felt like an imposter. An actor hired to play Ralph Castellucci.

The one constant in this storm of uncertainty should have been Giulietta and the child they would make together. Her child and his. Only now, thanks to his wife, it turned out that his dreams for the future were as shifting and ephemeral as his past.

And now she wanted him to share his feelings.

His jaw tightened. Why shouldn't he let her know what it felt like to be kept in the dark? 'I don't know what benefit that would serve.'

She was staring at him, her eyes blazing.

'But that's not what marriage is about, Ralph. You can't choose which parts of yourself you get to share. We're a couple. We're supposed to share everything—especially the truth.'

'It's good advice.' His eyes locked with hers. 'What a pity you don't apply it to yourself.'

She stared at him, the pulse in her throat leaping against her skin like a startled rabbit. 'I don't know what you're talking about.'

'You don't?' He reached into his pocket. 'Then allow me to refresh your memory.'

Stalking towards her, he tossed the blister pack onto the bed.

'These were in the bin in our bathroom.'

He watched her face stiffen with shock.

'You want to talk about honesty, *bella*? Then perhaps you'd like to explain why you've been *pretending* to try for a baby for months.'

CHAPTER FIVE

JULIET STARED AT Ralph in silence.

Shock was clawing at her, swamping her. Beneath her feet she could feel the *Alighieri* moving smoothly through the lagoon. Soon it would reach the choppier waters of the Adriatic, but she was already adrift and starting to drown in a treacherous sea of her own making.

She tried to speak, but her throat was dry and choked.

Heart pummelling her ribs, she glanced down at the packet. There were empty spaces where the pills had once been and now they gazed back at her like twenty-eight accusing eyes.

In her head, she had rationalised her behaviour. She had got married in haste to a man who had turned from soul mate to stranger in front of her eyes. It had broken her heart, but she'd decided she could, and would, live with her mistake.

But, no matter how badly she'd wanted a baby, she couldn't allow herself to bring a child into the world.

How could she? When every day she had felt herself and Ralph slipping further apart from each other? Watched the pure white brilliance of their love fading into darkness like a dying star?

Only now, faced with his real and justifiable anger, she felt her certainty fade. 'I can explain—'

'You said you wanted a baby.' His eyes narrowed and the cabin seemed to shrink in on her as he took a step closer. 'We talked about it three months ago and we decided that it was the right time. *We* decided that, Giulietta—not me. You said it was what you wanted.'

His hands—those beautiful long-fingered hands that had made pleasure pulse through her body—clenched at his sides. She swallowed past her panic, ripples of guilt spreading out over her skin like the wake from the *Alighieri*.

They had talked about having children.

She could remember the conversation almost word for word. It had been the exact opposite of the conversation they were having now. Easy, smooth-flowing, punctuated by laughter and smiles and kisses. So many kisses... Warm, sweet, soft at first, then more urgent, the heat of his lips demanding a response she had been more than happy to give, her body melting against his...

She pushed the memory away.

'I know I did. And it was what I wanted...' She faltered, her voice dropping.

It still is, she thought, an ache spreading through her chest. Holding Raffaelle at the christening party had been both a joy and an agony. But, if anything, she and Ralph were further apart now than they had ever been—like the earth from the sun at aphelion in its orbit.

He frowned down at her. 'Strange, then, that you would carry on taking a pill whose sole purpose is to stop that happening.'

His voice was rough-sounding, but it was the serrated edge to his gaze that made her skin feel as though it was being flayed from her body.

'I'm sorry.'

She meant it. She'd hated misleading him. But her words sounded meagre and inadequate even to her. As if she was speaking by rote, not from the heart.

Ralph clearly thought so too.

He swore beneath his breath. 'For what?' he asked abruptly. He was staring at her in disbelief, his handsome face harsh in the fading light of the cabin. 'For deceiving me for months? Lying to me?'

Her heart was pounding and she could barely breathe. The diamond ring on her finger felt like a leaden band.

'I didn't lie.'

He stared at her for a long time, as if he didn't know who she was. 'Only because I didn't actually ask if you'd come off the pill,' he said slowly. 'Idiot that I am, I didn't think I needed to. I just assumed you had.' His gaze didn't waver. 'Just out of interest, would you have told me the truth if I'd asked?'

How could she explain?

How could she put into words how she had felt?

The sliding panic, the sense of losing her grip, spinning out of control, and the creeping dread of knowing that she was moments away from impact but powerless to stop it.

To have done so would have meant talking about a life she had not just abandoned, but buried. It would have meant confessing more secrets, more lies—or 'unspoken truths' as she preferred to think of them.

When could she have told him about Juliet Jones? The small, scared, brittle child who had waited in her bedroom for the shouting to stop and waited in the playground, hoping someone would remember to pick her up after school. How could she have explained about living in a house where there had always been alcohol but no food?

She shivered inside.

Talking about it would have made it feel real again, and she couldn't have coped with that. That was why she'd fled to England five weeks ago. To put as much distance as possible between herself and those feelings.

'I don't know,' she said quietly.

There was another silence, thick and heavy like the silence that preceded a storm.

He took a breath, ran a hand over his face, swallowed.

For a moment she thought he was trying to think of a suitable response, but when finally he looked at her again she knew why he'd hesitated.

He hadn't been thinking. He was just too angry to speak. Not just angry, but coldly furious and barely hiding it.

She tried again. 'I didn't mean—'

'Di che diavolo parli!'

This time he swore out loud, and the anger in his voice sliced through the panicky drumroll of her heartbeat.

'"I didn't mean to" doesn't fly in this situation. You were taking a contraceptive pill. Fifty-six pills, in fact. That wasn't an accident or a mistake, Giulietta. It was deliberate.'

A dark flush of anger was highlighting his beautiful curving cheekbones.

'You didn't want to be pregnant.'

He shook his head.

'All these weeks you've been sitting in judgement of me, accusing me of being dishonest, when all the time you were playing me for a fool. You're such a hypocrite.'

Her breath caught in her throat. She took a step backwards, her panic giving way to anger. 'That's not fair,' she said, stung by his words, by their truth and their injustice.

His face was a hard mask. 'No, what's not fair is making me believe there was a chance you might be pregnant when you knew definitively that there couldn't be.'

She flinched inwardly. He was right, but he was ignoring his part in why she'd acted that way.

'I did want a baby when we talked about it.' Her fingers

curled into her palms. 'But then everything changed. You changed.'

Even before she had seen him with Vittoria he had become different. Gone had been the man who had taken her to the Trevi Fountain to watch the sun rise over the city and then produced a breakfast picnic of *maritozzo* and *ciambella* with fresh cherries.

They hadn't been able to get enough of each other...

But then everything had begun to change. Her husband had never been at home, and when he had been they'd hardly spoken.

His eyes were dark with frustration. 'So it's my fault you lied?'

She stared at him. 'No, that's not what I'm saying. I'm trying to tell you how it was. How we ended up like this.'

Her voice was rising now, and the tension and unhappiness of the last few weeks was enveloping her. It felt as if she was playing snakes and ladders—a game she loathed. Every time they seemed to be getting somewhere she landed on a snake and went slipping back to the start.

They would never sort this out.

The only way they had ever managed to communicate successfully was physically.

But sex couldn't resolve anything but lust.

Nor would having a baby tackle the raw emotions and complex issues they'd spent months circumnavigating.

A lump formed in her throat. 'You're not the man I married, Ralph.'

The silence tautened between them. Heart pounding, she watched his shoulders tense. There was a strange light in his eyes and his breathing wasn't quite steady.

'Finally,' he said quietly, 'we have something we can agree on.'

And before she could react, much less form a sentence, he turned and strode through the door.

Walking back through the boat, Ralph thought his hammering heart was going to break through his ribcage. He had waited so long to confront Giulietta, only nothing had gone according to plan. In fact, he couldn't have handled it any worse if he'd set out to do so.

In his head he'd played out various scenarios, and in all of them he'd stayed calm, coolly presenting the facts of her betrayal like a prosecuting lawyer. But the last forty-eight hours had made staying cool an impossibility.

His shoulders tensed.

More specifically, *his wife* had made staying cool impossible on so many levels.

He wasn't sure if it was her continued insistence that they get a divorce or the fact that after five weeks of abstinence his body was in a state of almost permanent discomfort, but as he'd carried her on board all his good intentions had been swept away by a toppling wave of anger.

It had been like nothing he'd ever known—a feeling so pure and absolute it had wiped out everything: all dignity and decorum and understanding.

His chest tightened.

He'd wanted answers, not a screaming match. He'd failed on both counts.

His stomach was tight, and aching as if he was hungry, but when he walked out onto the spacious on-deck lounge area he headed to the bar.

Leaning over the marble countertop, he reached for a bottle of his favourite whisky—a thirty-year-old single malt Laphroaig.

But maybe he should eat.

He glanced at the intercom. It would be no trouble to call downstairs and get the chef to prepare him a light supper. Then again, after his performance earlier the crew were probably hiding in the lifeboats.

And he also knew the ache in his stomach had nothing to do with lack of food. It had been there since Giulietta had fled from the *palazzo*.

Pushing aside the memory of that night, he snatched up a

tumbler and made his way over to one of the huge sofas. His wife might be the most infuriating woman on the planet, but he wasn't quite at the necking-it-from-the-bottle stage yet.

He unscrewed the top of the bottle, poured out two fingers of whisky and drank it in one gulp. It was a crime not to savour it, but right now he needed the hit of alcohol to dull his senses and the feeling of failure.

Then, maybe, he might be able to think about—

He frowned. What was it she had said? Oh, yes—how they had ended up like this.

Gritting his teeth, he poured another glass. This time, though, he rested it on the arm of the sofa.

Who was it who had said that people lost things that they wanted to lose? For him, meeting Giulietta in Rome had been the opposite. He had found the one woman he'd wanted to find.

Beautiful, smart, and free from the expectations of the world he lived in, she had wanted him for himself. Not for his wealth or his name or his connections. For her, he had been enough.

Or so he'd thought.

He still couldn't accept that he had got it wrong. But it wasn't just up to him.

His fingers tightened around the glass and he had to stop himself from tipping the contents down his throat.

'You're not the man I married.'

He breathed out unsteadily, her words replaying in his head. Had he changed? Yes and no.

When they'd met in Rome it had been a little over five months since his mother's deathbed confession. Six months since Vittoria had come to the house and tearfully confronted him with the letters she'd found.

His heart began beating faster. Love letters from *his* mother, Francesca, to *her* father, Niccolò. Intense, passion-filled letters that he'd struggled to read but found impossible to ignore. Particularly the one in which she begged Niccolò to meet her so that she could tell him her news.

At first his mother had refused to discuss it. It had only been in those last few days that she had finally confirmed what was hinted at in the letters.

Niccolò, not Carlo, was his father.

His mouth twisted.

And ever since then he'd been trying to decide what to do next. That was what the trip to Rome had been about. Getting some space from the family, from Verona, from the life that had been mapped out for him as heir-in-waiting to the Castellucci empire.

He'd wanted—needed—to do the right thing. The trouble was that then he hadn't been sure what that was. He still wasn't.

Saying nothing to Carlo was the simplest option—only that would mean living a lie for the rest of his life.

On the other hand, telling the truth would have devastating consequences.

The Castellucci name would be lost. Worse, the man who had raised him from birth and earned the right to be called his father would be without a son and heir.

Picking up his glass, he took a sip, holding the whisky in his mouth to savour the smoky, peaty flavour, the hint of lime and the salty sharp cleanness.

Ever since birth he'd been surrounded by family. Five hundred years of history flowed through his veins and the progression of his life had had an almost mathematical certainty to it.

But suddenly he'd never felt more alone, more hesitant, more unsure of himself.

And then he'd met Giulietta, and he'd seen a way forward to a shared future with a family that would share his own bloodline.

Closing his eyes, he blew out a breath.

'Is that a good idea?'

His heart kicked against his ribs and, opening his eyes, he glanced across the deck to where his wife was hovering by the bar. She was still wearing the cherry-patterned dress, but she had taken off her make-up and her feet were bare.

So she could run away faster? he thought, his pulse accelerating.

Aware that one wrong word would send her storming back to her cabin, he raised an eyebrow. 'Breathing?' He raised an eyebrow questioningly. 'I suppose that depends on if you'd rather be a widow or a divorcee.'

'I was talking about the whisky.'

As she took a step forward into the light he saw that she wasn't smiling. But she hadn't walked away. He watched her in silence, waiting...

'I'm sorry,' she said quietly. 'For what I said before. About you. I wasn't talking about Carlo not being your father.'

His fingers pressed against the glass. Hearing the truth spoken out loud made it suddenly shockingly real. And yet somehow it was a relief to finally admit even a fragment of his feelings.

He held her gaze. 'It's a bit of a sensitive subject.'

She bit her lip. 'And I'm sorry for not telling you I was still on the pill. I didn't plan to keep taking it,' she said slowly. 'I was going to stop when I came to the end of the cycle. Only then Carlo was ill—' She stopped.

'I remember.'

It had been less than a year after his mother's death. Carlo had been taken to the same hospital where she'd died. For over a week he'd been stricken with fear that he would lose his father too, and torn over whether to tell him the truth.

'Things were difficult.'

Looking back, he knew that he'd been distracted, distant—not just emotionally, but physically, in that he'd often stayed overnight at the hospital in case...

His throat tightened.

But he hadn't just been worried about Carlo. The thought of losing his father had made his plan to start a family of his own seem even more important—urgent, in fact. He hadn't meant it to, but it had taken over everything.

'It's been a long day.' Tilting his head back, he kept his voice steady and walked over to the bar. 'Why don't you join me?'

He had meant it innocently enough but, looking over at her, he saw that his remark had backfired.

'So that's it, is it?' she asked. 'We're just going to sit down and hit the bottle? I thought you wanted to talk.'

Her hands were clenched at her sides, and her glorious eyes were flashing with poorly concealed irritation.

'I mean, that *is* why you dragged me here in the first place, so I would have thought the least you could do is not walk off in the middle of a conversation,' she said hotly.

'Really? I could have sworn you said we were at the end of everything,' he said slowly.

'Don't get smart with me, Ralph.'

Her chin was jutting forward, and with her bare feet and her clenched fists she reminded him again of that cat he'd pulled from the storm drain. His finger brushed against the puckered skin where it had bitten him. What little patience he'd started the day with had almost completely gone.

'Oh, I'm not smart, *bella.* If I were I wouldn't have been hoodwinked by you into thinking you wanted a baby.'

He heard her breath hitch.

'I did want a baby. But babies aren't just an accessory.' Her eyes darted to his wrist. 'They're not some expensive watch. They're tiny little humans with feelings. They need love and security.'

'Are you seriously suggesting I wouldn't love my child?'

She raised her chin. '*Our* child, Ralph. Not yours—ours.' Her gaze locked with his. 'But I don't count, do I? That's the bottom line here.'

The gentle slap of the waves against the boat's hull filled the sudden silence on deck. Far out at sea, the sun was slipping beneath the horizon, the daylight transmuting into darkness.

'You're being foolish.'

She was impossible. Stubborn. Difficult. And scared.

A thought jolted him.

Just like his mother had been.

His shoulders tensed. He'd read those letters and he knew how trapped Francesca had felt in the first few months of her marriage to Carlo. Like Giulietta, she had fled. But not from the country. Instead she had sought comfort in the bed of Niccolò Farnese.

The idea that history might repeat itself—that he might drive his wife into the arms of another man—filled him with a fear and anger he found difficult to control. Anger with her, but mostly with himself.

He'd been a fool not to follow her to England.

A muscle bunched in his jaw. This time he wouldn't let her escape.

She took a step towards him, her hair spilling over her shoulders. 'No, this is foolish. Us trying to make our marriage work.'

His eyes clashed with hers. 'Our marriage worked just fine until you started making false accusations.'

'How can you say that? Our marriage was in pieces. That's why I thought you were having an affair.' She breathed out shakily. 'You were never there. You were either working or on this bloody boat.'

It was true. His father's illness had given him new responsibilities over the family's various charitable foundations, and, of course, he had to look after his aunts and his cousins.

And all the time, at every board meeting or lunch with his aunts, he'd felt a creeping sense of guilt...of being a fraud.

He glanced across the smooth wooden deck. It had only been here, on the *Alighieri*, that he'd felt 'at home'. Here, drifting out at sea, the rootlessness he'd felt on land had seemed to dissipate.

'I found it hard...being in Verona.'

She was staring at him in silence, and he realised that he had spoken out loud.

* * *

Juliet felt her breath catch. His words had startled her. Not their meaning, but their directness.

For weeks now they had been butting heads metaphorically. Or rather she had been butting her head against the brick wall of Ralph's refusal to discuss anything.

Looking up at his face now, she felt her heart contract. He looked tense, troubled, his features tight, and she felt some of her anger fade. 'You were upset.'

Doubly upset, she thought with a pang of guilt.

It would have been unbearable for him to see his father so ill, and so soon after his mother's death. And, of course, he'd also been carrying around the burden of when—*whether*—to tell Carlo the truth.

Ralph might seem strong and unbreakable, but she knew that the worst wounds were the ones beneath the surface.

His eyes found hers. 'I should have told you about my father.' He hesitated. 'I was going to, only then I found the pills, and you saw Vittoria with me, and everything got out of hand.'

And she had fled to England.

It was such a mess. All of it. And it was a mess of their own making. Both of them had held back when they should have opened up with each other.

A lump filled her throat. She felt suddenly helpless—the same kind of helpless she had felt as a child, when everything had been beyond her control. When nothing she'd said or done had seemed to make any difference to her situation.

She held her breath, held on to the panic rising in her chest. It was ironic but the only time she'd felt in control of her life had been with Ralph in Rome—before he'd even proposed to her, when they had been nothing more than lovers.

Except that 'nothing more' made it sound ordinary or just adequate, when in fact their being lovers had been the purest state of all.

Her hands felt clammy. And they had ruined it by rushing into marriage.

She turned to him and said, a little breathlessly, 'Has it ever crossed your mind that this can't be fixed?'

He stared at her for a long moment, and then he shook his head. 'We'll get through it,' he said.

'How?' She felt angry tears prickle her eyes. 'How can we get through this? Everything is wrong between us. Nothing works.'

She felt her heart thud against her ribs. He was standing so close she could feel the heat of his skin, see the heat in his gaze.

There was a long, burning silence.

'Not true,' he said softly. His eyes were fixed on her mouth, and they lingered a moment before rising to meet hers.

The sea was smooth, and beneath her bare feet the smooth wooden deck was solid, but suddenly she was fighting to retain her balance.

'Giulietta…'

He spoke her name gently. His hand when he touched her face was even more gentle. She was afraid to move, almost afraid to breathe. But the temptation to move closer, to touch and trace the shape of his beautiful mouth, made her shake inside.

'Giulietta…'

This time when he spoke her name his fingers slid through her hair, moving with a caressing slowness that stalled her heartbeat. His hands were tangling through her hair and he was tilting her head back, slanting his mouth over hers. She felt something unfurl inside her, like a flower opening its petals towards the sun, as she waited for his kiss.

His lips brushed against hers, their warm breath mingled, and then she leaned in closer, her mouth finding his, unable to tear herself away.

'Trust me, *bella*,' he whispered. 'We work.'

She felt his mouth drop to her neck, to the shadowed hollow at the base of her throat. *We.* That word again. Only this time she was honest with herself—could admit that she had come back to Verona not just for the christening but for this.

For him.

For the touch of his hands and the soft press of his lips on hers.

Head spinning, she stared at him. And then she ran her tongue along his lips.

He made a rough sound, half-growl, half-groan, and then, reaching down his hands, cupped her bottom and lifted her in one movement and carried her to the sofa. He laid her down and, lowering his head, took her mouth again.

'Ho voglia di scoparti qui adesso,' he said hoarsely.

She wanted him too and, reaching up, she clasped his face in her hands and pressed a frantic kiss to his mouth, her teeth catching against his lips.

He leaned into her and she felt the hard press of his erection against the softness of her belly. A moan rose in her throat. Sliding her arms over his shoulders, she pulled him closer, arching her spine, pushing her pelvis upwards, squirming against him, trying to ease the ache that was throbbing between her thighs.

He was reaching for the zip of her dress, but she batted his hand away. She didn't want to wait. She wanted it to be just like it had been in Rome that first time, when they had done it standing up against the bedroom door with his body supporting hers.

'I need you now,' she whispered.

Encircling her waist with his arm, he raised her slightly, and her body clenched as he slid his hand beneath her panties and drew them down over her bare legs. She whimpered, and his mouth found hers and he kissed her thoroughly, his tongue pushing deep into her mouth.

And then she was pulling him closer, her nipples brushing against the hard muscles of his chest, fingers tugging at his zip. Pulling him free, she tightened her hand around him and felt his control snap.

Holding her firmly, he thrust inside her, and she cried out in shock and relief as he began to move.

Her eyes closed. Heat was uncurling inside her, faster and faster, in time with his hips, and she was wrapping her legs around him, holding him close, her hands gripping his shoulders, her body convulsing around him as he erupted inside her with hot, liquid force.

CHAPTER SIX

RALPH WOKE WITH a start, his heart racing, muscles stretched taut. Opening his eyes, he stared around the cabin. It was still dark, but there was a silvery opalescence in the air and he guessed that it was not quite dawn.

For a minute or so he steadied himself, willing the panic to recede. Finally, he managed to breathe. He felt as though he'd been fighting, but it was just a dream. The same vivid dream, part nightmare, part panic attack, that had woken him on and off since his mother had told him the truth about his father.

A dream that seemed to be getting more intense, more vivid, more terrifying...

It always started the same way, with him walking into the Palazzo Gioacchino after work. Everything looked normal— except his mother was still alive and he could hear her and Carlo talking in the drawing room.

But when he walked into the room his father was alone, and instead of welcoming him home Carlo said, 'You shouldn't be here. You're not my son.'

His fingers tightened against the sheet, the memory of the

terror and the guilt pressing down on his ribs. So far, so familiar—but then this time in his dream his father had turned into Giulietta, who had shaken her head and said, 'You shouldn't be here. You're not my husband.'

From somewhere outside the sharp cry of a gull cut through his heartbeat and he felt a rush of relief, for even though he knew it was just a dream it had felt paralysingly real.

Beside him, he felt Giulietta shift in her sleep, and his body tensed as she rolled towards him. But as she settled against him he felt some of his tension ease.

It was called 'grounding'. Using something solid and certain to pull yourself back to reality.

And Giulietta was real. He could feel the heat of her body and the steady beat of her heart, her breath against his bare chest.

*S*he was real and she was here with him.

Against her will?

His hands clenched and then he breathed out slowly. On the boat, yes. But in his bed, no.

His groin tightened at the memory of her touch. It had been almost a rerun of that first time in Rome. There had been no time to savour any preliminaries, no slow, teasing exploration. They hadn't even taken off their clothes. It had been raw and urgent and necessary—a consummation of desire. She had wanted him as much as he'd wanted her.

But last night had to be more than just some mechanical satisfying of hunger.

Why else would she have led him back to this cabin? To this bed.

Thinking back to the moment before they'd kissed, he felt his breathing slow.

He had brought her onto the *Alighieri* wanting answers, wanting to punish her for her hypocrisy, for running away, for deceiving him, for wanting to abandon their marriage.

They had already argued twice—once in the car and then again after he'd tossed onto the bed in their cabin. But neither round had ended satisfactorily, and they had been squaring up to one another again, both of them simmering with rage and frustration.

And then she had looked up into his face and he had seen not just her anger, but her fear.

Her confusion.

Her uncertainty.

It had shaken him, for he understood all those feelings.

And somehow, in his understanding, the bitterness and all the *misunderstandings* of their shared history had dissolved, and they had come together as man and wife. Equals in the face of a shared and potent sexual attraction.

They had made love again and again. In the past, perhaps even in that moment, he would have told himself that sex—the one-of-a-kind sort of sex they shared, anyway—was enough. Should be enough to smooth the tensions in their relationship.

He knew now that it wasn't.

Trust was the issue here.

Giulietta's behaviour had surprised and angered him, and there was still a degree of anger beneath the surface. But the spark of his anger had been lit before they even met.

It had started to flicker way back, when his mother had first told him that Carlo was not his father and his place in the world, the person he'd believed himself to be, had vanished.

A pale pinkish-yellow light was filtering into the cabin now and, gazing down at her sleeping face, he felt his jaw tighten.

It was easy to understand the mistakes he'd made.

Betrayed by the past, feeling trapped in a present where he was torn between continuing to live a lie or ruining the lives of those he loved most by telling the truth, he had become fixated on the future. On having a child.

Only by not telling Giulietta the truth he had forfeited her trust and self-sabotaged his right to the baby he craved so badly.

It was all such a mess of lies and half-truths and secrets.

His body tensed.

And he was still holding back.

Understandably. Trust worked both ways.

And, yes, it didn't sit well with him, the part he'd played in making Giulietta think that her only option was to flee. But the fact was she had chosen to abandon him instead of fighting for their marriage.

His chest felt tight. It had been humiliating, trying to explain her absence to his family and their friends, and the threat of scandal had been the last thing he'd needed.

She moved against him again, her hand splaying out over his stomach, and he felt a kick of desire just below where her fingers lay twitching against his skin. He ached to pull her closer, to caress and kiss her awake.

It was an admission of sorts, her being here. Only he would be a fool to think that last night had resolved anything except a mutual sexual hunger.

She might be back in his bed, but he wanted her back in his life.

For good.

So he needed to work out how to persuade her that last night hadn't just been a one-off sexual encounter but the first step in their reconciliation.

Feeling calmer, he curved his arm around her waist, anchoring her against his body as he drifted back to sleep.

When he woke again, the bed was empty.

Rolling over, he picked up the remote control by the bed and opened the blinds, blinking as daylight flooded the cabin. It was a perfect day. In the flawless blue sky an apricot sun was already warming the air.

He glanced across the rumpled sheets, his pulse out of sync with his breathing. But where was his wife?

His shoulders tensed, and a rush of irritation flared over his skin. Did she really think she could run from this—from him?

His body had sung at her touch, and he knew he had made her feel the same way, but still she seemed bent on denying that fact.

It took him longer than he'd expected to track her down. She wasn't eating breakfast in the sunshine, or relaxing by the pool. Instead, he found her on the top deck.

He stopped in the doorway, his stomach clenching. Giulietta was less than five feet away. She was wearing peach-coloured shorts and a loose vest with a crossover back. Her hair was in a high ponytail and he could see the gleam of sweat on the lightly tanned skin of her shoulders.

But it was not her hair or her clothes or even her skin that made his breath catch.

It was her pose.

She was on her knees, leaning forward, with her arms stretched straight ahead and her bottom raised as though in supplication or surrender.

He knew it was a perfectly legitimate yoga position, designed to stretch the spine in both directions. But, predictably, it still took his brain less than three seconds to come up with a modified version of the same pose...this time involving him as well.

Pulse quickening, he found his eyes snagged on the cleft of her buttocks, and he struggled silently against the urge to reach and caress her there, as he had done only hours earlier.

He hadn't thought he'd made any noise... But maybe she had the same inbuilt radar as he did when it came to sensing each other's presence, because the muscles in her back and legs suddenly stiffened, like a deer catching the scent of a predator.

There was a stretch of silence as she rolled up her spine and sat back on her haunches, and then she stood up in one smooth movement and turned to face him.

He stepped out into the light. *'Buongiorno,'* he said softly. 'Or should I say *namaste?'*

The fringe of her dark lashes fluttered as she tilted her head back, her mouth moving into an approximation of a smile. *'Buongiorno* is fine.'

His fingers twitched. Last night he had felt as if she was his again, and it was tempting to reach out and pull her close, take her mouth with his. But, despite the clamour of his pulse, he stayed where he was.

'That pose looked familiar. It was the Melting Heart, wasn't it?'

She nodded slowly but, judging by the wary expression on her face, her heart hadn't been similarly affected by last night's encounter.

'That's one of the names for it. My teacher calls it the *ana-hatasana*. It's supposed to be good for tension.'

His eyes rested on her set, pale face. In that case, it wasn't working. She looked tense—nervous, even—and he was pretty sure he knew the reason why. It was the same reason she had not stayed in bed and waited for him to wake this morning.

Clearly they needed to talk about last night.

But they were on a boat in the middle of the Adriatic. Here, they were unmoored from the landlocked constraints of time. Surely he could wait a few moments?

Besides, he thought, as the smell of freshly brewed coffee drifted up from somewhere on board, he'd realised he was ravenously hungry.

'I'm guessing you haven't eaten,' he said slowly. 'Why don't you go and shower? Then we can get some breakfast.'

Fifteen minutes later she joined him on deck. She had changed her clothes, and her hair was still damp from the shower, but the wariness of her expression hadn't changed.

Keeping his expression intentionally bland, he waited while she served herself some fruit and muesli. 'Tea or coffee?' he asked.

'Tea, please.'

Leaning forward, he poured out the tea and added milk, his gaze drifting over the toned curves of her shoulders and arms. He liked what she was wearing. The sleeveless white shirt knotted at her waist and the flirty printed skirt reminded him of some Hitchcock heroine—Grace Kelly or Eva Marie Saint, maybe.

Except he couldn't imagine his wife as a cool, glacial blonde. She was too easy to stir to passion. And to anger.

Impulsively he leaned forward and tucked a stray tortoise-shell curl behind her ear. He felt her tense and, watching the flurry of conflicting emotions chase across her face, he felt his own body tighten too.

It was always there, simmering beneath the surface. One touch was all it took to remind both of them. The difference was she was still fighting it.

Lowering his hand, he leaned back in his seat. 'This is all very civilised,' he said softly.

Her eyes flickered up to meet his. 'You know what would be even more civilised? You turning the *Alighieri* round and taking me back to Venice.'

He held her gaze, letting the silence that followed her remark drift into the warm air.

Her lip curled. 'Doesn't it matter to you that I don't want this?'

'To be on the boat?'

'To be with you anywhere,' she snapped.

He let the silence that followed her remark deliberately lengthen. Then, 'In that case, I think now might be a good time to talk about what happened last night.'

Not just last night, Juliet thought, feeling heat feather her cheeks and her throat. They had reached for one another again and again as night had slipped into a new day.

She felt her pulse stumble.

How could she describe what had happened last night? It had been both inevitable and yet miraculous. Like adding potassium to water and standing back to watch it explode.

She didn't remember falling asleep, and when she'd woken she had momentarily thought that the warm pressure of Ralph's body next to hers was just a dream—some kind of hyper-realistic wish-fulfilment fantasy.

But of course it had been all too real.

She stared at him in silence. Even if she had any it was too late for regrets. But how could anyone regret such blissful sensual fulfilment?

Shifting in her seat, she thought back to the moment when she had finally stopped fighting the inevitable. Except that made her sound passive. Made it sound as if he had plundered her against her will like the heroine of some old Regency romance novel, when in fact their desire had been mutual.

She had matched his hunger. Shaking with eagerness, she had kissed him, pulled him hard against her and inside her aching body. It was she who had led him to their cabin.

It had been a fast and urgent no-holds-barred mating. With mouths, hands, reaching unashamedly for one another, bodies responding to an impulse as old as time.

And it had felt so good.

Glancing across the table, she felt her skin twitch as she remembered what lay beneath that pale blue striped knitted polo shirt and those faded linen shorts.

He had felt so good.

Hard where she was soft, his muscles smooth and taut, his skin warm and sleek. And she had wanted all of him. Skin on skin, the unthinkable freedom to taste, to touch, to savour the teasing, the slow foreplay and the swift passion.

Her eyes dropped to the deck. During her five weeks of self-inflicted celibacy she'd thought she was learning to live without him. She'd been wrong.

But it didn't matter how much she craved him, she was going to have to try harder to learn that particular lesson.

Her shoulders tightened as the words she'd thrown at him last night bumped into one another inside her head.

'Everything is wrong between us. Nothing works.'

He had proved his point: on one level they worked perfectly.

But to acknowledge that Ralph had the power to render her boneless with desire was to prove another point entirely. That sex was both the cure and the cause of their marital problems—an irresistible quick fix for when words failed as a means of communication.

A slow fix too, she thought, her cheeks heating as she remembered what had happened when they'd finally reached the cabin. Kisses had become caresses and their anger had grown formless, transfigured into passion of a different kind that overcame everything.

Last night's encounter was all part of the pattern of behaviour that had characterised their relationship from the start. It was hardly the basis for a good marriage. And as for having a baby—

Her heart jerked to a halt as a new, devastating thought barged to the front of her mind.

Around her, the warm air pulsed like a bass guitar at a rock concert and she gripped the arms of her chair. She felt suddenly breathless, dizzy, and something of what she was feeling must have shown in her face because he started to shake his head.

'Let me guess,' he said slowly. 'You're going to tell me that what happened was a mistake. That it means nothing and that it won't happen again.'

Actually, she wasn't.

A knot of panic was unravelling inside her chest.

So many times in the past she'd questioned how her mother could have made so many mistakes.

Now she knew.

She stared at him, not trusting herself to speak.

But she couldn't lie. Not after everything they had been through these last months. Not about this.

Her eyes found his. 'I'm not on the pill any more,' she said slowly. 'I stopped taking it just before I went back to England...' Her voice trailed away into silence.

She'd been in such a state—upset, angry, both hating him and missing him. When her period had finished it had felt like fate forcing her to choose a future.

Dazedly, she did some calculations in her head. *It might be okay...*

Heart pounding, she did the calculations once more. *Then again, it might not.*

'I'm about twelve days into my cycle.' *Make that thirteen this morning*, she corrected silently.

He was staring at her, his eyes steady, but she could sense his mind working swiftly through the implications of her words.

'You're saying you could be pregnant.'

He put the emphasis on 'could', but she still felt her pulse accelerate.

Yes, that was what she was saying. And, despite her panic, a shot of pure, shimmering happiness, bright as sunshine, more intoxicating than prosecco, flooded her veins.

She nodded. 'I don't know the odds, but it's definitely possible.'

Her heart thudded. She sounded like some clueless teenager. Worse—she sounded like her mother.

A cool spiderweb of shame wound over her skin. She'd spent so many years trying not to be Nancy Jones, smugly believing herself to be smarter, more stable, better... But she was worse. At least her mother had been only a teenager when she'd had unprotected sex and got pregnant.

She was twenty-five.

There was no excuse for behaving so irresponsibly.

But it had been so fast she hadn't been thinking straight. Truthfully, safe sex had been the last thing on her mind. Fast sex, slow sex, urgent sex, tender sex—but not safe sex.

His expression was unreadable. 'Why did you come off the pill?'

'I don't know.' How was she supposed to explain the chaotic, topsy-turvy flow of her thoughts back then? 'I suppose because I didn't think I needed to be on it any more.'

She watched his face harden infinitesimally, her stomach churning. More implied meanings...more unspoken truths.

'And if you are pregnant?'

His Italian accent was stronger now, muddying his vowels and softening his voice, and she felt her body start to hum beneath his steady gaze.

'Then we'll be having a baby—'

Her words stalled. It was still what she wanted, despite everything. Only it terrified her too—the idea that she might have replicated her own haphazard conception.

'You know nothing would make me happier if you were.'

He was staring at her, and his golden eyes were so incredibly gentle that it was all she could do not to cry. It was too easy to remember their shared hope in those few months of their marriage. Only so much had happened…so much had been revealed as fragile and illusory.

'I might not be,' she said quickly.

The silence stretched away from them, across the sparkling blue sea.

'There's only one way to find out for sure.'

Pushing back his seat, he stood up and pulled out his phone. She watched him walk away, nerves twisting in her throat, and then she stood up too. It was impossible to stay sitting. Her heart felt as though it might burst through her chest.

Trying to steady her breathing, she walked across the deck and braced herself against the handrail, her gaze fixed on the rippling jewel-coloured water.

She should never have come back to Verona. Then none of this would be happening.

Her whole body tensed.

Except then she might not be possibly pregnant, and even now, when she was awash with panic, she felt not just love but a yearning for the baby that might already be embedding itself inside her.

Her heartbeat stuttered as she remembered that moment at the christening when Luca had reached for Lucia, wrapping his arms around her and Raffaelle. Around them guests had stood chatting and laughing, and waiters had offered prosecco and canapés, but they'd had everything they needed.

She held her breath, feeling a tug in her belly like a magnet, and on its heels a swift, shameful envy at being untrammelled by doubt.

Her throat burned with tears.

But that was the difference. Lucia and Luca were meant to be together. They did not and never would know what it felt like to have a child with the wrong person. Or to be that child.

And what if she couldn't pull off being a mother?

The thought stabbed at her. She had tried and failed to be a good daughter and wife—why would being a mother be any different?

'That's sorted.'

His mood had shifted like the breeze coming off the water. The softness had faded from his eyes and his voice had the familiar cool authority of a man used to snapping his fingers and getting his own way.

Her fingers tightened against the cool metal. Abruptly, she turned and faced him, her chin jutting out. 'What are you talking about?'

'That was Dr de Masi. I've made an appointment at her clinic. She says she can do a pregnancy test when you come in.' His gaze held hers. 'Apparently you can do one as early as eight days after conception.'

Eight days.

So soon.

Needing to stop the panic rising in her throat, she resorted to anger. 'And that sorts everything out, does it?' She shook her head. 'Either I'm pregnant or I'm not and then life goes on?'

His gaze didn't shift from hers. 'That's not fair,' he said quietly.

It wasn't. But knowing that only made her feel more defensive.

'Yes, it is.' She couldn't stop the bitterness entering her voice. 'I know you, Ralph.'

'Clearly not.' Taking a step towards her, he caught her wrists, eyes locking with hers. 'If you did, you would know that I wasn't for one moment suggesting that life will just "carry on". But we do need to find out if you're pregnant.'

Her heartbeat stumbled. She couldn't fault the simple logic of his statement. Or his motives for contacting Dr de Masi. Monica de Masi was the obstetrician of choice for wealthy Veronese families. She had met her once and liked her.

But something inside her baulked at the idea of her and Ralph going to the clinic. It made it feel as if this was something they'd planned together as a couple, when actually the reverse was true.

'Can't we just get one of those tests you buy at a pharmacy?' she said, tugging free of his grip.

Their eyes met.

'The Clinica Filomena has an excellent reputation,' he said smoothly. 'And if the test is positive then we will have expert care on hand to advise us and answer questions.'

That was true—and again she couldn't fault his logic. But she knew that the real reason Ralph wanted to go to the clinic had nothing to do with expert care and advice.

He didn't trust her to tell him the truth.

Her fingers curled into fists, guilt and regret jabbing at her. She couldn't blame him. Certainly if their positions had been reversed she would have felt and acted the same way.

Only it hurt.

Not just the fact that he felt that way, but the fact that her actions had let distrust and doubt colour what might be the first few hours of their baby's life.

'I don't just want to buy some kit from the pharmacy,' he said quietly. 'I want to do this properly.'

She bit her lip. 'How can we do that? We've just blundered into it.'

Her mind twisted and turned away from the thought of her own careless conception. She knew that the setting had been somewhat shabbier—a bathroom at a raucous house party rather than a floating palace—but the occasion had shared the same reckless mix of sex and stupidity as her encounter with Ralph.

It made her feel sick.

'I was irresponsible and you were ignorant,' she said flatly.

Ralph's face was expressionless, and then a flicker of frustration crossed it. 'That's one way of looking at it,' he said. 'The other is that we wanted each other. Absolutely and unconditionally.' His thumbs bit into her shoulders. 'Do you know how rare that is, Giulietta? How incredible?'

Despite herself, she felt his words reach down deep inside her. Even now her body still sang from his touch. But that kind of passion carried a sting in the tail.

'It's not that rare.' Her mouth trembled. 'My parents felt like that every single time they had sex.'

She was talking too loudly, and too fast, and she wanted to stop but couldn't seem to call a halt. It was as if the words were like oil gushing from an uncapped well.

'It was what kept them together for so many years—even though their relationship was a disaster and they were completely wrong for one another.'

Ralph heard the break in her voice. It matched the one in his heart.

The thought that Giulietta could be carrying a child... their child...almost undid him. It was what he'd wanted for so long—ever since his mother's bombshell confession had cast him adrift.

It had been a double loss. Losing his mother and learning the truth about his father. He'd been numb with grief...eating standing up, barely sleeping.

It had only been after the funeral that he had been able to register the full extent of the damage, and in those terrible, endless, unnumbered days his life had collapsed like a house of cards.

Everything he'd taken for granted—familial bonds, ancestors stretching back five hundred years, a name that not only opened doors but took them off their hinges—all of it had been proved false.

He'd realised that the gleaming palace of his life had been built on the frailest of foundations. On his ignorance of the truth. But the instant that Giulietta had told him she might be pregnant he had felt as if an anchor had dropped to the seabed.

Not to know for certain was killing him.

He glanced over at her face, but she wouldn't meet his eyes.

Only he knew this wasn't just about him. Or even the possibility that she was pregnant.

He could see there was an exhaustion beneath her panic, as though she had been struggling with something for a long time. *Struggling alone.*

The thought jolted him.

He knew very little about her family or her background. So little, in fact, that what she had told him could be summed up in three sentences.

Her parents were separated.

When her mother had struggled to cope she had been placed with foster parents.

She had left home at sixteen and got a live-in job in the kitchen of a country house hotel.

At the time he hadn't given her reticence much thought. He'd been too distracted by his own unravelling family tree. But clearly it was the parts she'd edited out that mattered most.

Keeping his voice even, he said carefully, 'How long did they stay together?'

She hesitated, then shrugged. 'On and off for about ten years.'

Her eyes were still avoiding his. 'A decade is a long time to stay together,' he said quietly. 'Surely there must have been more to their relationship than sex.'

'There was.' Now she looked at him. 'There was anger. And resentment. And endless misunderstandings. But everything started and ended with sex.' She cleared her throat. 'You know, for a long time I thought that was what people meant by "fore-play"—arguing, making accusations, storming off.'

He heard her swallow.

'I wasn't planned. My parents barely knew each other when my mum got pregnant.'

Her shoulders were braced, limbs taut like a sprinter on the starting blocks, and he wanted to reach out and pull her close, smooth the tension from her body. But he didn't want her to run from him again.

'It was a disaster. They should never have been together. They certainly shouldn't have had a child. And I didn't want to be like them... I didn't want us to be like them. Only it's happened anyway.'

The ache in her voice swallowed him whole. For a few half-seconds he thought about the fears he'd kept hidden, and then he stopped thinking and caught her by the shoulders.

Her body tensed and she jerked against his hands, but he held her still. 'None of us get to choose our parents, *bella*. We don't get to choose how or when or where we're conceived.'

She stopped struggling.

'But we can choose how to live our lives—and you and I... we're not like your parents or mine. And we don't have to make a binary choice between fighting and breaking up.'

Watching her eyes widen, he steadied himself, and just for a moment he considered telling her more about his mother's affair.

But he couldn't bring himself to do so.

Instead, he captured her chin and tilted her face up so that she had to meet his gaze. 'We're going to do this our way, Giulietta. And whatever it takes I'll make it work. I promise.'

Her hands clenched. 'It's not that simple, Ralph.'

'Sure it is.' He spoke with a calmness he didn't feel. 'We go to the clinic. You take the test. And—'

'And then what?'

'I don't know,' he said simply. 'I don't have all the answers. But I do know that if you are pregnant then we can't be constantly at war. We need to be able to talk…to have a relationship for the sake of our child.'

He was choosing his words with the care of a violinist tuning his instrument.

'I know we have a lot of unresolved issues. But if I take you back to Verona then we'll have failed at the first hurdle.'

Something shifted in her eyes, like sunlight on water, and she stiffened for a heartbeat. And then he felt her relax just a fraction.

He relaxed a little too then. 'Look, we have a week until you can take the test. Why don't we spend it here?'

'Do you really need to ask that?' Her brown eyes widened and she twitched free of his grip. 'You brought me here against my will.'

He studied her face. Beneath the defiance she looked incredibly fragile. His heart was hammering his ribs. He felt like a diver standing on the edge of a board. It was all or nothing now. *Crunch time.*

'I can't change that. But if it's what you want then we can turn the boat around now. I'd prefer it if you stayed. Only this time, of your own volition.'

Her eyes flared. 'Why? So we can have sex again?'

Sex.

The word reverberated between them and, watching the pulse in her throat jump out at him, he had to stop himself from closing the gap between them and pressing his mouth against hers.

'That's not going to happen,' she said.

She sounded adamant, but as she spoke she swayed forward slightly, her body momentarily contradicting her words. He stared down at her, seeing his own hunger reflected in her eyes and in the flush of her cheeks, in the shiver running over her skin.

She was fighting for control.

He was too, his body reacting instantly, viscerally, to the quivering tension in the air.

Pulse trembling, he moved towards her, close enough that all it would take was one more step for him to curl his arm around her waist and join his mouth with hers. He wanted to pull her close as he had last night, as he had so many times in the past, but for this to work he needed to take sex out of the equation.

'You can have your own cabin. There'll be a lock on the door.' His body tensed in revolt, but the need to reassure her took priority over his hunger. 'In nine months' time we could be parents, *bella*. Surely we can call a truce and spend eight days together?' he said softly.

There was a pause. Then, 'Okay.'

Her voice was still taut, but her shoulders had relaxed and he felt a flood of relief. It was a long way from *till death us do part*, but they could start with that.

'I'll stay.' Her eyes clashed with his. 'But this doesn't change anything.'

She was right. Nothing had changed.

Whatever that test said, she was still his wife.

And eight days alone on a boat in the middle of the ocean should be plenty long enough to remind her that he was her husband.

CHAPTER SEVEN

SHRUGGING OFF HER ROBE, Juliet kicked off her flip-flops and dropped down onto one of the teak loungers that clustered around the on-deck pool like animals around a watering hole. She knew she could go for a dip, but it was her brain, not her body, that needed occupation, and she had come prepared.

Picking up her book, she flipped it open, tilting the spine back to avoid the glare of the sun. According to the blurb on the cover, it was 'a pulse-pounding thriller' promising 'an escape from reality'. But, glancing down at the first page, she felt a rush of frustration.

It was going to take a lot more than a fast-paced holiday read to match the drama of her own current situation, she thought, gazing away to the sparkling blue waters of the Adriatic. And as for escaping it…

Her mouth twisted. Right now, a lifeboat might be her best option.

It was just over an hour since she had agreed with Ralph that she would stay on the *Alighieri*.

It was only for eight days.

Hardly a lifetime.

But already she was wondering if she had made yet another mistake by agreeing to stay.

Only it would sound so juvenile to insist on going back now, when she was going to have to see him at the clinic anyway.

The clinic.

She felt her pulse stumble and her fingers twitch. But there was no point in reaching for her phone to check the calendar again. The facts hadn't changed.

They'd had unprotected sex yesterday.

And this morning.

More than once.

And at the time in her cycle when the chances of conception were at their greatest.

So, theoretically, she could be pregnant.

But, since it would be at least a week before she could confirm if she was having Ralph's baby, she was just going to have to wait.

Shifting against the cushions, she steadied her breathing. She hated waiting—hated feeling so uncertain about everything. It reminded her of being a child, shuttled between foster homes, her stomach cramping with hunger and a nagging unspecified dread.

She had learned to manage the feeling by living in the moment, and that had worked well for her. After moving out of her last foster parents' home she'd made a life for herself. She'd had friends, a rented flat, and her hobby—blogging about food—had turned into a job she loved.

Only then she'd fallen in love. And suddenly the past and the future had been all that mattered: Ralph's past, their future...

Just like that, all her doubts and fears had suddenly been unleashed again, so that for weeks—months, even—she'd felt out of depth.

But she'd never felt more confused than she did right now.

Lifting her arm to shade her face, she squinted across the deck at the docile blue sea.

Her head felt like a slot machine. Each time she thought she had a handle on what she was thinking and feeling something else happened and sent her thoughts spinning.

Her heartbeat skipped.

Like earlier.

They had been talking about her parents. Something he had said had caught her off balance and she had ended up unloading about her past.

She shivered in the sunlight. Not everything. Not the whole sordid story. Nobody needed to hear that. Just the part about the rows and the sex and the fact that she had been conceived without thought.

It was the first time she'd shared the ugliness of those years with anyone. Even just thinking about it had always made it seem too real again, so she'd buried the memories in the deepest corner of her mind.

But this morning, with Ralph, the truth had come tumbling out.

Heart hammering against her ribs, she thought back to that moment when he'd caught her arms, his golden eyes joining his hands to hold her captive.

'None of us get to choose our parents, bella. *We don't get to choose how or when or where we're conceived.'*

We.

Her shoulders tensed as she remembered how it had angered her at first, him talking about them in the first-person plural when they were, in effect, estranged.

But this time it hadn't angered her.

Instead it had been as if the last few months had never passed. She had wanted to hold and comfort him, had wanted his arms to close around her.

Picturing the defensive expression on his face, she felt a sudden rush of shame burn through her.

It wasn't hard to imagine his feelings—then or now.

To learn that the man who had raised him from birth was not his father would have been huge. Like an A-bomb detonating in his living room. And she should have been there to support him, but he'd been alone.

They had both been alone with their fears—both been caught up in the events of their pasts. Was it any surprise they had each been swamped by doubt and misunderstandings?

She closed the book.

It made her wonder how different things might be now if they had even once tried to face the past together as a couple, rather than separately as two individuals. If he hadn't kept the truth from her, and she had been able to trust him, would it have made a difference?

Hating that the answer to that question might possibly be yes, she blanked her mind and glanced across the deck. The boat was skirting the coastline now, and as her gaze snagged on a cluster of wildflowers clinging heroically to the cliffs she felt her pulse dart.

It was one of the many advantages of having your own private yacht. Space, independence, incomparable views... And, of course, if you wanted to, you could stake a claim to one of the many beautiful sandy beaches that were only accessible by water. Just like that you'd have your own completely private idyllic retreat, far from the chattering crowds of tourists.

Her heart beat a little faster as she thought back to the first time Ralph had taken her out on the *Alighieri*. They had driven across the country from Rome, picking up the *Alighieri* in Rimini and then drifting up the Adriatic coast towards Venice in the cool winter sunshine.

Sometimes they'd made it up on deck, but often they'd just stayed in bed, eating, talking, playing cards and making love as the coastline changed from the unbroken stretches of sand to dramatic eroded cliffs.

They'd dropped anchor in the early evening, just south of

the resorts of Rimini and Riccione. From the boat, the beach had been just a teasing sliver of gold, like a crescent moon. Up close it had been magical...otherworldly. A tiny scallop-shaped curve of sand overlooking an iridescent sea the colour of an abalone shell.

Beneath a flawless white moon they had swum in the cool aquamarine water, lost in the magic of being completely alone with each other, and then he had rolled her under him on the wet sand, his body covering hers as the foaming waves spilled over them...

There was a shout from the lower deck, a burst of laughter, and she was back on the *Alighieri* with the sun burning the air.

It wasn't fair.

It wasn't fair that she could recall it all so clearly.

She didn't want or need to be reminded of how it had felt. It was over, gone, lost... *Wasn't it?*

As the question fizzed inside her head a shadow fell over her face and, looking up, she felt her spine tense with an almost audible snap.

Ralph was standing beside the lounger, his phone in his hand, his body edged with sunlight.

She felt her stomach muscles curl as his gaze roamed over the three triangles of her rose-coloured bikini.

'Hi,' he said softly.

The air felt as though it was electrically charged. Suddenly all her senses were burning.

She cleared her throat. 'Hi.'

It was hard to look at him, but impossible to look away from his preposterously photogenic face.

'Luca called. He sent his love. And these.'

As she gazed up at him he nudged one of the other loungers closer to hers and sat down on it, resting one leg on the other with a familiar masculine confidence that made a pulse of heat tick over her skin.

Her fingers bit into the cover of the book.

She couldn't fault his dark blue swim-shorts or accuse him of underdressing. They were perfectly respectable. And yet they seemed deliberately designed to showcase his superb body: the taut chest, broad shoulders, curving biceps. And the skin that tasted as good as it looked.

She felt Ralph's eyes on her face and her heart thudded hard against her ribs as he held out his phone.

'Here. They're from the christening.'

Grateful for a reason to drag her gaze away from his power-ful frame, she took the phone.

She knew hearts couldn't melt but, glancing down at the screen, she felt as if hers was turning to liquid.

Slowly she swiped downwards.

People always said the camera didn't lie, and as far as Lucia and Luca were concerned that was true. They both looked radi-ant with a happiness that shone from within. But, gazing down at a picture of herself, Juliet wondered at her calm expression. She had been so tense all that day, yet there was no sign of the chaos churning beneath her skin.

Bending lower over the phone, she began scrolling down again—and then her fingers scuffed against the screen and a fluttering mass of butterflies rose up inside her stomach.

It was a photo of Ralph. He was holding Raffaelle and his face was serious. Solemn, almost, as if he was taking a pri-vate vow.

Her pulse jumped. She'd told herself there was nothing left between them but a physical attraction. Only gazing down at the photo she knew that it was more complicated than just pas-sion and possession.

With a hand that shook a little, she held out the phone. 'He's a good photographer.'

He stared at her steadily. 'Yes, he is.' His eyes flickered over her bikini again. 'I might take a dip in the pool before lunch. Would you care to join me?'

Her skin felt as if it was suddenly on fire. Being half naked on a lounger was one thing. Being half naked in a pool with Ralph in swim-shorts was something else entirely.

She managed a small, taut smile. 'I'll think I'll just read my book.'

There was a short pulsing silence as his eyes flickered over the cover and then he shrugged. 'Okay.'

Heart pounding, she watched as he tossed his phone onto the lounger and stood up. Relief washed over her as he executed a perfect dive into the pool and disappeared beneath the water.

An hour later it was time for lunch.

Forking the delicious antipasti of stuffed peppers, parmigiana and tiny pink prawns into her mouth, she was surprised to find she was really quite hungry. It was her favourite kind of food. Simple ingredients cooked well. But she knew it was more than the food.

It was easy being with him—easier than it should be, she thought. Easier than it had been even a few weeks ago. Easy, too, to see why she had fallen so deeply under his spell.

And might do so again?

She stared down at the cutlery, her eyes tracing the intricate embossed pattern on the handle of her spoon.

All she had to do was say the words. Only she'd felt like this before and been wrong. What if she was wrong again?

As they waited for their plates to be cleared away Ralph lounged back in his seat, tilting his face up to the sun. 'I was chatting to Franco earlier, and he told me about a place just down the coast where we can drop anchor.'

Her heart skipped. Could he read minds? Had that night beneath the stars stuck in his mind too? Or was it just coincidence?

His eyes met hers. 'I thought maybe we might go ashore.'

She held his gaze. 'You're not worried I might run away?'

A faint smile tugged the corners of his mouth. 'Should I be?'

They both knew it was a hypothetical question. She would need crampons to climb the cliffs that hugged the patches of sand edging this stretch of the coast. But she knew that he wanted to gauge her mood. To find out if their truce was holding.

Glancing past him, she focused her attention on the plunging sandstone cliffs. There was a part of her that was relieved to have a respite from fighting him.

She looked up to find him watching her, and suddenly she was conscious of every breath, of the heavy pulse pounding through her body.

He was on the other side of the table, but it felt as if there was no distance between them. She felt hot and tingly, as if his golden gaze had set off firecrackers beneath her skin.

No, Ralph didn't have to worry about her running away—but she should be worried about why she'd stayed.

Forcing herself to hold his gaze, she shook her head. 'Of course not. We made an agreement. I said I'd stay until the appointment with Dr de Masi, and that's what I'm going to do.'

Later, as they sped across the translucent water to the cove Franco had told them about, Ralph replayed her words inside his head, frustration swelling up inside him like the curling bow wave at the front of the dinghy.

She didn't trust him. Still.

But was that such a surprise? It required time to repair and restore trust.

He felt a rush of panic. What if he ran out of time, like his mother had?

His hands clenched. He wanted to scoop Giulietta into his arms as he'd done at the marina. Only this time he didn't want to let go of her.

But everything was so finely balanced at the moment. He didn't want to do anything that might risk them going backwards.

The cove was deserted—and beautiful. Powder-soft ivory-coloured sand, clear shallow water and the occasional piece of bleached driftwood.

He had hoped she might swim with him, but instead she lay down on the comfortable oversized cushions the crew had brought over earlier and began reading her book.

The water was perfect and, closing off his mind, he swam until his muscles ached.

Finally he'd had enough, and he made his way up the beach, his eyes fixed on his wife. She'd changed position. Now she was sitting with one arm curled around her knees, her tawny hair framing her face.

He felt his heart contract. She looked so young, and yet there was a tension to her shoulders as if she was carrying the weight of the world.

When he dropped down beside her she didn't look up from her book and, rolling onto his side, he sighed. 'I've got to say, this isn't doing much for my ego.'

There was a pause and then she lifted her face, frowning. 'What do you mean?'

'I'm not used to playing second fiddle—particularly to a book. Must be a real page-turner,' he prompted, sitting up.

There was another pause, and then she shrugged. 'Actually, I haven't managed to get past the first chapter.'

He raised an eyebrow. 'Really?' Ducking his head, he tipped the cover towards him. 'It says here it's "gripping, pacy, and utterly addictive".'

He watched the corners of her mouth lift.

'It probably is. I just can't concentrate.'

'Why not?

'I've got a lot on my mind.'

'So what's bothering you?' He screwed up his face. 'I mean, other than being abducted and possibly getting pregnant by a man you want to divorce.'

They stared at one another in silence, and then she smiled, and suddenly he was smiling too.

Then her mouth started to tremble. 'You make it so hard for me to fight you,' she said shakily.

The sheen of tears in her eyes made his body tense in shock. He'd never seen his wife cry. And he hated it that he had been the one to change that fact.

'That's because I don't want to fight with you any more, *bella.*' He kept his voice deliberately steady. 'I want to start again. Go back to the beginning.'

The beginning: Rome.

Memories of those first few days together moved smoothly inside his head like the picture strip in a spinning zoetrope.

It had been perfect.

Heat and passion.

Skin on skin.

And an all-encompassing need.

They might have met in Rome, but he didn't need to be in Verona to know that she was the one, his Giulietta. In that moment it was as if he could see the rest of his life with her at the centre. Only, through arrogance and stupidity, he had not just let her go, he had driven her from their home.

'Do you think we could do that, Giulietta? Do you think we could start over?'

His heart stumbled when she started shaking her head. 'I don't know if we can. I don't know if *I* can...'

Something in her voice reminded him of their conversation earlier, when she'd told him about her parents and their rows and their making up. There had been the same note of fatigue—defeat, even—and he felt suddenly out of his depth. He hadn't even managed to sort out his own problems. Why did he think he could help soothe her pain?

Because you're her husband, he told himself fiercely. *That's why.*

He took a breath. 'When did you last see them?' he said quietly. 'Your parents?'

She was silent for so long he thought he'd lost her, but then he realised she was searching for something to say that would be enough but not too much.

He knew that feeling well.

'I don't know,' she said finally. 'My dad was never really there. He was always coming and going. Mostly going.' Her lips twisted. 'I suppose I was probably about nine when he stopped coming back.'

She glanced past him, looking upwards, her eyes tracking the contrails of a plane across the sky.

'I don't remember the exact day, but it was October and it was foggy. He went out for bread and never came back.' Despite the heat of the sun, she sounded shivery. 'It was like the fog just swallowed him up...' Her words drifted into silence.

'And your mum?'

Now her eyes clashed with his, the brown dark and defensive.

'Why are you asking all these questions?' She had scooted away from him and she was holding the book in front of her chest like a shield.

'Because you're my wife,' he said quietly, reaching over and capturing her hand. 'And because I should have asked you when we first met.'

It hurt, admitting that to himself—to her. But at the time her past, her background, had been secondary to his. Or rather secondary to the earth-shattering repercussions of finding out that everything he had taken for granted was a lie.

He'd arrogantly assumed that nothing in her ordinary little life could be as devastating as finding out he wasn't a Castellucci.

He felt a rush of self-loathing. He'd had so much in his life, an excess of everything—*even fathers*—and yet he had failed to give his wife the reassurance and support she needed.

Across the beach, the waves were tumbling onto the sand, each one washing away the lacy patterns of the last. If only he could so easily erase the mistakes he'd made.

But, then again, maybe this shouldn't be easy.

Clearly she thought so too.

She pulled her hand free. Her mouth was trembling. 'But you didn't.'

'No, I didn't.' He pushed back against the regret. 'And that's on me. I let you down, and I hurt you. And I know I can't change what I did, but I will do everything in my power to earn your trust back.'

He could see the conflict in her eyes, the longing to believe his words vying with the hurt, and he hated it that he had so carelessly lost her trust.

She breathed out shakily. 'This isn't all on you. I was wrong too. I wouldn't have told you anything even if you had asked me about my parents. I didn't want you to know about them… about me.' Her voice was trembling now. 'Talking about it is so hard. It makes it all feel real again.'

He reached out and caught her hand again. 'Makes what feel real?' he asked gently.

'How it felt, living like that.'

This time, her fingers tightened around his.

'It wasn't just the rows. They were alcoholics. If they weren't out getting wasted, they were hungover and hopeless. When my dad left for good, my mum just gave up. One day she took some pills—'

The words sounded stark, ugly against the soft beauty of the beach. And there was a seam of pain in her voice now that made his stomach twist with rage. She had been nine years old…just a little girl.

'What happened?'

'I tried to dig them out of her mouth but she wouldn't wake up. So I called an ambulance. She was okay, but there was no one to look after me so I went to stay with Rebecca and Tim.'

She was curled over now, her shoulders hunched, as if she was surrounded by a pack of wolves. Maybe she felt that way.

'They were my first foster parents.'

First. For such a small word it packed a hell of a punch.

He stared at her small, tense body, his heart aching with emotions that felt too big to be contained. 'But there were others?'

She nodded. 'Lots of people like me...they just slip through the net. So I was lucky, really.'

He watched her fingers bunch into a fist. The gesture made his whole body hurt.

'I suppose it was just not knowing each time if there would be anyone there to catch me that was so terrible...'

His ribs ached.

For her, love had proved dangerous. What should have been solid—the love of her parents—had been consistently weak and unreliable, and yet she had not given up. Despite all those betrayals of her childhood she had let herself feel again, let herself love him.

Unlike him, she had faced her fears, her doubts, head-on, trusting to love, *trusting him.*

'What about now? Do you have anything to do with her?'

She cleared her throat. 'Not since I was sixteen. That's when we last spoke. She texts me sometimes, but I made the decision to cut her out of my life.'

She was looking at him, but not quite meeting his eyes.

'I know she's my mum, but being around her makes me feel so out of control, so powerless, and it scares me...'

Her voice wavered, and he had closed the gap between them and pulled her into his arms before he'd even realised what he was doing.

A sob caught in her throat and she crumpled against him. He held her tightly, stroking her silken hair and telling her over and over again that everything would be all right, swapping back and forth from English to Italian until finally she was calm.

'That's why you went back to England,' he said hoarsely. 'I'd made you feel powerless.'

He felt her shiver.

'I panicked. I thought it was something in me—something I was doing—and that was why you wanted someone else.'

Cupping her chin, he tipped her face up to his, fearing and knowing that he hadn't made his feelings for her sufficiently clear. 'I didn't want anyone else. I never have. I want you—all and every possible version of you.'

He felt her hands flutter against his chest and, looking down, felt heat flood his veins. Her eyes were wide and soft, her body pressing against his was softer still, and he was on the verge of kissing her.

But something held him back. The need to demonstrate that he wanted her for more than just sex. That he *needed* to be there for her.

And he needed her to be there for him.

His stomach clenched.

Could he tell her? Could he share his fears?

The dark, clammy panic rose inside him like an intruder, pinning him down and suffocating him. Heart swelling, he glanced down at her tear-stained face. Another time, maybe. This was about her, and her needs, not his, and she needed to know that she was deserving of love—his love.

'You don't need to be scared any more, *bella*. I'll always be there to catch you. Always.' Leaning down, he kissed her on the forehead, his hand moving over her cheek. 'I think we should get back to the boat now.'

Away from this secluded little beach, where he might be tempted to give in to lust or, worse, to the need to unburden the misery in his heart.

Stepping out of the shower, Juliet tucked the plush towel around her body, knotting it above her breasts. It wasn't late—not much past nine—but after a light supper she had retreated to her cabin, claiming tiredness.

And it was true. She felt exhausted and dazed. Just as if she'd just finished a race she had been training for all her life.

For so long she had dreaded talking about her childhood—had spent years avoiding the subject or telling a carefully edited version of her past. And yet she'd done it. She'd told Ralph the truth. And, although it had been distressing having to remember it all, it had been easier than she'd expected.

He'd made it easy for her.

Her heart bumped against her ribs.

She still couldn't quite believe everything that had happened since she'd returned to Verona. So much had changed in such a short time.

They had changed.

Take today. They had fought—*again*—but the difference was that this time they had finished the conversation. And they hadn't ended up having sex.

No thanks to her.

Remembering the moment when he'd told her he wanted her, she felt her skin grow suddenly warm.

Pressed against his beautiful bare chest, she had felt so weak in the face of her need for him that she had been seconds away from pulling his head down to hers and forgetting about the consequences.

Again.

Without thinking she moved her hand to her stomach, to the possible consequences of the last time she'd given in to just such an urge.

Her fingers trembled against the towel.

She might not be pregnant, but the possibility had broken the impasse between them. It had shown both of them that although they might be flawed, change was not just possible but in their hands.

Their hands.

His hands.

She felt her body tense and soften at the same time. He had the most instinctive sense of touch, reading her body like a healer. Only it wasn't her body she was talking about. He had helped heal the scars on her soul.

She felt calmer. But it was more than that. It was as though someone had shifted a burden from her shoulders so that she no longer felt like that unloved—worse, unlovable—little girl.

Her throat was suddenly so tight it was hard to breathe.

Not someone.

Ralph.

Pulse pounding, she walked over to the connecting door between their cabins and gently pushed it open.

Ralph was standing by the bed. He too was naked, except for the towel wrapped around his waist. He was rubbing his hair with another towel.

Glancing over at her, his face tensed. 'Giulietta—is something wrong?'

Dropping the towel, he crossed the cabin in two long strides. 'No. I…'

As her eyes slid over the powerful muscles of his chest she was momentarily lost for words. His body was just so perfect.

'Did you want to talk to me?' He was looking down at her, his beautiful golden eyes trained on her face.

She blinked, tried to refocus her brain. But she couldn't seem to think straight. Only why did she need to think at all? No thought was required for what she wanted—and she did want him, with an intensity and a freedom she had never felt before. Not even in Rome.

Then she had been…

Her heart was pounding so hard she thought it might burst. Taking a step forward, she leaned into him, her hands reaching up to capture his face. Tilting her head slightly, she brushed her lips against his.

'Kiss me.'

As she breathed the words into his mouth she felt him tense for a fraction of a second, and then his hands were sliding beneath the towel, fingers splaying against her back, his lips so warm and urgent that she felt a pit of need open up inside her.

Parting her lips, he kissed her more deeply, and then he pulled her closer, close enough that she could feel the thick outline of his erection pushing against her stomach.

She felt her breath tangle as he lifted her hair from her shoulder, tugging it sideways to expose the curve of her throat. And then he was licking her skin, running his tongue along her clavicle to the pulse leaping beneath the skin.

'La tua pelle sembra sete,' he said hoarsely. His eyes found hers, the pupils huge and shockingly dark against the gold of the iris. 'You want this.'

It was a statement of fact.

Licking her lips, she nodded slowly. 'Yes.'

He groaned as she began moving against him. *'Mi vuoi...'*

She shivered inside. Her body was tense. Hot. Damp. Her breasts felt heavy. She ached for his touch.

'Si,' she said softly, her hands reaching down to where the towel hugged his abs. *'Ti voglio così tanto.'*

CHAPTER EIGHT

HOOKING HER FINGERS beneath the damp fabric, she tugged gently, her pulse jumping in her throat as the towel slid to the floor. Now he was naked too. Naked and aroused. *Very* aroused.

'My turn,' he whispered softly.

Her mouth went dry as he reached out and pulled at the knot between her breasts. His face stilled, and she felt her muscles clench as he reached out to caress first her cheek and the curve of jaw, then lower to her taut ruched nipples.

She moaned softly as his fingers teased first one then the other. Her body tightened with need. She was so hot and hungry for him.

Her hand twitched against his skin. He was looking down at her in silence, his eyes like molten gold. 'You like that?' he said softly.

She nodded slowly, feeling an answering wetness between her thighs as he gently cupped her breasts in his hands and kissed her slowly and deeply.

Breathing out raggedly, she reached down and wrapped her hand around his hard length, a sharp heat shooting through her as he grunted against her mouth. Head swimming, she caressed the velvet-smooth skin, feeling him pulse in her hand.

'You're killing me, baby,' he groaned.

Batting her hand away, he lifted her up and lowered her onto the bed.

Gazing down at her, Ralph felt as though his skin was going to catch fire. She was so beautiful, and she was his to explore, to pleasure.

Leaning forward, he drew first one and then the other taut nipple into his mouth, his body tensing as the blunt head of his erection brushed against where she was already so wet for him.

He touched her lightly between her thighs. She felt slick and white-hot. Shaking with need, he ran his hands over her body as she arched upwards to meet his touch. For a moment he admired the smooth, flawless skin, the small breasts and the curve of her belly, and then, lowering his face, he kissed a path from her stomach to the triangle of fine dark hair.

Her fingers tightened on his head. She was moving restlessly, squirming against his mouth, and he slid his hand beneath the curve of her buttocks, lifting her up. He could feel tiny shivers of anticipation darting across her skin as he stroked her trembling thighs with his thumbs, inhaling her salty damp scent.

She was already swollen and, flattening his tongue, he began licking her clitoris with slow, precise strokes, again and again, until he was no longer conscious of anything but the pulse beating against his tongue and her soft moans.

Suddenly her hands jerked. 'No, not like this.' She was panting. 'I want you inside me.' Her eyes flared. 'You need a—'

'I'll get a condom.' His voice was husky.

They'd both spoken at once.

He rolled off the bed and Juliet watched dazedly, her breath trapped in her throat, as he tore open the foil. The need to touch, to taste, overwhelmed her and, cupping him in her hand, she leaned forward, flicking her tongue over the smooth polished head.

He made a rough sound in the back of his throat. Gripping her hair, he let her take him into her mouth, and then she felt him jerk away and he grabbed her wrist.

'Next time.'

With fingers that shook slightly he rolled the condom on, and then, dropping down on the bed, he pulled her onto his lap. She kissed him hungrily, nipping his lips with her teeth, and then he was holding her hips, raising her up, guiding himself into her body. His groan mixed with her gasp of pleasure as he slid into her.

Pulse hammering, she felt Ralph grip her waist, clamping her body to his as she started to roll back and forth.

Threading his fingers through her hair, he tipped back her head, baring her throat to his tongue and his lips. His hand moved to her clitoris, working in time with her frantically arching pelvis.

Juliet felt her pulse soar. 'Yes…' She moaned the word against his mouth, turning it from one syllable to five. Her skin was so hot and tight—but not as tight as she felt on the inside.

His thumb was pushing her to the edge, the fluttering ache between her legs was now impossible to ignore, and she shuddered helplessly, muscles rippling, her body gripping him, becoming his.

And then she cried out as he tensed, slamming into her, and there was nothing that mattered except Ralph and the power of his hard body driving into hers.

The shout filled her head and, jolted from sleep, Juliet struggled onto her side. The last thing she could remember was Ralph burying his face in her hair, his arms curving around her, anchoring her to his body as her heartbeat slowed.

Now her heart was hammering inside her ribcage.

She reached out.

In the darkness beside her Ralph was shuddering, his arms pushing against the covers.

'Ralph!'

She felt him tense as her voice echoed sharply round the silent cabin and, reaching out again, she fumbled for the light.

By the time she turned round he was sitting on the edge of the bed, his head in his hands.

'Ralph,' she said again, more softly this time. 'It's okay. You were having a nightmare but it's over now.'

He flinched as she touched his shoulder. His skin felt warm, but he was shivering as if he had a fever.

She stared down at him uncertainly. Ralph had always been a bad sleeper. But this didn't seem like the aftermath of a nightmare. He seemed barely aware of her presence and his breathing sounded jerky.

Sliding onto the floor, she knelt in front of him. 'You're going to be fine.'

Gently she reached up and took his hands in hers. He didn't reply, but she felt his fingers tighten around hers.

'It's okay, I'm not going anywhere. I'm going to stay right here,' she said quietly.

He still hadn't spoken, but he hadn't let go of her hands either and so, keeping her voice calm and fluid, she carried on talking.

She talked about the food they had shared that evening, and the pictures Luca had sent of the christening, until finally she felt his breathing grow steadier.

'Would you like a glass of water?' she asked.

For a moment she didn't think he would respond, but then he nodded.

'Wait a second,' she whispered.

Standing up, she went to the bathroom and filled a glass with water from the tap.

'Here.' She handed him the glass.

He took it without looking up. 'Thank you.'

His voice sounded frayed, as if he had torn it by shouting,

and she felt a sudden rage at whatever it was that had crept into his dreams.

'How are you feeling now?' She sat down beside him, keeping her movements small and her voice steady.

'Better.'

She watched as he ran a hand over his face.

'I'm sorry,' he said quietly.

'For what?' She hesitated a moment, then took his hand again.

'For waking you up like that. I didn't hurt you, did I?' Now he looked at her, his eyes desperately searching her face.

'No, of course you didn't hurt me.'

'I could have done. I didn't know what I was doing.'

He sounded distraught.

'You didn't do anything. You were just moving about and then you shouted something—'

But he was shaking his head. 'I'll sleep next door.'

He made as if to stand up, but she caught his arm.

'No, Ralph. You're not sleeping next door. If you do, then I'm coming with you.'

He stiffened, but didn't resist as she tugged him gently down onto the bed. His body was still trembling and, reaching round him, she grabbed a sweatshirt from the chair by the bed.

'Here—put this on.'

She watched as he pulled it over his head, breathing shakily into the silence of the cabin.

'It might help…' She hesitated, catching sight of the shuttered expression on his face, then tried again. 'It might help to talk about it.'

Her words hung in the air.

He glanced over at her and shook his head, then looked down at his hands. 'There's no need. It was just a nightmare…a bad dream. You said so yourself.'

She felt her heart beat faster.

Ever since she'd known him Ralph had slept badly, shifting restlessly and often waking in the night. The only exception to that pattern had been during those first few weeks in Rome—but of course then he had been on holiday.

This was different.

He had seemed disorientated, almost unaware of her and his surroundings. And scared. As if the nightmare hadn't stopped when he'd woken up.

She knew that feeling well.

'Is that what you think it was? Just a bad dream?'

Her question was level-toned, but she felt him go still. The silence echoed round the cabin.

Normally at this point he would either kiss her until she couldn't remember having asked the question, or give her one of those cool, enigmatic smiles that meant he was about to change the subject.

But this time he kept staring down at his hands. 'I don't know.'

She could hear the heaviness, the despair in his voice.

'I don't know,' he said again. 'I think it starts out as a bad dream.'

Starts.

So it wasn't a one-off.

'And then what happens?' she asked, and gazed away, giving him time.

The cabin was silent for a moment, and then he shrugged.

'I wake up and there's this weight crushing my chest.' He pressed a clenched hand against his breastbone. 'It feels as if something is sitting on me—like in that painting.'

'*The Nightmare*,' she said quietly.

Like most people, she knew the Fuseli painting. The image of a beautiful sleeping woman draped across a bed with a hunched creature with the face of a gargoyle crouching on her stomach was enough to give anyone nightmares.

She felt him shudder and, reaching out, prised his fingers apart and took his hand in hers again.

'I try to push it off me, but I can't, and then I realise I'm still asleep, and that I'm never going to wake up.'

It sounded terrifying. Doubly terrifying for an intensely physical man like Ralph.

She glanced down at the sculpted muscles of his thighs. He might be a billionaire businessman, with a highly trained security team tracking his every movement, but Ralph could take care of himself. Not only did he work out regularly, but he had been trained in the Russian martial art Systema.

'But you do wake up?' she said gently.

He nodded slowly. 'But I can't breathe. It's like I'm choking. The first time it happened I thought I was having a heart attack.'

It obviously hadn't been a heart attack, but it hadn't been just a bad dream either.

'Oh, Ralph...' As she whispered his name he turned to look at her, a muscle flickering in his jaw, and she felt her own heart twist.

'I thought it would stop.'

His eyes looked desperate and she nodded quickly.

'It will.' They were the only words she could force past the lump in her throat. 'But panic attacks don't go away on their own. There's usually a trigger.' She hesitated. 'What's the dream that starts it about? Or can't you remember?'

The sudden tension in his body told her that she was on the right track.

'I can remember it,' he said flatly.

There was a long silence, and then he inhaled sharply.

'It's always the same. I come home after work and everything seems normal, only my mother is still alive, and I can hear her and my father talking.'

Her throat was tight. No matter how bad her own pain had been, nothing could compete with hearing his...feeling his. It felt like a vice around her heart.

'I walk into the drawing room, but my father is alone, and

he turns to me and he says, "You shouldn't be here. You're not my son. You'll never be my son."'

He ran his hand over his face, and with a shock she realised that he was close to tears.

'You *are* his son,' she said fiercely. 'You've been his son for thirty years. His face lights up when you walk into the room. He loves you so much.'

'And I love him.' His voice was rough. 'And I don't want to keep lying to him. But I don't want to hurt him either.' He looked exhausted all of a sudden. 'He's already lost his wife. If I tell him the truth it'll be like losing her all over again.' A tremor started in his hands. 'If I tell him the truth he'll lose his son and heir too. He'll be the last of the Castelluccis.'

There was a long, dull silence. Juliet felt her pulse accelerate. She hadn't really registered the wider implications before, but Ralph was right. Without him, the Castellucci name would disappear.

Gazing over at his taut profile, she felt her heart twist. It must have been hard enough finding out his mother had been unfaithful and his father was not his father, but this was bigger than Ralph.

What he chose to do would have an impact on his entire family.

No wonder Francesca had held her secret close for so long. And yet something had pushed her to confess the truth...

'What did your mother want you to do?' she asked carefully. 'I know she couldn't bear to tell Carlo herself, but surely she wouldn't have told you if she didn't want him to know eventually.'

There was another silence, this one longer.

Then, 'She didn't want to tell me.' He met her eyes and his mouth twisted. 'Vittoria told me. She found some letters my mother wrote to her father, Niccolò, and she came to the house. She was so upset, making all kinds of accusations... Luckily I was there on my own.'

His hand clenched painfully around hers.

Luckily in some ways, she thought. But it would have been better for Ralph if Francesca and Carlo had been there. Then he would have been spared all these months of carrying the burden of guilt and uncertainty.

'Did you look at the letters?' she asked.

His beautiful mouth curved into a grimace. 'Yes. I don't know why. Maybe I shouldn't have. I suppose I wanted to prove her wrong, but I recognised her handwriting and it was clear that they'd been having an affair.'

He was silent again.

Gazing up at the smooth planes of his face, Juliet tried to imagine what it must have felt like to read those letters. The shock, the pain of betrayal, the burden of knowledge...

'Is that when you talked to your mother?' she said quietly.

He shook his head. 'That was the day they got her test results back from the hospital. They were both stunned...devastated... I couldn't—' Tears pricked the back of her eyes and he breathed out unsteadily.

She tightened her grip on his hand. 'Of course you couldn't. No one could.'

He was looking down at his hand in hers, his eyes locked on the signet ring on his little finger. 'Sometimes I think I should have just left it alone. Kept what Vittoria told me to myself. Only I couldn't. I think I knew that there was more to it.'

Juliet stared at him in silence. It was easy now to understand why he had found it so hard to confront the problems in their marriage. Look at what had happened last time he'd tried: his whole world had come tumbling down.

Her throat was tight and aching. It ached for him.

'What did she say when you did talk to her?' she asked.

'Nothing. She wouldn't talk about it.' There was a heaviness in his voice now, a note of finality. 'Not until the end. That's when she told me that Carlo wasn't my biological father.'

He looked up at Juliet and she saw his eyes were full of un-shed tears.

'I knew that anyway by then. I'd taken a DNA test. I just wanted her to say it to my face, so I could remember her telling me the truth.'

'And she did tell you the truth.' She spoke firmly, her hand tightening on his.

It felt like it had in Rome, when they had been so in tune with one another—only then it had been physical. This time he had stripped off more than just his clothes. He had bared his soul.

'She told you everything. The whole truth. Not just that she had an affair. But that Carlo wasn't your father. She didn't have to do that, but she did. Because she wanted you to have the choice. The choice she took from you before you were born.'

'But I don't want to choose.' His mouth twisted. 'I just want to do what's right.'

'You're already doing that,' she said slowly. 'You run your business. You take care of your family, your father—'

'I didn't take care of you.' The pain was there again, at the edges of his voice. 'I hurt you so badly you ran away.'

'We hurt each other—and I came back.'

His eyes found hers. 'For the christening.'

She held his gaze. 'For that too.' Reaching up, she cupped his face. 'Whatever you choose to do will be the right thing.'

She could feel his pain so acutely that it made her own eyes fill with tears, and without thinking she slid both arms around him and pulled him close.

He breathed out shakily. 'I miss her so much… I don't want to lose him as well.'

Light was starting to squeeze around the blinds and, her heart pounding, she took a breath. 'You can't lose him, Ralph. Carlo raised you, and he loves you, and no test can change that.' She forced a smile. 'DNA makes a baby, not a father. Trust me—I know.'

He pulled her closer, holding her tightly. 'You deserved so much better. You *deserve* so much better than this...than me.'

She could feel his heart beating in time with hers.

'I'm sorry...' He struggled with the words, a muscle working in his jaw. 'I'm sorry you had to see me like this.'

Pulling away slightly, she looked up at him. 'You're my husband. We took vows, remember? I know bad dreams and panic attacks aren't mentioned specifically, but I reckon they're covered by "in sickness and in health" or maybe "for better or worse".'

He looked up at her in silence, and her heart performed a perfect somersault as she felt the full impact of his beautiful golden eyes.

'What?' She frowned. 'What is it?'

He slid his hands into her hair and tilted her face up to his. 'That's the first time you've acknowledged that I'm your husband since you got back from England,' he said softly.

Watching her face, Ralph held his breath. There was a silence. Their eyes met.

She blinked, then looked down. 'I suppose it is.'

The cabin fell silent.

'So, I was wondering,' he said slowly, 'and hoping that maybe you might have changed your mind...'

As she looked up at him the glow from the bedside lamp lit up her face, emphasising both its softness and its strength.

'About getting a divorce. You see, I meant what I said on the beach about us trying again.' Reaching out, he touched her stomach gently. 'I want to spend the rest of my life with you. Have children with you. Grow old with you. Do you think we could do that, *bella*? Do you think we could try again?'

She held his gaze, and then slowly she nodded. 'Yes, I think we could.'

Her words—so simple, so honest—made his heart turn over

and emotion shudder through his body. He leaned in to kiss her, sliding his tongue over her lips and then into her mouth.

Her hands slid over his stomach, and he sucked in a breath and then tugged the sweatshirt over his head and reached for her...

When he woke, the sun was already high in the cloudless blue sky.

Giulietta was still asleep.

He stared down at her, holding his breath.

Her hair was a dark, swirling storm cloud on the pillow, and with her eyelashes feathering the curve of her cheekbone she looked exactly like an illustration in a book of fairy tales. A beautiful sleeping princess, trapped in a tower, waiting to be rescued by her prince.

His chest tightened.

Except that last night it had been he who had needed rescuing. He had been the one drowning in panic, and Giulietta had chased away his demons.

He dressed noiselessly and, resisting the urge to wake her with a kiss, made his way out onto the private deck beside their cabin.

It was another beautiful day, but as he walked into the sunlight he felt a rush of emotion that had nothing to do with the warm air or the sea or the sky. It was as if he had woken not just from a long sleep but from a living nightmare. He felt calmer than he had in months.

And it was all down to Giulietta.

His fingers tightened against the handrail.

Up until a few hours ago he'd barely been able to acknowledge the breathless, heart-hammering episodes that had been plaguing his nights, much less give them a name. But Juliet had done both. And more. She had agreed to give their marriage a second chance.

'Ralph...'

He turned, his heart missing a beat.

Juliet was standing in the doorway. Her hair was spilling over her shoulders in untidy curls and she was wearing the T-shirt he'd been wearing yesterday.

'Why didn't you wake me?' she said huskily.

Glancing down at her bare legs and imagining them wrapped around his waist, he felt his body harden.

Good question.

'I thought you needed to sleep.'

'Did *you* sleep?'

Hearing the concern in her voice, he felt his heart contract. 'Yes, I did.' He took a step towards her and pulled her against him. 'Thanks to you.'

He kissed her gently on the mouth, the tip of his tongue parting her lips briefly, and the hitch of her breath made him feel vertiginous with equal parts of hunger and relief.

'What was that for?' she asked.

'Lots of different things,' he said softly. 'Looking better in my T-shirt than I do.' Leaning forward, he kissed her again. 'Looking after me last night. And for agreeing to give us— *me*—a second chance.'

His words brought her eyes back to his. Gazing down at her face, he tightened his hands around her waist, his emotions almost too raw to contain so that he was suddenly afraid he might weep.

How could he have let it happen? That distance between them? He had come so close to losing her. To losing the one person who saw beneath the perfect façade...the one woman who knew him completely, inside and out.

And he knew her. He understood her now. He knew about the lonely little girl who had been raised by strangers and he understood her mistrust and her self-doubt.

That she had survived was miraculous.

Only she hadn't just survived. She had triumphed. And he was in awe of her strength, her determination, her courage.

There was nothing he wouldn't do for her, but mostly he wanted to hold her close, to wrap his body around hers.

Suddenly he was struggling to fill his lungs with air. He was so hungry for her. More than anything, he wanted to trail his lips along the warm silken skin of her throat, to savour that frantically beating pulse, to slide his hands beneath that T-shirt and skim his fingers over the peaks of her breasts. No boundaries. No restraint. No inhibitions.

He took a breath. 'I wish we could stay on the *Alighieri* for ever,' he whispered. 'Just you and me, sailing into a new dawn each day and drifting into the sunset at night.'

But... He didn't say it. He didn't need to.

'But we need to get back,' she said softly.

Watching his face still, Juliet felt her stomach flip over, and just for a few heart-stopping half-seconds she let her hands splay against his back as she felt the rigid press of his erection against her belly.

Heat was radiating through her body—the familiar, electrifying rush of desire for skin on skin, for his taste, his touch...

Only it was so much more than that.

On waking, she had felt memories of what had happened in the early hours of the morning fill her head. Their lovemaking, his panic attack, their conversation...and of course their reconciliation.

The last few days had changed so many things. She had talked to Ralph about her past—really talked—and his unconditional support had helped her to see herself and him in a different light.

But it had been seeing him so desperate, so distressed, or rather the fact that he had let her see him like that, that had blown away all thoughts of divorcing him.

He was her love, her life, her future—with or without a baby in her womb.

In a little over forty-eight hours they would be hosting the biggest party in town *together*—and this time it wouldn't just be an appearance of unity. This time it would be real.

Brushing his lips with her own, she tipped her head back and met his gaze head-on. 'We need to get back for the ball.'

She felt him tense.

The opera festival was a huge deal in Verona, but the Castellucci Ball was legendary in its own right. Not only was it a charitable fundraiser that raised seven-figure sums, it also gave guests a chance to mingle with celebrities from the world of art, fashion, film and music. It was the most important date in the family's social calendar. But she knew that wasn't the reason why his back suddenly felt like a rigid wall of muscle.

'Is Niccolò Farnese going to be there?' she asked quietly.

She knew he would be even before Ralph nodded. The Farneses were a powerful family—not as old as the Castelluccis, but still with connections stretching across Italy and beyond.

'With his wife.' He rubbed a hand across his eyes as if he wanted to block out the facts. 'And obviously Carlo will be there too.' His mouth twisted. 'It feels dangerous...all of us being there together. Like tempting fate.'

Hearing the strain in his voice, she felt a rush of self-loathing that she had considered letting him face this ordeal alone. 'Nothing is going to happen,' she said fiercely. 'I won't let it.'

His arms tightened around her. 'It feels like a betrayal...being there with both of them, neither of them knowing the truth...'

'You're not betraying anyone.' Her heart felt as if it was going to burst. She loved him so much that his pain was her pain. 'This is an impossible situation—nobody would know how to handle it, and most people wouldn't try. They'd just run away and hide.' She could feel his heart beating in time with hers. 'You're not doing that.'

He shifted against her, moving back slightly so that he could see her face.

Tilting her head back, she met his gaze. 'You're putting your feelings aside for Carlo and your family. You're going to smile and greet your guests and give them an evening to remember. And I'll be right by your side.'

He nodded slowly, his fingers curving over her belly. 'I'd like that.'

Her arm brushed against his. 'It's going to be fine. I promise. And when you're ready...when you've figured out how to say what you want to say...you can have a conversation with your father. Both of your fathers,' she said softly.

There was a silence. In the limitless sky above them the sun looked like a child's drawing. She heard him breathe out shakily.

'Thank you for doing this.'

She frowned. 'Doing what?'

He hesitated. 'Putting your feelings aside. I know you don't really enjoy the whole social scene, and that's partly my fault. No, it *is*,' he said as she started to protest. 'It was a lot to take on for anyone—much less someone who didn't even speak Italian.'

Reaching out, he pushed her hair behind her ear.

'Only I didn't think about that. I was so caught up with not being a Castellucci and I projected that onto you. I'm sorry.'

'I know you are.'

It was enough to know that he cared. She squeezed his hand, and saw his face relax a little.

'So, are you ready to turn the boat around?' she asked.

A shiver ran along his jaw as he glanced past her at the horizon, but then slowly he nodded.

She leaned into him, her heart beating in time with his.

The ramifications of his mother's affair had not been forgotten, but they would deal with it together. One day at a time.

The past was not going to come between them ever again.

CHAPTER NINE

TURNING ON THE SPOT, Juliet gazed into the mirror, her eyes moving critically over her reflection. She turned to the petite dark-haired woman beside her. 'What do you think?'

They were standing in the ornate master bedroom at the *palazzo*, but for once the gilt and marble setting was taking a back seat. Instead, it was the rail of jewel-bright dresses that held centre stage, their intricate beading and lustrous fabrics catching the morning sunlight and spraying rainbows across the room.

'I think you look exquisite. But it's what you think that matters, *cara*.'

Juliet grimaced. 'But I don't know what I think, Gia. That's why I have you.'

Before becoming a personal stylist, Gia Marazzi had worked for two of the largest fashion houses in Italy. Preternaturally calm and exceptionally pretty, Gia was the chicest woman she had ever met. She was also one of the nicest, and had become a friend as well as an advisor.

Gia shook her head. 'You have me because you don't like shopping.'

The look of disbelief on the stylist's perfectly made-up face as she spoke made Juliet burst out laughing. 'So would you if you had to go everywhere with a quartet of heavily armed over-muscular men tracking your every footstep.'

But that wasn't the only reason.

Before she'd met Ralph she'd never had enough money to really enjoy spending it on clothes. Marrying into the Castel-luccis had obviously changed that, but even after she'd married Ralph she'd still felt completely out of her depth and horribly conspicuous, so that even thinking about walking into the de-signer boutiques on Milan's Via Montenapoleone had been a toe-curlingly daunting prospect.

Back then she'd been so unsure of himself.

Or maybe sure only of one thing.

That it was simply a matter of time before Ralph realised the mistake he had made in marrying her. That sooner or later he would see her for who she was, and her fashion choices would just speed up the inevitable exposure.

Her heart bumped gently against her ribs.

Except he had seen who she was.

Sitting with her on that tiny little patch of sand, he had peeled back the layers she wore to protect herself against the world.

He knew who she was now.

He knew her and he wanted her.

The good, the bad, and even the ugly.

Ignoring the fluttering rush of unease that accompanied that resolute thought, she twisted round to face the mirror, holding out the full, heavy skirt.

This dress was the opposite of ugly.

In fact, it seemed ridiculous to criticise something so un-speakably lovely.

But... 'It just feels a little too structured, too emphatic.' She screwed up her face apologetically. 'Sorry, Gia. I know it's your favourite.'

'I do love it.' The stylist laughed. 'But *I'm* not going to be wearing it.' Running her hand lightly over the exquisite lace, Gia narrowed her eyes. 'And I do know what you mean. It's a dress that makes an unequivocal statement.'

'Yes, it does.'

The deep voice made Juliet stop mid-twirl. Glancing over her bare shoulder, she felt her mouth dry. Ralph was leaning against the door frame, his golden gaze fixed on her face, a smile tugging at the corners of his mouth.

Heat scuttled over her skin. Any ordinary man wearing black jeans and a charcoal-grey polo shirt would have looked underdressed beside all the glittering, embellished couture gowns. But that was the difference between Ralph and every other human. He didn't need a stylist or a rack of jaw-droppingly expensive clothes to make heads turn.

'It says my wife is unequivocally the most beautiful woman in the world.'

Juliet watched him walk towards her. 'You like it?' she asked. Her breath hitched in her throat as Ralph touched her lightly on the hip and she turned to face him.

They had arrived back in Verona yesterday afternoon. It had been a strange sensation, walking back into the *palazzo*—a kind of *déjà-vu*. Her home had seemed so familiar, and yet it had felt inexplicably different. Everything had felt lighter, brighter—almost as if it had been aired and redecorated in the time they'd been away.

But of course nothing had changed in a physical sense. It was just that so much had happened...so many things had changed between her and Ralph.

She felt a shimmer of pure happiness, warm like sunlight on her skin. It was as if the misery and uncertainty of the last few months had been erased and they had gone back to the beginning. Only the difference was that this time they were not stumbling around blindfolded. The past was an open book now.

It had been painful to admit their frailties and their fears, but they had come through the fire together and now they were stronger, wiser.

Closer.

She leaned into him, panic clutching at her stomach as she remembered how close she had come to walking away, to leaving this man who was her life blood, her breath, her heart, her soul.

'I like it a lot,' he said.

His fingers splayed against her waist. They were warm and firm and she felt her panic fade.

'It's a beautiful dress.' He stared down at her appraisingly. 'But I think the fabric is too rigid and the blue is too dark. You need something with a little more fluidity...*and heat.*'

Their eyes met and she sucked in a sharp breath as he brushed past her. Heart pounding, she watched as he pulled out a soft, swirling mass of primrose-coloured silk from the rail.

'That was my first choice,' she said softly. 'And I do really like it. But we thought it was a bit too sunny...'

'And you want moonlight?' he said softly, his eyes locking with hers. 'And music, and love, and romance? Isn't that how the song goes?'

Her stomach flipped over. When he looked at her like that there was no need to go to the opera. She could almost hear an orchestra playing.

'So...' his hand rested on a long silk jersey dress the colour of ripe Morello cherries '...how about this one?'

'Now, that was my first choice,' Gia purred approvingly.

Five minutes later Juliet was staring at her reflection again, and this time she didn't need to ask anyone how she looked. She could see the heat glittering in Ralph's eyes, and feel an answering heat flickering low in her belly as his gaze drifted over the smooth red silk.

'Yes,' he said quietly as she turned slowly on the spot.

The air hissed between them.

Yes, she thought silently.

From the front the dress looked simple enough—modest,

even, with its long sleeves and boat neckline. But from behind the fluid fabric was cut to a tantalising bottom-skimming V.

It was Gia who broke the pulsing silence. 'I think we can all agree that in this instance less is definitely more,' she said, with undisguised satisfaction.

Picking up her handbag, she sashayed across the room, kissed Juliet, and lifted her face for Ralph to graze her cheek.

'Clearly my services are no longer required, so I'll see you both at the Arena.' She paused. 'Unless you need help with your accessories?'

Shaking her head, Juliet took hold of Ralph's hand, a small smile tugging at the corners of her mouth. 'Thanks, Gia, but I already have the best accessory.'

There was a slight click as the door closed behind her. Ralph took a step forward and caught her against him, his hand low and flat on her back. Slowly she looked up into his face.

'Hi,' he said softly.

'Hi,' she whispered.

And then his mouth found hers and she felt her body turn boneless as he kissed her softly.

When they broke apart she caught his arms, her fingers pressing against the heat of his skin. 'I missed you.'

His lips curved up at the corners. 'I missed you too.'

Pulling her close, he rubbed his face against hers. The heat of his body and the warm, clean scent of his skin was making her head spin.

'I don't know how I'm ever going to go back to work,' he murmured. 'I can't bear being apart from you.'

The steady burn of his gaze made her an ache grow in her stomach. 'I can't bear it either.'

She could say that now—could admit her need for him without fearing that it was all they shared.

Which was lucky. Because right now it was a need that was making her feel as if she was melting from the inside out.

'I'd better get this dress back on the hanger.' Lifting the skirt with her foot, she flicked it to one side and cleared her throat. 'Could you help me?'

There was a slight pause, and then he nodded. 'With pleasure,' he said softly, moving closer.

His hands were gentle but firm as he turned her away from him, and her skin twitched as his fingers slid over the smooth fabric to the concealed zip.

As he pulled the dress down over her shoulders she felt her pulse accelerate. 'Wait a minute.' Grabbing the frame of the bed for balance, she bent over. 'Let me take my shoes off—'

He caught her wrist. 'No, keep them on.'

Ralph held his breath as she looked up at him, her soft brown eyes wide with longing, her cheeks flushed with the same hunger that was turning his body to stone.

He'd been on the phone all morning, going over the last-minute arrangements for the ball tomorrow. When he'd gone looking for Giulietta he'd actually forgotten that she would be trying on dresses with Gia. He'd just wanted to see her...to hear her voice. To touch base.

Only now he was with her he wanted to do so much more.

He wanted to kiss and caress and lick and stroke and tease.

Reaching out, he slid the dress slowly down over her stomach, holding her steady as she stepped free of the silky fabric. Now she was naked except for her simple white panties, and his eyes abseiled jerkily down her thighs to her skin-toned patent high heels.

For a moment he forgot to breathe. His body ached—*hell*, even his teeth ached because he wanted her so badly.

Her breasts were quivering slightly, the nipples already taut beneath his gaze, and as the blood surged down to his groin he thought he might actually pass out.

Almost without conscious thought, he slid one hand to the nape of her neck. The other moved to cup her breast as he kissed her softly, then more fiercely as he felt the slide of her tongue against his own.

His fingers moved from her breast to her hip and then, pushing past the waistband of her panties, he parted her thighs and with the delicate, measured precision of a *maestro pasticcere* found the nub of her clitoris.

He bit back a groan as her hand found his and she pressed his fingers against the damp fabric. She was already so wet for him.

Dropping to his knees, he slid his hands beneath her panties and pulled them gently down her legs. He took a breath, inhaling her scent. Then, resting his head against the cotton-soft skin of her thigh, his hands gripping her bottom to hold her steady, he traced a path between the dark curls, his flattened tongue merciless as she opened herself to him.

Her hands caught in his hair and he heard the sudden hitch in her breath, and then she was pulling him closer, crying out as she spasmed against his mouth. 'Let me!'

His erection was straining against the front of his jeans and she unzipped him, and then she was pushing him urgently onto the bed, her fingers wrapping around his fully aroused length.

'Ah, Giulietta...'

He breathed out her name, his fingers moving automatically to grip her hair as she knelt down in front of him and he felt her mouth slide over the swollen, heavy head of his erection.

Looking down, he felt his breath hiss between his teeth as he watched her guide him in, inch by inch.

When she ran her tongue over the raised ridge of his frenulum, he grunted. His head was swimming and his body felt as if it was dissolving, unravelling, the tug of her mouth acting with the gravitational force of a black hole.

He pulled out, panting, his heart raging, and then, standing up unsteadily, he turned her so that she was bending over the bed. Gazing down at the curve of her back, he felt his body tighten unbearably. He gripped her hips—and then he remembered.

'Don't move,' he said hoarsely. 'I'm just going to grab—'

'*No.*' She caught his hand. 'No. I don't—we don't need to. I don't want to.'

Her eyes were soft and dazed.

'Are you sure?'

She gave him an open-mouthed kiss by way of assent, and he kissed her back fiercely, drawing her up against his body.

Shivers of anticipation were rippling over her skin and, heart hammering, he pressed his erection against the soft cushion of her bottom. He lifted her hips and she backed up to meet him. Reaching under her stomach, he found her breast, brushing a thumb over the nipple, feeling it swell and harden.

Her soft moan acted like gasoline on the flames of his desire and, shifting slightly, he eased into her in one smooth movement. As her slick heat enveloped him he felt his control snap. His hands splayed against her back and he began to thrust inside her.

Moaning, she rocked against him, meeting his thrusts, her breath staccato, her whole body shaking now. He thrust harder and she gasped. He felt her jerk against him, and then he felt her fingers cupping him, squeezing gently, and he was jerking against her, a jagged cry jamming his throat, his body spilling into hers with molten force.

Breathing raggedly, he eased out of her and they both collapsed on the bed together.

He understood the significance of what they had just done—what she had allowed him to do.

It was a sign—a physical demonstration of her commitment to him, to their future, and the fact that she felt that way made an ache swell behind his ribs. The fact that she trusted him enough to show him so candidly, so passionately, almost undid him.

'What are you thinking about?' she asked,

Her hand was pressed against his shirt and, looking down, he saw that she was searching his face. In the past when she'd asked him that question he'd usually changed the subject. Or kissed her. Sometimes both. But now he gently smoothed her hair from her face and met her gaze.

'I was thinking about us. About how we met. About why I stopped that day.'

Her mouth tugged up at one corner. 'You're a gentleman and you saw a woman in distress.'

He frowned. 'No, that can't be it. I wasn't actually sure you were human, let alone female.'

'Hey!' She punched him lightly on the arm and he started laughing.

'To be fair, you looked like a drowned cat.' He caught her arm and pulled her closer. 'But you're right—I did think you needed help.'

His heart turned over as he remembered the electrifying jolt that had gone through his body, the absolute, unshakeable certainty that she was *the one*.

Reaching down, he brushed her cheek with his thumb. 'Only I was wrong. You were rescuing me.'

His life had been in a tailspin. But this woman—this beautiful, strong, loyal woman—had faced her own fears to stop him crash landing.

She stared at him steadily. 'We rescued each other.'

He brushed his lips across hers. 'And one very savage and ungrateful cat,' he said softly, gathering her against him as she buried her face in his shoulder, shaking with laughter.

For Juliet, the past twenty-four hours had seemed to pass in the space of a heartbeat, and now they were fast approaching the hour when the beautiful mirror-lined ballroom would be filled with guests.

But right now the room was empty.

The team in charge of staging the ball had worked almost non-stop to get everything in place, and from the polished parquet floor to the frescoed ceiling it all looked quite magical.

After the frantic efforts of the last few days, the silence now was intense, almost vertiginous. Or maybe that was guilt, she thought, glancing at the Rococo clock that stood at the end of the room.

Everyone else was busy getting ready. Glancing down at her cashmere robe and slippered feet, she bit her lip. She should be getting ready too. But she had wanted a private sneaky peek.

Turning slowly on the spot, she felt a rush of satisfaction.

Burnished silver bowls were filled with the palest pink roses, chandeliers glittered and the huge velvet curtains were beautifully swagged. All of it looked perfect.

Somewhere in the house a door slammed, and her heart started beating a little faster.

This year it needed to be more perfect than ever.

This year would be the first time in thirty years that the ball for three hundred carefully selected guests would not be hosted by Francesca and Carlo Castellucci.

This year she and Ralph would have that honour.

She felt a lurch of panic, as if the marble floor she was standing on had turned to ice.

Panic was understandable, she told herself quickly. It was not just an honour, but a responsibility.

Her breath caught in her throat. She should be feeling happy, and she had been happy back on the *Alighieri*, a kind of sweet, piercing happiness that had felt unassailable.

Her hand curved against her stomach. Whatever the future held, they would face it together.

Together.

Except the word seemed slippery, treacherous, unsteady—as if she was holding something that was too big for her hands, so that it was always on the verge of sliding between her fingers.

She glanced nervously up at the paintings above the mirrors, feeling the cool, assessing gaze of Ralph's ancestors.

It had been building, this feeling, as the hour of the ball had got ever closer. The familiar shifting doubts had been closing in on her like early-evening shadows. And now they were rising up and threatening to swallow her whole.

Turning away from the paintings, she glanced down at the name cards on the nearest table, her heart pounding as she read the beautiful italic writing.

Il Signor Castellucci
La Signora Castellucci

She took a deep breath, striving for calm.

It was crazy to feel so insecure, so inadequate.

She was married to the most glamorous man in the world—a man she loved, a man who loved her. And they had a seamless, innate understanding of each other, like skaters moving together with smooth synchronicity across a frozen lake.

Her chest ached sharply, as if she'd run out of breath.

Of course it was easy to spin and turn and leap when it was just the two of you on the ice. It would be harder when there were other people around to get in your way and trip you up.

But Ralph would be there to catch her if she fell. He had told her that—just as he had told her that he wanted *every* possible version of her. There was nothing to fear. Not from their guests and certainly not from a bunch of oil paintings.

From somewhere inside the house she heard the sound of voices coming from where Roberto was briefing the assembled waiting staff.

Her stomach fluttered. What was she doing? Standing here half-dressed with her hair in rollers, unpicking herself?

Tonight was a celebration. Plus, Anna was probably already upstairs, waiting to do her hair and make-up.

Blanking her mind, she turned and made her way back through the *palazzo*.

Forty minutes later the rollers were gone and in their place was a sleek, sculptured chignon.

All she had to do now was put on her dress.

Heart hammering, she checked her appearance in the mirror in their bedroom.

'It's got the night off.'

A ripple of quicksilver ran down her spine and she turned to where Ralph stood, watching her. Heat pulsed across her skin.

The first time she'd seen him in an evening suit she'd felt as though the world had tilted on its axis. And nothing had changed, she thought, her fingers gripping the chest of drawers to steady herself.

He wore a dark classic single-button tuxedo with peaked lapels, a white French-cuffed dress shirt, and superbly tailored trousers that hung perfectly to graze the tops of his handmade black Oxfords.

She frowned. 'I don't understand...'

He walked slowly towards her, his face unsmiling. 'The mirror. Not that you need to ask.' Reaching out, he touched her cheek gently. 'You are the fairest in the land.' His eyes held hers and then he smiled. 'But I think there's something missing.'

Reaching into his pocket, he pulled out a small square box. Her pulse stumbled as he flipped it open to reveal a pair of dark red pear-cut ruby earrings.

'Ralph, you didn't have to,' she whispered, touching them lightly. 'Oh, but they're so beautiful.'

He stared at her steadily. 'No, *you're* beautiful. They're just baubles.'

As she put the earrings on her eyes met his in the reflection of the mirror, and the slow, lambent burn of his gaze made her skin feel hot and tight.

Reaching out, he flicked one of the delicate jewels with his finger, and she felt her pulse beat in time with the oscillating pendant.

'You're going to be the belle of the ball tonight. But you're always my *bella* Giulietta.'

She felt her stomach clench. More than anything she wanted

to believe him. To believe that she had a right to be here, to be his wife. *Unconditionally.*

Smiling back at his reflection, she cleared her throat. 'You scrub up pretty well yourself.'

His answering smile seemed to press down on her pubic bone and suddenly, illogically, breathing made her breathless.

'Thank you for these, Ralph.'

He was standing behind her, so close she could feel his warm breath feathering the nape of her neck. The weight of his hand felt sensual, intimate, possessive...

'It's my pleasure,' he said softly.

She felt his fingers splay against the bare skin of her back and lightning skittered down her spine. It would be so easy to move her head a little, to turn into him and seek his lips, to lose herself and her fears in the firm, insistent press of his mouth...

He groaned. 'Don't look at me like that, *bella.*'

She bit her lip. 'Sorry.'

'No, I'm sorry.' A muscle tightened in his jaw. 'I'm just a bit tense.'

'It's going to be fine.' The desperation she'd heard in his voice, his willingness to share his fear, made her fingers tighten around his. 'I'll be there to make sure it is.'

It hurt her—hurt with a debilitating relentless intensity—to know that she had come so close to breaking that vow that she had let her fears and insecurities come between them.

'I wish—' He screwed up his face, stopped.

'Wish what?' She looked up at him, and kept looking until he shook his head.

'It's stupid. I just wish we knew about the baby already.'

She felt his words, and the longing in his eyes, tug at her heart. She felt the same way. The thought of walking into the Verona Arena knowing that she was carrying Ralph's child almost undid her. She wanted it so badly.

They both did.

As he pulled her against him his phone buzzed from across

the room. It would be Marco, letting them know that the car was ready for them.

'I'll tell him we need a bit longer,' she said quickly. Her head was buzzing. Her throat felt as though it was closing up.

'No, it's fine.' Catching her hand in his, he lifted it to his mouth and kissed it gently. 'I'm ready if you are.'

For one wild moment she wanted to ask him whether this was real. Whether all this intimacy and certainty would fade like it had before, after Rome.

But she was being stupid.

Ralph had made it clear that he loved her—every version of her.

He'd told her that.

And, yes, they were just words, but they had come from the heart and she needed to trust in them. To trust in him and their incredible intuitive understanding of each other.

Stomach lurching, she steadied her nerves and forced a smile. 'I am.'

The journey into the city was surprisingly swift. As VIPs, the Castelluccis had a police escort, and they were waved past the lines of traffic.

The opera was packed—a sell-out, in fact. Fourteen thousand people waiting excitedly for a performance of *La Traviata*.

She had never seen so many people—so many beautiful, well-connected people—but she didn't care. There was only one face that mattered to her.

But she could sense that her husband was searching the crowd for one face.

Her pulse accelerated. She knew that, for him, tonight was not just about 'moonlight and music and love and romance'. It was about putting ghosts to rest and making a silent, heartfelt prayer for the future.

She felt Ralph's hand tense in hers as Carlo Castellucci stepped towards them, handsome in his dark suit.

'*Ciao*, Giulietta, *mia cara*, you look divine. Ralph, *mio figlio*.'

Watching the two men embrace, she felt her tears sting her eyes. Whatever their DNA might say, they were father and son, and she knew that nothing, not even the truth, could come between them.

But would that be true for her and Ralph?

Suddenly she was struggling not to cry, and it was a relief when the orchestra began to tune up and they took their seats.

Darkness fell, and the hum of voices settled into silence It was time to light the *mocoleto*—the candles handed out to the audience in homage to the ancient history of the Arena as a place of entertainment.

'Here.' Ralph bent forward, lighting her candle with his.

'Ralph, I just need to—'

'I know I don't—'

They both spoke at once.

She stared at him, her heart beating fast and out of time. 'You first,' she said quickly.

Their eyes met above the tiny, fluttering flames.

'I know I don't say it enough,' he said, 'but I love you, Giulietta. You...our baby...' he rested his hand against her stomach '...you're everything I've ever wanted.'

In the flickering circle of light, his face was so serious, so beautiful, so essential to her. She could hear the hope, the yearning in his voice, and then she thought about the excruciating loneliness she'd felt in London.

Her mouth was dry, her throat tight.

She couldn't ask him now if he'd meant what he said—couldn't break the spell of his words.

Instead she leaned into him, their mouths fusing as the beautiful, sweeping score by Verdi rose from the orchestra pit and soared upwards to the starry sky.

CHAPTER TEN

GAZING AROUND THE crowded ballroom, Ralph knew he should be feeling satisfied with how the evening was progressing—and part of him was more than satisfied.

Everything was going exactly as planned.

The tables from dinner had been cleared away and waiters with trays of drinks were moving smoothly between the women in their shimmering dresses and the men in their monochromatic evening wear. Beneath the ornate Venetian glass chandeliers people were dancing and talking and laughing.

All that remained was for him to introduce the auction. But tonight was always going to be about more than giving people a good time and raising money.

This was Francesca Castellucci's event.

His mother had started it in the first year of her marriage and, thanks to her, it had grown from being a small soirée for family and friends to a major social event.

Glancing across the room, he felt his shoulders tense.

His mother had not only been beautiful and vivacious, she'd

made things happen—only for months now he'd been struggling to come to terms with some of those things.

But stepping into her shoes this evening had made him understand her more, had made him realise that she hadn't been just his mother. She had been a woman with strengths and flaws.

And he missed her. Every day.

Only thanks to the woman walking towards him now he'd been able to face the past and move forward in his life to embrace the wonderful present.

He glanced over at Giulietta, his eyes lingering on her flat stomach beneath the clinging silk of her dress. Being here with her tonight was not just about the present, but the future—a new and exciting future. A future that might already be growing inside her.

His heart began to beat a little faster.

He'd wanted a baby before, but back then it had only been a possibility. Here, tonight, at the ball founded by his mother and with both his fathers in attendance, it felt more real, somehow, and more insistent. It was a wordless, elemental need to have something of his own—a continuation of his bloodline.

'Are you okay?' Her hand found his.

He was having to lean into her to make himself heard above the hum of laughter and conversation, and as her warm breath grazed her throat he felt a flicker of corresponding heat in his groin.

He had a strong urge to scoop her into his arms and carry her upstairs. To lose himself in the heat and intensity of their coupling.

But he was a little bit older and wiser now.

Refusing to face the past had nearly destroyed his marriage and he would not make the same mistake again. And his past was here in this room.

Both the *passato prossimo* and the *imperfecto*.

His gaze travelled from Carlo Castellucci to where Niccolò

Farnese stood, with his wife Marina and his daughter Vittoria—Ralph's half-sister—his head bent in conversation with the lead tenor from the evening's performance.

As though sensing his gaze, Vittoria looked up and smiled across the room, but then his heart bumped against his ribs as he realised that his half-sister wasn't smiling at him, but at Juliet. And his wife was smiling too.

Reaching out, he caught her by the waist, his thumbs gently brushing over the smooth silk of her dress. 'I'm better than okay,' he said softly.

There was a clinking of silver on glass, and a hush fell on the room. Turning, Ralph saw that Carlo was standing slightly apart, a glass and a knife in his hand.

'I know this year I've taken a bit of a back seat in the arrangements for our family's annual ball, but I hope Ralph won't mind if I say a few words before the start of tonight's auction.'

It wasn't on the running order, but Ralph shook his head. 'Of course not, Papà.'

Carlo smiled. 'Thank you—and thank you to all of you for coming here tonight. As you know, the money raised goes to the charitable foundation set up by my late wife, and it really does make a difference to people's lives.'

He waited for the enthusiastic applause to die down and then began speaking again.

'I miss Francesca,' he said simply. 'And I don't think I will ever not miss her. But it's not Francesca I want to talk about tonight. It's my son, Ralph, without whose strength and support I would have gone under.'

Ralph felt a tug at his heart as Carlo turned to face him.

'I'm in no need of charity, but he makes a difference to my life every day, and I don't think I've made that clear enough. So I'd like to remedy that now, if I may.' Holding up his glass, his father smiled across the room. 'To Ralph. For making a difference to me.'

As everyone lifted their glasses and repeated the toast Ralph felt a sharp sting of love and guilt for the man who had raised him.

Voices were buzzing in his head. Suddenly it was an effort to breathe. He felt dizzy—nauseous, almost.

He hid it well. His handsome face was smooth, and a smile pulled at his mouth so that nobody would know he was deeply moved.

Except Giulietta.

Without thinking, he leaned into her soft body and kissed her.

'It's okay,' she whispered softly against his mouth. 'It's okay.'

He pulled her closer, his fingers seeking the curve of her spine like a rock climber searching for a handhold. The pain in his chest felt as if it would never leave.

'Ralph...'

It was Carlo, smiling, calm.

'Sorry, Giulietta. I wonder if it would be possible to have a quick word with my son? I promise not to keep him long.'

Beside him, he felt Giulietta nod.

'Of course. There's someone I've been meaning to speak to all evening,' she said quickly, squeezing his hand before she let it go. 'Take as long as you need.'

As long as you need.

The words echoed inside his head as he followed Carlo into the drawing room, where he'd imagined them talking so many times in his dreams. But how long would it take before he would be ready to honour this man with the truth?

He shut the door, expecting his father to sit down, but instead Carlo walked over to where someone—probably Roberto—had put out a decanter of whisky and two glasses.

Clearly his father had planned this... His heart began to pound. Except Carlo didn't drink whisky as a rule.

'Here.' His father held out a glass. 'I hope you don't mind me taking you away from the party—it's just that we haven't seen much of one another lately, and...well, tonight is your mother's night. It always will be.'

Ralph nodded, his chest tightening at the hollowed-out note in his father's usually polished voice. 'I know, Papà.'

Carlo smiled unsteadily. 'I let her down, Ralph.'

'No!' The word exploded from his lips as he shook his head. 'You loved her, Papà. You took care of her.'

'Yes, I did.' His father nodded, his smile fading. 'But I still let her down. You see, she asked me to do something...something important...and I haven't. I couldn't. I was too scared. Too scared of losing you too.'

Ralph frowned. His head felt strange, flimsy and thin, as if it were made of paper. 'I don't understand, Papà.'

Except he did.

Around him the room seemed to fold in on itself, and he gripped the back of an armchair to get his balance back.

'You know,' he said shakily.

'That I'm not your biological father? Yes.'

There was a brightness to Carlo's eyes as he nodded.

'Your mother told me just after she found out she was pregnant with you.' His mouth twisted. 'I know you're angry with her, and that's completely understandable. But please don't judge her. She made a bad choice and she was so ashamed. That's why she found it so hard to talk to you about it.' Carlo's gaze was clear and unflinching. 'But we were both at fault, Ralph.'

Ralph met his father's eyes. 'I believe you.'

Marriages might look balanced to an outsider, but he knew from his own experience that they were a perpetually shifting equation of power and need and expectation.

'But we never stopped loving one another, and both of us wanted to make our marriage—*our family*—work.' Carlo took a deep breath. 'That's why we decided not to tell you until you were old enough to understand. And, of course, Niccolò and Marina had started their own family.'

'Vittoria…' Ralph said quietly.

'Yes, Vittoria.' Carlo gave him a small, stiff smile. 'When she came to the house your mother was devastated. She had no idea that Niccolò had kept those letters.' Reaching out, Carlo gripped Ralph's arm. 'She hated it that you found out that way. It was wrong, and unfair, and we should have told you. I know that now, and there's no excuse except that we both loved you so much and were scared of how you'd react.'

Ralph saw that tears were sliding down his father's handsome face.

'Before she died she made me promise to tell you everything—only I couldn't make myself do it.'

'I should have come to you.' Ralph didn't even try to hide the emotion in his voice. 'I should have talked to you.'

'No.' Carlo was shaking his head. 'You've grown into a fine young man but I'm the adult here, and you'll always be my child…*my son.'* He took another breath. 'That is if you still want to be.'

Ralph couldn't speak, but words were unnecessary for what he needed to say and, stepping forward, he embraced his father.

Carlo's arms hugged him close. 'I want you to know that I will support you in everything you want to do—including getting to know Niccolò.' Loosening his grip, he smiled shakily. 'And your mother felt the same way.'

'Thank you, Papà.'

'No, thank *you, mio figlio.'* His father squeezed his shoulder. 'And believe me when I say that you *are* a Castellucci, Ralph. Our family bond goes beyond blood and that in the end is all that matters: family.'

Ralph felt his heart swell. More than anything, he wanted to tell his father that Giulietta might be pregnant. It would be the perfect gift to repay Carlo's love and loyalty. A chance to demonstrate his own love and commitment to the family that had raised him.

But he would need to run it past Juliet first...

After Carlo and Ralph had left the ballroom, Juliet turned and walked over to where a dark-haired woman with eyes like her husband was looking up at a beautiful Titian.

'Vittoria,' she said quietly.

'Juliet.'

There had been no need for introductions as both women had reached out to embrace each other.

As they stepped apart, Vittoria held on to Juliet's hand. 'I'm so sorry for the trouble I've caused. When I found the letters I freaked out. I thought Ralph was the only one who would understand, and he was so kind and patient.'

She screwed up her face.

'Only I didn't think about how it would look. I didn't think about anything or anyone but myself.'

Her fingers tightened around Juliet's.

'Do you think you can forgive me?'

'Of course I can forgive you,' Juliet said gently.

How could she not?

Up close, the similarities between the half-siblings were subtle, but irrefutable—the shape and colour of their eyes, the line of their noses...

'You were thinking about your family. And, actually, you did me—both of us—a favour.'

Breathing out shakily, Vittoria glanced over her shoulder. 'I should be getting back. My father wants me to bid on that BVLGARI bracelet. It's a surprise for my mum so he's taken her out to see the gardens.' She smiled. 'But perhaps we could go out to lunch one day.'

Juliet took a quick breath, steadied her voice. 'I'd like that. I'd like that very much.'

She watched Vittoria leave, then turned back to look up at the Titian. She had been terrified to approach Vittoria, but now she was glad she'd done it. Perhaps they might even become friends.

'There you are...'

Ralph was by her side. 'Ralph, I was—' she began, but he caught her hand.

'I need to talk to you.'

She searched his face, his eyes, and knew without having to ask that he had told his father the truth.

Heart hammering, she let him lead her through the house and up the stairs to their bedroom. As he pushed the door shut he turned and clasped her face, his thumbs stroking her cheeks as he stared down at her.

Her hands gripped his arms. His whole body was trembling. 'You told him, didn't you?' she said gently. 'About not being his son.'

She felt his shoulders shift, the muscles in his chest tighten.

'I didn't have to. He already knew.'

'I don't understand...' She stared at him, blinking.

'My mother told him right at the start when she found out she was pregnant. She told him she'd had an affair, and that she wanted to try and make things work between them.'

She bit into her lip. 'And they did.' Tears filled her eyes. 'They must have loved each other very much.'

'They did.' His mouth twisted. 'You know that was the hardest thing for me—thinking that it had all been a sham, an act. But it wasn't.'

She gripped his arms more tightly. 'I'm so happy for you, Ralph—and for Carlo.'

He breathed out shakily. 'They did think about telling me the truth, but then Niccolò and Marina had Vittoria, and everyone seemed happy.'

She nodded. 'I talked to Vittoria. She's really nice.'

'She is. She found it hard at the beginning...' He paused, his eyes locking with hers. 'But she's like all the women in my life. Strong and smart.'

She shook her head. 'You did this, Ralph, not me. It was you and Carlo.'

'No, I couldn't have done it without you. I would have just kept on burying myself in work and pushing you away.' His arm tightened around her waist. 'You pushed back. You made me realise that if I didn't deal with my past I'd lose everything.' He touched her stomach lightly. 'And I have so much to lose.'

His eyes on hers were bright with unshed tears of love and longing.

'Not just our marriage, but our future.' He breathed out shakily. 'It was so hard not telling him that you could be pregnant. I didn't say anything, but I know it would mean so much to him. I thought perhaps we could call him from the clinic.'

The eagerness in his voice made her shake inside. But, forcing a smile to her face, she nodded, and he slid his hand round the nape of her neck, drawing her close.

For a moment they just leaned into one another, his tears mingling with hers. She couldn't breathe. Her throat seemed to have shrunk, so that it felt as if she was having to squeeze her words out.

'So, how does Carlo feel about you talking to Niccolò?'

'He understands why I'd want to, and I will talk to him…'

'But not tonight?'

Their eyes met and he shook his head, his mouth tipping up at one corner. 'No, not tonight. I have other priorities—' He broke off, his face tensing as he glanced down at his watch. 'Like the auction.'

'So go.' She pressed her hands against his chest. 'Go on. I'm just going to tidy myself up a bit and then I'll follow.'

'Are you sure?' He looked uncertain.

'Of course. I'll be down in a minute. Go.'

Left alone, she walked into the bathroom and held her hands

under the cold tap. Thanks to Anna, her mascara hadn't run, but she could feel her pulse leaping in her wrists.

Lifting her head, she stared at her face. Like most girls growing up, she had pored over pictures of her favourite celebrities, thinking that if only she could look like them her life would be different...*better*.

Now, though, staring at her own glossy lips, her smoky eyes and artfully flushed cheeks, she knew that anyone could look the part. It was how you felt on the inside that mattered.

And she felt as if everything was crumbling to dust...all her hopes and certainties.

She turned off the tap, watching the water spiral down the plughole. For so long she had been scared of the past. Scared of repeating her parents' mistakes, of becoming a person she didn't want to be against her will.

Now, though, she could see that the past wasn't the threat. It was the present. The here and now. The person she was.

And if that person wasn't carrying Ralph's baby, what then?

Her heart pounded like a cannon against her ribs.

Earlier in the ballroom, before the ball had started, she'd reminded herself that Ralph had told her he loved her—every version of her.

And he'd been telling the truth. She knew that. Speaking from the heart.

But what his heart wanted more than anything was for her to be pregnant.

Only what would happen if she wasn't?

They had grown so close in the past few days—surely nothing could come between them.

Except it had after Rome.

And how could she be sure that it wouldn't again?

How could she be sure of anything?

Her whole life had been spent second-guessing her parents, and how many times had she got it wrong?

She couldn't breathe. Everything was tangling inside her.

If only she could talk to someone.

Not Ralph. She couldn't bear even thinking that she might see doubt in his face, distance in his eyes.

There was no one. She was alone.

'*Sold!* To Signor Gino Rosso. *Grazie*, Gino.' Smiling, Ralph banged the gavel down as a ripple of applause filled the ballroom. 'And now, I'm going to hand over to my cousin, Felix. But please keep bidding, people. Remember, it's all for a very good cause.'

Still smiling, Ralph made his way through the tables and chairs, his eyes fixed on the huge double doors at the end of the room. But as he left the ballroom his smile faded. After the noise of the ball the house felt oddly silent, and he glanced down at his watch, frowning.

It had been at least thirty minutes since he'd left Giulietta upstairs, and he'd half expected to meet her on her way to find him. Only the hallway was empty.

His shoulders tensed. Surely it couldn't take her that long to tidy herself up?

There was no reason to think that anything was wrong, but he still took the stairs two at a time.

Their bedroom was in darkness and, switching on the lights, he saw that it was empty. The bathroom was empty too, and for a moment he stood in the doorway, unsure of what to do.

And then a chill slid over his skin as he realised the doors to the balcony were open.

And then he was walking swiftly, fear blotting out all thought.

'Giulietta,' he said hoarsely.

She was sitting on the marble floor, hugging her knees, face lowered.

His limbs felt like lead, but his thoughts were spinning uncontrollably. *Had she hurt herself? Was she ill?*

He was by her side in three strides. Crouching down, he touched her gently. 'What is it, *bella*? Are you okay?'

As she looked up at him a tear rolled down her cheek. He felt her pain inside him, and it was more terrible than anything he'd ever experienced because it was *her* pain.

He sat down beside her and pulled her onto his lap. Holding her close, he let her cry, his fingertips drawing slow circles against her hair until finally a shuddering breath broke from her throat.

'Tell me what it is and I will fix it,' he told her.

She shook her head. 'You can't fix it, Ralph.'

Her voice sounded small and cramped, and a thin sweat spread over his body. 'Then I'll fight it.'

He stared at her, the muscles in his arms bunching. He was desperate to do something—anything—to take away the pain in her voice.

Shaking her head again, she breathed in a shaky breath. 'You can't fight it. It's me.'

His heart jumped. There was something about her posture, the way she was curled in on herself, as though she was trying to hold on to something. Or had already lost it.

'Has something happened?'

She looked up at him, her gaze searching his face. 'You mean with the baby?'

'I suppose I do,' he said quietly. 'But if something's happened to the baby, then it's happened to you too, *bella*.'

Reaching out, Ralph stroked her face gently. Fresh tears spilled down her cheeks.

'Nothing's happened,' she said. 'But what if it had? What if it does?'

She looked down, biting her lip. 'I know how much you want this baby to be real, Ralph. I know how important it is right now for you and your father, for your family...'

He brought her closer against him. 'I do want this baby to be real for my father, and for us, but—'

He swallowed, remembering what it had felt like to walk into their bedroom and find it empty that first time, and then again tonight. Seeing her curled up in a ball like that had been even more devastating.

Burying his face against her hair, he breathed out shakily. 'But when I found you I wasn't thinking about the baby. I thought you were hurt,' he whispered. 'And I didn't care about anything else. You're all that matters to me.'

It was true.

Downstairs, with Carlo, the idea of a baby had seemed so urgent to him, so imperative—only now he realised that this woman, their love was enough.

'But what about…?' She hesitated, her eyes seeking his. 'Will you mind if I'm not pregnant? I mean, I know that's the reason—'

'It was never the reason.' He cupped her face in his hands and kissed her softly. 'You're the reason, *bella*. I love you. Yes, I want you to be pregnant, but if you're not then we'll try again. And if you can't get pregnant then we'll adopt.' His expression gentled. 'In fact, we should do that anyway.'

For a few seconds Ralph rested his forehead against hers, and she felt her heart slow in time with his.

'My life is so blessed already, and I'm sorry that I made you feel that it wasn't—that you weren't enough. Because you are.' His hand moved gently through her hair. 'And I'd give up all of this in a heartbeat, for you.'

She glanced out at the beautiful moonlit grounds. 'You don't need to go that far,' she said, letting a teasing smile tug at the corners of her mouth.

The answering gleam in his eyes seemed to push through her skin.

Reaching out and gripping his jacket, she drew him closer. 'I love you. Ralph. I never stopped loving you, even when I didn't want to—even when I was scared to love you.'

Above them, the sky was starting to grow pale.

His golden gaze drifted slowly across her face, searching,

seeing everything. She felt his love warm her skin, filling her with heat, and she closed her eyes against another hot rush of tears.

'*E ti amo, Giulietta,*' he said softly, drawing her face close to his. 'You're my sun, my light, my life. Whatever happens, you're all I need. For ever.'

Juliet gazed up at his face…a face that was as familiar, as necessary to her as the sun now rising behind the hills.

And her love for him was as eternal as his for her. Feeling the first rays of light reach over the balcony she leaned into his body, closing her eyes as his mouth found hers.

EPILOGUE

'THERE YOU ARE.' Lucia rushed forward. 'We were getting worried. I thought we might have to send out a search party.'

Shaking his head, Luca shifted Raffaelle from one arm to the other. 'I wasn't worried.'

Smiling, Juliet leaned in to kiss her friend. 'Sorry. Honestly, everything that could go wrong did. We woke up late. I dripped nail polish on my dress. Then Charlie wanted a feed...' She held up her face for Luca to kiss her, and then bent down to kiss Raffaelle. 'Hi, Rafi. And then we had to change him.'

'By "we" she means *me*.'

Turning, Juliet felt a rush of love. Ralph was standing beside her. But it wasn't just her tall, dark, handsome and dangerously tempting husband who was making her heart swell.

It was the beautiful dark-haired baby in his arms.

She felt Ralph's gaze on her face, the tight focus of his clear, golden-eyed love, and with it a vertiginous rush of happiness brighter and more vivid than the stained-glass windows of the church.

It was nearly a year since that week when she and Ralph had

found their way back to one another. A week that had started with doubt and despair and ended with hope and reconciliation.

But not with a pregnancy.

Remembering that moment in the clinic when Dr de Masi had told them the test was negative, she drew a breath. She had wept. But Ralph had held her close and told her how much he loved her and needed her, and that when it was meant to happen it would.

And it had.

Two months later she'd been pregnant.

And nine months after that Charles Francesco Castellucci had been born.

And today was his christening.

Not the usual Castellucci christening, with half the world's media tripping over themselves for a photo, but a small, private ceremony for just close friends and the family.

And they were her family too.

Ralph had been determined to make that happen—determined, too, to build on the positives from his own experience for the next generation of Castelluccis.

At that moment, the youngest member of that generation gave a short, imperious shout.

She bent over her son, breathing in his scent. He stared up at her, his small fist pressed against Ralph's shirt, his golden eyes widening as she dropped a kiss on his forehead.

'Are you ready?'

Looking up, she met Ralph's gaze. They had come so far, she thought. A year ago they had been separated by doubt and mistrust, facing their fears alone. Now they had no secrets. They talked all the time. And they still hadn't run out of ways to say, 'I love you.'

Leaning into him, she caught his arm. 'Yes, we should go in.' She smiled. 'Your fathers will be waiting.'

Ralph put his hand lightly on her hip bone and drew her against his body.

His fathers.

A year ago he had been falling apart. Everything he had taken for granted in his life had been in question. He'd felt torn, conflicted, guilty—and excruciatingly lonely.

Living what had felt like a lie, but terrified of the truth, he'd avoided his family and pushed Giulietta to the point of leaving him.

But she had made him fight for what he wanted.

And she had fought with him. For him. For them.

Without her he would still be lost at sea, running from a past he couldn't change and in the process destroying the future he craved.

Now, though—thanks to her—he had not one but two fathers waiting in the church for the ceremony to start.

It had taken some time before he'd been ready to reach out to his biological father, but he was glad he had. He liked Niccolò a lot, and Marina had been generous in giving them the space they needed to connect.

So now he felt like the luckiest man alive.

His eyes locked with Giulietta's and he felt his heart turn over.

He was the luckiest man alive.

She was the sexiest, strongest, smartest woman in the world, and together they had made a beautiful, healthy son.

Chest tightening, he glanced down at Charlie. His son was so soft and small he fitted into his arm with room to spare, but his love for him was boundless. As it was for his wife.

'Do you want to take him?'

Juliet turned to Ralph. 'No.' She shook her head. 'He's happy where he is.'

'And you? Are you happy where you are?' he asked softly.

Juliet met his eye. 'I'm happy where *you* are.'

He held out his hand. Smiling, she took it, and they walked into the church together.

* * * * *

The Sicilian
Doctor's Proposal
Sarah Morgan

Dear Reader,

The next best thing to actually being on a holiday is imagining that you're on a holiday, which is why *The Sicilian Doctor's Proposal* is set in Cornwall. I have several favorite holiday destinations, but the north coast of Cornwall, with its wild, rocky coastline and fierce sea, comes very near the top of the list and makes a perfect setting for a summer romance.

GP Alice Anderson doesn't believe that love exists, and no amount of matchmaking on the part of her friends is going to convince her otherwise. She gives her all to her patients and she isn't interested in relationships.

But then her new colleague, Gio Moretti, arrives in the tiny Cornish fishing village and suddenly her summer becomes red hot. Gio is determined to persuade her that not only does love exist, but that it exists for the two of them.

A reserved Englishwoman and a red-blooded, passionate Sicilian was an interesting combination to explore, and I loved discovering the contrasts between these two extremely different characters. Alice is the serious one who takes a scientific approach to everything. Gio is a warmhearted, romantic Sicilian who believes in love and the strength of the family. I hope you enjoy reading their story.

Sarah

For the Blue Watch at Bethel Street
with many thanks for the tour and the talk!

PROLOGUE

'I DON'T BELIEVE in love. And neither do you.' Alice put her pen down and stared in bemusement at her colleague of five years. Had he gone mad?

'That was before I met Trish.' His expression was soft and far-away, his smile bordering on the idiotic. 'It's finally happened. Just like the fairy-tales.'

She wanted to ask if he'd been drinking, but didn't want to offend him. 'This isn't like you at all, David. You're an intelligent, hard-working doctor and at the moment you're talking like a—like a...' *A seven-year-old girl?* No, she couldn't possibly say that. 'You're not sounding like yourself,' she finished lamely.

'I don't care. She's the one. And I have to be with her. Nothing else matters.'

'Nothing else matters?' On the desk next to her the phone suddenly rang, but for once Alice ignored it. 'It's the start of the summer season, the village is already filling with tourists, most of the locals are struck down by that horrid virus, you're telling me you're leaving and you don't think it matters? Please, tell me this is a joke, David, please tell me that.'

Even with David working alongside her she was working flat out to cope with the demand for medical care at the moment. It wasn't that she didn't like hard work. Work was her life. *Work had saved her.* But she knew her limits.

David dragged both hands through his already untidy hair. 'Not leaving exactly, Alice. I just need the summer off. To be with Trish. We need to decide on our future. We're in love!'

Love. Alice stifled a sigh of exasperation. Behind every stupid action was a relationship, she mused silently. She should know that by now. She'd seen it often enough. Why should David be different? Just because he'd *appeared* to be a sane, rational human being—

'You'll hate London.'

'Actually, I find London unbelievably exciting,' David confessed. 'I love the craziness of it all, the crowds of people all intent on getting somewhere yesterday, no one interested in the person next to them—' He broke off with an apologetic wave of his hand. 'I'm getting carried away. But don't you ever feel trapped here, Alice? Don't you ever wish you could do something in this village without the whole place knowing?'

Alice sat back in her chair and studied him carefully. She'd never known David so emotional. 'No,' she said quietly. 'I like knowing people and I like people knowing me. It helps when it comes to understanding their medical needs. They're our responsibility and I take that seriously.'

It was what had drawn her to the little fishing village in the first place. And now it felt like home. And the people felt like family. *More than her own ever had.* Here, she fitted. She'd found her place and she couldn't imagine living anywhere else. She loved the narrow cobbled streets, the busy harbour, the tiny shops selling shells and the trendy store selling surfboards and wetsuits. She loved the summer when the streets were crowded with tourists and she loved the winter when the beaches were empty and lashed by rain. For a moment she thought of London with its muggy, traffic-clogged streets and then she thought of her beautiful house. The house overlooking the broad sweep of the sea. The house she'd lovingly restored in every spare moment she'd had over the past five years.

It had given her sanctuary and a life that suited her. A life that was under her control.

'Since we're being honest here…' David took a deep breath and straightened, his eyes slightly wary. 'I think you should consider leaving, too. You're an attractive, intelligent woman but you're never going to find someone special buried in a place like this. You never meet anyone remotely eligible. All you think about is work, work and work.'

'David, I don't want to meet anyone.' She spoke slowly and clearly so that there could be no misunderstanding. 'I love my life the way it is.'

'Work shouldn't be your life, Alice. You need love.' David stopped pacing and placed a hand on his chest. 'Everyone needs love.'

Something inside her snapped. 'Love is a word used to justify impulsive, irrational and emotional behaviour,' she said tartly, 'and I prefer to take a logical, scientific approach to life.'

David looked a little shocked. 'So, you're basically saying that I'm impulsive, irrational and emotional?'

She sighed. It was unlike her to be so honest. *To reveal so much about herself.* And unlike her to risk hurting someone's feelings. On the other hand, he was behaving very oddly. 'You're giving up a great job on the basis of a feeling that is indefinable, notoriously unpredictable and invariably short-lived so yes, I suppose I am saying that.' She nibbled her lip. 'It's the truth, so you can hardly be offended. You've said it yourself often enough.'

'That was before I met Trish and discovered how wrong I was.' He shook his head and gave a wry smile. 'You just haven't met the right person. When you do, everything will make sense.'

'Everything already makes perfect sense, thank you.' She

reached for a piece of paper and a pen. 'If I draft an advert now, I just might find a locum for August.'

If she was lucky.

And if she wasn't lucky, she was in for a busy summer, she thought, her logical brain already involved in making lists. The village with its pretty harbour and quaint shops might not attract the medical profession but it attracted tourists by the busload and her work increased accordingly, especially during the summer months.

David frowned. 'Locum?' His brow cleared. 'You don't need to worry about a locum. I've sorted that out.'

Her pen stilled. 'You've sorted it out?'

'Of course.' He rummaged in his pocket and pulled out several crumpled sheets of paper. 'Did you really think I'd leave you without arranging a replacement?'

Yes, she'd thought exactly that. All the people she'd ever known who'd claimed to be 'in love' had immediately ceased to give any thought or show any care to those around them.

'Who?'

'I have a friend who is eager to work in England. His qualifications are fantastic—he trained as a plastic surgeon but had to switch because he had an accident. Tragedy, actually.' David frowned slightly. 'He was brilliant, by all accounts.'

A plastic surgeon?

Alice reached for the papers and scanned the CV. 'Giovanni Moretti.' She looked up. 'He's Italian?'

'Sicilian.' David grinned. 'Never accuse him of being Italian. He's very proud of his heritage.'

'This man is well qualified.' She put the papers down on her desk. 'Why would he want to come here?'

'You want to work here,' David pointed out logically, 'so perhaps you're just about to meet your soulmate.' He caught her reproving look and shrugged. 'Just joking. Everyone is entitled to a change of pace. He was working in Milan, which might explain it but, to be honest, I don't really know why he wants to come here. You know us men. We don't delve into details.'

Alice sighed and glanced at the CV on her desk. He'd probably only last five minutes, but at least he might fill the gap while she looked for someone to cover the rest of the summer.

'Well, at least you've sorted out a replacement. Thanks for that. And what happens at the end of the summer? Are you coming back?'

David hesitated. 'Can we see how it goes? Trish and I have some big decisions to make.' His eyes gleamed at the prospect. 'But I promise not to leave you in the lurch.'

He looked so happy, Alice couldn't help but smile. 'I wish you luck.'

'But you don't understand, do you?'

She shrugged. 'If you ask me, the ability to be ruled by emotion is the only serious flaw in the human make-up.'

'Oh, for goodness' sake.' Unexpectedly, David reached out and dragged her to her feet. 'It's out there, Alice. Love. You just have to look for it.'

'Why would I want to? If you want my honest opinion, I'd say that love is just a temporary psychiatric condition that passes given sufficient time. Hence the high divorce rate.' She pulled her hands away from his, aware that he was gaping at her.

'A temporary psychiatric condition?' He gave a choked laugh and his hands fell to his sides. 'Oh, Alice, you *have* to be joking. That can't really be what you believe.'

Alice tilted her head to one side and mentally reviewed all the people she knew who'd behaved oddly in the name of love. There were all too many of them. Her parents and her sister included. 'Yes, actually.' Her tone was flat as she struggled with feelings that she'd managed to suppress for years. Feeling suddenly agitated, she picked up a medical journal and scanned the contents, trying to focus her mind on fact. Facts were safe and comfortable. Emotions were dangerous and uncomfortable. 'It's exactly what I believe.'

Her heart started to beat faster and she gripped the journal more tightly and reminded herself that her life was under her control now. She was no longer a child at the mercy of other people's emotional transgressions.

David watched her. 'So you still don't believe love exists? Even seeing how happy I am?'

She turned. 'If you're talking about some fuzzy, indefinable emotion that links two people together then, no, I don't think that exists. I don't believe in the existence of an indefinable emotional bond any more than I believe in Father Christmas and the tooth fairy.'

David shook his head in disbelief. 'But I *do* feel a powerful emotion.'

She couldn't bring herself to put a dent in his happiness by saying more, so she stepped towards him and took his face in her hands. 'I'm pleased for you. Really I am.' She reached up and kissed him on the cheek. 'But it isn't "love". She sat back down and David studied her with a knowing, slightly superior smile on his face.

'It's going to happen to you, Alice.' He folded his arms across his chest and his tone rang with conviction. 'One of these days you're going to be swept off your feet.'

'I'm a scientist,' she reminded him, amusement sparkling in her blue eyes as they met the challenge in his. 'I have a logical brain. I don't believe in being swept off my feet.'

He stared at her for a long moment. 'No. Which is why it's likely to happen. Love strikes when you're not looking for it.'

'That's measles,' Alice said dryly, reaching for a pile of results that needed her attention. 'Talking of which, little Fiona Ellis has been terribly poorly since her bout of measles last winter. I'm going to check up on her today. See if there's anything else we can do. And I'm going to speak to Gina, the health visitor, about our MMR rates.'

'They dipped slightly after the last newspaper scare but I

thought they were up again. The hospital has been keeping an eye on Fiona's hearing,' David observed, and Alice nodded.

'Yes, and I gather there's been some improvement. All the same, the family need support and we need to make sure that no one else in our practice suffers unnecessarily.' She rose to her feet and smiled at her partner. 'And that's what we give in a small community. Support and individual care. Don't you think you'll miss that? In London you'll end up working in one of those huge health centres with thousands of doctors and you probably won't get to see the same patient twice. You won't know them and they won't know you. It will be completely impersonal. Like seeing medical cases on a production line.'

She knew all the arguments, of course. She understood that a large group of GPs working together could afford a wider variety of services for their patients—psychologists, chiropodists— but she still believed that a good family doctor who knew his patients intimately was able to provide a superior level of care.

'You'll like Gio,' David said, strolling towards the door. 'Women always do.'

'As long as he does his job,' Alice said crisply, 'I'll like him.'

'He's generally considered a heartthrob.' There was a speculative look on his face as he glanced towards her. 'Women go weak at the knees when he walks into a room.'

Great. The last thing she needed was a Romeo who was distracted by everything female.

'Some women are foolish like that.' Alice stood up and reached for her jacket. 'Just as long as he doesn't break more hearts than he heals, then I really don't mind what he does when he isn't working here.'

'There's more to life than work, Alice.'

'Then go out there and enjoy it,' she advised, a smile on her face. 'And leave me to enjoy mine.'

CHAPTER ONE

GIOVANNI MORETTI STOOD at the top of the narrow cobbled street, flexed his broad shoulders to try and ease the tension from the journey and breathed in the fresh, clean sea air. Above him, seagulls shrieked and swooped in the hope of benefiting from the early morning catch.

Sounds of the sea.

He paused for a moment, his fingers tucked into the pockets of his faded jeans, his dark eyes slightly narrowed as he scanned the pretty painted cottages that led down to the busy harbour. Window-boxes and terracotta pots were crammed full with brightly coloured geraniums and tumbling lobelia and a smile touched his handsome face. Before today he'd thought that places like this existed only in the imagination of artists. It was as far from the dusty, traffic-clogged streets of Milan as it was possible to be, and he felt a welcome feeling of calm wash over him.

He'd been right to agree to take this job, he mused silently, remembering all the arguments he'd been presented with. Right to choose this moment to slow the pace of his life and leave Italy.

It was early in the morning but warm, tempting smells of baking flavoured the air and already the street seemed alive with activity.

A few people in flip-flops and shorts, who he took to be tourists, meandered down towards the harbour in search of early morning entertainment while others jostled each other in their eagerness to join the queue in the bakery and emerged clutching bags of hot, fragrant croissants and rolls.

His own stomach rumbled and he reminded himself that he hadn't eaten anything since he'd left Milan the night before. Fast food had never interested him. He preferred to wait for the real thing. And the bakery looked like the real thing.

He needed a shower and a shave but there was no chance of that until he'd picked up the key to his accommodation and he doubted his new partner was even in the surgery yet. He glanced at his watch and decided that he just about had time to eat something and still time his arrival to see her just before she started work.

He strolled into the bakery and smiled at the pretty girl behind the counter. *'Buongiorno*—good morning.'

She glanced up and caught the smile. Her blue eyes widened in feminine appreciation. 'Hello. What can I offer you?'

It was obvious from the look in those eyes that she was prepared to offer him the moon but Gio ignored the mute invitation he saw in her eyes and studied the pastries on offer, accustomed to keeping women at a polite distance. He'd always been choosy when it came to women. Too choosy, some might say. 'What's good?'

'Oh—well…' The girl lifted a hand to her face, her cheeks suddenly pink. 'The *pain au chocolat* is my favourite but the almond croissant is our biggest seller. Take away or eat in?'

For the first time Gio noticed the small round tables covered in cheerful blue gingham, positioned by the window at the back of the shop. 'Eat in.' It was still so early he doubted that his partner had even reached the surgery yet. 'I'll take an almond croissant and a double espresso. *Grazie.*'

He selected the table with the best view over the harbour. The coffee turned out to be exceptionally good, the croissant wickedly sweet, and by the time he'd finished the last of his breakfast he'd decided that spending the summer in this quaint little village was going to be no hardship at all.

'Are you on holiday?' The girl on the till was putting croissants into bags faster than the chef could take them from the oven and still the queue didn't seem to diminish.

Gio dug his hand into his pocket and paid the bill. 'Not on holiday.' Although a holiday would have been welcome, he mused, his eyes still on the boats bobbing in the harbour. 'I'm working.'

'Working?' She handed him change. 'Where?'

'Here. I'm a doctor. A GP, to be precise.' It still felt strange to him to call himself that. For years he'd been a surgeon and he still considered himself to be a surgeon. But fate had decreed otherwise.

'You're our new doctor?'

He nodded, aware that after driving through the night he didn't exactly look the part. He could have been evasive, of course, but his new role in the community was hardly likely to remain a secret for long in a place this small. And, anyway, he didn't believe in being evasive. What was the harm in announcing himself? 'Having told you that, I might as well take advantage of your local knowledge. How does Dr Anderson take her coffee?'

All that he knew about his new partner was what David had shared in their brief phone conversation. He knew that she was married to her job, very academic and extremely serious. Already he'd formed an image of her in his mind. Tweed skirt, flat heels, horn-rimmed glasses—he knew the type. Had met plenty like her in medical school.

'Dr Anderson? That's easy.' The girl smiled, her eyes fixed on his face in a kind of trance. 'Same as you. Strong and black.'

'Ah.' His new partner was obviously a woman of taste. 'And what does she eat?'

The girl continued to gaze at him and then seemed to shake herself. 'Eat? Actually, I've never seen her eat anything.' She shrugged. 'Between the tourists and the locals, we probably keep her too busy to give her time to eat. Or maybe she isn't that interested in food.'

Gio winced and hoped it was the former. He couldn't imagine developing a good working partnership with someone who wasn't interested in food. 'In that case, I'll play it safe and take her a large Americano.' Time enough to persuade her of the benefits of eating. 'So the next thing you can do is direct me to the surgery. Or maybe Dr Anderson won't be there yet.'

It wasn't even eight o'clock.

Perhaps she slept late, or maybe—

'Follow the street right down to the harbour and it's straight in front of you. Blue door. And she'll be there.' The girl pressed a cap onto the coffee-cup. 'She was up half the night with the Bennetts' six-year-old. Asthma attack.'

Gio lifted an eyebrow. 'You know that?'

The girl shrugged and blew a strand of hair out of her eyes. 'Around here, everyone knows everything.' She handed him the coffee and his change. 'Word gets around.'

'So maybe she's having a lie-in.'

The girl looked at the clock. 'I doubt it. Dr Anderson doesn't sleep much and, anyway, surgery starts soon.'

Gio digested that piece of information with interest. If she worked that hard, no wonder she took her coffee strong and black.

With a parting smile at the girl he left the bakery and followed her instructions, enjoying the brief walk down the steep cobbled street, glancing into shop windows as he passed.

The harbour was bigger than he'd expected, crowded with

boats that bobbed and danced under the soft seduction of the sea. Tall masts clinked in the soft breeze and across the harbour he saw a row of shops and a blue door with a brass nameplate. The surgery.

A few minutes later he pushed open the surgery door and blinked in surprise. What had promised to be a small, cramped building proved to be light, airy and spacious. Somehow he'd expected something entirely different—somewhere dark and tired, like some of the surgeries he'd visited in London. What he hadn't expected was this bright, calming environment designed to soothe and relax.

Above his head glass panels threw light across a neat waiting room and on the far side of the room a children's corner overflowed with an abundance of toys in bright primary colours. A table in a glaring, cheerful red was laid with pens and sheets of paper to occupy busy hands.

On the walls posters encouraged patients to give up smoking and have their blood pressure checked and there were leaflets on first aid and adverts for various local clinics.

It seemed that nothing had been forgotten.

Gio was just studying a poster in greater depth when he noticed the receptionist.

She was bent over the curved desk, half-hidden from view as she sifted through a pile of results. Her honey blonde hair fell to her shoulders and her skin was creamy smooth and untouched by sun. She was impossibly slim, wore no make-up and the shadows under her eyes suggested that she worked harder than she should. She looked fragile, tired and very young.

Gio's eyes narrowed in an instinctively masculine assessment.

She was beautiful, he decided, and as English as scones and cream. His eyes rested on her cheekbones and then dropped to her perfectly shaped, soft mouth. He found himself thinking of summer fruit—strawberries, raspberries, redcurrants...

Something flickered to life inside him.

The girl was so absorbed in what she was reading that she hadn't even noticed him and he was just about to step forward and introduce himself when the surgery door swung open again and a group of teenage boys stumbled in, swearing and laughing.

They didn't notice him. In fact, they seemed incapable of noticing anyone, they were so drunk.

Gio stood still, sensing trouble. His dark eyes were suddenly watchful and he set the coffee down on the nearest table just in case he was going to need his hands.

One of them swore fluently as he crashed into a low table and sent magazines flying across the floor. 'Where the hell's the doctor in this place? Matt's bleeding.'

The friend in question lurched forward, blood streaming from a cut on his head. His chest was bare and he wore a pair of surf shorts, damp from the sea and bloodstained. 'Went surfing.' He gave a hiccup and tried to stand up without support but failed. Instead he slumped against his friend with a groan, his eyes closed. 'Feel sick.'

'Surfing when you're drunk is never the best idea.' The girl behind the desk straightened and looked them over with weary acceptance. Clearly it wasn't the first time she'd had drunks in the surgery. 'Sit him down over there and I'll take a look at it.'

'You?' The third teenager swaggered across the room, fingers tucked into the pockets of his jeans. He gave a suggestive wink. 'I'm Jack. How about taking a look at me while you're at it?' He leaned across the desk, leering. 'There are bits of me you might be interested in. You a nurse? You ever wear one of those blue outfits with a short skirt and stockings?'

'I'm the doctor.' The girl's eyes were cool as she pulled on a pair of disposable gloves and walked round the desk without giving Jack a second glance. 'Sit your friend down before he falls down and does himself more damage. I'll take a quick look at him before I start surgery.'

Gio didn't know who was more surprised—him or the teen-agers.

She was the doctor?

She was Alice Anderson?

He ran a hand over the back of his neck and wondered why David had omitted to mention that his new partner was stunning. He tried to match up David's description of a serious, academic woman with this slender, delicate beauty standing in front of him, and failed dismally. He realised suddenly that he'd taken 'single' to mean 'mature'. And 'academic' to mean 'dowdy'.

'*You're* the doctor?' Jack lurched towards her, his gait so unsteady that he could barely stand. 'Well, that's good news. I love a woman with brains and looks. You and I could make a perfect team, babe.'

She didn't spare him a glance, refusing to respond to the banter. 'Sit your friend down.' Her tone was firm and the injured boy collapsed onto the nearest chair with a groan.

'I'll sit myself down. Oh, man, my head is killing me.'

'That's what happens when you drink all night and then bang your head.' Efficient and businesslike, she pushed up the sleeves of her plain blue top, tilted his head and took a look at the cut. She parted the boy's hair gently and probed with her fingers. Her mouth tightened. 'Well, you've done a good job of that. Were you knocked out?'

Gio cast a professional eye over the cut and saw immediately that it wasn't going to be straightforward. Surely she wasn't planning to stitch that herself? He could see ragged edges and knew it was going to be difficult to get a good cosmetic result, even for someone skilled in that area.

'I wasn't knocked out.' The teenager tried to shake his head and instantly winced at the pain. 'I swallowed half the ocean, though. Got any aspirin?'

'In a minute. That's a nasty cut you've got there and it's near your eye and down your cheek. It's beyond my skills, I'm afraid.' She ripped off the gloves and took a few steps backwards, a slight frown on her face as she considered the options. 'You need to go to the accident and emergency department up the coast. They'll get a surgeon to stitch you up. I'll call them and let them know that you're coming.'

'No way. We haven't got time for that.' The third teenager, who hadn't spoken up until now, stepped up to her, his expression threatening. 'You're going to do it. And you're going to do it here. Right now.'

She dropped the gloves into a bin and washed her hands. 'I'll put a dressing on it for you, but you need to go to the hospital to get it stitched. They'll do a better job than I ever could. Stitching faces is an art.'

She turned to walk back across the reception area but the teenager called Jack blocked her path.

'I've got news for you, babe.' His tone was low and insulting. 'We're not going anywhere until you've fixed Matt's face. I'm not wasting a whole day of my holiday sitting in some hospital with a load of sickos. He doesn't mind a scar. Scars are sexy. Hard. You know?'

'Whoever does it, he'll be left with a scar,' she said calmly, 'but he'll get a better result at the hospital.'

'No hospital.' The boy took a step closer and stabbed a finger into her chest. 'Are you listening to me?'

'I'm listening to you but I don't think you're listening to me.' The girl didn't flinch. 'Unless he wants to have a significant scar, that cut needs to be stitched by someone with specific skills. It's for his own good.'

It happened so quickly that no one could have anticipated it. The teenager backed her against the wall and put a hand round her throat. 'I don't think you're listening to me, babe. It's your bloody job, Doc. Stitch him up! *Do it.*'

Gio crossed the room in two strides, just as the teenager uttered a howl of pain and collapsed onto the floor in a foetal position, clutching his groin.

She'd kneed him.

'Don't try and tell me my job.' She lifted her hand to her reddened throat. Her tone was chilly and composed and then she glanced up, noticed Gio for the first time and her face visibly paled. For a moment she just stared at him and then her gaze flickered towards the door, measuring the distance. Gio winced inwardly. It was obvious that she thought he was trouble and he felt slightly miffed by her reaction.

He liked women. Women liked him. And they usually responded to him. They chatted, they flirted, they sent him long looks. The look in Dr Anderson's eyes suggested that she was calculating ways to injure him. All right, so he hadn't had time to shave and change, but did he really look that scary?

He was about to introduce himself, about to try and redeem himself in her eyes, when the third teenager stepped towards the girl, his expression threatening. Gio closed a hand over his arm and yanked him backwards.

'I think it's time you left. Both of you.' His tone was icy cool and he held the boy in an iron grip. 'You can pick up your friend in an hour.'

The teenager balled his fists, prepared to fight, but then eyed the width of Gio's shoulders. His hands relaxed and he gave a slight frown. 'Whazzit to do with you?'

'Everything.' Gio stepped forward so that his body was between them and Dr Anderson. 'I work here.'

'What as?' The boy twisted in his grip and his eyes slid from Gio's shoulders to the hard line of his jaw. 'A bouncer?'

'A doctor. One hour. That's how long I estimate it's going to take to make a decent job of his face. Or you can drive to the hospital.' Gio released him, aware that Alice was staring at him in disbelief. 'Your choice.'

The teenager winced and rubbed his arm. 'She...' he jerked his head towards the doctor '...said he needed a specialist doctor.'

'Well, this is your lucky day, because I am a specialist doctor.'

There was a long pause while the teenager tried to focus.

'You don't look anything like a doctor. Doctors shave and dress smart. You look more like one of those—those...' His words slurred and he swayed and waved a hand vaguely. 'Those Mafia thugs that you see in films.'

'Then you'd better behave yourself,' Gio suggested silkily, casting a glance towards his new partner to check she was all right. Her pallor was worrying him. He hoped she wasn't about to pass out. 'Leave now and come back in an hour for your friend.'

'You're not English.' The boy hiccoughed. 'What are you, then? Italian?'

'I'm Sicilian.' Gio's eyes were cold. *'Never* call me Italian.'

'Sicilian?' A nervous respect entered the teenager's eyes and he licked his lips and eyed the door. 'OK.' He gave a casual shrug. 'So maybe we'll come back later, like you suggested.'

Gio nodded. 'Good decision.'

The boy backed away, still rubbing his arm. 'We're going. C'mon, Rick.' He loped over to the door and left without a backward glance.

'Dios, did he hurt you?' Gio walked over to the girl and lifted a hand to her neck. The skin was slightly reddened and he stroked a finger carefully over the bruising with a frown. 'We should call the police now.'

She shook her head and backed away. 'No need. He didn't hurt me.' She glanced towards the teenager who was still sprawled over the seats of her waiting room and gave a wry shake of her head. 'If you're Dr Moretti, we'd better see to him before he's sick on the floor or bleeds to death over my chairs.'

'It won't hurt him to wait for two minutes. You should call the police.' Gio's tone was firm. He didn't want to be too graphic about what might have happened, but it was important that she acknowledge the danger. It hadn't escaped him that if he hadn't decided to arrive at the surgery early, she would have been on her own with them. 'You should call them.'

She rubbed her neck. 'I suppose you're right. All right, I'll do it when I get a minute.'

'Does this happen often? I imagined I was coming to a quiet seaside village. Not some hotbed of violence.'

'There's nothing quiet about this place, at least not in the middle of summer,' she said wearily. 'We're the only doctors' surgery in this part of the town and the nearest A and E is twenty miles down the coast so, yes, we get our fair share of drama. David probably didn't tell you that when he was persuading you to take the job. You can leave now, if you like.'

His eyes rested on her soft mouth. 'I'm not leaving.'

There was a brief silence. A silence during which she stared back at him. Then she licked her lips. 'Well, that's good news for my patients. And good news for me. I'm glad you arrived when you did.'

'You didn't look glad.'

'Well, a girl can't be too careful and you don't exactly look like a doctor.' A hint of a smile touched that perfect mouth. 'Did you see his face when you said you were Sicilian? I think they were expecting you to put a hand in your jacket and shoot them dead any moment.'

'I considered it.' Gio's eyes gleamed with humour. 'But I've only had one cup of coffee so far today. Generally I need at least two before I shoot people dead. And you don't need to apologise for the mistake. I confess that I thought you were the receptionist. If you're Alice Anderson, you're nothing like David's description.'

'I can imagine.' She spoke in a tone of weary acceptance. 'David is seeing the world through a romantic haze at the moment. Be patient with him. It will pass, given time.'

He laughed. 'You think so?'

'Love always does, Dr Moretti. Like many viruses, it's a self-limiting condition. Left alone, the body can cure itself.'

Gio searched her face to see if she was joking and decided that she wasn't. Filing the information away in his brain for later use, he walked over to retrieve the coffee from the window-sill. 'If you're truly Dr Anderson, this is for you. An ice breaker, from me.'

She stared at the coffee with sudden hunger in her eyes and then at him. 'You brought coffee?' Judging from the expression on her face, he might have offered her an expensive bauble from Tiffany's. She lifted a hand and brushed a strand of hair out of her eyes. Tired eyes. 'For me? Is it black?'

'*Si.*' He smiled easily and handed her the coffee, amused by her response. 'You have fans in the bakery who know every detail of your dietary preferences. I was told "just coffee" so I passed on the croissant.'

'There's no such thing as "just coffee". Coffee is wonderful. It's my only vice and currently I'm in desperate need of a caffeine hit.' She prised the lid off the coffee, sniffed and gave a whimper of pleasure. 'Large Americano. Oh, that's just the best smell...'

He watched as she sipped, closed her eyes and savoured the taste. She gave a tiny moan of appreciation that sent a flicker of awareness through his body. He gave a slight frown at the strength of his reaction.

'So...' She studied him for a moment and then took another sip of coffee. Some of the colour returned to her cheeks. 'I wasn't expecting you until tomorrow. Not that I'm complaining, you understand. I'm glad you're early. You were just in time to save me from a nasty situation.'

'I prefer to drive when the roads are clear. I thought you might appreciate the help, given that David has already been gone two days. We haven't been formally introduced. I'm Gio Moretti.' He wanted to hold her until she stopped shaking but he sensed that she wouldn't appreciate the gesture so he kept his distance. 'I'm your new partner.'

She hesitated and then put her free hand in his. 'Alice Anderson.'

'I gathered that. You're really *not* what I expected.'

She tilted her head to one side. 'You're standing in my surgery having frightened off two teenage thugs by your appearance and you're telling me *I'm* not what *you* expected?' There was a hint of humour in her blue eyes and his attention was caught by the length of her lashes.

'So maybe I don't fit anyone's image of a conventional doctor right at this moment...' he dragged his gaze away from her face and glanced down at himself with a rueful smile '...but I've been travelling all night and I'm dressed for comfort. After a shave and a quick change of clothes, I will be ready to impress your patients. But first show me to a room and I'll stitch that boy before his friends return.'

'Are you sure?' She frowned slightly. 'I mean, David told me you didn't operate any more and—'

'I don't operate.' He waited for the usual feelings to rise up inside him. Waited for the frustration and the sick disappointment. Nothing happened. Maybe he was just tired. Or maybe he'd made progress. 'I don't operate, but I can certainly stitch up a face.'

'Then I'm very grateful and I'm certainly not going to argue with you. That wound is beyond my skills and I've got a full surgery starting in ten minutes.' She looked at the teenager who was sprawled across the chairs, eyes closed, and sighed. 'Oh, joy. Is it alcohol or a bang on the head, do you think?'

'Hard to tell.' Gio followed her gaze and shook his head slowly. 'I'll stitch him up, do a neurological assessment and then we'll see. Is there anyone who can help me? Show me around? I can give you a list of what I'll need.'

'Rita, our practice nurse, will be here in a minute. She's very experienced. Her asthma clinic doesn't start until ten so I'll send her in.' Her eyes slid over him. 'Are you sure you're all right with this? We weren't expecting you until tomorrow and if you've been travelling all night you must be tired.'

'I'm fine.' He studied her carefully, noting the dark shadows under her eyes. 'In fact, I'd say that you're the one who's tired, Dr Anderson.'

She gave a dismissive shrug. 'Goes with the job. I'll show you where you can work. We have a separate room for minor surgery. I think you'll find everything you need but I can't be sure. We don't usually stitch faces.'

He followed her down the corridor, his eyes drawn to the gentle swing of her hips. 'Do you have 5/0 Ethilon?'

'Yes.' She pushed open a door and held it open while he walked inside. 'Is that all you need?'

'The really important thing is to debride the wound and align the tissues exactly. And not leave the stitches in for too long.'

Her glance was interested. Intelligent. 'I wish I had time to watch you. Not that I'm about to start suturing faces,' she assured him hastily, and he smiled.

'Like most things, it's just a question of practice.'

She opened a cupboard. 'Stitches are in here. Gloves on the shelf. You're probably about the same size as David. Tetanus et cetera in the fridge.' She waved a hand. 'I'll send Rita in with the patient. I'll get on with surgery. Come and find me when you've finished.'

'Alice.' He stopped her before she walked out of the door. 'Don't forget to call the police.'

She tilted her head back and he sensed that she was wrestling with what seemed like a major inconvenience then she gave a resigned sigh.

'I'll do that.'

CHAPTER TWO

ALICE SPOKE TO RITA, called the police and then worked flat out, seeing patients, with no time to even think about checking on her new partner.

'How long have you had this rash on your eye, Mr Denny?' As she saw her tenth patient of the morning, she thought gratefully of the cup of coffee that Gio Moretti had thought to bring her. It was the only sustenance she'd had all day.

'It started with a bit of pain and tingling. Then it all went numb.' The man sat still as she examined him. 'I suppose all that began on Saturday. My wife noticed the rash yesterday. She was worried because it looks blistered. We wondered if I'd brushed up against something in the garden. You know how it is with some of those plants.'

Alice picked up her ophthalmoscope and examined his eye thoroughly. 'I don't think it's anything to do with the garden, Mr Denny. You've got quite a discharge from your eye.'

'It's very sore.'

'I'm sure it is.' Alice put the ophthalmoscope down on her desk and washed her hands. 'I want to test your vision. Can you read the letters for me?'

The man squinted at the chart on her wall and struggled to recite the letters. 'Not very clear, I'm afraid.' He looked worried. 'My eyes have always been good. Am I losing my sight?'

'You have a virus.' Alice sat down and tapped something into her computer. Then she turned back to the patient. 'I think you have shingles, Mr Denny.'

'Shingles?' He frowned. 'In my eye?'

'Shingles is a virus that affects the nerves,' she explained, 'and one in five cases occur in the eye—to be technical, it's the ophthalmic branch of the trigeminal nerve.'

He pulled a face. 'Never was much good at biology.'

Alice smiled. 'You don't need biology, Mr Denny. But I just wanted you to know it isn't uncommon, unfortunately. I'm going to need to refer you to an ophthalmologist—an eye doctor at the hospital. Is there someone who can take you up there?'

He nodded. 'My daughter's waiting in the car park. She brought me here.'

'Good.' Alice reached for the phone and dialled the clinic number. 'They'll see you within the next couple of days.'

'Do I really need to go there?'

Alice nodded. 'They need to examine your eye with a slit lamp—a special piece of equipment that allows them to look at your eye properly. They need to exclude iritis. In the meantime, I'll give you aciclovir to take five times a day for a week. It should speed up healing time and reduce the incidence of new lesions.' She printed out the prescription on the computer as she waited for the hospital to answer the phone.

Once she'd spoken to the consultant, she quickly wrote a letter and gave it to the patient. 'They're really nice up there,' she assured him, 'but if you have any worries you're welcome to come back to me.'

He left the room and Alice picked up a set of results. She was studying the numbers with a puzzled frown when Rita walked in. A motherly woman in her early fifties, her navy blue uniform was stretched over her large bosom and there was a far-away expression on her face. 'Pinch me. Go on, pinch me hard. I've died and gone to heaven.'

Alice looked up. 'Rita, have you seen Mrs Frank lately? I ran some tests but the results just don't make sense.' She'd examined the patient carefully and had been expecting something entirely different. She studied the results again. Perhaps she'd missed something.

'Forget Mrs Frank's results for a moment.' Rita closed the door behind her. 'I've got something far more important for you to think about.'

Alice didn't look up. 'I thought she had hypothyroidism. She had all the symptoms.'

'Alice...'

Still absorbed in the problem, Alice shook her head. 'The results are normal.' She checked the results one more time and checked the normal values, just in case she'd missed something. She'd been so *sure.*

'Alice!' Rita sounded exasperated. 'Are you even listening to me?'

Alice dragged her eyes away from the piece of paper in her hand, still pondering. Aware that Rita was glaring at her, she gave a faint smile. 'Sorry, I'm still thinking about Mrs Frank,' she admitted apologetically. 'What's the matter?'

'Dr Giovanni Moretti is the matter.'

'Oh, my goodness!' Alice slapped her hand over her mouth and rose to her feet quickly, ridden with guilt. 'I'd *totally* forgotten about him. How could I?'

Rita stared at her. 'How could you, indeed?'

'Don't! I feel terrible about it.' Guilt consumed her. And after he'd been so helpful. 'How could I have done that? I showed him into the room, made sure he had what he needed and I *promised* to look in on him, but I've had streams of patients this morning and I completely forgot his existence.'

'You forgot his existence?' Rita shook her head. 'Alice, how could you *possibly* have forgotten his existence?'

'I know, it's dreadful! I feel terribly rude.' She walked briskly round her desk, determined to make amends. 'I'll go and check on him immediately. Hopefully, if he'd needed any help he would have come and found me.'

'Help?' Rita's tone was dry. 'Trust me, Alice, the guy doesn't need any help from you or anyone else. He's slick. Mr Hotshot. Or I suppose I should call him Dr Hotshot.'

'He's finished stitching the boy?' She glanced at her watch for the first time since she'd started surgery and realised with a shock that almost an hour and a half had passed.

'Just the head, although personally I would have been happy to see him do the mouth as well.' Rita gave a snort of disapproval. 'Never heard such obscenities.'

'Yes, they were pretty drunk, the three of them. How does the head look?'

'Better than that boy deserves. Never seen a job as neat in my life and I've been nursing for thirty years,' Rita admitted, a dreamy expression on her face. 'Dr Moretti has *amazing* hands.'

'He used to be a surgeon. If he's done a good job and he's finished, why did you come rushing in here telling me he was having problems?'

'I never said he was having problems.'

'You said something was the matter.'

'No.' Rita closed her eyes and sighed. 'At least, not with him. Only with me. I think he's fantastic.'

'Oh.' Alice paused by the door. 'Well, he arrived a day early, brought me coffee first thing, sorted out a bunch of rowdy teenagers and stitched a nasty cut so, yes, I think he's fantastic, too. He's obviously a good doctor.'

'I'm not talking about his medical skills, Alice.'

'What are you talking about, then?'

'Alice, he's *gorgeous*. Don't tell me you haven't noticed!'

'Actually, I thought he looked a mess.' Her hand dropped from the doorhandle and she frowned at the recollection. 'But he'd been travelling all night.'

'A mess?' Rita sounded faint. 'You think he looks a *mess*?'

Alice wondered whether to confess that she'd thought he looked dangerous. Strangely enough, the teenagers hadn't bothered her. They were nothing more than gawky children and she'd had no doubts about her ability to handle them. But when she'd looked up and seen Gio standing there...

'I'm sure he'll look more respectable when he's had a shower and a shave.' Alice frowned. 'And possibly a haircut. The boy was in such a state, I didn't think it mattered.'

'You didn't even notice, did you?' Rita shook her head in disbelief. 'Alice, you need to do something about your life. The man is sex on a stick. He's a walking female fantasy.'

Alice stared at her blankly, struggling to understand. 'Rita, you've been married for twenty years and, anyway, he's far too young for you.'

Rita gave her a suggestive wink. 'Don't you believe it. I like them young and vigorous.'

Alice sighed and wished she didn't feel so completely out of step with the rest of her sex. Was she the only woman in the world who didn't spend her whole life thinking about men? Even Rita was susceptible, even though she'd reached an age where she should have grown out of such stupidity.

'He doesn't look much like a doctor,' she said frankly, 'but I'm sure he'll look better once he's shaved and changed his clothes.'

'He looks every inch a man. And he'd be perfect for you.'

Alice froze. 'I refuse to have this conversation with you again, Rita. And while we're at it, you can tell that receptionist of ours that I'm not having it with her either.'

Rita sniffed. 'Mary worries about you, as I do, and—'

'I'm not interested in men and both of you know that.'

'Well, you should be.' Rita folded her arms and her mouth clamped into a thin line. 'You're thirty years of age and—'

'Rita!' Alice interrupted her sharply. 'This is not a good time.'

'It's never a good time with you. You never talk about it.'

'Because there's nothing to talk about!' Alice took a deep breath. 'I appreciate your concern, really, but—'

'But you're married to your work and that's the way you're staying.' The older woman rose to her feet and Alice sighed.

'I'm happy, Rita.' Her voice softened slightly as she saw the worry in the older woman's face. 'Really I am. I like my life the way it is.'

'Empty, you mean.'

'Empty?' Alice laughed and stroked blonde hair away from her face. 'Rita, I'm so busy I don't have time to turn round. My life certainly isn't empty.'

Rita pursed her lips. 'You're talking about work and work isn't enough for anybody. A woman needs a social life. A man. Sex.'

Alice glanced pointedly at her watch. 'Was there anything else you wanted to talk about? I've got a surgery full of patients, Rita.'

And she was exhausted, hungry and thirsty and fed up with talking about subjects that didn't interest her.

'All right. I can take a hint. But the subject isn't closed.' Rita walked to the door. 'Actually, I did come to ask you something. Although he doesn't need your help, Gio wants two minutes to discuss the boy with you before he sends him out. Oh, and the police are here.'

Alice stood up and removed a bottle of water from the fridge in her consulting room. She couldn't do anything about the hunger, but at least she could drink. 'I don't have time for them right now.'

'If what Gio told me is correct, you're going to make time.' Suddenly Rita was all business. 'They can't go round behaving like that. And you need to lock the door behind you if you come in early in the morning. You might have been the only person in the building. You were careless. Up half the night with the little Bennett girl and not getting enough sleep as usual, no doubt.'

'Rita—'

'You'll tell me I'm nagging but I worry about you, that's all. I care about you.'

'I know you do.' Alice curled her hands into fists, uncomfortable with the conversation. Another person—*a different person to her*—would have swept across to Rita and given her a big hug, but Alice could no more do that than fly. Touching wasn't part of her nature. 'I know you care.'

'Good.' Rita gave a sniff. 'Now, drink your water before you die of dehydration and then go and see Gio. And this time take a closer look. You might like what you see.'

Alice walked back to her desk and poured water into a glass. 'All right, I'll speak to Gio then I'll see the police. Ask Mary to give them a coffee and put them in one of the empty rooms. Then see if she can placate the remaining patients. Tell them I'll be with them as soon as possible.' She paused to drink the water she'd poured and then set the glass on her desk. 'Goodness knows if I'll get through them all in time to do any house calls.'

'Gio is going to help you see the patients once he's discharged the boy. For goodness' sake, don't say no. It's like the first day of the summer sales in the waiting room. If he helps then we might all stand a chance of getting some lunch.'

'The letting agent is dropping the keys to his flat round here. He needs to get settled in. He needs to rest after the journey and shave the designer stubble—'

'Any fool can see he's a man with stamina and I don't see his appearance hampering his ability to see patients,' Rita observed, with impeccable logic. 'We're just ensuring that the surgery is going to be crammed for weeks to come.'

'Why's that?'

'Because he's too gorgeous for his own good and all the women in the practice are going to want to come and stare.'

Alice opened the door. 'What exactly is it about men that turns normally sane women into idiots?' she wondered out loud, and Rita grinned.

'Whoever said I was sane?'

With an exasperated shake of her head, Alice walked along the corridor and pushed open the door of the room they used for minor surgery. 'Dr Moretti, I'm so sorry, I've had a steady stream of patients and I lost track of the time.'

He turned to look at her and for a brief, unsettling moment Alice remembered Rita's comment about him being a walking fantasy. He was handsome, she conceded, in an intelligent, devilish and slightly dangerous way. She could see that some women would find him attractive. Fortunately she wasn't one of them.

'No problem.' His smile came easily. 'I've just finished here. I don't need anyone to hold my hand.'

'Shame,' Rita breathed, and Alice shot her a look designed to silence.

Gio ripped off his gloves and pushed the trolley away from him. 'I think he's safe to discharge. He wasn't knocked out and his consciousness isn't impaired. Fortunately he obviously drank less than his friends. I see no indication for an X-ray or a CT scan at the moment. He can be discharged with a head injury form.' He turned to the boy, his expression serious. 'I advise you to stay off the alcohol for a few days. If you start vomiting, feel drowsy, confused, have any visual disturbances or experience persistent headache within the next forty-eight hours, you should go to the A and E department at the hospital. Either way, you need those stitches out in four days. Don't forget and don't think it's cool to leave them in.'

The boy gave a nod and slid off the couch, his face ashen. 'Yeah. I hear you. Thanks, Doc. Are the guys outside?'

'They're having a cosy chat with the police,' Rita told him sweetly, and the boy flushed and rubbed a hand over his face.

'Man, I'm sorry about that.' He shook his head and breathed out heavily. 'They were a bit the worse for wear. We were at an all-night beach party.' He glanced sideways at Alice, his expression sheepish. 'You OK?'

She nodded. 'I'm fine.' She was busy looking at the wound. She couldn't believe how neat the sutures were.

The boy left the room, escorted by Rita.

'You did an amazing job, thank you so much.' Alice closed the door behind them and turned to Gio. 'I never would have thought that was possible. That cut looked such a mess. So many ragged edges. I wouldn't have known where to start.'

But obviously he'd known exactly where to start. Despite appearances. If she hadn't seen the results of his handiwork with her own eyes, she would still have struggled to believe that he was a doctor.

When David had described his friend, she'd imagined a smooth, slick Italian in a designer suit. Someone safe, conservative and conventional in appearance and attitude.

There was nothing safe or conservative about Gio.

He hovered on the wrong side of respectable. His faded T-shirt was stretched over shoulders that were both broad and muscular and a pair of equally faded jeans hugged his legs. His face was deeply tanned, his jaw dark with stubble and his eyes held a hard watchfulness that suggested no small degree of life experience.

She tried to imagine him dressed in a more conventional manner, and failed.

'He'll have a scar.' Gio tipped the remains of his equipment into the nearest sharps bin. 'But some of it will be hidden by his hair. I gather from Rita that you have a very long queue out there.'

Remembering the patients, exhaustion suddenly washed over her and she sucked in a breath, wondering for a moment how she was going to get through the rest of the day. 'I need to talk to the police and then get back to work. I'm sorry I don't have time to give you a proper tour. Hopefully I can do that tomorrow, before you officially start.'

'Forget the tour.' His eyes scanned her face. 'You look done in. The girl who made your coffee told me that you were up in the night, dealing with an asthma attack. You must be ready for a rest yourself. Let's split the rest of the patients.'

She gave a wan smile. 'I can't ask you to do that. You've been travelling all night.' It occurred to her that he was the one who ought to look tired. Instead, his gaze was sharp, assessing.

'You're not asking, I'm offering. In fact, I'm insisting. If you drop dead from overwork before this afternoon, who will show me round?'

His smile had a relaxed, easy charm and she found herself responding. 'Well, if you're sure. I'll ask Mary to send David's patients through to you. If you need any help just buzz me. Lift the receiver and press 3.'

CHAPTER THREE

'WHAT A DAY!' Seven hours later, Gio rubbed a hand over his aching shoulder and eyed the waiting room warily. Morning surgery had extended into the afternoon well-woman clinic, which had extended into evening surgery. Even now the telephone rang incessantly, two little boys were playing noisily in the play corner and a harassed-looking woman was standing at the reception desk, wiggling a pram in an attempt to soothe a screaming baby. 'I feel as though I have seen the entire population of Cornwall in one surgery. Is it always like this?'

'No, sometimes it's busy.' Mary, the receptionist, replaced the phone once again and gave him a cheerful smile as she flicked through the box of repeat prescriptions for the waiting mother. 'Don't worry, you get used to it after a while. I could try locking the door but it would only postpone the inevitable. They'd all be back tomorrow. There we are, Mrs York.' She handed over a prescription with a flourish and adjusted her glasses more comfortably on her nose. 'How are those twins of yours doing, Harriet? Behaving themselves?'

The young woman glanced towards the boys, her face pale.

'They're fine.' Her tone had an edge to it as she pushed the pre-scription into her handbag. 'Thanks.'

The baby's howls intensified and Mary stood up, clucking. She was a plump, motherly woman with curling hair a soft shade of blonde and a smiling face. Gio could see that she was dying to get her hands on the baby. 'There, now. What a fuss. Libby York, what do you think you're doing to our eardrums and your poor mother's sanity?' She walked round the recep-tion desk, glanced at the baby's mother for permission and then scooped the baby out of the pram and rested it on her shoulder, cooing and soothing. 'Is she sleeping for you, dear?' Despite the attention, the baby continued to bawl and howl and Harriet gritted her teeth.

'Not much. She—' The young woman broke off as the boys started to scrap over a toy. 'Stop it, you two!' Her tone was sharp. 'Dan! Robert! Come here, now! Oh, for heaven's sake...' She closed her eyes and swallowed hard.

The baby continued to scream and Gio caught Mary's eye and exchanged a look of mutual understanding. 'Let me have a try.' He took the baby from her, his touch firm and confident, his voice deep and soothing as he switched to Italian. The baby stopped yelling, hiccoughed a few times and then calmed and stared up at his face in fascination.

At least one woman still found him interesting in a dishev-elled state, he thought with a flash of amusement as he recalled Alice's reaction to his appearance.

Mary gave a sigh of relief and turned to Harriet. 'There. That's better. She wanted a man's strength.' She put a hand on the young mother's arm. It was a comforting touch. 'It's hard when they're this age. I remember when mine were small, there were days when I thought I'd strangle them all. It gets easier. Before you know it they're grown.'

Harriet looked at her and blinked back tears. Then she cov-ered her mouth with her hand and shook her head. 'Sorry—oh, I'm being so stupid!' Her hand dropped and she sniffed. 'It's just that I don't know what to do with them half the time. Or what to do with me. I'm so tired I can't think straight,' she muttered, glancing towards the baby who was now calm in Gio's arms. 'This one's keeping the whole family awake. It makes us all cranky and those two are so naughty I could—' She broke off and caught her lip between her teeth. 'Anyway, as you say, it's all part of them being small. There's going to come a time when I'll wish they were little again.'

With a forced smile and a nod of thanks, she leaned across and took the baby from Gio.

'How old is the baby?' There was something about the woman that was worrying him. He didn't know her, of course, which didn't help, but still…

'She'll be seven weeks tomorrow.' Harriet jiggled the baby in her arms in an attempt to keep her calm.

'It can be very hard. My sister had her third child two months ago,' Gio said, keeping his tone casual, 'and she's certainly struggling. If the baby keeps crying, bring her to see me. Maybe there's something we can do to help.'

'Dr Moretti has taken over from Dr Watts,' Mary explained, and Harriet nodded.

'OK. Thanks. I'd better be getting back home. She needs feeding.'

'I can make you comfortable in a room here,' Mary offered, but the woman shook her head and walked towards the door, juggling pram and baby.

'I'd better get home. I've got beds to change and washing to put out.' She called to the boys, who ignored her. 'Come on!' They still ignored her and she gave a growl of exasperation and strapped the baby back in the pram. Libby immediately started crying again. 'Yes, I know, I know! I'm getting you home right now!' She glared at the twins. 'If you don't come now I'm leaving you both here.' Her voice rose slightly and she reached out and grabbed the nearest boy by the arm. 'Do as you're told.'

They left the surgery, boys arguing, baby crying. Mary stared after them, her fingers drumming a steady rhythm on the desk. 'I don't like the look of that.'

'No.' Gio was in full agreement. There had been something about the young mother that had tugged at him. 'She looked stretched out. At her limit.'

Mary looked at him. 'You think there's something wrong with the baby?'

'No. I think there's something wrong with the mother, but I didn't want to get into a conversation that personal with a woman I don't know in the reception area. A conversation like that requires sensitivity. One wrong word and she would have run.'

'Finally. A man who thinks before he speaks...' Mary gave a sigh of approval and glanced up as Alice walked out of her consulting room, juggling two empty coffee-cups and an armful of notes.

She looked even paler than she had that morning, Gio noted, but perhaps that was hardly surprising. She'd been working flat out all day with no break.

'Did I hear a baby screaming?' She deposited the notes on the desk.

'Libby York.' Mary turned her head and stared through the glass door into the street where Harriet was still struggling with the boys. As they disappeared round the corner, she turned back with a sigh. 'You were great, Dr Moretti. Any time you want to soothe my nerves with a short spurt of Italian, don't let me stop you.'

Gio gave an apologetic shrug. 'My English doesn't run to baby talk.'

Alice frowned, her mind focused on the job. 'Why was Harriet in here?'

'Picking up a repeat prescription for her husband.' Mary's mouth tightened and her eyes suddenly clouded with worry. 'I knew that girl when she was in primary school. The smile never left her face. Look at her now and her face is grim. As if she's holding it together by a thread. As if every moment is an effort. If you ask me, she's close to the edge.'

'She has three children under the age of six. Twin boys of five. It's the summer holidays so she has them at home all day.' Alice frowned slightly. Considered. 'That's hard work by anyone's standards. Her husband is a fisherman so he works pretty long hours. Her mother died a month before the baby was born and there's no other family on the scene that I'm aware of. On top of that her delivery was difficult and she had a significant post-partum haemorrhage. She had her postnatal check at the hospital with the consultant.'

She knew her patients well, Gio thought as he watched her sifting through the facts. She was making mental lists. Looking at the evidence in front of her.

'Yes.' Mary glanced at her. 'It might be that.'

'But you don't think so?'

'You want my opinion?' Mary pressed her lips together as the telephone rang yet again. 'I think she's depressed. And Dr Moretti agrees with me.'

'A new baby is hard work.'

'That's right. It is.' Mary reached out and picked up the receiver. 'Appointments line, good afternoon.' She listened and consulted the computer for an appointment slot while Alice ran a hand through her hair and turned to Gio.

'Did she seem depressed to you?'

'Hard to be sure. She seemed stressed and tired,' he conceded, wondering whether she gave all her patients this much thought and attention when they hadn't even asked for help. If so, it was no wonder she was tired and overworked.

'I'll talk to the Gina, the health visitor, and maybe I'll call round and see her at home.'

'You haven't got time to call and see everyone at home.' Mary replaced the receiver and rejoined the conversation. 'She was David's patient, which means she's now Dr Moretti's responsibility. Let him deal with it. Chances are she'll make an appointment with him in the next couple of days. If she doesn't, well, I'll just have to nudge her along.'

To Gio's surprise, Alice nodded. 'All right. But keep an eye on her, Mary.'

'Of course.'

Alice put the cups down and lifted a journal that was lying on the desk.

She had slim hands, he noticed. Delicate. Like the rest of her. It seemed unbelievable that someone so fragile-looking could handle such a punishing workload. She glanced up and caught him looking at her. 'If you want to know anything about this town or the people in it, ask Mary or Rita. They went to school together and they've lived here all their lives. They actually qualify as locals.' She dropped the journal back on the desk and looked at Mary. 'Did the letting agent drop off Dr Moretti's keys?'

'Ah—I was building up to that piece of news.' Mary pulled a face and adjusted her glasses. 'There's a slight problem with the let that David arranged.'

'What problem?'

Mary looked vague. 'They've had a misunderstanding in the office. Some junior girl didn't realise it was being reserved for Dr Moretti and gave it away to a bunch of holidaymakers.' She frowned and waved a hand. 'French, I think.'

Alice tapped her foot on the floor and her mouth tightened. 'Then they'll just have to find him something else. Fast.' She cast an apologetic glance at Gio. 'Sorry about this. You must be exhausted.'

Not as exhausted as she was, Gio mused, wondering whether she'd eaten at all during the day. Whether she ever stopped thinking about work. At some point, Rita had produced a sandwich and an excellent cup of coffee for him but that had been hours earlier and he was ready for something more substantial to eat. And a hot bath. His shoulder was aching again.

'Not that easy.' Mary checked the notes she'd made. 'Nothing is free until September. Schools are back by then. Demand falls a bit.'

'September?' Alice stared. 'But it's still only July.'

Gio studied Mary carefully. Something didn't feel quite right. She was clearly a caring, hospitable woman. Efficient, too. And yet she seemed totally unconcerned about his apparent lack of accommodation. 'You have an alternative plan?'

'Hotels,' Alice said firmly. 'We just need to ring round and see if—'

'No hotels,' Mary said immediately, sitting back in her chair and giving a helpless shrug. 'Full to the brim. We're having a good season, tourist-wise. Betty in the newsagent reckons it's been the best July since she took over from her mother in 1970.'

'Mary.' Alice's voice was exasperated. 'I don't care about the tourists and at the moment I don't care about Betty's sales figures, but I do care about Dr Moretti having somewhere to live while he's working here! You have to do something. And you have to do it right now.'

'I'm trying a few letting agents up the coast,' Mary murmured, peering over the top of her glasses, 'but I'm getting nowhere at the moment. Might need an interim plan. I know.' Her face brightened with inspiration. 'He can stay with you. Just until I find somewhere.'

There was a long silence and something flashed in Alice's eyes. Something dangerous. 'Mary.' There was an unspoken threat in her voice but Mary waved a hand airily.

'You're rattling around in that huge house in the middle of nowhere and it isn't safe at this time of year with all those weirdos on the beach and—'

'Mary!' This time her tone was sharp and she stepped closer to the desk and lowered her voice. 'Mary, don't you dare do this. Don't you *dare*.'

'Do what?'

'Interfere.' Alice gritted her teeth. 'He can't stay with me. That isn't a solution.'

'It's a perfect solution.' Mary smiled up at her innocently and Gio saw the frustration in Alice's face and wondered.

'You've gone too far this time,' she muttered. 'You're embarrassing me and you're embarrassing Dr Moretti.'

Not in the least embarrassed, Gio watched, intrigued. He wouldn't have been at all surprised if she was going to throw a punch. It was clear that she believed that Mary had in some way orchestrated the current problem.

Adding weight to his theory, the older woman looked over the top of her glasses, her gaze innocent. *Far too innocent.* 'It's the perfect solution while I look for somewhere else. Why not?'

'Well, because I...' Alice sucked in a breath and ran a hand over the back of her neck. 'You know I don't—'

'Well, now you do.' Mary beamed, refusing to back down. 'It's temporary, Alice. As a favour to the community. Can't have our new doctor sleeping rough in the gutter, can we? Are you ready to go, Rita?' She stood up as the practice nurse walked into reception. 'What a day. I'm going to pour myself a large glass of wine and put my feet up. Can we call in at Betty's on the way? I need to pick up a local paper. See you in the morning. Oh, and by the way...' She turned to Gio with a wink. 'I suggest you order a take-away for dinner. Our Dr Anderson is a whiz with patients but the kitchen isn't her forte.'

They left with a wave and Gio watched as Alice's hands clenched and unclenched by her sides.

He broke the tense silence. 'You look as though you're looking for someone to thump.'

She turned and blinked, almost as if she'd forgotten his existence. As if he wasn't part of her problem. 'Tell me something.' Her voice was tight. 'Is it really possible to admire and respect someone and yet want to strangle them at the same time?'

He thought of his sisters and nodded. 'Definitely.'

He noticed that she didn't use the word 'love' although it had taken him less than five minutes to detect the warmth and affection running between the three women.

'I want to be so *angry* with the pair of them.' Her hand sliced through the air and the movement encouraged wisps of her hair to drift over her eyes. 'But how can I when I know—' she broke off and let out a long breath, struggling for control. 'This isn't anything to do with you. What I mean is...' Her tone was suddenly tight and formal, her smile forced, 'you must think I'm incredibly rude, but that wasn't my intention. It's just that you've stepped into the middle of something that's been going on for a long time and—'

'And you don't like being set up with the first available guy who happens to walk through the door?'

Her blue eyes flew to his, startled. 'It's that obvious? Oh, this is so embarrassing.'

'Not embarrassing.' He watched as the colour flooded into her cheeks. 'But interesting. Why do your colleagues feel the need to interfere with your love life?'

She was a beautiful woman. He knew enough about men to know that a woman like her could have the male sex swarming around her without any assistance whatsoever.

She paced the length of the waiting room and back again, working off tension. 'Because people have a stereotypical view of life,' she said, her tone ringing with exasperation. 'If you're not with a man, you must want to be. Secretly you must long to be married and have eight children and a dog. And if you're not, you're viewed as some sort of freak.'

Gio winced. 'Eight is definitely too many.' He was pleased to see a glimmer of humour in her eyes.

'You think so?'

'Trust me.' He tried to coax the smile still wider. Suddenly he wanted to see her smile. Really smile. 'I am one of six and the queue for the bathroom was unbelievable. And the battle at the meal table was nothing short of ugly.'

The smile was worth waiting for. Dimples winked at the side of her soft mouth and her eyes danced. Captivated by the dimples, Gio felt something clench inside him.

She was beautiful.

And very guarded. He saw something in the depths of her blue eyes that made him wonder about her past.

Still smiling, she gave a shake of her head. 'I know they mean well but they've gone too far this time. It's even worse than that time on the lifeboat.'

'The lifeboat?'

'Believe me, you don't want to know.' She sucked in a breath and raked slim fingers through her silky blonde hair. 'Let's look at this logically. I'm assuming Mary was telling the truth about your flat having fallen through—'

'You think she might have been lying?'

'Not lying, no. But she's manoeuvred it in some way. I don't know how yet, but when I find out she's going to be in trouble. Either way, at the moment, it looks as though you're going to have to stay with me. Aggh!' She tilted her head backwards and made a frustrated sound. 'And I'll never hear the last of it! Every morning they're going to be looking at me, working out whether I've fallen in love with you yet. Nudging. Making comments. I'll kill them.'

He couldn't keep the laughter out of his voice. 'Is that what you're afraid of? Do you think you're going to fall in love with me, Dr Anderson?'

She looked at him and the air snapped tight with tension. 'Don't be ridiculous!' Her voice was slightly husky. 'I don't believe in love.'

Could she feel it? Gio wondered. Could she feel what he was feeling?

'Then where is the problem?' He spread lean, bronzed hands and flashed her a smile. 'There is no risk of you falling in love with me. That makes me no more than a lodger.'

But a lodger with a definite interest.

'You don't know what they're like. Every moment of the day there will be little comments. Little asides. They'll drive us mad.'

'Or we could drive them mad. With a little thought and application, this could work in your favour.'

Her glance was suspicious. 'How?'

'Mary and Rita are determined to set you up, no?'

'Yes, but—'

'Clearly they believe that if they put a man under your nose, you will fall in love with him. So—I move in with you and when they see that you have no trouble at all resisting me, they will give up.'

She stared at him thoughtfully. 'You think that will work?'

'Why wouldn't it?'

'You don't know them. They don't give up easily.' The tension had passed and she was suddenly crisp and businesslike. 'And, to be honest, I don't know if I can share a house with someone. I've lived alone since I was eighteen.'

It sounded lonely to him. 'I can assure you that I'm house trained. I'm very clean and I pick up after myself.'

This time there was no answering smile. 'I'm used to having my own space.'

'Me, too,' Gio said smoothly. Was that what the problem was? She liked her independence? 'But Mary said that your house is large...'

'Yes.'

'Then we need hardly see each other.' In truth he'd made up his mind that he'd be seeing plenty of her but decided that the way to achieve that was a step at a time. He was fascinated by Alice Anderson. She was complex. Interesting. Unpredictable. And he knew instinctively that any show of interest on his part would be met with suspicion and rejection. If he looked relaxed and unconcerned about the whole situation, maybe she would, too. 'And think of it this way—' he was suddenly struck by inspiration '—it will give you a chance to brief me fully on the practice, the patients, everything I need to know.'

She looked suddenly thoughtful and he could see her mentally sifting through what he'd just said. 'Yes.' She gave a sharp nod. 'You're right that it will give us plenty of opportunity to talk about work. All right.' She took a deep breath, as if bracing herself. 'Let's lock up here and make a move. Where did you park?'

'At the top of the hill, in the public car park.'

'There are three spaces outside the surgery. You can use one of those from now on.' She delved into her bag and removed a set of keys. 'I'll give you a lift to your car. Let's go.'

CHAPTER FOUR

STILL FUMING ABOUT Mary and Rita, Alice jabbed the key into the ignition and gripped the steering-wheel.

She'd been thoroughly outmanoeuvred.

Why had she been foolish enough to let them arrange accommodation? Why hadn't she anticipated that they'd be up to their usual tricks? Because her mind didn't work like theirs, she thought savagely, that was why.

Vowing to tackle the two of them as soon as Gio wasn't around, Alice drove away from the car park, aware that his low black sports car was following close behind her.

Her mind on Mary and Rita, she changed gear with more anger than care and then winced at the hideous crunch. Reminding herself that her car wasn't up to a large degree of abuse, she forced herself to take a calming breath.

They'd set her up yet again, she knew they had. Rita and Mary. The two mother figures in her life. And they'd done it without even bothering to meet the man in question. Somehow they'd both decided that an attractive single guy was going to be perfect for her. It didn't matter that they'd never even met him, that they knew absolutely nothing about him. He was single and she was single and that was all it should take for the magic to kick in.

Anger spurted inside her and Alice thumped the steering-wheel with the heel of her hand and crunched the gears again. They were a pair of interfering old—old…

She really wanted to stay angry but how could she be when she knew that they were only doing it because they cared? When she remembered just how good they'd been to her since her very first day in the practice?

No, better to go along with their little plan and prove to them once and for all that love just didn't work for her. Gio Moretti was right. If she did this, maybe then they'd finally get the message about the way she wanted to live her life.

Yes, that was it. They obviously believed that Gio Moretti was the answer to any woman's prayers. When they realised that he wasn't the answer to hers, maybe they'd leave her alone. She'd live with him if only to prove that she wasn't interested. Since they considered him irresistible, her ability to resist him with no problem should prove something, shouldn't it?

Satisfied with her plan, she gave a swift nod and a smile as she flicked the indicator and took the narrow, winding road that led down to her house.

Her grip on the steering-wheel relaxed slightly. And living with him wouldn't be so bad. Gio seemed like a perfectly civilised guy. He was intelligent and well qualified. His experience in medicine was clearly very different to hers. She would certainly be able to learn from him.

And as for the logistics of the arrangement, she would put him in the guest room at the top of the house that had an *en suite* bathroom so she need never see him. He could come and go without bothering her. They need never have a conversation that didn't involve a patient. And when Mary and Rita saw how things were, they'd surely give up their quest to find her love.

Having satisfied herself that the situation wasn't irredeemable, she stepped on the brake, pulled in to allow another car to pass on the narrow road and drove the last stretch of road that curved down towards the sea.

The crowds of tourists dwindled and immediately she felt calmer.

This was her life. Her world.

The tide was out, the mudflats stretched in front of her and birds swooped and settled on the sandbanks. Behind her were towering cliffs of jagged rock that led out into the sea, and in front of her was the curving mouth of the river, winding lazily inland.

Cornwall.

Home.

Checking that he was still behind her, she touched the brake with her foot, turned right down the tiny track that led down to the water's edge and turned off the engine.

The throaty roar of the sports car behind her died and immediately peace washed over her. For a moment she was tempted to kick her shoes off and walk barefoot, but, as usual, time pressed against her wishes. She had a new lodger to show round and some reading that she needed to finish. And she was going to have to cook something for dinner.

With a shudder of distaste she stepped out of the car feeling hot, sticky and desperate for a cool shower. Wondering when the weather was finally going to break, she turned and watched as Gio slid out of his car and glanced around him. It was a long moment before he spoke.

'This place is amazing.' His hair gleamed glossy dark in the sunlight and the soft fabric of his T-shirt clung to his broad, powerful shoulders. There was a strength about him, an easy confidence that came with maturity, and Alice was suddenly gripped by a shimmer of something unfamiliar.

'Most people consider it to be lonely and isolated. They lecture me on the evils of burying myself somewhere so remote.'

'Do they?' He stood for a moment, legs planted firmly apart

in a totally masculine stance, his gaze fixed on the view before him. 'I suppose that's fortunate. If everyone loved it here, it would cease to be so peaceful. You must see some very rare birds.'

'Over fifty different species.' Surprised by the observation, she leaned into her car to retrieve her bag, wondering whether he was genuinely interested in wildlife or whether he was just humouring her. Probably the latter, she decided. The man needed accommodation.

She slammed her car door without bothering to lock it and glanced at his face again. He looked serious enough.

He removed a suitcase from his boot. 'How long have you lived here?'

'Four years.' She delved in her bag for the keys and walked up the path. 'I found this house on my second day here. I was cycling along and there it was. Uninhabited, dilapidated and set apart from everything and everyone.' *Just like her.* She shook off the thought and wriggled the key into the lock. 'It took me a year to do it up sufficiently to live in it, another two years to get it to the state it's in now.'

He removed his sunglasses and glanced at her in surprise. 'You did the work yourself?'

She caught the look and smiled. 'Never judge by appearances, Dr Moretti. I have hidden muscles.' She pushed open the front door and stooped to pick up the post. 'I'll show you where you're sleeping and then meet you in the kitchen. I can fill you in on everything you need to know while we eat.'

She deposited the post, unopened, on the hall table and made a mental note to water the plants before she went to bed.

'It's beautiful.' His eyes scanned the wooden floors, which she'd sanded herself and then painted white, lifted to the filmy white curtains that framed large, picture windows and took in the touches of blue in the cushions and the artwork on the walls. He stepped forward to take a closer look at a large watercolour she had displayed in the hall. 'It's good. It has real passion. You can feel the power of the sea.' He frowned at the signature and turned to look at her. 'You paint?'

'Not any more.' She strode towards the stairs, eager to end the conversation. It was becoming too personal and she was always careful to avoid the personal. 'No time. Your room is at the top of the house and it has its own bathroom. It should be perfectly possible for us to lead totally separate lives.'

She said it to reassure herself as much to remind him and took the stairs two at a time and flung open a door. 'Here we are. You should be comfortable enough here and, anyway, it's only short term.' She broke off and he gave a smile.

'Of course.'

'Look, I don't mean to be rude and I'm thrilled that you're going to be working here, but I'm just not that great at sharing my living space with anyone, OK?' She shrugged awkwardly, wondering why she felt the need to explain herself. 'I'm selfish. I'm the first to admit it. I've lived on my own for too long to be anything else.'

And it was the way she preferred it. It was just a shame that Rita and Mary couldn't get the message.

He strode over to the huge windows and stared at the view. 'You're not being rude. If I lived here, I'd protect it, too.' He turned to face her. 'And I'm not intending to invade your personal space, Alice. You can relax.'

Relax?

His rich accent turned her name into something exotic and exciting and she gave a slight shiver. There would be no relaxing while he was staying with her.

'Then we won't have a problem.' She backed towards the door. 'Make yourself at home. I'm going to take a shower and change. Come down when you're ready. I'll be in the kitchen. Making supper.'

Her least favourite pastime. She gave a sigh of irritation as she left the room. She considered both cooking and eating to be a monumental waste of time but, with a guest in the house, she could hardly suggest that they skip a meal in favour of a bowl of cereal, which was her usual standby when she couldn't be bothered to cook.

Which meant opening the fridge and creating something out of virtually nothing. She just hoped that Gio Moretti wasn't too discerning when it came to his palate.

Her blue eyes narrowed and she gave a soft smile as she pushed open the door to her own bedroom and made for the shower, stripping off clothes as she walked and flinging them on the bed.

If the way to a man's heart was through his stomach, she was surprised that Mary and Rita had given their plan even the remotest chance of success.

It didn't take a genius to know that it was going to be hard for a man to harbour romantic notions about a woman who had just poisoned him.

When Gio strolled into the kitchen after a shower and a shave, she was grating cheese into a bowl with no apparent signs of either skill or enthusiasm. He watched with amusement and no small degree of interest and wondered who had designed the kitchen.

It was a cook's paradise. White slatted units and lots of glass reflected the light and a huge stainless-steel oven gleamed and winked, its spotless surface suggesting it had never been used. In fact, the whole kitchen looked as though it belonged in a show home and it took him less than five seconds of watching the usually competent Alice wrestle with a lump of cheese to understand why.

At the far end of the room French doors opened onto the pretty garden. Directly in front of the doors, positioned to make the most of the view, was a table covered in medical magazines, a few textbooks and several sheets of paper covered in neat handwriting.

He could picture her there, her face serious as she read her way through all the academic medical journals, checking the facts. He'd seen enough to know that Alice Anderson was comfortable with facts. Possibly more comfortable with facts than she was with people.

He wondered why.

In his experience, there was usually a reason for the way people chose to live their lives.

'Cheese on toast all right with you?' She turned, still grating, her eyes fixed on his face. 'Oh...'

'Something is wrong?'

She blew a wisp of blonde hair out of her eyes. 'You look... different.'

He smiled and strolled towards her. 'More like a doctor?'

'Maybe. Ow.' She winced as the grater grazed her knuckles and adjusted her grip. 'I wasn't expecting guests, I'm afraid, so I haven't shopped. And I have to confess that I loathe cooking.' Her blonde hair was still damp from the shower and she'd changed into a pair of linen trousers and a pink top. She looked young and feminine and a long way from the brisk, competent professional he'd met earlier. The kitchen obviously flustered her and he found her slightly clumsy approach to cooking surprisingly appealing. In fact, he was fast discovering that there were many parts of Alice Anderson that he found appealing.

'Anything I can do?' Wondering if he should take over or whether that would damage her ego, he strolled over to her, lifted a piece of cheese and sniffed it. 'What is it?'

'The cheese?' She turned on the grill and watched for a moment as if not entirely confident that it would work. 'Goodness knows. The sort that comes wrapped in tight plastic. Cheddar or something, I suppose. Why?'

He tried not to wince at the vision of cheese tightly wrapped in plastic. 'I'm Italian. We happen to love cheese. Mozzarella, fontina, ricotta, marscapone...'

'This is just something I grabbed from the supermarket a few weeks ago. It was covered with blue bits but I chopped them off.

I assumed they weren't supposed to be there. I don't think they were there when I bought it.' She dropped the grater and stared down at the pile of cheese with a distinct lack of enthusiasm. 'There should be some salad in the fridge, if you're interested.'

He opened her fridge and stared. It was virtually empty. Making a mental note to shop at the earliest convenient moment, he reached for a limp, sorry piece of lettuce and examined it thoughtfully. 'I'm not bothered about salad,' he murmured, and she glanced up, her face pink from the heat of the grill, her teeth gritted.

'Fine. Whatever. This is nearly ready.' She pulled out the grill pan and fanned her hand over the contents to stop it smoking. 'I'm not that great a cook but at least it's food, and that's all that matters. Good job I'm not really trying to seduce you, Dr Moretti.' She flashed him a wicked smile as she slid the contents of the grill pan onto two plates. 'If the way to a man's heart is through his stomach, I'm completely safe.'

She wasn't joking about her culinary skills. Gio stared down at the burnt edges of the toast and the patchy mix of melted and unmelted cheese and suddenly realised why she was so slim. It was a good job he was starving and willing to eat virtually anything. Suddenly he understood Mary's suggestion that they get a take-away. 'Did you eat lunch today?'

She fished knives and forks out of a drawer and sat down at the table, pushing aside the piles of journals and books to make room for the plates. 'I can't remember. I might have had something at some point. So what's your opinion on Harriet?' She pushed cutlery across the table and poured some water. 'Do you think she is depressed?'

He wondered if she even realised that she was talking about work again.

Did she do it on purpose to avoid a conversation of a more personal nature?

He picked up a fork and tried to summon up some enthusiasm for the meal ahead. It was a challenge. For him a meal was supposed to be a total experience. An event. A time to indulge the palate and the senses simultaneously. Clearly, for Alice it was just a means of satisfying the gnawing in her stomach.

Glancing down at his plate, he wondered whether he was going to survive the experience of Alice's cooking or whether he was going to require medical attention.

She definitely needed educating about food.

'Is Harriet depressed? It's possible. I'll certainly follow it up.' He cautiously tasted the burnt offering on his plate and decided that it was the most unappetizing meal he'd eaten for a long time. 'Postnatal depression is a serious condition.'

'And often missed. She was fine after the twins but that's not necessarily significant, of course.' Alice finished her toasted cheese with brisk efficiency and no visible signs of enjoyment and put down her fork with an apologetic glance in his direction. 'Sorry to eat so quickly. I was starving. I don't think I managed to eat at all yesterday.'

'Are you serious?'

'Perfectly. We had a bit of a drama in the bay. The lifeboat was called out to two children who'd managed to drift out to sea in their inflatable boat.' She broke off and sipped her drink. 'I spent my lunch-hour over with the crew, making sure they were all right. By the time I finished I had a queue of people in the surgery. I forgot to eat.'

To Gio, who had never forgotten to eat in his life, such a situation was incomprehensible. 'You need to seriously rethink your lifestyle.'

'You sound like Mary and Rita. I happen to like my lifestyle. It works for me.' With a fatalistic shrug she finished her water and stood up. 'So, Dr Moretti, what can I tell you about the practice to make your life easier? At this time of year we see a lot of tourists with the usual sorts of problems. Obviously, on top of the locals, it makes us busy, as you discovered today.'

All she thought about was work, he reflected, watching as she lifted a medical journal from the pile on the table and absently scanned the contents. She was driven. Obsessed. 'Do you do a minor accident clinic?'

'No.' She shook her head and dropped the journal back on the pile. 'David and I tried it two years ago but, to be honest, there were days when we were swamped and days when we were sitting around. We decided it was better just to fit them into surgery time. We have a very good relationship with the coastguard and the local paramedics. Sometimes they call on us, sometimes we call on them. We also have a good relationship with the local police.'

'The police?' His attention was caught by the gentle sway of her hips as she walked across the kitchen. Her movements were graceful and utterly feminine and from nowhere he felt a sharp tug of lust.

Gritting his teeth, he tried to talk sense into himself.

They were colleagues.

He'd known her for less than a day.

'Beach parties.' She lifted the kettle and filled it. 'At this time of year we have a lot of teenagers just hanging out on the beach. Usually the problem's just too much alcohol, as you saw this morning. Sometimes it's drugs.'

To hide the fact that he was studying her, Gio glanced out towards the sea and tried to imagine it crowded with hordes of teenagers. *Tried to drag his mind away from the tempting curve of her hips.* 'Looks peaceful to me. It's hard to imagine it otherwise.'

She rested those same hips against the work surface while she waited for the kettle to boil. 'They don't come down this far. They congregate on the beach beyond the harbour. The surf is good. Too good sometimes, and then we get a fair few surfing accidents, as you also noticed this morning. Coffee?'

Gio opened his mouth to say yes and then winced as he saw her reaching into a cupboard for a jar. 'You are using instant coffee?'

She pulled a face. 'I know. It's not my favourite either, but it's better than nothing and I've run out of fresh. One of the drawbacks of living out here is that both the supermarket and the nearest espresso machine are a car ride away.'

'Not any more.'

'Don't tell me.' She spooned coffee into a mug. 'You've brought your own espresso machine.'

'Of course. It was a key part of my luggage. Along with a large supply of the very best beans.'

She stilled, the spoon still in her hand. 'You're not serious?'

'Coffee is extremely serious,' he said dryly. 'If you expect me to work hard, I need my daily fix, and if today is anything to go by then I'm not going to have time to pop up the hill to that excellent bakery.'

She scooped her hair away from her face and there was longing in her eyes. 'You're planning to make fresh coffee every morning?'

'*Si.*' He wondered why she was even asking the question when it seemed entirely normal to him. 'It is the only way I can get through the day.'

The smile spread across her face. 'Now, if Mary had mentioned that, I would have cancelled your flat with the letting agent myself.' She licked her lips, put down the spoon, a hunger in her eyes. 'Does your fancy machine make enough for two cups?'

He decided that if it guaranteed him one of her smiles, he'd stand over the machine all morning. 'A decent cup of coffee to start your day will be part of my fee for invading your space,' he offered. Along with the cooking, but he decided to wait a while before breaking that to her in case she was offended. 'So tell me about Rita and Mary.' He wanted to know about their relationship with her. Why they felt the need to set her up.

He wanted to know everything there was to know about Alice Anderson.

'They've worked in the practice for ever. Twenty-five years at least. Can you imagine that?' She shook her head. 'It helps, of course, because they know everything about everyone. History is important, don't you think, Dr Moretti?'

He wondered about her history. He wondered what had made a beautiful woman like her choose to bury herself in her work and live apart from others. It felt wrong. Not the setting, he mused as he glanced out of the window. The setting was perfect. But in his opinion it was a setting designed to be shared with someone special.

Realising that she was waiting for an answer, he smiled, amused by her earnest expression. She was delightfully serious. 'I can see that history is important in general practice.'

'It gives you clues. Not knowing a patient's history is often like trying to solve a murder with no access to clues.' Her eyes narrowed. 'I suppose as a surgeon, it's different. It's more task orientated. You get the patient on the operating table and you solve the problem.'

'Not necessarily that simple.' He sat back in his chair, comfortable in her kitchen. *In her company.* The problems of the past year faded. 'In plastic surgery the patient's wishes, hopes, dreams are all an important part of the picture. Appearance can affect people's lives. As a society, we're shallow. We see and we judge. As a surgeon you have to take that into account. You need to understand what's needed and decided whether you can deliver.'

'You did face lifts? Nose jobs?'

He smiled. It was a common misconception and it didn't offend him. 'That wasn't my field of speciality,' he said quietly. 'I did paediatrics. Cleft palates, hare lips. In between running my clinic in Milan, I did volunteer work in developing countries. Children with unrepaired clefts lead very isolated lives. Often they can't go to school—they're ostracised from the community, no chance of employment...'

She was staring at him, a frown in her blue eyes as if she was reassessing him. 'I had no idea.' She picked up her coffee, but her focus was on him, not the mug in her hand. 'That's so interesting. And tough.'

'Tough, rewarding, frustrating.' He gave a shrug. 'All those things. Like every branch of medicine, I suppose. I also did a lot of training. Showing local doctors new techniques.' He waited for the dull ache of disappointment that always came when he was talking about the past, but there was nothing. Instead he felt more relaxed than he could ever recall feeling.

'It must have been hard for you to give it up.'

He shrugged and felt a twinge in his shoulder. 'Life sometimes forces change on us but sometimes it's a change we should have made ourselves if we only had the courage. I was ready for a change.'

He sensed that she was going to ask him more, delve deeper, and then she seemed to withdraw.

'Well, there's certainly variety in our practice. If you're good with babies, you can run the baby clinic. David used to do it.'

She was talking about work again, he mused. 'Immunisations, I assume?' Always, she avoided the personal. *Was she afraid of intimacy?*

'That and other things.' She sipped at her coffee. 'It's a really busy clinic. We expanded its remit a few months ago to encourage mothers to see us with their problems during the clinic rather than making appointments during normal surgery hours. It means that they don't have to make separate appointments for themselves and we reduce the number of toddlers running around the waiting room.' Her fingers tightened on the mug. 'I have to confess it isn't my forte.'

'I've seen enough of your work to know that you're an excellent doctor.' He watched as the colour touched her cheekbones.

'Oh, I can do the practical stuff.' She gave a shrug and turned her back on him, dumping her mug in the sink. 'It's everything that goes with it that I can't handle. All the emotional stuff. I'm terrible at that. How are you with worried mothers, Dr Moretti?' She turned and her blonde hair swung gently round her head.

Was she afraid of other people's emotions or her own? Pondering the question, he flashed her a wicked smile. 'Worried women are my speciality, Dr Anderson.'

She threw back her head and laughed. 'I'll just bet they are, Dr Moretti. I'll just bet they are.'

Alice woke to the delicious smells of freshly ground coffee, rolled over and then remembered Gio Moretti. Living here. In her house.

She sat upright, pushed the heavy cloud of sleep away and checked the clock. 6 a.m. He was obviously an early riser, like her.

Tempted by the smell and the prospect of a good cup of coffee to start her day, she padded into the shower, dressed quickly and followed her nose.

She pushed open the kitchen door, her mind automatically turning to work, and then stopped dead, taken aback by the sight of Gio half-naked in her kitchen.

'Oh!' She'd assumed he was up and dressed, instead of which he was wearing jeans again. This time with nothing else. His chest was bare and the muscles of his shoulders flexed as he reached for the coffee.

He was gorgeous.

The thought stopped her dead and she frowned, surprised at herself for noticing and more than a little irritated. And then she gave a dismissive shrug. So what? Despite what Rita and Mary obviously thought, she was neither blind nor brain dead. And it wasn't as if she hadn't experienced sexual attraction before. She had. The important thing was not to mistake it for 'love'.

He turned to reach for a cup and she saw the harsh, jagged scars running down his back. 'That looks painful.'

The minute she said the words she wished she hadn't. Was he sensitive about it? Perhaps she wasn't supposed to mention it. If he was the type of guy that spent all day staring in the mirror, then perhaps it bothered him.

'Not as painful as it used to. *Buongiorno.*' He flashed her a smile and handed her a cup, totally at ease in her kitchen. 'I wasn't expecting you up this early. I have to have coffee before I can face the shower.'

'I know the feeling.' Wondering how he got the scar, she took the cup with a nod of thanks and wandered over to the table, trying not to look in his direction.

She might not believe in love but she could see when a man was attractive and Gio Moretti was certainly attractive. When she'd said he could have her spare room, she hadn't imagined he'd be walking around her house half-naked. It was unsettling and more than a little distracting.

She sat down. Her body suddenly felt hot and uncomfortable and she slid a finger around the neck of her shirt and glanced at the sun outside. 'It's going to be another scorcher today.' Even though she made a point of not looking in his direction, she sensed his gaze on her.

'You're feeling hot, Alice?'

Something in his voice made her turn her head. Her eyes met hers and an unexpected jolt shook her body. 'It's warm in here, yes.' She caught her breath, broke the eye contact and picked up her coffee, but not before her brain had retained a clear image of a bronzed, muscular chest covered in curling dark hairs. He was all muscle and masculinity and her throat felt suddenly dry. She took a sip of coffee. 'This is delicious. Thank you.'

Still holding her cup, she stared out of the window and tried to erase the memory of his half-naked body. She wasn't used to having a man in her kitchen. It was all too informal. Too intimate.

Everything she avoided.

To take her mind off the problem she did what she always did. She thought about work.

'Rita has a baby clinic this afternoon,' she said brightly, watching as a heron rose from the smooth calm of the estuary that led to sea and flew off with a graceful sweep of its wings.

'Invariably she manages it by herself but sometimes she needs one of us to—'

'Alice, *cara*.' His voice came from behind her, deep and heavily accented. 'I need at least two cups of coffee before I can even think about work, let alone talk about it.' His hands came up and touched her shoulders and she stiffened. She wasn't used to being touched. No one touched her.

'I just thought you should know that—'

'This kitchen has the most beautiful view.' He kept his hands on her shoulders, his touch light and relaxed. 'Enjoy it. It's still early. Leave thoughts of work until later. Look at the mist. Enjoy the silence. It's perfect.'

She sat still, heart pounding, thoroughly unsettled. Usually her kitchen soothed her. Calmed her. But today she could feel the little spurts of tension darting through her shoulders.

It was just having someone else in the house, she told herself. Inevitably it altered her routine.

Abandoning her plan to read some journals while drinking her coffee as she usually did, she stood up and firmly extricated herself from his hold.

'I need to get going.' Annoyed with herself and even more annoyed with him, she walked across the room, taking her cup with her. 'I'll meet you at the surgery later.'

His eyes flickered to the clock on the wall. 'Alice, it's only 6.30.' His voice was a soft, accented drawl. 'And you haven't finished your coffee.'

'There's masses of paperwork to plough through.' She drank the coffee quickly and put the cup on the nearest worktop. 'Thank you. A great improvement on instant.'

His eyes were locked on her face. 'You haven't had breakfast.'

'I don't need breakfast.' What she needed most of all was space. Air to breathe. The safety of her usual routine. She backed out of the door, needing to escape. 'I'll see you later.'

Grabbing her bag and her jacket, she strode out of the house, fumbling for her keys as she let the door swing shut behind her.

Oh, bother and blast.

Instead of starting her day in a calm, organised frame of mind, as she usually did, she felt unsettled and on edge and the reason why was perfectly obvious.

She didn't need a lodger and she certainly didn't need a lodger that she noticed, she thought to herself as she slid into the sanctuary of her car.

And she was *definitely* going to kill Mary when she saw her.

He made her nervous.

She claimed not to believe in love and yet there was chemistry between them. An elemental attraction that he'd felt from the first moment. And it was growing stronger by the minute.

Gio made himself a second cup of coffee and drank it seated at the little table overlooking the garden and the sea.

She was serious, academic and obviously totally unaccustomed to having a man in her life. He'd felt the sudden tension in her shoulders when he'd touched her. Felt her discomfort and her sudden anxiety.

He frowned and stretched his legs out in front of him.

In his family, touching was part of life. Everyone touched. Hugged. Held. It was what they did. But not everyone was the same, of course.

And, for whatever reason, he sensed that Alice wasn't used to being touched. *Wasn't comfortable being touched.*

The English were generally more reserved and emotionally distant, of course, so it could be that. He drained his coffeecup. Or it could be something else. Something linked with the reason he was sitting here now instead of in a flat in another part of town.

Why had Mary seen the need to interfere?

Why did she think that Alice needed help finding a man in her life?

And, given his distaste for matchmaking attempts, why wasn't he running fast in the opposite direction?

Why did he suddenly feel comfortable and content?

The question didn't need much answering. Everything about Alice intrigued him. She was complex and unpredictable. She had a beautiful smile but it only appeared after a significant amount of coaxing. She was clever and clearly caring and yet she herself had humbly confessed that she wasn't good with emotions.

And she was uncomfortable with being touched.

Which was a shame, he thought to himself as he finished his coffee. Because he'd made up his mind that he was going to be touching her a lot. So she was going to have to start getting used to it.

CHAPTER FIVE

MARY SAILED INTO the surgery just as Alice scooped the post from the mat. 'You're early.' There was disappointment in her expression, as if she'd expected something different. 'So—did you have a lovely evening?'

'Wonderful. Truly wonderful.' Alice dropped the post onto the reception desk to be sorted and gave a wistful sigh, deriving wicked satisfaction from the look of hope that lit Mary's face. 'I must do it more often.'

'Do what more often?'

'Go home early, of course.' Alice smiled sweetly. 'I caught up on so many things.'

Mary's shoulders sagged. 'Caught up on what? How was your lodger?'

'Who?' Alice adopted a blank expression and then waved a hand vaguely. 'Oh, you mean Dr Moretti? Fine, I think. I wouldn't really know. I hardly saw him.'

Mary dropped her bag with a thump and a scowl. 'You didn't spend the evening together?'

'Not at all. Why would we? He's my lodger, not my date.'

Alice leaned forward and picked up the contents of her in tray. 'But he does make tremendous coffee. I suppose I have you to thank for that, given that you arranged it all.'

'You already drink too much coffee,' Mary scolded as they both walked towards the consulting rooms. She caught Alice's arm in a firm grip. 'Are you serious? You didn't spend any time with him at all?'

Alice shrugged her off. 'None.'

'If that's true, you're a sad case.' Her eyes narrowed. 'You're teasing me, aren't you?'

'All right, I'll tell you the truth.' Thoroughly enjoying herself now, Alice threw Mary a saucy wink as she pushed open the door to her room. 'I'm grateful to you, really I am. Even I can see that Gio Moretti is handsome. I don't suppose they come much handsomer. If I have to share my house with someone I'd so much rather it was someone decorative. I could hardly concentrate on my breakfast this morning because he was standing in my kitchen half-naked. *What* a body!' She gave an exaggerated sigh and pressed her palm against her heart. 'I'd have to be a fool not to be interested in a man like him, wouldn't you agree?'

'Alice—'

'And I'm certainly not a fool.' She dropped her bag behind her desk. 'Anyway, I just want you to know that we've been at it all night like rabbits and now I've definitely got him out of my system so you can safely find him somewhere else to live, you interfering old—'

'*Buongiorno.*'

The deep voice came from the doorway and Alice whirled round, her face turning pink with embarrassment. She caught the wicked humour in his dark eyes and cursed inwardly.

Why had he chosen that precise moment to walk down the corridor?

He lounged in her doorway, dressed in tailored trousers and a crisp cotton shirt that looked both expensive and stylish. The

sleeves were rolled up to his elbows, revealing bronzed forearms dusted with dark hairs. The laughter in his eyes told her
that he'd heard every word. 'You left without breakfast, Dr
Anderson. And after such a long, taxing night...' He lingered
over each syllable, his rich, Italian accent turning the words
into something decadent and sinful '...you need to replenish
your energy levels.'

Mary glanced between them, her expression lifting, and
Alice suppressed a groan. Friendly banter. Teasing. All designed to give Mary totally the wrong idea. And she'd been
the one to start it.

'Finally, someone else to scold you about not eating proper
meals.' Mary put her hands on her hips and gave a satisfied
nod. 'If Dr Moretti values his stomach lining, he'll take over
the cooking.'

'I'm perfectly capable of cooking,' Alice snapped, sitting
down at her desk and switching on her computer with a stab of
her finger. 'It's just that I don't enjoy it very much and I have so
many other more important things to do with my time.'

'Like work.' Mary looked at Gio. 'While you're at it, you
might want to reform her on that count, too.' She walked out
of the room, leaving Alice glaring after her.

'I've decided that David had the right idea after all. London
is looking better all the time. In London, no one cares what the
person next to them is doing. No one cares whether they eat
breakfast, work or don't work. And for sure, no one cares about
the state of anyone else's love life.' She hit the return key on the
keyboard with more force than was necessary, aware that Gio
was watching her, a thoughtful expression in his dark eyes. His
shoulders were still against the doorframe and he didn't seem
in any hurry to go anywhere.

'She really cares about you.'

Alice stilled. He was right, of course. Mary did care about
her. And she'd never had that before. Until she'd arrived in

Smuggler's Cove, she'd never experienced interference as a result of caring.

'I know she does.' Alice bit her lip. 'I wish I could convince her that I'm fine on my own. That this is what I want. How I want to live my life.'

His gaze was steady. 'Sounds lonely to me, Dr Anderson. And perhaps a bit cowardly.'

'Cowardly?' She forgot about her computer and sat back in her chair, more than a little outraged. 'What's that supposed to mean?'

He walked further into the room, his eyes fixed on her face. 'People who avoid relationships are usually afraid of getting hurt.'

'Or perhaps they're just particularly well adjusted and evolved,' Alice returned sweetly. 'This is the twenty-first century and we no longer all believe that a man is necessary to validate and enhance our lives.'

'Is that so?' His gaze dropped to her mouth and she felt her heart stumble and kick in her chest.

With a frown of irritation she turned her head and concentrated on her computer screen. Why was he looking at her like that? Studying her? As if he was trying to see deep inside her mind? Her fingers drummed a rhythm on the desk. Well, that was a part of herself that she kept private. Like all the other parts.

She looked up, her expression cool and discouraging. 'We don't all have to agree on everything, Dr Moretti. Our differences are what make the world an interesting place to live. And now I'm sure you have patients to see and I know that I certainly do.' To make her point, she reached across her desk and pressed the buzzer to alert her first patient. 'Oh, and please don't give Mary and Rita the impression that we're living a cosy life together. They'll be unbearable.'

'But surely the point is to prove that we can be cosy and yet you can still resist me,' he reminded her in silky tones, and she stared at him, speechless. 'Isn't that the message you want them to receive? Unless, of course, you are having trouble resisting me.'

'Oh, please!' She gave an exclamation of impatience and looked up just as the patient knocked on the door. 'Let's just move on.'

'Yes, let's do that.' He kept his hand on the doorhandle, his eyes glinting darkly, 'but at least try and keep this authentic. For the record, you would not get me out of your system in one night, *cara mia.*'

Her mouth fell open and she searched in vain for a witty reply. And failed.

His smile widened and he wandered out of the room, leaving her fuming.

Alice took refuge in work and fortunately there was plenty of it.

Her first patient was a woman who was worried about a rash on her daughter's mouth.

'She had this itchy, red sore and then suddenly it turned into a blister and it's been oozing.' The mother pulled a face and hugged the child. 'Poor thing. It's really bothering her.'

Alice took one look at the thick, honey-coloured crust that had formed over the lesion and made an instant diagnosis. *Impetigo contagiosa,* she decided, caused by *Staphyloccocus aureus* and possibly group A beta-haemolytic streptococcus. This was one of the things she loved about medicine, she thought as she finished her examination and felt a rush of satisfaction. You were given clues. Signs. And you had to interpret them. Behind everything was a cause. It was just a question of finding it.

In this case she had no doubt. 'She has impetigo, Mrs Wood.' She turned back to her computer, selected a drug and pressed the print key. 'It's a very common skin condition, particularly in children. As it's only in one area I'm going to give you some cream to apply to the affected area. You need to wash the skin several times a day and remove the crusts. Then apply the cream. But make sure you wash your hands carefully because it's highly contagious.'

'Can she go back to nursery?'

Alice shook her head. 'Not until the lesions are cleared. Make sure you don't share towels.'

Mrs Wood sighed. 'That's more holiday I'll have to take, then. Being a working mother is a nightmare. I wonder why I bother sometimes.'

'It must be difficult.' Alice took the prescription from the printer and signed it. 'Here we are. Come back in a week if it isn't better.'

Mrs Wood left the room clutching her prescription and Alice moved on to the next patient. And the next.

She was reading a discharge letter from a surgeon when her door opened and Gio walked in, juggling two coffees and a large paper bag.

'I'm fulfilling my brief from Mary. Breakfast.' He flashed her a smile, kicked the door shut with his foot and placed everything on the desk in front of her. He ripped open the bag and waved a hand. 'Help yourself.'

She sat back in her chair and stared at him in exasperation. She never stopped for a break when she was seeing patients. It threw her concentration and just meant an even longer day. 'I've still got patients to see.'

'Actually, you haven't. At least, not at this exact moment. I checked with Mary.' He sat down in the chair next to her desk. 'Your last patient has cancelled so you've got a break. And so have I. Let's make the most of it.'

She stared at the selection of croissants and muffins. 'I'm not really hungry but now you're here we could quickly run through the referral strategy for—'

'Alice.' He leaned forward, a flash of humour in his dark eyes. 'If you're about to mention work, hold the thought.' He pushed the bag towards her. 'I refuse to discuss anything until I've seen you eat.'

The scent of warm, freshly baked cakes wafted under her nose. 'But I—'

'Didn't eat breakfast,' he reminded her calmly, 'and you've got the whole morning ahead of you. You can't get through that workload on one cup of black coffee, even though it was excellent.'

She sighed and her hand hovered over the bag. Eventually her fingers closed over a muffin. 'Fine. Thanks. If I eat this, will you leave me alone?'

'Possibly.' He waited until she'd taken a bite. 'Now we can talk about work. I'm interested in following up on Harriet. You mentioned that there's a baby clinic this afternoon. Is she likely to attend?'

'Possibly.' The muffin was still warm and tasted delicious. She wondered how she could have thought she wasn't hungry. She was starving. 'Rita would know whether she's down for immunisation. Or she may just come to have the baby weighed. Gina is around this morning, too. It would be worth talking to her. I've got a meeting with her at eleven-fifteen, to talk about our MMR rates.'

'I'll join you. Then I can discuss Harriet.'

'Fine.' Her gaze slid longingly at the remaining muffins. 'Can I have another?'

'Eat.' He pushed them towards her and she gave a guilty smile.

'I'll cook supper tonight in return.' She thought she saw a look of alarm cross his face but then decided she must have imagined it.

'There's no need, I thought we could—'

'I insist.' It was the least she could do, she thought, devouring the muffin and reached for another without even thinking. She loathed cooking, but there were times when it couldn't be avoided. 'Last night's supper of cheese on toast was hardly a gourmet treat. Tonight I'll do a curry.' She'd made one once before and it hadn't turned out too badly.

'Alice, why don't you let me—' He broke off and turned as the door opened and Rita walked in.

'Can you come to the waiting room? Betty needs advice.'

Alice brushed the crumbs from her lap and stood up. 'I'll come now. Nice breakfast. Thanks.'

Dropping the empty bag in the bin on his way past, Gio followed, wondering if she even realised that she'd eaten her way through three muffins.

It was almost eleven o'clock, and she'd been up since dawn and working on an empty stomach until he'd intervened.

Something definitely needed to be done about her lifestyle.

He gave a wry smile. Even more so if he was going to be living with her. After sampling her cheese on toast, he didn't dare imagine what her curry would be like, but he had a suspicion that the after-effects might require medication.

He walked into the reception area and watched while she walked over to the couple standing at the desk.

'Betty? What's happened?'

'Eating too quickly, that's what happened.' Betty scowled at her husband but there was worry in her eyes. 'Thought I'd cook him a nice bit of fish for breakfast, straight from the quay, but he wasn't looking what he was doing and now he's got a bone lodged in his throat. And, of course, it has to be right at peak season when the shop's clogged with people spending money and I can't trust that dizzy girl on her own behind the counter. If we have to go to A and E it will be hours and—'

'Betty.'

Gio watched, fascinated, as Alice put a hand on the woman's arm and interrupted her gently, her voice steady and confident. 'Calm down. I'm sure we'll manage to take the bone out here, but if not—' She broke off as the door opened again and another woman hurried in, her face disturbingly pale, a hand resting on her swollen stomach. 'Cathy? Has something happened?'

'Oh, Dr Anderson, I've had the most awful pains this morning. Ever since I hung out the washing. I didn't know whether

I should just drive straight to the hospital but Mick has an interview later this morning and I didn't want to drag him there on a wild-goose chase. I know surgery has finished, but have you got a minute?'

Obviously not for both at the same time, Gio reflected with something close to amusement. No wonder Alice looked tired. She never stopped working. Surgery was finished and still the patients were crowding in. Had he really thought that he was in for a quiet summer?

He glanced towards the door, half expecting someone else to appear, but there was no one. 'Point me in the direction of a pair of Tilley's forceps and I'll deal with the fishbone,' he said calmly, and Alice gave a brief nod, her eyes lingering on Cathy's pale face.

'In your consulting room. Forceps are in the top cupboard above the sink. Thanks.'

Her lack of hesitation impressed him. She might be a workaholic but at least she didn't have trouble delegating, Gio mused as he introduced himself to the couple and ushered them into the consulting room.

'If you'll have a seat, Mr...?' He lifted an eyebrow and the woman gave a stiff smile.

'Norman. Giles and Betty Norman.' Her tone was crisp and more than a little chilly, but he smiled easily.

'You'll have to forgive me for not knowing who you are. This is only my second day here.'

Betty Norman gave a sniff. 'We run the newsagent across the harbour. If you were local, you'd know that. There have been Normans running the newsagent for five generations.' She looked at him suspiciously, her gaze bordering on the unfriendly. 'That's a foreign accent I'm hearing and you certainly don't look English.'

'That's because I'm Italian.' Gio adjusted the angle of the light. 'And I may be new to the village, Mrs Norman, but I'm not new to medicine so you need have no worries on that score.'

He opened a cupboard and selected the equipment he was going to need. 'Mr Norman, I just need to shine a light in your mouth so that I can take a better look at the back of your throat.'

Betty dropped her handbag and folded her arms. 'Well, I just hope you can manage to get the wretched thing out. Some surgeries insist you go to A and E for something like this but we have a business to run. A and E is a sixty-minute round trip at the best of times and then there's the waiting. Dr Anderson is good at this sort of thing. Perhaps we ought to wait until she's finished with young Cathy.'

Aware that he was being tested, Gio bit back a smile, not remotely offended. 'I don't think that's a trip you're going to be making today, Mrs Norman,' he said smoothly, raising his head briefly from his examination to acknowledge her concerns. 'And I don't think you need to wait to see Dr Anderson. I can understand that you're wary of a new doctor but I can assure you that I'm more than up to the job. Why don't you let me try and then we'll see what happens?'

She stared at him, her shoulders tense and unyielding, her mouth pursed in readiness to voice further disapproval, and then he smiled at her and the tension seemed to ooze out of her and her mouth relaxed slightly into a smile of her own.

'Stupid of me to cook fish for breakfast,' she muttered weakly, and Gio returned to his examination.

'Cooking is never stupid, Mrs Norman,' he murmured as he depressed her husband's tongue to enable him to visualise the tonsil. 'And fish is the food of the gods, especially when it's eaten fresh from the sea. I see the bone quite clearly. Removing it should present no difficulty whatsoever.'

He reached for the forceps, adjusted the light and removed the fishbone with such speed and skill that his patient barely coughed.

'There.' He placed the offending bone on a piece of gauze. 'There's the culprit. The back of your throat has been slightly scratched, Mr Norman, so I'm going to give you an antibiotic and ask you to come back in a day for me to just check your throat. If necessary I will refer you to the ENT team at the hospital, but I don't think it will come to that.'

Mr Norman stared at the bone and glanced at his wife, an expression of relief on his face.

'Well—thank goodness.'

She picked up her handbag, all her icy reserve melted away. 'Thank the doctor, not goodness.' She gave Gio a nod of approval. 'Welcome to Smuggler's Cove. I think you're going to fit in well.'

'Thank you.' He smiled, his mind on Alice and her soft mouth. 'I think so, too.'

Alice watched from the doorway, clocked the killer smile, the Latin charm, and noted Betty's response with a sigh of relief and a flicker of exasperation. Why was it that the members of her sex were so predictable?

She'd briefly examined Cathy and what she'd seen had been enough to convince her that a trip to hospital was necessary for a more detailed check-up. Then she'd returned to the consulting room, prepared to help Gio, only to find that her help clearly wasn't required.

Not only had he removed the fishbone, which she knew could often be a tricky procedure, but had obviously succeeded in winning over the most difficult character in the village.

It amused her that even Betty Norman wasn't immune to a handsome Italian with a sexy smile and for a moment she found herself remembering David's comment about women going weak at the knees. Then she allowed herself a smile. *Not every woman.* Her knees were still functioning as expected, despite Mary's interference.

She could see he was handsome, and she was still walking with no problem.

Clearing her throat, she walked into the room. 'Everything OK?'

But she could see that everything was more than OK. Betty had melted like Cornish ice cream left out in the midday sun.

'Everything is fine.' Betty glanced at her watch, all smiles now. She patted her hair and straightened her blouse. 'I can be back behind the counter before that girl has a chance to make a mistake. Nice meeting you Dr... I didn't catch your name.'

'Moretti.' He extended a lean, bronzed hand. 'Gio Moretti.'

His voice was a warm, accented drawl and Betty flushed a deep shade of pink as she shook his hand. 'Well, thank you again. And welcome. If you need any help with anything, just call into the newsagent's.' She waved a hand, flustered now. 'I'd be more than happy to advise you on anything local.'

Gio smiled. 'I'll remember that.'

'By the way...' She turned to Alice. 'Edith doesn't seem herself at the moment. I can't put my finger on it but something isn't right. It may be nothing, but I thought you should know, given what happened to her last month.'

'I'll check on her.' Alice frowned. 'You think she might have fallen again?'

'That's what's worrying me.' Betty reached for her handbag. 'Iris Leek at number thirty-six has a key if you need to let yourself in. I tried ringing her yesterday for a chat, but I think she was away at her sister's.'

'I'll call round there this week,' Alice promised immediately. 'I was going to anyway.'

Betty smiled. 'Thank you, dear. You may not have been born here but you're a good girl and we're lucky to have you.' She turned to Gio with a girlish smile. 'And doubly lucky now, it seems.'

The couple left the surgery and Alice shook her head in disbelief. 'Well, you really charmed her. Congratulations. I've never seen Betty blush before. You've made a conquest.'

His gaze was swift and assessing. 'And that surprises you?'

'Well, let's put it this way—she's not known for her warmth to strangers unless they're spending money in her shop.'

'I thought she was a nice lady.' He switched off the light and tidied up the equipment he'd used. 'A bit cautious, but I suppose that's natural.'

'Welcome to Smuggler's Cove,' Alice said lightly. 'If you can't trace your family back for at least five generations, you're a stranger.'

'And how about you, Alice?' He paused and his dark gold eyes narrowed as they rested on her face. 'From her comments, you obviously aren't a local either. So far we've talked about work and nothing else. Tell me about yourself.'

His slow, seductive masculine tones slid over her taut nerves and soothed her. It was a voice designed to lull an unsuspecting woman into a sensual coma.

'Alice?'

Alice shook herself. She wasn't going to be thrown off her stride just because the man was movie-star handsome. She'd leave that to the rest of the female population of the village. 'There's nothing interesting to say about me. I'm very boring.'

'You mean you don't like talking about yourself.'

He was sharp, she had to give him that. 'I came here after I finished my GP rotation five years ago so, no, I don't qualify as a local,' she said crisply, delivering the facts as succinctly as possible. In her experience, the quickest way to stop someone asking questions was to answer a few. 'But I'm accepted because of the job I do.'

'And it's obviously a job you do very well. So where is home to you? Where are your family?'

Her blood went cold and all her muscles tightened. 'This is my home.'

There was a brief pause and when he spoke again his voice was gentle. 'Then you're lucky, because I can't think of a nicer place to live.' His eyes lingered on her face and then he strolled across the room to wash his hands. 'Do you often do night visits?'

Relieved that he'd changed the subject, some of the tension left her. 'Not since the new GP contract. Why?'

'Because I was told that the other night you were up with a child who had an asthma attack.'

'Chloe Bennett.' She frowned. 'How do you know that?'

He dried his hands. 'I was talking to the girl in the coffee-shop yesterday. Blonde. Nice smile.'

Alice resisted the temptation to roll her eyes. 'Katy Adams.' Obviously another conquest.

'Nice girl.'

Knowing Katy's reputation with men, Alice wondered if she should warn her new partner that he could be in mortal danger. She decided against it. A man who looked like him would have been fending off women from his cradle. He certainly wouldn't need any help from her.

'Chloe Bennett is a special case,' she explained briskly. 'Her mother has been working hard to control her asthma and give her some sort of normal life at school. It's been very difficult. She has my home number and I encourage her to use it when there's a problem, and that's what happened the night before last. I had to admit her in the end but not before she'd given me a few nasty moments.'

'I can't believe you give patients your home number.'

'Not every patient. But when the need is real...' She gave a shrug. 'It makes perfect sense from a management point of view. I'm the one with all the information. It means Chloe gets better care and her mother doesn't have to explain her history all the time.'

'You can't be there for everyone all the time. It isn't possible.'

'But continuity makes sense from a clinical point of view.' She frowned as she thought of it. 'In Chloe's case it means that a doctor unfamiliar with her case doesn't have to waste time taking details from a panicking parent when it's dark outside and the child can't breathe properly.'

'I can clearly see the benefits for your patients.' His eyes, dark and disturbingly intense, searched hers in a way that she found unsettling. 'But the benefits for you are less clear to me. It places an enormous demand on your time. On your life.'

'Yes, well, my job is important to me,' she said quickly, wondering whether there was anyone left in the world who felt the way she did about medicine. 'For me the job isn't about doing as little as possible and going home as early as possible. It's about involving yourself in the health of a community. About making a real difference to people's lives. I don't believe that a supermarket approach to health care is in anyone's interests.' She broke off and gave an awkward shrug, spots of colour touching her cheeks as she reflected on the fact that she was in danger of becoming carried away. 'Sorry. It's just something I feel strongly about. I don't expect you to understand. You probably think I'm totally mad.'

'On the contrary, I think your patients are very fortunate. But in all things there has to be compromise. How can you be awake to see patients—how can you be truly at your best— when you've been up half the night?' He strolled towards her and she felt her whole body tense in a response that she didn't understand.

She'd always considered herself to be taller than average but next to him she felt small. Even in heels she only reached his shoulder. Unable to help herself, she took a step backwards and then immediately wished she hadn't. 'You don't need to worry about me, Dr Moretti,' she said, keeping her tone cool and formal to compensate for her reaction. 'I'm not short of stamina and I really enjoy my life. And my patients certainly aren't suffering.'

'I'm sure they're not.' He gave a slow smile and raised an eyebrow. 'Does it make you feel safer, Alice?'

She took another step backwards. 'Does what make me feel safer?'

'Calling me Dr Moretti.' His expression was thoughtful. 'You do it whenever I get too close. Does it help give you the distance you need?'

She felt her heart pump harder. 'I don't know what you're talking about.'

'Was it a man?' He lifted a hand and tucked a strand of blonde hair behind her ear, his fingers lingering. 'Tell me, Alice. Was it a man who hurt you? Is that why you live alone and bury yourself in work? Is that why you don't believe in love?'

With a subtle movement that was entirely instinctive she moved her head away from his touch. 'You're obviously a romantic, Dr Moretti.'

'You're doing it again, *tesoro*,' he said softly, his hand suspended in midair as he studied her face. 'Calling me Dr Moretti. It's Gio. And of course I'm romantic.'

'I'm sure you are.' She tilted her head, her smile mocking. 'All men are when it suits their purpose.'

He raised an eyebrow. 'You're suggesting that I use romance as some sort of seduction tool? You're a cynic, Alice, do you know that?'

Was it even worth defending herself? 'I'm a realist.' Her tone was cool. 'And you're clearly an extremely intelligent man. You should know better than to believe in all that woolly, emotional rubbish.'

'Ah, but you've overlooked one important fact about me.' His eyes gleamed dark and dangerous as he slid a hand under her chin and forced her to look at him. 'I'm Sicilian. We're a romantic race. It's in the blood. It has nothing to do with seduction and everything to do with a way of life. And a life is nothing without love in it.'

'Oh, please.' She rolled her eyes. 'I'm a scientist. I prefer to deal with the tangible. I happen to believe that love is a myth and the current divorce statistics would appear to support my view.'

'You think everything in this world can be explained given sufficient time in a laboratory?'

'Yes.' Her tone was cool and she brushed his hand away in a determined gesture. 'If it can't then it probably doesn't exist.'

'Is that right?' He looked at her as if he wanted to say something more but instead he smiled. 'So what do you do to relax around here? Restaurants? Watersports?'

For some reason her heart had set up a rhythmic pounding in her chest. 'I read a lot.'

'That sounds lonely, Dr Anderson,' he said softly. 'Especially for someone as young and beautiful as you.'

Taken aback and totally flustered, she raked a hand through her blonde hair and struggled for words. 'I—If you're flirting with me, Dr Moretti, it's only fair to warn you that you're wasting your time. I don't flirt. I don't play those sorts of games.'

'I wasn't flirting and I certainly wasn't playing games. I was stating a fact.' He said the words thoughtfully, his eyes narrowed as they scanned her face. 'You are beautiful. And very English. In Sicily, you would have to watch that pale skin.'

'Well, since I have no plans to visit Sicily, it isn't a problem that's likely to keep me awake at night.' Her head was buzzing and she felt completely on edge. There was something about him—something about the way he looked at her...

Deciding that the only way to end the conversation was to leave the room, she headed for the door.

'Wait. Don't run,' he said gently, his fingers covering hers before she could open the door.

His hand was hard. Strong. She turned, her heart pounding against her chest when she realised just how close he was.

'We have to meet Gina and—'

'What are you afraid of, Alice?'

'I'm not afraid. I'm just busy.' There was something in those dark eyes that brought a bubble of panic to her throat and her insides knotted with tension.

'You don't have to be guarded around me, Alice.' For a brief moment his fingers tightened on hers and then he let her go and took a step backwards, giving her the distance she craved. 'People interest me. There's often such a gulf between the person on the surface and the person underneath. It's rewarding to discover the real person.'

'Well, in my case there's nothing to discover, so don't waste your time.' She opened the door a crack. 'You're a good-looking guy, Dr Moretti, you don't need me to tell you that. I'm sure you can find no end of women willing to stroll on the beach with you, fall into bed, fall in love or do whatever it is you like to do in your spare time. You certainly don't need me. And now we need to meet Gina. She'll be waiting.'

CHAPTER SIX

GIO SPENT THE rest of the day wondering about Alice. Wondering about her past.

She'd claimed that it hadn't been a man who'd forged her attitude to love, but it had to have been someone. In his experience, no one felt that strongly about relationships unless they'd been badly burned.

He tried to tell himself that it wasn't his business and that he wasn't interested. But he was interested. Very. And she filled his mind as he worked his way through a busy afternoon surgery.

The patients were a mix of locals and tourists and he handled them with ease and skill. Sore throats, arthritis, a diabetic who hadn't brought the right insulin on holiday and a nasty local reaction to an insect bite.

The locals lingered and asked questions. Where had he worked last? Had he bought a wife with him? Was he planning on staying long? The tourists were eager to leave the surgery and get on with their holiday.

Gio saw them all quickly and efficiently and handled the more intrusive questions as tactfully as possible, his mind distracted by thoughts of Alice. She was interesting, he mused as he checked glands and stared into throats. Interesting, beautiful and very serious.

Slightly prickly, wary, definitely putting up barriers. But underneath the front he sensed passion and vulnerability. He sensed that she was afraid.

He frowned slightly as he printed out a prescription for eye drops and handed it to his last patient.

There had been no mention of a social life in her description of relaxation. And David had definitely said that his partner had no time for anything other than work.

'You finished quickly today.' She walked into the room towards the end of the afternoon, just as his patient left. 'Any problems?'

'No. No problems so far.' He shook his head and leaned back in his chair. 'Should I have expected some?'

'People round here are congenitally nosy. You should have already realised that after twenty minutes in the company of the Normans this morning.' This time she stood near the door. Keeping a safe distance. 'This is a small, close-knit community and a new doctor is bound to attract a certain degree of attention. I bet they've been asking you no end of personal questions. Do you answer?'

'When it suits me. And when it doesn't...' he gave a shrug '...let's just say I was evasive. So, Dr Anderson, what next? I've asked about you but you haven't asked anything about me and you're probably the only one entitled to answers, given that we're working closely together.'

Their eyes met briefly and held for a long moment. Then she looked away. 'I've read your CV and that's all that matters. I'm not interested in the personal, Dr Moretti. Your life outside work is of no interest to me whatsoever. I really don't feel the need to know anything about you. You're doing your job. That's all I care about.'

Gio studied her in thoughtful silence. There was chemistry there. He'd felt it and he knew she'd felt it, too. Felt it and rejected it. Her face was shuttered. Closed. As if a protective shield had been drawn across her whole person.

Why?

'Make sure you have your key tonight because I have two house calls to make on the way home, so I'll be a bit late. Then I'm going to call at the supermarket and pick up the ingredients for a curry.' What exactly went into a curry? She knew she'd made it once before but she had no precise recollection of the recipe. 'How was the mother and baby clinic?'

'Fun. Interesting. But no Harriet.'

Alice frowned. 'Did you talk to Gina after our meeting?'

'At length. Interestingly enough, she's found it very hard to see Harriet. Every time she tries to arrange a visit Harriet makes an excuse, but she said that she'd sounded quite happy on the phone so she hasn't pushed. She thinks Harriet is just under a normal amount of strain for a new mother but she's promised to make another attempt at seeing her.'

'And what do you think?'

His gaze lifted to hers. 'After what I saw in the waiting room, I need to talk to her before I can answer that question.'

Alice grabbed her keys and popped her head into the nurse's room to say goodbye to Rita. 'I'm off. If Harriet comes to see you for anything in the next few days, make sure you encourage her to make an appointment with Dr Moretti.'

'I certainly will.' Rita returned a box of vaccines to the fridge and smiled. 'If you ask me, the man is a real find. Caring, warm and yet still incredibly masculine. You two have a nice evening together.'

'Don't you start. It isn't a date, Rita,' Alice said tightly. 'He's my lodger, thanks to Mary.'

Only somewhere along the way he'd forgotten his role. Lodgers weren't supposed to probe and delve and yet, from what she'd seen so far, Gio just couldn't help himself. Probing and delving seemed to be in his blood. Even with Harriet, he'd refused to take her insistence that she was fine at face value. Clearly he didn't intend to let the matter drop until he'd satisfied himself that she wasn't depressed.

Alice watched absently as Rita closed the fridge door. But, of course, at least where the patients were concerned, that was a good thing. It was his job to try and judge what was wrong with them. To pick up signs. Search for clues. To see past the obvious. She just didn't need him doing it with *her*.

'It's not Mary's fault the letting agency made a mess of things,' Rita said airily as she washed her hands. 'And if he were my lodger, I'd be thanking my lucky stars.'

'Well, you and I are different. And we both know that the letting agency wouldn't have made a mess of things without some significant help from certain people around here.' Alice put her hands on her hips and glared. 'And just for the record, in case you didn't get the message the first two hundred times, I don't need you to set me up with a man!'

'Don't you?' Rita dried her hands and dropped the paper towel in the bin. 'Strikes me you're not doing anything about it yourself.'

'Because, believe it or not, being with a man isn't compulsory!'

Reaching the point of explosion, Alice turned on her heel and strode out to her car before Rita had a chance to irritate her further. That day had been one long aggravation, she decided as she delved in her bag for her keys. All she wanted was to be left in peace to live her life the way she wanted to live it. What was so wrong with that?

Climbing into her car, she closed the door and shut her eyes.

Breathe, she told herself firmly, trying to calm herself down. Breathe. In and out. Relax.

Beside her, the door was pulled open. 'Alice, *tesoro,* are you all right?'

Her eyes opened. Gio was leaning into the car, his eyes concerned.

'I'm fine.' Gripping the wheel tightly, she wondered whether the sight of a GP screaming in a public place would attract attention. 'Or at least I will be fine when people stop interfering with my life and leave me alone. At least part of this is your fault.' She glared at him and his eyes narrowed.

'My fault?'

'Well, if you weren't single and good-looking, they wouldn't have been able to move you into my house.'

He rubbed a hand across his jaw and laughter flickered in his eyes. 'You want me to get married or rearrange my features?'

'No point. They'd just find some other poor individual to push my way.' Her tone gloomy, she slumped back in her seat and shook her head. 'Sorry, this really isn't your fault at all. It's just this place. Maybe David was right to get away. Right now I'd pay a lot to live among people who don't know who on earth I am and can't be bothered to find out. I must get going. I've got house calls to make on my way home.'

Unfortunately her car had other ideas. As she turned the key in the ignition the engine struggled and choked and then died.

'Oh, for crying out loud!' In a state of disbelief Alice glared at the car, as if fury alone should be enough to start it. 'What is happening to my life?'

Gio was still leaning on the open door. 'Do you often have problems with it?'

'Never before.' She tried the ignition again. 'My car is the only place I can get peace and quiet these days! The only place I can hide from people trying to pair me off with you! And now even that has died!'

'Shh.' He put a hand over her lips, his eyes amused. 'Calm down.'

'I can't calm down. I've got house calls to make and no transport.'

'I'm leaving now.' His tone was calm and reasonable as he

gestured to the low, sleek sports car parked next to hers. 'We'll do the calls together.'

'But—'

'It makes perfect sense. It will help me orientate myself a little.'

'What's happening?' Mary hurried up, a worried expression on her face. 'Is it your car?'

'Yes.' Alice hissed the word through gritted teeth. 'It's my car.'

'Give me the keys and I'll get it taken care of,' Mary said immediately, holding out her hand. 'I'll call Paul at the garage. He's a genius with cars. In the meantime, you go with Dr Moretti.'

A nasty suspicion unfolded like a bud inside her. 'Mary...' Alice shook her head and decided she was becoming paranoid. No matter how much Mary wanted to push her towards Gio, she wasn't capable of tampering with a car. 'All right. Thanks.'

Accepting defeat, she climbed out of her car, handed the keys to Mary and slid into Gio's black sports car.

He pressed a button and the roof above her disappeared in a smooth movement.

She rolled her eyes. 'Show-off.'

He gave her a boyish grin, slid sunglasses over his eyes and reversed out of the parking space.

The last thing she saw as they pulled out of the surgery car park was the smug expression on Mary's face.

He drove up the hill, away from the harbour, with Alice giving directions.

'I'm embarrassed turning up at house calls in this car,' she mumbled as they reached the row of terraced houses where Edith lived. 'It's hardly subtle, is it? Everyone will think I've gone mad.'

'They will be envious and you will give them something interesting to talk about. Is this the lady that Betty was talking about earlier?' Gio brought the car to a halt and switched off the engine.

'Yes. Edith Carne.' Alice reached for her bag. 'She's one of David's patients but she had a fall a few weeks ago and I just want to check on her because she lives on her own and she's not one to complain. You don't have to come with me. You're welcome to wait in the car. Who knows? Keep the glasses on and you might get lucky with some passing female.'

'But I am already lucky,' he said smoothly, leaning across to open the door for her, 'because you are in my car, *tesoro*.'

She caught the wicked twinkle in his dark eyes and pulled a face. 'Save the charm, Romeo. It's wasted on me.' She climbed out of the car and walked towards the house, her hair swinging around her shoulders, frustration still bubbling inside her.

'If she's David's patient, she's going to be mine,' Gio pointed out as he caught up with her, 'so this is as good a time as any to make her acquaintance. It's logical.'

It was logical, but still she would have rather he'd waited in the car. Having him tailing her flustered her and put her on edge. She needed space to calm herself. Normally she loved her work and found it absorbing and relaxing but today she felt restless and unsettled, as if the door to her tidy, ordered life had been flung wide open.

And it was all thanks to Mary and Rita, she thought angrily, and their interfering ways.

If she hadn't been living with the man, she could have easily avoided him. The surgery was so busy that often their paths didn't often cross during the day.

The evenings were a different matter.

Pushing aside feelings that she didn't understand, she rang the doorbell and waited. 'Her husband died three years ago,' she told Gio, 'and they were married for fifty-two years.'

He raised an eyebrow. 'And you don't believe in love?'

'There are lots of reasons why two people stay together.' She tilted her head back and stared up at the bedroom window through narrowed eyes. 'But love doesn't come into it, in my opinion. Why isn't she answering?'

'Does she have family?'

'No. But she has lots of friends in the village. She's lived here all her life.' Alice rang the bell again, an uneasy feeling spreading through her.

'Why did she fall last time? Does anyone know?'

'I don't think they found anything. The neighbour called an ambulance. She had a few cuts and bruises but nothing broken. But I know David was worried about her.' And now she was worried, too. Why wasn't Edith answering the door? She sighed and jammed her fingers through her hair. 'All right. I suppose I'll have to go next door and get the key, but I hate the thought of doing that.' Hated the thought of invading another person's privacy.

'Could she have gone out?' Gio stepped across the front lawn and glanced in through the front window. 'I can hear voices. A television maybe? But I can't see anyone.'

Alice was on the point of going next door to speak to the neighbour when the door opened.

'Oh, Edith.' She gave a smile of relief as she saw the old lady standing there. 'We were worried about you. We thought you might have fallen again. I wanted to check on how you're feeling.'

'Well, that's kind of you but I'm fine, dear.' Edith was wearing a dressing-gown even though it was late afternoon, and the expression on her face was bemused. 'No problems at all.'

Alice scanned Edith's face, noting that she looked extremely pale and tired. Something wasn't right.

'Can I come in for a minute, Edith? I'd really like to have a chat and check that everything's all right with you. And I need to introduce you to our new doctor.' She flapped a hand towards Gio. 'He's taken over from David. Come all the way from Sicily. Land of *canolli* and volcanoes that misbehave.'

'Sicily? Frank and I went there once. It was beautiful.' Edith's knuckles whitened on the edge of the door. 'I'm fine, Dr Anderson. I don't need to waste your time. There's plenty worse off than me.'

'Consider it a favour to me.' Gio's voice was deep and heavily accented. 'I am new to the area, Mrs Carne. I need inside information and I understand you've lived here all your life.'

'Well, I have, but—'

'Please—I would be so grateful.' He spread his hands, his warm smile irresistible to any female, and Edith looked into his dark eyes and capitulated.

'All right, but I'm fine. Completely fine.'

At least Gio used his charm on the old as well as the young, Alice thought as they followed Edith into the house. Wondering whether she was the only one who felt that something wasn't right, she glanced at Gio but his attention was focused on the old lady.

'This is a lovely room.' His eyes scanned the ancient, rose-coloured sofa and the photographs placed three deep on the window-sill. 'I can see that it is filled with happy memories.'

'I was born in this house.' Edith sat down, folded her hands in her lap and stared at the empty fireplace. 'My parents died in this house and Frank and I carried on living here. I've lived here all my life. I can see the sea from my kitchen window.'

'It's a beautiful position.' Gio leaned towards a photograph displayed on a table next to his right hand. 'This is you? Was it taken in the garden of this house?'

Edith gave a nod and a soft smile. 'With my parents. I was five years old.' She stared wistfully at the photo, her hands clasped in her lap. 'The garden was different then, of course. My Frank loved the garden. I used to joke that he loved his plants more than me.'

Gio lifted the photo and took a closer look. 'It must be lovely to walk in the garden that he planted.'

Alice shifted impatiently in her chair. What was he talking about? And why wasn't he asking Edith questions about her blood pressure and whether she'd felt dizzy lately? What was the relevance of the garden, for goodness' sake?

Edith was staring at him, a strange expression in her eyes. 'Very few people understand how personal a garden can be.'

'A garden tells you so much about a person,' Gio agreed, replacing the photo carefully on the table. 'And being there, you share in their vision.'

Edith twisted her hands in her lap. 'Just walking there makes me feel close to him.'

Alice frowned, wondering where the conversation was leading. True, Edith was much more relaxed than she'd been when they'd arrived and she had to admit that Gio had a way with people, but why were they talking about gardening? She wanted to establish some facts. She wanted to find out whether Edith had suffered another fall but Gio seemed to be going down an entirely different path.

She forced herself to sit quietly and breathed an inaudible sigh of relief when Gio eventually steered the talk round to the topic of Edith's health. It was so skillfully done that it seemed like a natural direction for the conversation.

'I can barely remember the fall now,' Edith said dismissively, 'it was so long ago.'

'A month, Edith,' Alice reminded her, and the old lady sniffed, all the tension suddenly returning to her slim frame.

'I was just clumsy. Not looking where I was going. Tripped over the carpet. It won't happen again—I'm being really careful.'

Alice glanced around the room. The carpet was fitted. There were no rugs. The carpet in the hall and on the stairs had been fitted, too. Her eyes clashed with Gio's and she knew that he'd noticed the same thing.

'Can I just check your pulse and blood pressure?' He opened his bag and removed the necessary equipment. 'Just routine.'

'I suppose so...'

Gio pushed up the sleeve of her dressing-gown and paused.

'That's a nasty bruise on your arm,' he commented as he wrapped the blood-pressure cuff around her arm. 'Did you knock yourself?'

Edith didn't look at him. 'Just being a bit careless walking through the doorway.'

Without further comment Gio checked her pulse, blood pressure and pulse and then eased the stethoscope out of his ears. 'When you went into hospital after your fall, did anyone say that your blood pressure was on the low side?'

Edith shook her head. 'Not that I remember. They just sent me home and told me they'd set up another appointment in a few months. I'm fine. Really I am. But it was good of you to call in.' She stood up, the movement quite agitated. 'I'll come to the surgery if I need any help. Good of you to introduce yourself.'

Not giving them a chance to linger, she hurried them out of the front door and closed it.

'Well.' Standing on the doorstep, staring at a closed door, Alice blinked in amazement. 'What was all that about? She's normally the most hospitable woman in the community. From her reaction today, you would have thought we were planning to take her away and lock her up.'

'I think that's exactly what she thought.' Gio turned and walked down the path towards his car.

'What do you mean?' She caught up with him in a few strides. 'You're not making sense.'

He unlocked the car doors. 'I think your Mrs Carne has had more falls since David saw her. But she isn't ready to confess.' He slid into the car while Alice gaped at him from the pavement.

'But why?' It seemed simple to Alice. 'If she's falling then she should tell us and we'll try and solve it.'

The engine gave a throaty roar and he drummed long fingers on the steering-wheel while he waited for her to get into the passenger seat. 'Life isn't always that simple, is it?'

She climbed in next to him and fastened her seat belt. 'So why wouldn't she tell us?'

'General practice is very like detective work, don't you think?' He glanced towards her. 'In hospital you see only the patient. At home you have the advantage of seeing the patient in their own environment and that often contains clues about the person they are. About the way they live their lives.'

'And what clues did you see?'

'That her whole life is contained in that house. There were photographs of her parents, her as a child, her husband. There were cushions that she'd knitted on a sofa that I'm willing to bet belonged to her mother. The garden had been planted by her husband.'

Alice tried to grasp the relevance of what he was saying and failed. 'But that's all emotional stuff. What's that got to do with her illness?'

'Not everything about a patient can be explained by science alone, Alice.' He checked the rear-view mirror and pulled out. 'She doesn't want us to know she's falling because she's afraid we're going to insist she leaves her home. And she loves her home. Her home is everything to her. It contains all her memories. Take her from it and you erase part of her life. Probably the only part that matters.'

He was doing it again, Alice mused, delving deep. Refusing to accept people at face value.

She stared ahead as he drove off down the quiet road and back onto the main road. 'Take a left here,' she said absently, her mind still on their conversation. 'Aren't you making it complicated? I mean, if Edith is falling, we need to find the reason. It's that simple. The rest isn't really anything to do with us.'

'The rest is everything to do with us if it affects the patient. You're very afraid of emotions, aren't you, Alice?' His voice was soft and she gave a frown.

'We're not talking about me.'

'Of course we're not.' There was no missing the irony in his tone but she chose to ignore it.

'So now what do we do?'

'I want to check on a couple of things. Look at the correspondence that came out of her last appointment and speak to the doctor who saw her before I go crashing in with my diagnosis.'

'Which is?' The wind picked up a strand of hair and blew it across her face. 'You think you know why she's falling?'

'Not for sure, no. But certainly there are clues.' He eased the car round a tight corner, his strong hands firm on the wheel. 'Her heart rate is on the slow side and her blood pressure is low. What do you know about CSS?'

'Carotid sinus syndrome. I remember reading a UK study on it a few years ago.' Alice sifted through her memory and her brow cleared. 'They linked it to unexplained falls in the elderly. It can result in syncope—fainting. Are you saying that you think—?' She broke off and Gio gave a shrug that betrayed his Latin heritage.

'I don't know for sure, of course, but it's certainly worth considering. It's important that elderly patients who fall are given cardiovascular assessment. Do you think this happened in her case?'

'Not to my knowledge. We'll check the notes and, if not, we'll refer her immediately.' The wind teased her hair again and Alice slid a hand through the silky strands and tried to anchor them down. 'Well done. That was very smart of you. And all that stuff about her house and the way she was feeling...' She frowned, angry and disappointed with herself. 'I wouldn't have thought of that.'

'That's because you work only with facts and not emotions, but the truth is that the two work together. You can't dissociate them from each other, Alice. Emotions are a part of people's lives.' He gave her a quick glance, a slight smile touching his mouth, a challenge in his dark eyes. 'And she was definitely in love with her husband.'

She tipped her head back against the seat and rolled her eyes upwards. 'Don't let's go there again.'

'You heard the way she talked about him. You saw the look on her face. Do you really think she didn't love him?'

'Well, obviously you're going to miss someone if you've lived with them for over fifty years,' Alice said tetchily, 'and I'm sure they were best friends. I just don't believe in this special, indefinable, woolly emotion that supposedly binds two people together.'

'You don't believe in love at first sight?'

'Nor on second or third sight,' Alice said dryly, letting go of her hair and pointing a finger towards a turning. 'You need to take a right down there so that I can pick up some dinner.'

He followed her instructions and turned into the supermarket car park. 'Listen, about dinner. You cooked last night. Perhaps I ought to—'

'No need. I've got it. Back in five minutes.' She slammed the door and braced herself for her second least favourite pastime after cooking. Shopping for the ingredients.

Later, wondering whether his taste buds would ever recover, Gio drank yet another glass of water in an attempt to quench the fire burning in his mouth. 'Alice, tomorrow it's my turn to cook.'

'Why would you want to do that?'

Was it all right to be honest? He gave a wry smile and risked it. 'Because I want to live?'

Because he respected his stomach far too much to eat another one of her meals and because he needed to show her that there was more to eating than simply ingesting animal and plant material in any format.

She sighed and dropped her fork. 'All right, it tasted pretty awful but I'm not that great at curry. I think I might have got my tablespoons mixed up with my teaspoons. Does it really matter?'

'When you're measuring chilli powder? Yes,' he replied dryly. 'And, anyway, I'm very happy to cook from now on. I love to cook. I'll do you something Italian. You'll enjoy it.'

She pushed her plate away, the contents only half-eaten. 'We eat to live, Gio, not the other way round. The body needs protein, carbohydrate, fats and all that jazz in order to function the way it should. It doesn't care how you throw them together.'

She was all fact, he thought to himself. All fact and science. As far as she was concerned, if it couldn't be explained by some fancy theory then it didn't exist.

It would be fun to show her just what could be achieved with food, he decided. And atmosphere.

At least she'd stopped jumping every time he walked into the room. It was time to make some changes. Time to push her out of her comfort zone.

He tapped his foot under the table, his mind working. Maybe it was time to show Dr Alice Anderson that there was more to life than scientific theory. That not everything could be proven.

Maybe it was time for her to question her firmly held beliefs. But before that he needed to deal with his indigestion.

'Let's go for a walk on the beach.'

She shook her head and dumped the remains of the totally inedible curry in the bin. 'I need to catch up on some reading. You go. Take a left at the bottom of the garden, along the cycle path for about two hundred metres and you reach the harbour. Go to the end and you drop straight down onto the beach. You can walk for miles if the tide is out. Once it comes in you have to scramble up the cliffs to the coast path.'

'I want you to come with me.' Not giving her a chance to shrink away from him, he reached out a hand and dragged her to her feet. 'The reading can wait.'

'I really need to...' Her hand wriggled in his as she tried to pull away, but he kept a tight hold and used his trump card. Work.

'I want to talk about some of David's patients.' He kept his expression serious. Tried to look suitably concerned. 'It's obvious to me that the only time we're going to have for discussion is during the evenings. And I have so many questions.'

He struggled to think of a few, just in case he needed to produce one.

'Oh.' She thought for a moment and then gave a shrug. 'Well, I suppose that makes sense, but we don't have to go out. We could do it here and—'

'Alice, we've been trapped inside all day. We both need some air.' Letting go of her hand, he reached out and grabbed her jacket from the back of the door. 'Let's walk.'

'Have you come across a specific problem with a patient? Who is on your mind?'

He racked his brains to find someone to talk about, knowing that if he didn't start talking about work immediately, she'd vanish upstairs and spend the rest of the evening with her journals and textbooks, as she had the previous evening.

'I thought we could talk about the right way to approach Harriet.' He stepped through the back door and waited while she locked it. 'You know her after all.'

'Not that well. She was David's patient. Mary knows her, she might have some ideas.'

She slipped the keys into her pocket and they walked down to the cycle way. Although it was still only early evening, several cyclists sped past them, enjoying the summer weather and the wonderful views.

The tide was far out, leaving sandbanks exposed in the water.

'It's beautiful.' Gio stared at the islands of sand and Alice followed his gaze.

'Yes. And dangerous. The tide comes in so fast, it's lethal.' She stepped to one side to avoid another cyclist. 'There are warnings all over the harbour and the beach, but still some tourists insist on dicing with death. Still, it keeps the lifeboat busy.'

They reached the harbour and weaved a path through the crowds of tourists who were milling around, watching the boats and eating fish and chips on the edge of the quay.

Gio slipped a hand in his pocket. 'Ice cream, Dr Anderson?'

'I don't eat ice cream.' She was looking around her with a frown. 'Bother. We shouldn't have come this way.'

'Why not?'

'Because I've just seen at least half a dozen people who know me.'

'And what's wrong with that?' He strolled over to the nearest ice-cream shop and scanned the menu. Vanilla? Too boring. Strawberry? Too predictable.

'Because if I've seen them, then they've seen me.' She turned her head. 'With you.'

'Ah.' Cappuccino, he decided. 'And surely that's a good thing.'

'Why would fuelling town gossip possibly be a good thing?'

'Because you want to prove that you don't want a relationship.' He wandered into the shop and ordered two cones. 'In order to do that, you at least have to be seen to be mixing with members of the opposite sex. If you do that and still don't fall in love then eventually everyone will just give up trying. If you don't, they'll just keep fixing you up.'

She glared at him and he realised that the lady selling the ice creams was listening avidly.

'Perfect evening for a walk, Dr Anderson. We don't see you in here often enough. That will be three pounds forty, please.' The woman took the money with a smile and turned to Gio. 'You must be our new doctor. Betty told me all about you.'

'That's good. Saves me introducing myself.' Gio pocketed the change and picked up the ice creams with a nod of thanks and a few more words of small talk.

Outside he handed a cone to Alice.

'I said I didn't want one.'

'Just try it. One lick.'

'It's—'

'It's protein, Dr Anderson.' He winked at her and she raised an eyebrow.

'How do you work that out?'

'All that clotted cream.' He watched, noting with satisfaction the smile that teased the corners of her mouth. He was going to teach her to relax. To loosen up. To enjoy herself.

'It's a frozen lump of saturated fat designed to occlude arteries,' she said crisply, and he nodded.

'Very possibly. But it's also a mood lifter. An indulgence. A sensory experience. Smooth. Cold. Creamy. Try it.'

She stared at him. 'It's ice cream, Gio. Just ice cream.' She waved a hand dismissively and almost consigned the ice cream to the gutter. 'The body doesn't need ice cream in order to function efficiently.'

'The body may not *need* ice cream,' he conceded, 'but it's extremely grateful to receive it. Try it and find out. Go on—lick.'

With an exaggerated roll of her eyes she licked the cone. And licked again. 'All right, so it tastes good. But that's just because of the coffee. You know I love coffee.' The evening sunlight caught the gold in her hair and her blue eyes were alight with humour. 'It's my only vice.'

Looking at the way her mouth moved over the ice cream, he decided that before the summer was finished Alice would have expanded her repertoire of vices. And he was going to help her do it.

'Lick again and close your eyes,' he urged her, ignoring the fact that his own ice cream was in grave danger of melting.

She stared at him as if he were mad. 'Gio, I'm not closing my eyes with half the town watching! I have to work with these people long after you've gone! I need to retain my credibility. If I stand in the harbour with my eyes closed, licking ice cream, they'll never listen to me again.'

'Stop trying to be so perfect all the time. And stop worrying about other people.' She was delightfully prim, he thought, noticing the tiny freckles on her nose for the first time. He doubted she'd ever let her hair down in her life.

And he was absolutely crazy about her.

The knowledge knocked the breath from his lungs. 'Close

your eyes, or I'll throw you in the harbour.' His voice was gruff. 'And that will seriously damage your credibility.'

How could he possibly be in love with a woman he'd only known for a couple of days?

'Oh, fine!' With an exaggerated movement she squeezed her eyes shut and he stepped closer, tempted by the slight pout of her lips.

Suppressing the desire to kiss her until her body melted like the ice cream in her hand, he reminded himself that it was too soon for her.

He was going to take it slowly. Take his time. *Coax her out of her shell.*

'Now lick again and tell me what you taste. Tell me what it makes you feel. What it reminds you of.'

Her lick was most definitely reluctant. 'Ice cream?' Receiving no response to her sarcasm, she licked again and he waited. And waited. But she said nothing.

'Don't you go straight back to your childhood?' He decided that he was going to have to prompt her. Clearly she'd never played this game before. 'Seaside holidays, relaxation? All the fun of being young?'

There was a long silence and then her eyes opened and for a brief moment he saw the real Alice. And what he saw shocked and silenced him. He saw pain and anguish. He saw hurt and disillusionment. But most of all he saw a child who was lost and vulnerable. Alone.

And then she blanked it.

'No, Dr Moretti.' Her voice had a strange, rasping quality, as if talking was suddenly difficult. 'I don't see that. And I'm not that keen on ice cream.' Without giving him time to reply, she tossed it in the nearest bin and made for the beach, virtually breaking into a run in her attempt to put distance between them.

CHAPTER SEVEN

AT THE BOTTOM of the path, Alice slowed her pace and took several gulps of air. Her stomach churned and she felt light-headed and sick but most of all she felt angry with herself for losing control.

Oh, damn, damn damn.

How could she have let that happen? How could she have revealed so much? And because she had, *because she'd been so stupid,* he was going to come after her and demand an explanation. He was that sort of man. The sort of man who always looked beneath the surface. The sort of man who delved and dug until he had access to all parts of a person.

And she didn't want him delving. She didn't want him digging.

She bent down, removed her shoes and stepped onto the sand, intending to walk as far as possible, as fast as possible. *Even though she knew that even if she were to run, it wouldn't make any difference.* The problems were inside her and always would be, and she knew from experience that running couldn't change the past. Couldn't change the feelings that were part of her.

But she'd learned ways to handle them, she reminded herself firmly as she breathed in deeply and unclenched her hands. Ways that worked for her. It was just a question of getting control back. Of being the person she'd become.

She stared at the sea, watching the yachts streak across the bay, the wind filling their brightly coloured sails. Breathing in the same strong sea breeze, she struggled to find the familiar feeling of calm, but it eluded her.

She was concentrating so hard on breathing that the feel of Gio's hand on her shoulder made her jump, even though she'd been expecting it.

Her instinct was to push him away, but that would draw attention that she didn't want. She could have run but that, she told herself, would just make it even harder later. It would just delay the inevitable conversation. So she decided to stay put and give him enough facts to satisfy him. Just enough and no more.

She turned to face him and dislodged his hand in the process. Immediately she wished she'd thought to wear sunglasses. Or a wide-brimmed hat. Anything to give her some protection from that searching, masculine gaze.

She felt exposed. Naked.

Wishing she'd decided to run, she hugged herself with her arms and looked away, gesturing towards the beach with a quick jerk of her head. 'You can walk along here for about an hour before the tide turns.' The words spilled out like girlish chatter. 'Then you have to climb up to the coast path if you don't want to get cut off.'

'Alice—'

'It's a nice walk and you always lose the crowds about ten minutes out of the harbour.' The wind picked up a strand of her hair and threw it across her face, but she ignored it. 'It will take you about an hour and a half to reach the headland.'

He stepped closer and his hands closed over her arms. 'Alice, don't!' He gave her a little shake. 'Don't shut me out like this. I said something to upset you and for that I'm sorry.'

'You don't need to be sorry. You haven't done anything wrong.' She tilted her head back and risked another glance at his face. And saw kindness. Kindness and sympathy. The combination untwisted something that had been knotted inside her for years and she very nearly let everything spill out. Very nearly told him exactly how she was feeling. But she stopped herself. Reminded herself of how she'd chosen to live her life. 'I just don't happen to like ice cream that much.'

'Alice...' He tried to hold her but she shrugged him off, swamped by feelings that she didn't want to feel.

'I'm sorry, but I need to walk.'

He muttered something in Italian and then switched to English. 'Alice, wait!' With his long stride, he caught up with her easily. 'We need to talk.' His Italian accent was stronger than ever, as if he was struggling with the language.

'We don't need to talk.' She walked briskly along the sand, her shoes in one hand, the other holding her hair out of her eyes. This far up the beach the sand was soft and warm, cushioning the steady rhythm of her feet and causing her to stumble occasionally. 'I don't want to talk! Not everyone wants to talk about everything, Gio.'

'Because you're afraid of your own emotions. Of being hurt. That's why you prefer facts.' He strode next to her, keeping pace. 'You've turned yourself into a machine, Alice, but emotions are the oil that makes the machine work. Human beings can't function without emotions.'

She walked faster in an attempt to escape the conversation. 'You don't need to get into my skin and understand me. And I don't need healing.'

'Most people need healing from something, Alice. It's—*Dios,* can you stop walking for a moment?' Reaching out, he grabbed her shoulders and turned her, his fingers firm on her flesh as he held her still. 'Stop running and have a conversation. Is that really so frightening?'

'You want facts? All right, I'll give you the facts. You and

Edith obviously have lots of happy childhood memories. I don't.'
Her heart thumped steadily against her chest as her past spilled
into her present. 'It's as simple as that. Ice cream doesn't remind
me of happy holidays, Gio. It reminds me of bribes. A way of
persuading me to like my mother's latest boyfriend. A way of
occupying me for ten minutes while my father spent romantic time with his latest girlfriend. Ice cream was a salve to the
conscience while they told me I needed to live in a different
place for a while because I was getting in the way of *"love".'*
Her heart was beating, her palms were sweaty and feelings of
panic bubbled up inside her. Feelings that she hadn't had for a
very long time.

Gio sucked in a breath. 'This was your childhood?'

'Sometimes I was a ping-pong ball, occasionally I was a
pawn but mostly I was just a nuisance.'

'And now?' He frowned and his grip on her arms tightened.
'Your parents are divorced?'

'Oh, several times. Not just the once.' She knew her tone
was sarcastic and brittle but she couldn't do anything about it.
Couldn't be bothered to hide it any more. Maybe if he understood the reasons for the way she was, he'd leave her alone. 'You
know what they say—practice makes perfect. My parents had
plenty of practice. They are quite expert at divorce.'

His eyes were steady on her face. Searching. 'And you?'

'Me? I survived.' She spread her hands. 'Here I am. In one
piece.'

He shook his head. 'Not in one piece. Your belief in love has
been shattered. They took that from you with their selfish behaviour.' He lifted a hand and touched her cheek. 'My beautiful Alice.'

Her breathing hitched in her throat and her shoulders stiffened. 'Don't feel sorry for me. I like my life. I don't need fairy-
tales to be happy.' She tensed still further as he slid a hand over
her cheek, his thumb stroking gently. 'What are you doing?'

'Offering you comfort. A hug goes a long way to making

things better, don't you think?' His voice was soft. 'Touch is important.'

'I'm not used to being touched.' She stood rigid, not moving a muscle. 'I don't like being touched.'

'Then you need more practice. Everyone likes being touched, as long as it's in the right way.'

He was too close and it made her feel strange. His voice made her feel strange.

'Enough.' Shaken and flustered, she took a step backwards. Broke the contact. 'You just can't help it, can you? I've only known you for a short time but during that time I've seen how you always have to dig and delve into a person's life.'

'Because the answers to questions often lie below the surface.'

She scraped her hair out of her eyes. 'Well, I don't need you to delve and I don't want you to dig. There are no questions about my life that you need to answer. I'm not one of your patients with emotional needs.'

'Everyone has emotional needs, Alice.'

'Well, I don't. And I don't have to explain myself to you! And I don't need you to understand me. I didn't ask to take this walk and I didn't ask for your company. If you don't like the way I am then you can go back to the house.'

'I like the way you are, *cara mia*.' Without warning or hesitation, his hands cupped her face and he brought his mouth down on hers, his kiss warm and purposeful.

Alice stood there, frozen with shock while his mouth moved over hers, coaxing, tempting, growing more demanding, and suddenly a tiny, icy part of herself started to melt. The warmth started to spread and grew in intensity until she felt something explode inside her. Something delicious and exciting that she'd never felt before.

Feeling oddly disconnected, she tried to summon up logic and reason. *Any minute now she was going to pull away.* But his arms slid round her, his hold strong and powerful, and still his mouth plundered and stole the breath from her body. *She was going to punch him somewhere painful.* But his fingers stroked her cheek and his tongue teased and danced and coaxed a response that she'd never given to any man before.

In the end it was Gio who suspended the kiss. 'My Alice.' He lifted his head just enough to breathe the words against her mouth. 'They hurt you badly, *tesoro.*'

She felt dazed. Drugged. Unable to speak or think. She tried to open her eyes but her eyelids felt heavy, and as for her knees—hadn't David said something about knees?

'Dr Anderson!' A sharp young voice from directly behind her succeeded where logic had not. Her eyes opened and she pulled away, heart thumping, cheeks flaming.

'Henry?' Her voice cracked as she turned to acknowledge the ten-year-old boy behind her. Flustered and embarrassed, she stroked a hand over her cheeks in an attempt to calm herself down. 'What's the matter?'

Henry pointed, his expression frantic. 'They're cut off, Dr Anderson. The tide's turning.'

Beside her, Gio ran a hand over the back of his neck and she had the satisfaction of seeing that he was no more composed than she was.

For a brief, intense moment their eyes held and then she turned her attention back to Henry, trying desperately to concentrate on what he was saying.

And it was obviously something important. He was hopping on the spot, his expression frantic, his arms waving wildly towards the sea.

'Who is cut off from what?' She winced inwardly as she listened to herself. Since when had she been unable to form words properly? To focus on a problem in hand?

'The twins. They were playing.'

'Twins?' Alice shielded her eyes from the evening sun and stared out across the beach, her eyes drawn to two tiny figures playing on a small, raised patch of sand. All around them the sea licked and swirled, closing off their route back to the beach. They were on a sand spit and the tide was turning. 'Oh, no...'

Finally she understood what Henry had been trying to tell her and she slid her hand in her pocket and reached for her mobile phone even as she started to run towards the water. 'I'll call the coastguard. Where's their mother, Henry? Have you seen Harriet?' She was dialling as she spoke, her finger shaking as she punched in the numbers, aware that Gio was beside her, stripping off as he ran.

The boy shook his head, breathless. 'They were on their own, I think.'

Alice spoke to the coastguard, her communication brief and succinct, and then broke the connection and glanced around her. They couldn't possibly have been on their own. They were five years old. Harriet was a good mother. She wouldn't have left them.

And then she saw her, carrying the baby and weighed down by paraphernalia, walking along the beach and calling for the twins. Searching. She hadn't seen them. Hadn't seen the danger. And Alice could hear the frantic worry in her voice as she called.

'You go to Harriet, I'll get the twins,' Gio ordered, running towards the sea, his long, muscular legs closing the distance.

The tide was still far out but she knew how fast it came in, how quickly those tempting little sand spits disappeared under volumes of seawater.

She ran with him, aware that Henry was keeping up with them. 'Henry, go to the cliff and get us a line.' She barked out the instruction, her throat dry with fear, her heart pounding. 'You know the line with the lifebuoy.' She knew the dangers of entering the water without a buoyancy aid. 'Gio, wait. You have to wait. You can't just go in there.'

For a moment the kiss was forgotten. The ice cream was forgotten. Nothing mattered except the urgency of the moment. Two little boys in mortal danger. *The weight of responsibility.*

'In a few more minutes those children will be out of reach.'

Alice grabbed his arm as they ran. Tried to slow him. Tried to talk sense into him. The sand was rock hard now as they approached the water's edge and then finally she felt the damp lick of the sea against her toes and stopped. 'You're not going into that water without a line. Do you know how many people drown in these waters, trying to save others?' Her eyes skimmed his body, noticed the hard, well-formed muscles. He had the body of an athlete and at the moment it was clad only in a pair of black boxer shorts.

'Stop giving me facts, Alice.' His expression was grim. 'They're five years old,' he said roughly, 'and they're not going to stand like sensible children on that spit of sand and wait to be rescued. What do you want me to do? Watch while they drown? Watch while they die?' Concern thickened his accent and she shook her head.

'No, but—'

'Get me a buoyancy aid and go to Harriet,' he urged as he stepped into the water. He caught her arm briefly, his eyes on her face. 'And remember emotions when you talk to her, Alice. It isn't always about facts.'

He released her and Alice swallowed and cast a frantic glance up the coast. She knew the lifeboat would come from that direction. Or maybe the coastguard would send the helicopter. Either way, she knew they needed to hurry.

From the moment he plunged into the water she could see that Gio was a strong swimmer, but she knew that the tides in this part of the bay were lethal and she knew that it would only take minutes for the water level to rise. Soon the spit of sand that was providing the twins with sanctuary would vanish from under their feet.

She could hear them screaming and crying and closed her eyes briefly. And then she heard Harriet's cry of horror.

'Oh, my God—my babies.' The young mother covered her

mouth with her hand, her breathing so rapid that Alice was afraid she might faint.

'Harriet—try and stay calm.' *What a stupid, useless thing to say to a mother whose two children were in danger of drowning.* She took refuge in facts, as she always did. 'We've called the coastguard and Dr Moretti is going to swim out to them. Henry Fox is getting the buoyancy aid.'

'Neither of them can swim,' Harriet gasped, her eyes wild with panic, and Alice remembered what Gio had said about remembering emotions.

She swallowed and felt helpless. She just wasn't in tune with other people's emotions. She wasn't comfortable. What would Gio say? Certainly not that the ability to swim wouldn't save the twins in the lethal waters of Smuggler's Cove.

'They don't need to swim because the coastguard is going to be here in a moment,' she said finally, jabbing her fingers into her hair and wishing she was better with words. She just didn't know the right things to say. And then she remembered what Gio had said about touch. Hesitantly she stepped closer to Harriet and slipped an arm round her shoulders.

Instantly Harriet turned towards her and clung. 'Oh, Dr Anderson, this is all my fault. I'm a useless mother. Terrible.'

Caught in the full flood of Harriet's emotion, Alice froze and wished for a moment that she'd been the one to go in the water. She would have been much better at dealing with tides than with an emotional torrent.

'You're a brilliant mother, Harriet,' she said firmly. 'The twins are beautifully mannered, tidy, the baby is fed—'

'But that isn't really what being a mother is,' Harriet sniffed, still clinging to Alice. 'A childminder can do any of those things. Being a mother is noticing what your child really needs. It's the fun stuff. The interaction. And I'm so tired, I just can't do any of it. They wanted to go to the beach so I took them, but I was too tired to actually play with them so I sat feeding the baby and then I just lost sight of them and they wandered off.'

Alice watched as Gio climbed onto another sand spit. Between him and the twins was one more strip of water. Treacherous water.

And then she heard the clack, clack, clack of an approaching helicopter and breathed a sigh of relief. Gio didn't even need to cross the water now. The coastguard could—

'No! Oh, no, don't try and get in the water,' Harriet shrieked, moving away from Alice and running towards the water's edge. 'Oh, Dr Anderson, my Dan is trying to get into the water.'

Gio saw it too and shouted something to the boys before diving into the sea to cross the last strip of water. He used a powerful front crawl but even so Alice could see that he was being dragged sideways by the fast current.

It was only after he pulled himself safely onto the strip of sand that Alice realised that her fingernails had cut into her palms.

She saw him lift one of the twins and take the other by the hand, holding them firmly while the coastguard helicopter hovered in position above them.

The sand was gradually disappearing as the tide swirled and reclaimed the land, and a crowd of onlookers had gathered on the beach and were watching the drama unfold.

Alice bit her lip hard. The helicopter crew would rescue them all. Of course they would.

Still with her arm round Harriet, she watched as the winchman was lowered down to the sand to collect the first child.

The baby was screaming in Harriet's arms but she just jiggled it vaguely, all her attention focused on her twins.

'Let me take her.' Alice reached across and took the baby and Harriet walked into the sea, yearning to get to the boys. 'Hold it, Harriet.' With a soft curse Alice held the baby with one arm and used the other to grab Harriet and hold her back. 'Just wait. They're fine now. Nothing's going to happen to them.' Providing the coastguard managed to pick up the second child and Gio before the tide finally closed over the rapidly vanishing sand spit.

Discovering new depths of tension within herself, Alice watched helplessly as the winchman guided the first child safely into the helicopter and then went down for the second.

By now Gio's feet were underwater and he was holding the child high in his arms, safely away from the dangerous lick of the sea.

The helicopter held its position, the crowd on the beach grew and there was a communal sigh of relief as the winchman picked up the second child, attached the harness and then guided him safely into the helicopter.

'Oh, thank God!' Harriet burst into tears, her hands over her face. 'Now what?' She turned to Alice. 'Where are they taking them?'

'They'll check them over just in case they need medical help,' Alice told her, her eyes fixed on Gio who was now up to mid-thigh in swirling water. She raked fingers through her hair and clamped her teeth on her lower lip to prevent herself from crying out a warning. What was the point of crying out a warning when the guy could see perfectly well for himself what was happening?

'Will they take them to the hospital?' Harriet was staring up at the helicopter but Alice had her gaze fixed firmly on Gio.

There was no way he'd be able to swim safely now. The water was too deep and the current was just too fierce.

The crowd on the beach must have realised it too because a sudden silence fell as they waited for the helicopter to lower the winchman for a third time.

And finally Harriet saw...

'He's risking his life.' She said the words in hushed tones, as if she'd only just realised what was truly happening. 'Oh, my God, he's risking his life for my babies. And now he's going to—'

'No, he isn't.' Alice snapped the words, refusing to allow her to voice what everyone was thinking. 'He's going to be fine, Harriet,' she said, as much to convince herself as the woman standing next to her in a serious state of anxiety. 'They're lowering the winchman again.'

What was the Italian for *you stupid, brave idiot*? she wondered as she watched Gio exchange a few words with the winchman and then laugh as the harness was attached. They rose up in the air, swinging slightly as they approached the hovering helicopter.

Alice closed her eyes briefly as he vanished inside. For a moment she just felt like sinking onto the sand and staying there until the panic subsided. Then her mobile phone rang. She answered it immediately. It was Gio.

'Twins seem fine but they're taking them to hospital for a quick check.' His voice crackled. 'Tell Harriet I'll bring them home. It isn't safe for her to drive in a state of anxiety and shock and by the time she gets up to the house, picks up the car and drives to the hospital, I'll be home with them.'

Deciding that it wasn't the right moment to yell at him, she simply acknowledged what he'd said and ended the call. 'They seem fine but they're going to take them to the hospital for a check. Dr Moretti will bring them home, Harriet,' she said quietly. 'Let's go back to your house now and make a cup of tea. I don't know about you, but I need one.'

Gio arrived back at the house three hours later. Three long hours during which she'd had all too much time to think about *that kiss* and the fact that she'd told him far more about herself than she'd intended.

Annoyed with herself, confused, Alice abandoned all pretence of reading a medical journal and was pacing backwards and forwards in the kitchen, staring at the clock, when she finally heard the doorbell. She closed her eyes and breathed a sigh of relief.

She opened the door and lifted an eyebrow, trying to regain some of her old self. Trying to react the way she would have reacted before *that kiss*. 'Forgot your key?'

He was wearing a set of theatre scrubs and he looked broad-shouldered and more handsome than a man had a right to look. She sneaked a look at his firm mouth and immediately felt a sizzle in her veins.

'Careless, I know. I went swimming and I must have them in my trousers.' He strolled past her with a lazy grin and pushed the door closed behind him. Suddenly her hallway seemed small.

'Talking of swimming...' she took a step backwards and kept her tone light '...you certainly go to extreme lengths to pull the women, Dr Moretti. Plunging into the jaws of death and acting like a hero. Does it work for you?'

He paused, his eyes on hers, his expression thoughtful. 'I don't know. Let's find out, shall we?' Without warning, he reached out a hand and jerked her against him, his mouth hovering a mere breath from hers. 'We have unfinished business, Dr Anderson.'

He kissed her hard and she felt her knees go weak but she didn't have the chance to think about the implications of that fact because something hot and dangerous exploded in her body. She wound her arms round his neck for support. *Just for support.*

He gave a low groan and dug his fingers into her hair, tilting her head, changing the angle, helping himself to her mouth.

'You taste good, *cara mia,*' he muttered, trailing kisses over her jaw and then back to her mouth. He kissed her thoroughly. Skilfully. And then lifted his head, his breathing less than steady. 'I'm addicted to your mouth. It was one of the first things I noticed about you.'

Her head swam dizzily and she tried to focus, but before she could even remember how to regain control he lowered his head again.

With a soft gasp, she tried to speak. 'Stop...' His lips had found a sensitive spot on her neck and she was finding it impossible to think straight. With a determined effort, she pushed at his chest. 'We have to stop this.'

'Why?' His mouth returned to hers, teasing and seducing. 'Why stop something that feels so good?'

Her head was swimming and she couldn't concentrate. 'Because I don't do this.'

'Then it's good to try something new.' He lifted his head, his smile surprisingly gentle. 'Courage, *tesoro*.'

Her fingers were curled into the hard muscle of his shoulders and she remembered the strength he'd shown in the water.

'Talking of courage, you could have drowned out there.'

His eyes searched hers. Questioning. 'You're telling me you were worried, Dr Anderson?' He lifted a hand and gently brushed her cheek. 'Better not let Mary hear you say that. She'll be buying a hat to wear at our wedding.'

'Oh, for goodness' sake.' She knew he was teasing but all the same the words flustered her and she pulled away, trying not to look at his mouth. Trying not to think about the way he kissed. About the fact that she wanted him to go on kissing her. 'What took you so long, anyway? I was beginning to think you'd gone back to Italy.'

'I hurried the twins through A and E, we got a ride home with one of the paramedics and then I dropped them home.'

'And that took three hours? Did you drive via Scotland?'

'You really were worried. Careful, Alice.' His voice was soft, his gaze searching. 'You're showing emotion.'

She flushed and walked past him to the kitchen. 'Given the distance between here and the hospital, with which I'm entirely familiar, I was expecting you back ages ago. And you didn't answer your mobile.'

'I was with Harriet.' He followed her and went straight to the espresso machine. 'She had a nasty shock and she was blaming herself terribly for what happened. She needed TLC.'

And he would have given her the comfort she needed, because he was that sort of man. He was good with people's emotions, she thought to herself. Unlike her.

'I stayed with her for the first two hours,' she muttered, raking fingers through her hair, feeling totally inadequate, 'but she just kept pacing and saying she was a terrible mother. And I didn't know what to say. I'm hopeless at giving emotional comfort. If she'd cut her finger or developed a rash, I would have been fine. But there was nothing to see. She was just hysterical and miserable. I did my best, but it wasn't good enough. I was useless.'

He glanced over his shoulder, his eyes gentle. 'That's not true. You're not hopeless or useless. Just a little afraid, I think. Emotions can be scary things. Not so easily explained as some other things. You'll get better with practice. She's calmer now.' Reaching across the work surface, Gio opened a packet of coffee-beans and tipped them into a grinder. 'And she definitely has postnatal depression.'

Alice stared. 'You're sure?'

'Certain.'

'So what did you do?'

'I listened.' He flicked a switch, paused while the beans were ground and then gave a shrug. 'Sometimes that's all a person needs, although, in Harriet's case, I think she does need something more. Tomorrow she is coming to see me and we are going to put together a plan of action. I think her condition merits drug treatment but, more importantly, we need to get her emotional support. Her husband isn't around much and she needs help. She needs to feel that people love and care for her. She needs to know that people mind how she's feeling. She doesn't have family to do that, so we need to find her the support from elsewhere.'

Alice watched him. He moved around the kitchen the same way he did everything. With strength and confidence. 'You really believe that family holds all the answers, don't you?'

'Yes, I do.' He emptied the grinder and turned to look at her. 'But I realise that you may find that hard to understand, given your experience of family life. You haven't ever seen a decent example, so why would you agree with me?'

She stiffened. 'Look, I wish I'd never mentioned it to you. It isn't important.'

'It's stopped you believing in love, so it's important.'

'I don't want to talk about it.'

'That's just because you're not used to talking about it. A bit like kissing. You'll be fine once you've had more practice.'

The mere mention of kissing made her body heat. 'I don't want more practice! I hate talking about it!'

'Because it stirs up emotions and you're afraid of emotions. Plenty of people have problems in their past, but it doesn't have to affect the future. Only if you let it. Family is perhaps the most important thing in the world, after good health.' His voice was calm as he started making the coffee, his movements steady and methodical. It seemed to her as she watched that making coffee was almost a form of relaxation for him.

'Is that how it happens in Italy? I mean Sicily?' She corrected herself quickly and saw him smile.

'In Sicily, family is sacred.' He watched as coffee trickled into the cup, dark and fragrant. 'We believe in love, Alice. We believe in a love that is special, unique and lasts for a lifetime. I'm surrounded by generations of my family and extended family who have been in love for ever. Come with me to Sicily and I will prove it to you.'

He was teasing, of course. He had to be teasing. 'Don't be ridiculous.'

'You have been to Sicily?' She shook her head and took the coffee he handed to her.

'No.'

His smile was lazy and impossibly attractive. 'It is a land designed to make people believe in romance and passion. We have the glittering sea to seduce, and the fires of Etna to flame the coldest heart.' He spoke in a soft, accented drawl and she rolled her eyes to hide how strongly his words affected her.

'Drop the sweet talk. It's wasted on me, Dr Moretti. Romance is just a seduction tool.'

And she'd had three long hours to think about seduction.

Three long hours to think about the kiss on the beach.

And the way he'd plunged into the water after two small children in trouble.

And now she also had to think about the way he'd spent his evening with a vulnerable, lonely mother with postnatal depression.

Bother.

She was really starting to like the man. And notice things about him. Things that other women probably noticed immediately. Like his easy, slightly teasing smile and the thick, dark lashes that gave his eyes a sleepy look. A dangerous look. The way, when he talked to a woman, he gave her his whole attention. His rich, sexy accent and the smooth, confident way that he dealt with every problem. And the way he shouldered those problems without walking away.

It was just the kiss, she told herself crossly as she drank her coffee. The kiss had made her loopy. Up until then she really hadn't looked at him in *that way.*

'Did you pick up my clothes?' He strolled over to her and she found herself staring at his shoulders. He had good shoulders.

'Sorry?'

'My clothes.' He lifted an eyebrow, his eyes scanning her face. 'Did you pick them up from the beach?'

'Oh.' She pulled herself together and dragged her eyes away from the tangle of dark hairs at the base of his throat. 'Yes. Yes, I did. I put them on the chair in your room.'

Heat curled low in her pelvis and spread through her limbs. Sexual awareness, she told herself. The attraction of female to male. Without it, the human race would have died out. It was a perfectly normal chemical reaction. *It's just that it wasn't normal for her.* She tried to shut the feeling down. Tried to control it. But it was on the loose.

'Thanks.' He was watching her. 'It would have been hard to

explain that to Mary if some helpful bystander had delivered them to the surgery tomorrow.'

She folded her arms across her chest in a defensive gesture. 'It would have made Mary's day.'

'So would this, I suspect.' He lowered his head and kissed her again, his mouth lingering on hers.

This time she didn't even think about resisting. She just closed her eyes and let herself feel. Allowed the heat to spread through her starving body. Her nerves sang and hummed and when he finally lifted his head she felt only disappointment.

It was amazing how quickly a person could adapt to being touched, she thought dizzily.

'I—We...' She lifted a hand to her lips and then let it drop back to her side, suddenly self-conscious. 'You've got to stop doing that.' But even she knew the words were a lie and he gave a smile as he walked towards the door.

'I'm going to keep doing it, *cara mia*.' He turned in the doorway. Paused. His eyes burned into hers. 'So you're just going to have to get used to it.'

CHAPTER EIGHT

GIO LOOKED AT Harriet and felt his heart twist. She looked so utterly miserable.

'Crazy, isn't it?' Her voice was little more than a whisper. 'I have this beautiful, perfect baby and I'm not even enjoying having her. I snap at the twins and yesterday I was so miserable I didn't even notice that they'd wandered off.'

'Don't be so hard on yourself and never underestimate a child's capacity for mischief,' Gio said calmly. 'They are young and adventurous, as small boys should be.'

'But I can't cope with them. I'm just so tired.' Her eyes filled. 'I snap at Geoff and he says that suddenly he's married to a witch, and I really can't face sex…' She blushed, her expression embarrassed. 'Sorry, I didn't mean to say that. Geoff would kill me if he thought I was talking about our sex life in the village.'

'This isn't the village,' Gio said gently. 'It's my consulting room and I'm a doctor. And it's important that you tell me everything you are feeling so that I can make an informed judgement on how to help you.'

Her eyes filled and she clamped a hand over her mouth,

struggling for control. 'I'm sorry to be so pathetic, it's just that I'm so tired. I'll be fine when I've had some sleep—the trouble is I don't get any. I'm so tired I ought to go out like a light but I can't sleep at all and I'm totally on edge all the time. I'm an absolutely *terrible* mother. And do you know the worst thing?' Giving up her attempts at control, she burst into heartbreaking sobs. Gio reached across his desk for a box of tissues, his eyes never leaving her face.

'Tell me.'

'I'm so useless I don't even know what my own baby wants.' Wrenching a tissue from the box, she blew her nose hard. 'She's my third child and I find myself sitting there, staring at her while she's crying, totally unable to move. And I worry about everything. I worry I'm going to go to her cot in the morning and find she's died in the night, I worry that she's going to catch something awful and I won't notice—'

Gio put his hand over hers. 'You're describing symptoms of anxiety, Harriet, and I think—'

'You think that I'm basically a completely terrible mother and a hideously pathetic blubbery female.' She blew her nose again and he shook his head and tightened his grip on her hand.

'On the contrary, I think you are a wonderful mother.' He hesitated, choosing his words carefully. 'But I think it's possible that you could be suffering from depression.'

She frowned. Dropped the tissue into her bag. 'I'm just tired.'

'I don't think so.' He kept his hand on hers and she clamped her lower lip between her teeth, trying not to cry.

'I can't be depressed. Oh, God, I just need to pull myself together.'

'Depression is an illness. It isn't about pulling yourself together.'

Her eyes filled again and she reached for another tissue. 'Do you mean depressed as in postnatal depression?'

'Yes, that's exactly what I think.'

Tears trickled down her face. 'So maybe this isn't just about me being useless?'

'You're not useless. In fact, I think the opposite.' He shook his head, a look of admiration on his face. 'How you are coping with three children under the age of six and postnatal depression, I just don't know.'

'I'm not coping.'

'Yes, you are. Just not as well as you'd like. And you're not enjoying yourself.' Gio let go of her hand and turned back to his desk, reaching for a pad of paper. 'But that's going to change, Harriet. We're going to sort this out for you.'

She blew her nose. 'My husband will just tell me to pull myself together and snap out of it.'

'He won't say that,' Gio scribbled on a pad, 'because I'm going to talk to him. Many people are ignorant about the true nature of postnatal depression, he isn't alone in that. Once I explain everything to him, he will give you the support you need. I've spoken to Gina, the health visitor, and done some research. This is a group that I think you might find helpful.' He handed her the piece of paper and she looked at it.

'It's only in the next village.'

Gio nodded. 'Will you be able to get there?'

'Oh, yes. I can drive.' She stared at the name. 'Do I have to phone?'

'I've done it. They're expecting you at their next meeting, which happens to be tomorrow afternoon. You can take the twins and the baby, there'll be someone there to help.'

Harriet looked at him. 'Do I need drugs?'

'I'd like to try talking therapy first and I want to see you regularly. If you don't start to feel better then drug treatment might be appropriate. Let's see how we go.'

Harriet slipped the paper into her bag and gave a feeble smile. 'I feel a bit better already, just knowing that this isn't all my fault.'

'None of it is your fault.' Gio rose to his feet and walked her to the door. 'Go to the meeting and let me know how you get on.'

Alice parked her newly fixed car outside her house and stared at the low black sports car that meant that Gio was already back from his house calls.

Bother. She'd been hoping that he'd work late.

It had been almost a week since the episode on the beach. A week during which she'd virtually lived in the surgery in order to put some distance between her and Gio. A week during which she'd drunk endless cups of black coffee and eaten nothing but sandwiches at her desk. A week during which she'd been cranky and thoroughly unsettled. It was as if her neat, tidy life had been thrown into the air and had landed in a different pattern. And she didn't know how to put it back together.

What she did know was that it was Gio's fault for kissing her.

And Mary's fault for arranging for him to lodge with her.

Pushing open the front door, she was stopped by the smell.

'Well, well. The wanderer returns. I was beginning to think you'd taken root in the surgery.' Gio emerged from the kitchen and her heart stumbled and jerked. A pair of old, faded jeans hugged his hard thighs and his black shirt was open at the neck. 'If you hadn't returned home at a decent hour, I was coming to find you.'

Even dressed so casually he looked handsome and—she searched for the word—exotic?

'I had work to do. And now I'm tired.' She had to escape. Had to get her mind back together. 'I'm going straight up to bed, if you don't mind.'

'Alice.' His tone was gentle and there was humour in his eyes. 'It's not even eight o'clock, *tesoro*. If you are going to try and avoid me, you're going to have to think of a better excuse than that. You've kept your distance for a week. It's long enough, I think.'

Something in his tone stung. He made her feel like a coward. 'Why would I try and avoid you?'

'Because I make you uncomfortable. I make you talk when you'd rather be silent and I make you feel when you'd rather stay numb.'

'I don't—'

'And because I kissed you and made you want something that you've made a point of denying yourself for years.'

'I don't—'

'At least eat with me.' He held out a hand. 'And if after that you want to go to bed, I'll let you go.'

She kept her hands by her sides. 'You've cooked?'

'I like cooking. I've made a Sicilian speciality. It's too much for one person and, anyway, I need your opinion.' His hand remained outstretched and there was challenge in his dark eyes.

Muttering under her breath about bullying Italian men, she took his hand and felt his strong fingers close firmly over hers.

Instead of leading her into the kitchen, he took her into the dining room. The dining room at the back of the house that she never used. The dining room that was now transformed.

All the clutter was gone and tiny candles flickered on every available surface. The smells of a warm summer evening drifted in through the open French doors.

The atmosphere was intimate. Romantic.

Something flickered inside her. Panic? She turned to him with a shake of her head. 'No, Gio. This isn't what I do, I—'

He covered her lips with his fingers. 'Relax, *tesoro*. It's just dinner. Food is always more enjoyable when the atmosphere is good, and the atmosphere in this room is perfect. Go and take a shower and change. Dinner is in fifteen minutes.'

She stared after him as he strolled back to the kitchen. The guy just couldn't help himself. He'd obviously decided that she needed rescuing from her past and he thought he was the one to do it. The one to show her that romance existed.

She stared at the candles and rolled her eyes. Well, if he

thought that a few lumps of burning wax were going to make her fall in love, he was doomed to disappointment.

Telling herself that she was only doing it because she was hot and uncomfortable, she showered and changed into a simple white strap top and a green silk skirt that hugged her hips softly and then fell to mid-thigh.

Staring at her reflection in the mirror, she contemplated make-up and decided against it. She didn't want to look as though she was making an effort. She didn't want him getting the wrong idea.

With that thought on her mind, she walked back into the dining room and came straight to the point.

'I know that some women would just drop to their knees and beg for a man who does all this.' She waved a hand around the room. 'But I'm not one of them. Really. I'm happy with a sandwich eaten under a halogen light bulb. So if you're trying to make me fall in love with you, you're wasting your time. I just thought we ought to get that straight right now, before you go to enormous effort.'

'I'm not trying to make you fall in love with me. True love can't be forced,' he said softly as he pulled the cork out of a bottle of wine, 'and it can't be commanded. True love is a gift, *cara mia*. Freely given by both parties.'

'It's a figment of the imagination. A serious hallucination,' she returned, her tone sharper than she'd intended. 'A justification for wild, impulsive and totally irrational behaviour, usually between two people who are old enough to know better.'

'That isn't love.' He pushed her towards the chair that faced the window. 'From what you've told me, you haven't seen an example of love. But you will do. I intend to show you.'

She rolled her eyes and watched while he filled her glass. 'What are you? My fairy godmother?'

His smile broadened. 'Do I look like a fairy to you?'

She swallowed hard and dragged her eyes away from the laughter in his. No. He looked like a thoroughly gorgeous man.

And he was standing in her dining room about to serve her dinner.

'All right.' She gave a shrug that she hoped looked suitably casual. 'I'm hungry. Let's agree to disagree and just eat.'

The food was delicious.

Never in her life had she ever tasted anything so sublime. And through it all Gio topped up her wineglass and kept up a neutral conversation. He was intelligent and entertaining and she forgot her plan to eat as fast as possible and then escape to her room. Instead she ate, savouring every mouthful, and sipped her wine. And all the time she listened as he talked.

He talked about growing up on Sicily and about his life as a surgeon in Milan. He talked about the differences in medicine between the two cultures.

'So...' She reached for more bread. 'Are you going to tell me why you had to give up surgery as a career? Or am I the only one who has to spill about my past?'

'It's not a secret.' He lounged across the table from her, his face bronzed and handsome in the flickering candlelight. 'I was working in Africa. We were attacked by rebels hoping to steal drugs and equipment that they could sell on.' He gave a shrug and lifted his glass. 'Unfortunately the damage was such that I can't operate for any length of time.'

She winced. 'I'm sorry, I shouldn't have asked.'

'It's part of my life and talking about it doesn't make it worse. In a way I was lucky. I took some time off and went home to my family.' He continued to talk, telling her about his sisters and his brother, his parents, his grandparents and numerous aunts, uncles and cousins.

'You were lucky.' She put her glass down on the table. 'Having such good family.'

'Yes, I was.' He passed her more bread. 'Luckier than you.'

'She took me to the park once—my mother.' She stared at her plate, the memory rising into her brain so clearly that her hands curled into fists and her shoulders tensed. 'She was meeting her lover and I was the excuse that enabled her to leave the house without my dad suspecting anything. Although I doubt he would have cared because he was seeing someone, too. Only she didn't know that.'

She looked up, waiting for him to display shock or distaste, but Gio sat still, his eyes on her face. Listening. It occurred to her that he was an excellent listener.

She shrugged. 'Anyway, I was playing on the climbing frame. They were sitting on the seat. Kissing. Wrapped up in each other.' She licked dry lips. 'I remember watching two other children and envying them. Their mothers were both hovering at the bottom of the climbing frame, hands outstretched. They said things like "be careful" and "watch where you put your feet" and "that's too high, come down now". My mother didn't even glance in my direction.' She broke off and ran a hand over the back of her neck, the tension rising inside her. 'Not even when I fell. And in the ambulance she was furious with me and accused me of sabotaging her relationship on purpose.'

Gio reached across the table and took her hand. But still he didn't speak. Just listened, his eyes holding hers.

She chewed her lip and flashed him a smile. 'Anyway, he was husband number two and life just carried on from there, really. She went through two more— Oh, sorry.' She gave a cynical smile that was loaded with pain. 'I should say she "fell in love" twice more before I was finally old enough to leave home.'

'And your sister?'

Alice rubbed her fingers over her forehead. 'She's on her second marriage. She had high hopes of doing everything differently to our parents. She still believed that true love existed. I think she's finally discovering that it doesn't. I've never told anyone any of this before. Not even Rita and Mary. They know I'm not in touch with my parents, but that's all they know.'

It had grown dark while she was talking and through the open doors she could hear the sounds of the night, see the flutter of insects drawn by the flickering candlelight.

Finally Gio spoke. 'It's not surprising that you don't believe that love exists. It's hard to believe in something that you've never seen. You have a logical, scientific brain, Alice. You take a problem-solving approach to life. Love is not easily defined or explained and that makes it easy to dismiss.'

She swallowed. How was it that he seemed to understand her so well? And why had she just told him so much? She looked suspiciously at her wineglass but it was still half-full and her head was clear. She waited for regret to flood through her but instead she felt strangely peaceful for the first time. 'If love really existed then the divorce rate wouldn't be so high.'

'Or maybe love just isn't that easy to find, and that makes it even more precious. Maybe the divorce rate is testament to the fact that love is so special that people are willing to take a risk in order to find it.'

She shook her head. 'What people feel is sexual chemistry and, if they're lucky, friendship. But there isn't a whole separate emotion called love that binds people together.'

'Because you haven't seen it yet.' He studied her face. 'True love is selfless and yet the emotion you saw was greedy and selfish. They allowed you to fall and they weren't there to catch you.'

Instinctively she knew he wasn't just talking about the incident on the climbing frame.

She lifted her glass. 'So, if you believe in love, Dr Moretti, why aren't you married with eight children?' Her eyes challenged him over the rim of her glass and he smiled.

'Because you don't choose when to love. Or even who to love. You can't just go out and find it in the way that you can find friendship or sex. Love chooses you. And chooses the time. For some people it's early in life. For others...' he gave a shrug that showed his Latin heritage '...it's later.'

She frowned. 'So you're waiting for Signorina Right to just bang on your door?' Her tone had a hint of sarcasm and he smiled.

'No. She gave me a key.' Something in his gaze made her heart stop.

Surely he wasn't saying…

He couldn't be suggesting…

She put her glass down. 'Gio—'

'Go to bed, *tesoro*,' he said softly. 'The other thing about love is that it can't be controlled. Not the emotion and not the timing. It happens when it happens.'

She stared at him. 'But—'

He rose to his feet and smiled. 'Sleep well, Alice.'

Gio left via the back door, knowing that if he didn't leave the house, he'd join her in her bedroom.

It had taken every ounce of willpower to let her walk away from him.

But he knew instinctively that they'd taken enough steps forward for one night. She'd talked—really talked—perhaps for the first time in her life and he could tell that she was starting to relax around him.

Which was how he wanted it to be.

They'd come a long way in a short time.

He breathed in the warm, evening air and strolled down towards the sea, enjoying the comfort of the semi-darkness.

It felt strange, he thought to himself as he walked, to have fallen in love with a woman who didn't even believe that love existed.

After that night, the evenings developed a pattern and, almost a month after he'd arrived in the surgery, Alice sat staring out of the window of her consulting room, wondering what Gio would be cooking for dinner.

It was so unlike her to dream about food, but since he'd taken over the cooking she found herself looking forward to the evenings.

Sometimes they ate in the dining room, sometimes they ate

in her garden and once he'd made a picnic and they'd taken it down to the beach.

Thinking, dreaming, she missed the tap on the door.

It was friendship, she decided, and she liked it.

She could really talk to him and he was an excellent listener. And she enjoyed working with him. He was an excellent doctor.

And, of course, there was sexual chemistry. She wasn't so naïve that she couldn't recognise it. She'd even experienced it before, to a lesser degree, with a man she'd dated a few times at university. Not love, but a chemical reaction between a man and a woman. And it was there, between her and Gio.

But since the incident on the beach, he hadn't kissed her again.

Hadn't made any attempt to touch her.

The door behind her opened. 'Alice?'

Why hadn't he touched her since?

'Dr Anderson?'

Finally she heard her name, and turned to find Mary standing in the doorway. 'Are you on our planet?'

'Just thinking.'

'Dreaming, you mean.' Mary looked at her curiously and then handed her a set of notes. 'You've got one extra. The little Jarrett boy has a high temperature. I don't like the look of him so I squeezed him in.'

'That's fine, Mary.' She took the notes. 'Thanks.'

She pulled herself together, saw Tom Jarrett and then walked through to Reception with the notes just as Gio emerged from his consulting room, with his hand on Edith Carne's shoulder.

He was so tactile, Alice thought to herself, observing the way he guided the woman up the corridor, his head tilted towards her as he listened.

Touching came entirely naturally to him, whereas she—

'The cardiology referral was a good idea,' he said to her as he strolled back from reception and saw her watching him.

'They're treating Edith and it appears that they've found the cause of her falls.'

'You mean, you found the cause. She never would have—'

A series of loud screams from Reception interrupted her and she exchanged a quick glance with Gio before hurrying to the reception area just as a mother came struggled through the door, carrying a sobbing child. He was screaming and crying and holding his foot.

Alice stepped towards them. 'What's happened?'

'I don't know. We were on the beach and then suddenly he just started screaming for no reason.' The mother was breathless from her sprint from the beach and the child continued to howl noisily. 'His foot is really red and it's swelling up.'

Gio picked up the foot and examined it. 'Erythema. Oedema. A sting of some sort?'

Alice tilted her head and looked. 'Weaver fish,' she said immediately, and glanced towards Mary. 'Get me hot water, please. Fast.'

Mary nodded and Gio frowned. 'What?'

'If you're expecting the Italian translation you're going to be waiting a long time,' Alice drawled, her fingers gentle as she examined the child's foot, 'but basically weaver fish are found in sandy shallows around the beaches down here. It has venomous spines on its dorsal fin and that protrudes out of the sand. If you tread on it, you get stung.'

The mother shook her head. 'I didn't see anything on the sand.'

'It's a good idea to keep something on your feet when you're walking in the shallows at low water,' Alice advised, taking the bucket of water that Mary handed her with a nod of thanks. 'All right, sweetheart, we're going to put your foot in this water and that will help the pain.'

She tested the water quickly to check that it wasn't so hot that it would burn the child and then tried to guide the child's foot into the water. He jerked his leg away and his screams intensified.

'We really have to get this into hot water.' Alice looked at the mother. 'Heat inactivates the venom. After a few minutes in here, the pain will be better. Trust me.'

'Alex, please...' the mother begged, and tried to reason with her son. 'You need to put your foot in the bucket for Mummy. Please, darling, do it for Mummy.'

Alex continued to yell and bawl and wriggle and Gio rubbed a hand over his roughened jaw and crouched down. 'We play a game,' he said firmly, sounding more Italian than ever. He produced a penny from his pocket, held it up and then promptly made it disappear.

Briefly, Alex stopped crying and stared. 'Where?'

Gio looked baffled. 'I don't know. Perhaps if you put your foot in the bucket, it will reappear. Like magic. Let's try it, shall we?'

Alex sniffed, hesitated and then tentatively dipped his foot in the water. 'It's hot.'

'It has to be hot,' Alice said quickly, guiding his foot into the water. 'It will take the pain away.'

She watched gratefully as Gio distracted Alex, producing the coin from behind the child's ear and then from his own ear.

Alex watched, transfixed, and Gio treated him to ten minutes of magic, during which time the child's misery lessened along with the pain.

'Oh, thank goodness,' the mother said, as Alex finally started smiling. 'That was awful. And I had no idea. I've never even heard of a weaver fish.'

'They're not uncommon. There were five hundred cases along the North Devon and Cornwall coast last year,' Alice muttered as she dried her hands on the towel that Mary had thought to provide. 'Keep his foot in the bucket for another ten minutes at least and give him some paracetamol and antihistamine when you get home. He should be fine but if he isn't, give us a call.'

'Thank you so much.' The mother looked at her gratefully. 'What would I have done if you'd been shut?'

'Actually, lots of the cafés and surf shops around here keep a bucket just for this purpose so it's worth remembering that. But the best advice is to avoid walking near the low-water mark in bare feet.'

Alice walked over to the reception desk and Gio followed.

'Weaver fish? What is this weaver fish?' He spoke slowly, as if he wasn't sure he was pronouncing it correctly.

'Nobody knows exactly what is in weaver fish venom but it contains a mixture of biogenous amines and they've identified 5-hydroxytryptamine, epinephrine, norepinephrine and histamine.' She angled her head. 'Alex was probably stung by *Echiichthys vipera*—the lesser weaver fish.'

Gio lifted a brow. 'Implying that there is a greater weaver fish?'

She nodded. '*Trachinus draco*. There are case reports of people being stung. Often fisherman. We've seen one in this practice. It was a few years ago, but we sent him up to the hospital to be treated. The symptoms are severe pain, vomiting, oedema, syncope—in his case, the symptoms lasted for a long time.'

He smiled at her and she frowned, her heart beating faster as she looked into his eyes.

'What? Why are you looking at me like that?'

'Because I love it when you give me facts.' He leaned closer to her, his eyes dancing. 'You are delightfully serious, Dr Anderson, do you know that? And I find you incredibly sexy.'

'Gio, for goodness' sake.' Her eyes slid towards Mary, who was filling out a form with the mother. But she couldn't drench the flame of desire that burned through her body.

And he saw that flame.

'We're finished here.' Gio's voice was low and determined. 'Let's go home, Dr Anderson.'

'But—'

'It's home, or it's your consulting room with the door locked. Take your pick.'

She chose home.

CHAPTER NINE

THEY BARELY MADE it through the front door.

The tension that had been building for weeks reached break-ing point as she fumbled with her key in the lock, aware that he was right behind her, his hand resting on the small of her back.

Gio's fingers closed over hers and guided. Turned the key. And then he was nudging her inside and shouldering the door closed.

For a moment they both stood, breathing heavily, poised on the edge of something dangerous.

And then they cracked. Both moved at the same time, mouths greedy, hands seeking.

'I need you naked.' He ripped at Alice's shirt, sending but-tons flying across the floor, and she reciprocated, fumbling with his buttons while her breath came in tiny pants.

'Me, too. Me, too.' And all the time a tiny voice in her head was telling her that she didn't do this sort of thing.

She ignored it and slipped his shirt from his shoulders, revel-ling in the feel of warm male flesh under her hands. 'You have a perfect body, Dr Moretti.'

He gave a groan and slid his hands up her back, his eyes feasting on the swell of her breasts under her simple lacy bra. He spoke softly in Italian and then scooped her into his arms and carried her up the stairs to her bedroom.

'I don't understand a word you're saying, but I suppose it might be better that way. I like it.' With a tiny laugh she buried her head in his neck, breathed in the tantalising scent of aroused male and then murmured in protest as he lowered her onto the bed. 'I want you to carry on holding me. Don't let me go.'

'No chance.' With a swift movement he removed his trousers and came down on top of her, his hands sliding into her hair, his mouth descending to hers. 'And this from the girl who hated being touched.'

He was touching her now. Everywhere. His hands seeking, seducing, soothing all at the same time.

'That was before—' She arched under him, burning to get closer still to his hard, male body while his hands explored ever curve of hers. 'Before...'

'Before?' His hand slid over her breast and she realised in a daze that she hadn't even felt him remove her bra.

'Before you.' The flick of his tongue over her nipple brought a gasp to her throat and she curled a leg around him, the ache in her pelvis intensifying to unbearable proportions. 'Before I met you.' The touch of his mouth was skilful and sinful in equal measures and she closed her eyes and felt the erotic pull deep in her stomach.

'You're beautiful.' His mouth trailed lower and his fingers dragged at her tiny panties, sliding them downwards, leaving her naked.

She slid a hand over the hard planes of his chest, felt his touch grow more intimate. His fingers moved over her, then his mouth, and she offered herself freely, wondering what had happened to her inhibitions.

Drowning in sensation, she shifted and gasped and finally he rose over her and she reached for him, desperate.

'Now.' Her eyes were fevered and her lips were parted. 'I need you now. Now.'

And he gathered her against him and took her, his possessive thrust bringing a gasp to her lips and a flush to her cheeks. For a moment he stilled, his eyes locked on hers, his breathing unsteady. And then he lowered his head and his mouth covered hers in a kiss that was hot and demanding, his powerful body moving against hers in a rhythm that created sensations so exquisitely perfect that she cried out in desperation.

Her skin was damp from the heat and her fingers raked his back as the sensation built and threatened to devour her whole.

She toppled fast, falling into a dark void of ecstasy, and immediately he slowed the pace, changing the rhythm from desperate to measured, always the one in control.

With a low moan she opened her eyes and slid her arms round his neck. 'What are you doing?'

'Making love to you.' He spoke the words against her lips, the hot brand of his mouth sending her senses tumbling in every direction. 'And I don't ever want to stop.'

She didn't want him to stop either and she arched her back and moved her hips until she felt the change in him. Felt his muscles quiver and his skin grow slick, heard the rasp of his breath and the increase in masculine thrust.

And then she felt nothing more because he drove them both forward until they reached oblivion and fell, tumbling and gasping into a whirlpool of sexual excitement that sucked them both under.

She lay there, eyes closed, struggling for breath and sanity. His weight should have bothered her, but it didn't.

And she was relieved that he didn't seem able to move either.

Eventually he lifted his head and nuzzled her neck gently, his movements slow and languid. 'Are we still alive?' With a fractured groan he rolled onto his back, taking her with him. 'You need to wear more clothes around the house. I find it hard to resist you when you're naked.'

Her eyes were still closed. 'It's your fault that I'm naked.'

'It is?' He stroked her hair away from her face and something about the way he was touching her made her open her eyes. And she saw.

'Gio—'

'I love you, Alice.'

Her heart jerked. Jumped. Kick-started by pure, blind panic. 'No need to get all mushy on me, Dr Moretti. You already scored.'

'That's why I'm saying it now. If I'd said it when we were making love then you would have thought it was just the heat of the moment. If I said it over dinner with candles and wine, you would have said it was the romance of the moment. So I'm saying it now. After we've made love. Because that's what we just did.'

'I don't need to hear this.' She tried to wriggle away from him but he held her easily, his powerful body trapping hers.

'Yes, you do. The problem is that you're not used to hearing it. But that's going to change because I'm going to be saying it to you a lot. A few weeks ago you weren't used to talking or touching but you do both those now.'

'This is different.' Her heart was pounding. 'It was just sex, Gio. Great sex, admittedly, but nothing more.'

His mouth trailed over her breast and she groaned and tried to push him away. 'Stop. You're not playing fair.'

'I'm in love with you. And I'm just reminding you how you feel about me.' He lifted his head, a wicked smile in his eyes, and she ran a hand over her shoulder, trying not to lick her lips. He had an incredible body and every female part of her craved him.

But that was natural, she reminded herself. 'It's sexual attraction,' she said hoarsely, trying to concentrate despite the skilled movement of his mouth and hands. 'If sexual attraction didn't exist then the human race would have died out long ago.

It isn't love.' She gave a low moan as his fingers teased her intimately. 'Gio...'

'Not love?' He rolled onto his back and positioned her above him. 'Fine, Dr Anderson. Then let's have sex. At the moment I don't care what you call it as long as you stop talking.'

A week later, Alice walked into work with a smile on her face and a bounce in her step.

And she knew why, of course.

It was her relationship with Gio. And she was totally clear about her feelings. Friendship and sex. It was turning out to be a good combination. In a month or so he'd probably be leaving and that would be fine. Maybe they'd stay in touch. Maybe they wouldn't. Either way, she felt fine about it. She felt fine about everything.

And the fact that he always said 'I love you' and she didn't just didn't seem to matter any more. It didn't change the way things were between them.

The truth was, they were having fun.

Mary caught her as she walked into her consulting room. 'You're looking happy.'

'I am happy.' She dropped her bag behind the desk and turned on her computer. 'I'm enjoying my life.'

'You weren't smiling this much a month ago.'

A month ago Gio hadn't been in her life.

She frowned slightly at the thought and then dismissed it. What was wrong with enjoying a friendship?

'Professor Burrows from the haematology department at the hospital rang.' Mary handed her a piece of paper. 'He wants you to call him back on this number before ten o'clock. And I've slotted in Mrs Bruce because she's in a state. She had a scan at the hospital and they think the baby has a cleft palate. She's crying in Reception.'

Alice looked up in concern. 'Oh, poor thing. Send her straight in.' She flicked on her computer while Mary watched, her eyes searching.

'It's Gio, isn't it?'

'What is?'

'The reason you're smiling. So relaxed. You're in love with him, Alice.'

'I'm not in love.' Alice lifted her head and smiled sweetly. 'And the reason I know that is because there's no such thing. But I'm willing to admit that I like him a lot. I respect and admire him as a doctor. He's a nice man.'

And he was great in bed.

Mary looked at her thoughtfully. 'A nice man? Good, I'm glad you like him.'

Alice felt slightly smug as she buzzed for her first patient. Really, in her opinion, it all went to prove that love just didn't exist. In many ways Gio was perfect. He was intelligent and sharp and yet still managed to be kind and thoughtful. He was a terrific listener, a great conversationalist and a spectacular lover. What more could a girl want in a man?

The answer was nothing. But still she didn't feel anything that could be described as love. And when he left to return to Italy, as he inevitably would, she'd miss him but she wouldn't pine.

Which just went to prove that she'd been right all along.

There was a tap on the door and she looked up as Mrs Bruce entered, her face pale and her eyes tired.

'I'm sorry to bother you, Dr Anderson,' she began, but Alice immediately shook her head.

'Don't apologise. I understand you had a scan.'

Mrs Bruce sank into the chair and started to sob quietly. 'And they think the baby has a cleft palate.' The tears poured down her cheeks and she fumbled in her bag for a tissue. 'There was so much I wanted to ask. I had all these questions...' Her voice cracked. 'But the girl couldn't answer any of them and now I have to wait to see some consultant or other and I can't even remember his name.' The sobs became gulps. 'They don't know what it's like. The waiting.'

'It will be Mr Phillips, the consultant plastic surgeon, I expect.' Alice reached for her phone and pressed the button that connected her to Gio's room. 'Dr Moretti? If you could come into my room for one moment when you've finished with your patient, I'd be grateful.'

Then she replaced the receiver and stood up. 'You poor thing.' She slipped an arm around the woman's shoulders and gave her a hug without even thinking about it. 'You've had a terrible shock. But there's plenty that can be done, trust me. There's an excellent cleft lip and palate team at the hospital. They serve the whole region and I promise that you won't leave this surgery until you know more about what to expect, even if I have to ring the consultant myself.'

Mrs Bruce blew her nose hard and shook her head. 'She isn't even born yet,' she said in a wavering voice, 'and already I'm worried that she's going to be teased and bullied at school. You know what kids are like. They're cruel. And appearance is everything.'

Alice gave her another squeeze and then looked up as Gio walked into the room.

'Dr Moretti—this is Mrs Bruce. The hospital have told her that her baby has a cleft palate and she's terribly upset, which is totally understandable. They don't seem to have given her much information so I thought you might be able to help reassure her about a few things. Answer some questions for her.'

'It's just a shock, you know?' Mrs Bruce clung to Alice's arm like a lifeline and Gio nodded as he pulled out another chair and sat down next to her.

'First let me tell you that I trained as a plastic surgeon,' he said quietly, 'and I specialised in the repair of cleft lips and palates so I know a lot about it.'

Mrs Bruce crumpled the tissue in her hand. 'Why are you a GP, then?'

Gio pulled a face and spread his hands. 'Unfortunately life does not always turn out the way we intend. I had an accident which meant I could no longer operate for long periods. So I changed direction in my career.'

'So you've operated on children with this? Can you make them look normal?'

'In the hands of a skilled surgeon the results can be excellent but, of course, there are no guarantees and there are many factors involved. A cleft lip can range in severity from a slight notch in the red part of the upper lip...' he gestured with his finger '...to a complete separation of the lip, extending into the nose. The aim of surgery is to close the separation in the first operation and to achieve symmetry, but that isn't always possible.'

He was good, Alice thought to herself as she sat quietly, listening along with the mother. Really good.

Mrs Bruce sniffed. 'Will they do it straight away when she's born?'

'They usually wait until the baby is ten weeks old. The repair of a cleft palate requires more extensive surgery and is usually done when the child is between nine and eighteen months old so that it is better able to tolerate the procedure.'

'Is it a huge operation?'

'In some children a cleft palate may involve only a tiny portion at the back of the roof of the mouth or it might be a complete separation that extends from front to back.' Gio reached for a pad and a pen that was lying on Alice's desk. 'It will make more sense if I draw you a picture.'

Mrs Bruce watched as his pen flew over the page, demonstrating the defect and the repair. 'How will she be able to suck if her mouth is—?' She broke off and gave a sniff. 'If her mouth looks like that?'

'There are special bottles that will help her feed.' Gio put the pad down on the desk. 'Looking after the child with a cleft lip and palate has to be a team approach, Mrs Bruce. She may need help with feeding, with speech and other aspects of her development. The surgeon is really only one member of the team. You will have plenty of support, be assured of that.'

Alice sat patiently while Gio talked, reassuring the mother, answering questions and explaining as best he could.

Finally, when she seemed calmer, he reached for the pad again and scribbled a number on a piece of paper. 'If you have other worries, things you think of later and wish you'd asked, you can call me,' he said gently, handing her the piece of paper.

She stared at it. 'You're giving me your phone number?'

He nodded. 'Use it, if you have questions. If the hospital tells you something you don't understand. Or you can always make an appointment, of course.'

'Thank you.' Mrs Bruce gave him a shaky smile and then turned to Alice and squeezed her hand. 'And thank you, too, Dr Anderson.'

'We'll tackle the problem together, Mrs Bruce,' Alice said firmly. 'She'll be managed by the hospital, but never forget that you're still our patient.' She watched Mrs Bruce—a much happier Mrs Bruce—leave the room and then turned to Gio. 'Thanks for that. I didn't have a clue what to say to her. And I don't know much about cleft palates. Will the baby have long-term problems?'

Gio pulled a face. 'Possibly many. They can be very prone to recurrent middle-ear infections, which can lead to scarring of the ossicular chain in the middle ear, and that can damage hearing or even cause deafness.'

'Why are they susceptible to ear infections?'

'In cleft babies, the muscle sling across the palate is incomplete, divided by the cleft, so they can't pull on the eustachian tube,' he explained. 'Also, scar formation following the postnatal correction of cleft lip and palate can lead to abnormal soft tissue, bone and dental growth. There has been some research looking at the possibilities of operating *in utero* in the hope of achieving healing without scarring.'

This was his area. His speciality. And she was fascinated. 'What else?'

'Sometimes there is a gap in the bone, known as the alveolar defect. Then the maxillary facial surgeon will do an alveolar bone graft.'

There was something in his face that made her reach out and touch his arm. 'Do you miss it, Gio?'

'Sometimes.' He gave a lopsided smile. 'Not always.'

'Well, you were great with her. I knew you would be.'

'You were good with her, too.' He shot her a curious look. 'Do you even realise how much you've changed.'

'Changed? How have I changed?' She went back to her chair and hit a button on her computer.

'You were touching a patient and you were doing it instinctively. You were offering physical comfort and emotional support.'

Alice frowned. 'Well, she was upset.'

'Yes.' Gio's voice was soft. 'She was. And you coped well with it. Emotions, Alice. Emotions.'

'What exactly are you implying?'

'That you're getting used to touching and being touched.' He strolled to the door. 'All I have to do now is persuade you to admit that you love me. Tomorrow I'm taking you out to dinner. Prepare yourself.'

'That's nice.' Her breath caught at the look in his eyes. She didn't love him. *She had absolutely nothing to worry about because she didn't love him.* 'Where are we going?'

'My favourite place to eat in the whole world.'

'Oh.' She felt a flicker of surprise. Knowing Gio's tastes for the spectacular, she was surprised that there was anywhere locally that would satisfy him. Perhaps he'd discovered somewhere new. 'I'll look forward to it.'

It took a considerable amount of planning and a certain amount of deviousness on his part, but finally he had it all arranged.

He was gambling everything on a hunch.

The hunch that she loved him but wasn't even aware of it herself.

She'd lived her whole life convinced that love didn't exist, so persuading her to change her mind at this stage wouldn't be easy.

Words alone had failed and so had sexual intimacy, so for days he'd racked his brains for another way of proving to her that love existed. That she could let herself feel what he already knew that she felt.

And finally he'd come up with a plan.

A plan that had involved a considerable number of other people.

And now all he could do was wait. Wait and hope.

Alice had just finished morning surgery the following day when Gio strolled into the room.

'Fancy a quick lunch?' His tone was casual and she gave a nod, surprised by how eager she was to leave work and spend time with him.

'Why not?' It was just because she enjoyed his company and was making the most of it while he was here. What was wrong with that?

She followed him out of the surgery, expecting him to turn and walk up the street to the coffee-shop. Instead, he turned left, round the back of the building and towards the surgery car park.

'You're taking the car?' She frowned. 'Where are we going?'

'Wait and see.' He held the door of his car open and she slipped into the passenger seat, a question in her eyes.

'We can't go far. We have to be back for two o'clock.'

He covered his eyes with a pair of sunglasses and gave her a smile. 'Stop thinking about work for five minutes.'

It was on the tip of her tongue to tell him that she hardly thought about work at all these days, but something stopped her. If she made a comment like that, he'd read something into it that wasn't there.

Wondering where he could possibly be taking her and thinking that he was acting very strangely, Alice sat back in her seat and pondered some of the problems that she'd seen that morning. And found she couldn't concentrate on any of them.

It was Gio's fault, she thought crossly. Going out for lunch with him was too distracting. She should have said no.

The wind played with her hair and she caught it and swept it out of her eyes. And noticed where they were.

'This is the airport.' She glanced behind her to check that she wasn't mistaken. 'Gio, this is the road to the airport. Why are we going to the airport?'

He kept driving, his hands steady on the wheel. 'Because I want to.'

'You want to eat plastic sandwiches in an airport?'

'You used to live on plastic sandwiches before you met me,' he reminded her in an amused voice, and she laughed.

'Maybe I did. But you've given me a taste for pasta. Gio, what is going on?' They'd arrived at the small airport and everything seemed to be happening around her.

Before she could catch her breath and form any more questions, she was standing on the runway, at the foot of a set of steps that led into the body of an aircraft.

'Go on. We don't want to miss our slot.' Gio walked up behind her, carrying two cases and she stared at them.

'What are those?'

'Our luggage.'

'I don't have any luggage. I was just coming out for a sandwich.' She brushed the hair out of her eyes, frustrated by the lack of answers she was receiving to her questions. 'Gio, what is going on?'

'I'm taking you to my favourite place to eat.'

'That's this evening. It's only one o'clock in the afternoon.'

She watched as a man appeared behind them and took the cases onto the plane. 'Who's he? What's he doing with those?'

'He's putting them on the plane.' Gio took her arm. 'We're leaving at one o'clock because it takes a long time to get there, and we're going by plane because it's the best way to reach Sicily.'

'Sicily?' Her voice skidded and squeaked. 'You're taking me to *Sicily*?'

'You'll love it.'

Had he gone totally mad? 'I'm sure I'll love it and maybe I'll go there one day, but not on a Thursday afternoon when I have a well-woman clinic and a late surgery!' She looked over her shoulder, ready to make a dash back to the car, but he closed a hand over her arm and urged her onto the steps.

'Forget work, *tesoro*. It's all taken care of. David and Trisha are taking over for five days.'

'David?' With him so close behind her, she was forced to climb two more steps. 'What's he got to do with this? He's in London.'

'Not any more. He's currently back in your surgery, pre- paring for your well-woman clinic.' He brushed her hair away from her face and dropped a gentle kiss on her mouth. 'When did you last have a holiday, Alice?'

'I haven't felt the need for a holiday. I like my life.' She took another step upwards, her expression exasperated. 'Or, rather, I liked my life the way it was before everyone started interfering!'

He urged her up another step. 'I'll do you a deal—if, after this weekend, you want to go back to your old life, I'll let you. No arguments.'

'But I can't just—'

He nudged her forwards. 'Yes, you can.'

'You're kidnapping me in broad daylight!'

'That's right. I am.' His broad shoulders blocked her exit and she made a frustrated sound in her throat and turned and stomped up the remaining steps.

This was totally ridiculous!

It was—

She stopped dead, her eyes widening as she saw the cabin. It was unlike any plane she'd ever seen before. Two soft creamy leather sofas faced each other across a richly carpeted aisle. A table covered in crisply laundered linen was laid for lunch, the silver cutlery glinting in the light.

Her mouth dropped.

'This isn't a plane. It's a living room.' Glancing over her shoulder, she realised that she'd been so distracted by the fact he was planning to take her away, she hadn't been paying attention. 'We didn't come through the airport the normal way.'

'This is a private plane.' He pushed her forward and nodded to the uniformed flight attendant who was smiling and waiting for them to board.

'Private plane?' Not knowing what else to do, she walked towards the sofas, feeling bemused and more than a little faint. 'Whose private plane?'

He sat down next to her. 'My brother, Marco, has made quite a success of his olive oil business.' Gio's tone was smooth as he leaned across to fasten her seat belt before placing another kiss on her cheek. 'It has certain compensations for the rest of his family. And now, *tesoro,* relax and prepare to be spoiled.'

She wished he'd stop touching her.

She couldn't think or concentrate when he touched her and she had a feeling that she was really, really going to need to concentrate.

CHAPTER TEN

THE MOMENT THE plane landed, Alice knew it was possible to fall in love. With a country, at least.

And as they drove away from the airport and along the coast, the heat of the sun warmed her skin and lifted her spirits. It was summer in Cornwall, of course, but somehow it didn't feel the same.

As she relaxed in her seat and watched the country fly past, all she knew was that that she'd never seen a sky more blue or a sea that looked more inviting. As they drove, the coast was a golden blur of orange and lemon orchards and she wanted to beg Gio to stop the car, just so that she could pick the fruit from the tree.

As if sensing the change in her, he reached across and rested a hand on her leg, his other hand steady on the wheel. 'It is beautiful, no?'

'Wonderful.' She turned to look at him. 'Where are we going?'

'Always you ask questions.' With a lazy smile in her direction, he returned his hand to the wheel. 'We are going to dinner, *tesoro.* Just as I promised we would.'

The warmth of the sun and the tantalising glimpses of breath-taking coastline and ancient historical sights distracted her from delving more deeply, and it was early evening when Gio pulled off the main road, drove down a dusty lane and into a large courtyard.

Alice was captivated. 'Is this where we're staying? It's beautiful. Is it a hotel?'

'It has been in my family for at least five generations,' Gio said, opening the boot and removing the cases. 'It's home.'

'Home?' The smile faded and she felt nerves flicker in the pit of her stomach. 'You're taking me to meet your parents.'

'Not just my parents, *tesoro.*' He slammed the boot shut and strolled over to her, sliding a hand into her hair and tilting her head. 'My whole family. Everyone lives in this area. We congregate here. We exchange news. We show interest in each other's lives. We offer support when it's needed and praise when it's deserved and quite often when it isn't. But most of all we offer unconditional love. It's what we do.'

'But I—'

'Hush.' He rested a finger on her lips to prevent her from speaking. 'You don't believe in love, Alice Anderson, because you've never seen it. But after this weekend you will no longer be able to use that excuse. Welcome to Sicily. Welcome to my home.'

She looked a little lost, he thought to himself, seated among his noisy, ebullient family. A little wary. As if she had no idea how to act surrounded by a large group of people who so clearly adored each other.

As his mother piled the table high with Sicilian delicacies, his father recounted the tale of his latest medical drama in his severely restricted English and Gio saw Alice smile. And respond.

She was shy, he noticed. Unsure how to behave in a large group. But they drew her into the conversation in the way that his family always welcomed any guest at their table. The language was a mix of Italian and English. English when they addressed her directly and could find the words, Italian when the levels of excitement bubbled over and they restarted to their native tongue with much hand waving and voice raising, which would have sent a lesser person running for cover. His grand-mother spoke only a Sicilian dialect and his younger sister, Lucia, acted as interpreter, her dark eyes sparkling as she was given the opportunity to show off her English in public.

And gradually Alice started to relax. After eating virtually nothing, he saw her finally lift her fork. He intercepted his mother's look of approval and understanding.

And knew that he'd been right to bring her.

The buzz of conversation still ringing in her ears, Alice fol-lowed Gio out into the semi-darkness. 'Where are we going?'

'I don't actually live in the house any more.' He took her hand and led her towards a track that wound through a citrus orchard towards the sea. 'Years ago my brother and I built a small villa at the bottom of the orchard. The idea was to let it to tourists but then we decided we wanted to keep it. He's long since moved to something more extravagant but I keep this place as a bolthole. I love my family but even I need space from them.'

'I thought they were lovely.' She couldn't keep the envy out of her voice and suddenly she stopped walking and just stood and stared. Tiny lights illuminated the path that ran all the way to the beach. The air was warm and she could smell the fruit trees and hear the lap of the sea against the sand. 'This whole place is amazing. I just can't imagine it.'

'Can't imagine what?'

'Growing up here. With those people.' She took her hand away from his and reached out to pick a lemon from the near-est tree. It fell into her hand, complete with leaves and stalk, and she stared at it, fascinated. 'It's no wonder you believe in love, Dr Moretti. I think it would be possible to believe in just about anything if you lived here.'

He stepped towards her. Took her face in his hands. 'And do you believe in it, Alice? You met my family this evening. My parents have been together for almost forty years, my grandparents for sixty-two years. I believe that my great-grandparents were married for sixty-five years, although no one can be sure because no one can actually remember a time when they weren't together.' His thumb stroked her cheek. 'What did you see tonight, Alice? Was it convenience? Friendship? Any of those reasons you once gave me for people choosing to spend their lives together?'

Her heart was thumping in her chest and she shook her head slowly. 'No. It was love.' Her voice cracked as she said the words. 'I saw love.'

'Finally.' Gio closed his eyes briefly and murmured something in Italian. 'Let's go—I want to show you how I feel about you.'

It was tender and loving, slow and drawn out, with none of the fevered desperation of their previous encounters. Flesh slid against flesh, hard male against soft female, whispers and muttered words the only communication between them.

The bedroom of the villa opened directly onto the beach and she could hear the sounds of the sea, feel the night air as it flowed into the room and cooled them.

Long hours passed. Hours during which they feasted and savoured, each reluctant to allow the other to sleep.

And finally, when her body was so languid and sated that she couldn't imagine ever wanting to move again, he rolled onto his side and looked into her eyes.

'I love you, Alice.' His voice was quiet in the semi-darkness. 'I want you to be with me always. For ever. I want you to marry me, *tesoro.*'

'No, Gio.' The word made her shiver and she would have backed away but he held her tightly.

'Tonight you admitted that love exists.'

'For some other people maybe.' She whispered the words, almost as if she was afraid to speak them too loudly. 'But not for me.'

'Why not for you?'

'Because I don't—I can't—'

'Because when you were a child, your mother let you fall.' He lifted a hand and stroked the hair away from her face. 'She let you fall and now you don't trust anyone to be there to catch you. Isn't that right, Alice?'

'It isn't—'

'But you have to learn to trust. For the first time in your life you have to learn.' His mouth hovered a mere breath away from hers. 'You can fall, Alice. You can fall, *tesoro,* and I'll be standing here ready to catch you. Always. That's what love is. It's a promise.'

Tears filled her eyes. 'You make it sound so perfect and simple.'

'Because it is both perfect and simple.'

'No.' She shook her head and let the tears fall. 'That is what my mother thought. Every time she was with a man she had these same feelings and she thought they were love. But they turned out to be something entirely different. Something brittle and destructive. My father was the same. And I have their genes. I believe that *you* can love, but I don't believe the same of myself. I can't do it. I'm not capable of it.'

'You are still afraid.' He brushed the tears away with his thumb. 'You think that you are still that little girl on the climbing frame, but you're not. Over the past few weeks I've watched you and I've seen you learning to touch and be touched. I've seen you becoming comfortable with other people's emotions. All we need to do now is make you comfortable with your own.'

'It won't work, Gio. I'm sorry.'

Their bags were packed and Gio was up at the house having a final meeting with his brother about family business. She hovered in the courtyard, enjoying the peace and tranquillity of the setting.

After four days of lying on the beach and swimming in the pool, she should have felt relaxed and refreshed. Instead, she felt tense and miserable. And the last thing she wanted was to go home.

From the courtyard of the main house she stared down through the citrus orchard to the sea and then glanced behind her, her eyes on the summit of Mount Etna, which dominated the skyline.

'We will miss you when you've gone. You must come again soon, Alice.' Gio's mother walked up behind her and gave her a warm hug.

'Thank you for making me feel so welcome.' The stiffness inside her subsided and she hugged the older woman back, envying Gio his family.

'Anyone who has taught my Gio to smile again will always be welcome here.'

Alice pulled away slightly. 'He always smiles.'

'Not since the accident. He was frustrated. Sad. Grieving for the abilities that he'd lost. His ability to help all those poor little children. You have shown him that a new life is possible. That change can be good. You have given him a great deal. But that is what love is all about. Giving.'

Alice swallowed. 'I haven't—I don't—'

'You will come and see us again soon. You must promise me that.'

'Well, I…' she licked her lips, 'Gio will probably want to bring some other girl—'

His mother frowned. 'I doubt it.' Her voice was quiet. 'You are the first girl he has ever brought home, Alice.'

The first girl?

Alice stared at her and the other woman smiled.

'He has had girlfriends, yes, of course. He is an attractive, healthy young man so that is natural. But love…' She gave a fatalistic shrug. 'That only happens to a man once in a lifetime, and for my Giovanni it is now. Don't take too long to realise that you feel the same way, Alice. To lose something so precious would be nothing short of a tragedy.'

With that she turned and walked back across the courtyard into the house, leaving Alice staring after her.

Gio stood on the beach and stared out to sea, unable to drag himself away. Disappointment sat in his gut like a lead weight that he couldn't shift.

He'd relied on this place, *his home,* to provide the key he needed. To unlock that one remaining part of Alice that was still hidden away. But his plan had failed.

Maybe he'd just underestimated the depth of the damage that her parents had done to her.

Or maybe he was wrong to think that she loved him. Maybe she didn't love him at all.

'Gio?' Her voice sounded tentative, as if she wasn't sure of her welcome, and he turned with a smile. It cost him in terms of effort but he was determined that she shouldn't feel bad. None of this was her fault. None of it.

He glanced at his watch. 'You're right—we should be leaving. Are you ready?'

'No. No, I'm not, actually.' She stepped away from him, a slender figure clothed in a blue dress that dipped at the neck and floated past her knees. Her feet were bare and she was wearing a flower in her hair.

The transformation was complete, he thought to himself sadly. A few weeks ago her wardrobe had all been about work. Practical skirts and comfortable shoes. Neat tops with tailored jackets.

Now she looked relaxed and feminine. Like the exquisitely beautiful woman that she was.

'Well, you have five more minutes before we have to leave.'

He prompted her gently. 'If there are still things you need to fetch, you'd better fetch them fast.'

'There's nothing I need to fetch.' In four days on the beach her pale skin had taken on a soft golden tone and her blonde hair fell silky smooth to her shoulders. 'But there are things that I need to say.'

'Alice—'

'No, I really need to be allowed to speak.' She stood on tip-toe and covered his lips with her fingers, the way he'd done to her so many times. 'I didn't realise. I didn't realise that giving up surgery had meant so much to you. You hid that well.'

He tensed. 'I—'

'It's nice to know that other people hide things, too. That it isn't just me. It makes me realise that everyone has things inside them that they don't necessarily want to share.' She let her fingers drop from his mouth. 'It doesn't stop you from moving forward. It's nice to know that, even though you didn't smile for a while, you're smiling again now. And it's nice to know that I'm the only woman that you've ever brought home.'

'You've been speaking to my mother.'

'Yes.' She glanced down at her feet. Curled her toes into the sand. 'And I want it to stay that way. I want to be the first and last woman that you ever bring here. I should probably tell you that I'm seriously in love with your mother. And your sisters and brother, grandparents, uncles and aunts.'

'You are?' Hope flickered inside him, and the tiny flicker grew as she lifted her head and looked at him, her blue eyes clear and honest.

'You're right that I'm afraid. I'm afraid that everything that's in my past might get in the way of our future. I'm afraid that I might mess everything up.' She swallowed and took a deep breath, her hands clasped in front of her. 'I'm afraid of so many things. But love only happens once in a lifetime and it's taken me this long to find it so I can't let my fear stand in my way.' She held out her hand and lifted her chin. 'I'm ready to climb,

Gio, if you promise that you'll be there to catch me. I'm ready to marry you, if you'll still have me.'

He took her hand, closed his eyes briefly and pulled her hard against him. 'I love you and I will always love you, even when you're ninety and you're still trying to talk to me about work when all I want to do is lie in the sun and look at my lemon trees.'

She looked up at him, eyes shining, and he felt his heart tumble. 'I have another confession to make—I haven't actually been thinking about work as much lately.'

'Is that so, Dr Anderson?' His expression was suddenly serious. 'And that's something that we haven't even discussed. What we do about work. Where we are going to live.' Did she want to stay in Cornwall? Was she thinking of moving to Italy?

She shrugged her shoulders. 'It doesn't matter.'

He couldn't hide his surprise. 'Well, I—'

'What matters is us,' she said quietly, her hand still in his. 'You've shown me that. I love you, Gio, and I always will. I believe in love now. A love that can last. This place makes me believe that. You make me believe it.'

For the first time in his adult life words wouldn't come, so he bent his head and kissed her.

* * * * *

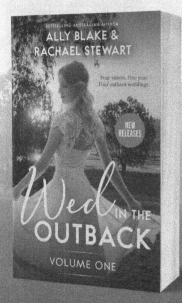
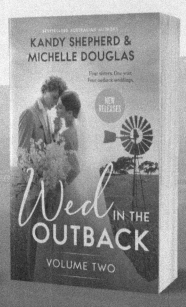

Subscribe and fall in love with a Mills & Boon series today!

You'll be among the first to read stories delivered to your door monthly and enjoy great savings.

WE SIMPLY LOVE ROMANCE